Swords & Eagles

Swords & Eagles
Two Adventures of the Napoleonic Wars

The Sword Hand of Napoleon

The Eagle of the Empire

Cyrus Townsend Brady

LEONAUR

Swords & Eagles
Two Adventures of the Napoleonic Wars
The Sword Hand of Napoleon
and
The Eagle of the Empire
by Cyrus Townsend Brady

First published under the titles
The Sword Hand of Napoleon
and
The Eagle of the Empire

Leonaur is an imprint of Oakpast Ltd

Copyright in this form © 2010 Oakpast Ltd

ISBN: 978-0-85706-371-7 (hardcover)
ISBN: 978-0-85706-372-4 (softcover)

http://www.leonaur.com

Publisher's Notes

The opinions of the authors represent a view of events in which he
was a participant related from his own perspective,
as such the text is relevant as an historical document.

The views expressed in this book are not necessarily
those of the publisher.

Contents

The Sword Hand of Napoleon

Contents

To Robert Hobart Davis
Great Editor. True Man. Good Friend

Preface

And now comes the, to me, most delightful task—the writing of the preface. I set about it blithely. The story has been dictated, transcribed, corrected, revised, serialised; the galley and page proofs have been carefully gone over with great attention; the pictures have been made; the publication campaign talked over and plans laid; the format of the book, the colour scheme for the cover, the unique wrapper, have all been attended to—everything is finished. The book is ready save for these few words.

Why did I write this story? Well, for one thing because I was asked to do so, but mainly because I wanted to. In the first place it is just the kind of a story I like to write: I delight in it. It deals with a great character—albeit a bad one!—which I have made the subject of long study, and is laid in a period with which I am measurably familiar. And then it brings before the reader what is of the very essence of the dramatic, a contrast so striking and so vivid that no one can fail to note it and dwell upon it. Napoleon with six hundred thousand men behind him on the banks of the Niemen in spring, and Napoleon with six hundred thousand men still behind him on the banks of the Niemen in winter—that does not sound very striking; but when you think that most of the six hundred thousand behind him in winter were dead men who had been alive in spring and then when you consider how they died, it is different.

And another reason for the book is the chance it gives me to dilate upon Marshal Ney. He was not the noblest of the marshals, nor the greatest. His character was full of faults. He made fatal blunders at Bautzen—really I think that the decisive battle of the later Napoleonic wars—and at Quatre-Bras. But what a fighter the big red-head was! And how gallant and brave. And how tragic was his end. With all his faults I love him still.

I neither love nor admire Napoleon. My sober judgement arrived at after long study and reflection inclines me to characterise him in words which would not be popular with the unthinking. But I cannot escape from his fascination and in spite of his transcendental egotism, his overweening selfishness, his utterly heartless indifference, I cannot fail to see his genius. It is hard to come down to the ordinary levels in dealing with so vast and complex a character. Indeed, in writing a novel in which he figures he is apt to monopolise the attention of the author to the exclusion of the romance. In the century since Waterloo there has grown up a Napoleon myth and it is still growing. I have tried to show the man as he was.

Some of the pre-publication critics who have read this story have looked at it from the historical or biographical point of view and declare that there is too much Napoleon in it and not enough story, while others from the fictional standpoint have said quite the reverse, there was too much story in it and not enough Napoleon. Naturally at this writing I agree with neither. I think the proportion between romance and history justly set forth. I may think differently later, but not now.

Between the two opinions—or three counting my own!—shall my book fall to the ground? Well, dear reader, in the language of the day, that is up to you. When you pay your money for the book—or get it from the public library, which is cheaper!—you can at least make your choice. If you decide that the book from either view point, or both, or all three, is worth while you may expect another one next spring to deal with the Emperor at bay in France and at Waterloo, upon which I am already engaged, and which will bear the title of *The Eagle of the Empire*. Will that announcement be a stimulus or a deterrent to the success of this book, I wonder?

Cyrus Townsend Brady.

Rectory of the Church of the Ascension
Mt. Vernon, New York,
January, 1914.

Prologue

THE ARMY OF THE NATIONS

At one o'clock in the morning of June the twenty-fourth, in the year of Our Lord, eighteen hundred and twelve, a horseman galloped hurriedly up a steep hill overlooking a broad valley through which meandered gently a wide river. Throwing the reins to a sentry who challenged him, he leaped to the ground in front of a large tent and giving the password for the night, stepped toward it. Back of the tent and on either side numerous other tents were erected. Officers and men flitted hastily and silently through the encampment on various pressing errands. Glowing heaps of embers showed where camp fires had blazed and there were lights in many of the tents indicating wakeful occupants.

As the clatter of the horse's hoofs died away the entrance flaps of the largest tent were parted and a rather stout, not to say heavy set, little man in a plain grey overcoat with a three-cornered black hat on his head, stepped out into the night. The full moon was now low on the horizon. It was due to set in little more than two hours, but with the diffused twilight of the high latitudes, it gave sufficient illumination to reveal the approaching horseman's figure to the greatest man of his time, the Emperor Napoleon. Dropping the reins of the horse, the sentry came quickly to a present with his piece in salute. As if by magic the news that the Emperor was awake and out was communicated to the occupants of the other tents and from them poured a stream of brilliantly uniformed officers of the General Staff who gathered about their great chieftain ready for service and waiting for him to break the silence.

On every hand, back of the crest of the hill and extending down toward the river's brink, rose great forests of mighty pines. Beneath their wide spread branches to the ears of the men on the hill came

15

through the night confused noises, subdued, somewhat unreal and yet distinctly heard above the sough of the wind through the tall tops of the great trees. A sound of life, human and animal, voices indescribable and indistinguishable, hushed, controlled, but rising, falling, beating and throbbing like a great muffled heart. A clinking, clashing, rolling, creaking, low breathed diapason of tumult with here and there "dim drums throbbing in the hills half heard" and thin faint notes of bugles, "horns of elfland softly blowing" within the forest glades.

The little man in the grey coat hearkened a moment and then threw a sharp look around him which seemed to comprehend the heavens above and the earth beneath in its swift glance. An officer led a splendidly accoutred white horse into the circle back of him.

"Do you take the bridle, Roustan," said the Emperor quietly to a tall Mameluke in the picturesque dress of his Oriental land who had followed him closely. "Who have we here?" he continued, stepping toward the horseman, who at the appearance of the Emperor had stopped by the sentry, having resumed the bridle of his own tired horse.

"A messenger from General Éblé, Sire," said the horseman, drawing himself still more erect and saluting.

"Ha!" exclaimed the Emperor, "and what says he?"

"The pontoon bridges are ready, Sire."

All night long had been heard the sounds of hammering, the movement of boats, the grinding of timbers being lashed together. Napoleon reflected for the first time that at that moment the sound of this work had ceased to contribute its quota to the noises of the night.

"The army can cross now?" he asked.

"At your pleasure. Sire."

"Very good."

The Emperor walked apart from the rest who stood in tense silence back of him and stepped closer to the edge of the bank which here fell away sharply for several hundred feet. The moonlight was reflected in silver crescents and circles on the wind-broken wavelets of the slow moving river. In front of him, several hundred yards apart, three broad, black lines, seen darkly against the broken reflections, spanned the stream. Many lights twinkled in groups on the ends nearest him and lights appeared here and there on the long lines which marked the pontoon bridges just completed by the engineers.

The country opposite had been reconnoitred and patrolled by a squadron of light cavalry which had been ferried across in boats, but as a precaution against surprise the approaches on either side had been covered by massed batteries of heavy guns, supported by divisions of infantry and cavalry. The keen-eyed soldier, standing on the roof of the world as it were, thought he could detect the reflection of the waning moon on brass or polished steel where his artillery lay ready to speak open-mouthed his defiance to his enemies. He could see further with the naked eye and further still with his mind's eye than most men, perhaps any man, in all that vast mass beneath his feet, sheltered under the pines, restless and instinct with life, waiting for a word. But even he could not see all!

They say Caesar paused at the Rubicon, probably Xerxes looked long at the Hellespont, Alexander may have hesitated at the Granicus and doubtless Hannibal weighed well the difficulties of the passage of the snow-covered Alps. So Bonaparte stopped at the Niemen. Xerxes made his crossing only to meet defeat and disaster unparalleled in military history up to that date. The story of his retreat with all its horrors has never been told, but a soldier like Napoleon could understand what it might be. Alexander fighting his way over the Granicus conquered that part of the world which had not yet acknowledged his prowess and the supremacy of his arms only to die of excess at thirty-three! Hannibal's career of conquest finally brought him to Capua, to Zama and the poison cup, the only resource of the hunted exile in a foreign land. Caesar in passing the Rubicon, turned Rome from a Republic into an Empire for his successors, only to fall by assassins' swords. What would Napoleon do with Russia and what would Russia do with him!

Before the Emperor stretched miles of plains covered in part with vast forests and extending elsewhere for leagues in uncovered *steppes*. Away, far across the world, over the long distance that lay between him and the rising sun lay the immemorial East. When scarcely more than a boy he had sought to conquer the Orient by way of the Delta of the Nile and the plains of Arabia and had failed. Now in the full and splendid vigour of his ripened manhood was he to fail again in the northern land in his advance in the same direction? For, in his grandiose mind, one way to India lay across the half oriental Muscovy, and ultimately to penetrate the East farther than Alexander, was already within the scope of his far-reaching plan.

Between that defeat on the shores of the ancient sea in the land called "Holy" and this projected advance into the wilds of Russia, a land by singular coincidence also called "Holy," lay such a career of conquest and triumph as the world had never seen. If all the exploits of the greatest captains of the past were rolled into one the aggregate of achievement would not equal the accomplishments of this one small man in the grey coat, who stood on the hill overlooking the River Niemen pausing reflectively a moment before he gave the order to advance.

He was then at the very summit of his power, the acme of his magnificence, the zenith of his glory. In the pursuance of his ambition he had attained the giddiest height upon which mortal had ever poised himself. The army that he had assembled comprised representatives of not less than sixteen different nationalities who spoke as many languages and thrice as many dialects. It included a great multitude from Sunny Italy, from the once Greek Island of Sicily, from Corsica of the Vendetta, from the banks of the tawny Tiber, from majestic Rome, from beauty-loving Florence, from the lofty heights of the Apennines. There were smaller detachments from the banks of the Ebro and the Tagus in Spain and Portugal, marching side by side with regiments of their hereditary enemies from the Low Countries, dyked Holland and rich Belgium. Legions of Polish Cavalry from the Vistula led by descendants of the Jagellons swarmed on the flanks. White coated Austrians, Hungarians and Bohemians marched by the side of blue-coated Prussians, Bavarians, Westphalians, Wurtembergers, divisions from the newly created Confederation of the Rhine were followed by sunny Saxons, savage Croats, faithful Swiss. And above all there were the veterans of France.

Soldiers who had followed their Eagles all over the world were there. Men who had battled on the plains of Esdraelon by the waters of Megiddo in Asia. Men who had fought in Cleopatra's famous land at Aboukir and within the shadow of the pyramids in Africa. Men who had battled in the islands of the New Continent of America. The Conquerors of Italy, of Prussia, of Austria, of Germany, of Spain were there. Men who had hoisted the tri-colour over every capital in Europe. Men of Arcola, of Marengo, of Austerlitz, of Friedland, of Somo-Sierra, of Eylau and of Wagram. The Imperial Guard, heroes of a hundred pitched battles, the Young Guard burning with ambition to show themselves worthy of their elders, the Corps of Davoust, the strategist, and tactician, of Oudinot the fearless captain, of Eugene the Viceroy of Italy, of the noble and incorruptible MacDonald, of the hard fighting and soon to be immortal Ney, of the greatest of cavalrymen Murat, and of other marshals, generals and officers, of distinction

18

without number. To mention their names even is to unfold the history of their times, and to call the roll of their exploits is to recite the golden records of this world's glory.

All the world was there in the army of this new Caesar Augustus. Yet not all the world. The Orient was without representation, save in the graceful person of the faithful Roustan, the Egyptian. There was no contingent of red-coated, stubborn English. They were hammering away on other marshals, striving to bring Portugal and Spain into submission. There was no Scandinavian contingent under that Bernadotte whom, as he was wont to say, was once a Marshal of France and now only the Prince Royal of Sweden. That old soldier and comrade of the Emperor was arrayed on the side of his enemies. And there were above all, concentrated somewhere in the depths of the forests yonder, or spread abroad upon the limitless expanse of *steppes*, the Russians, more formidable in retreat in the defence of their native land than in any other military manoeuvre they attempted. Napoleon had defeated them often but he had never disgraced them.

On the banks of that very River Niemen further down at Tilsit a few years before two Emperors, he of France and Alexander of Russia, young, boyish, enthusiastic, bewitched by the glory and glamour of Napoleon had discussed the destinies of mankind. There Alexander the son of Rurik of the great house of Romanoff had divided the world with the little Corsican who was an ancestor himself and not a descendant! Now between the two Emperors yawned a great gulf of broken faith and mistrust, mutual jealousy and thwarted ambition, suspicion and hatred, which separated them forever. Could any army, however great, however puissant, however numerous, bridge that utter severance into which human passion had reft their former compact?

But aside from England, Sweden and Russia, the world was at Napoleon's feet. He did well to call his force the Army of the Nations. Back in Dresden a month before he had held splendid court—"the Congress of Kings" so styled—at which Emperors, Kings, Archdukes, Royal Princes, the heads of great, of ancient, of powerful houses had gathered from all over Europe to pay him homage, to do him honour. Fortune, as was well said of another ruler, had denied him no attribute of greatness except—in the views of his enemies—virtue! He had built his tower of Babel—a simile in view of the confusion of tongues among those he commanded that night which is not inappropriate—until it reached into the heavens.

The human being is not designed for omnipotence, the human

frame, the human body, the human mind, the human soul are alike and together unequal to it. Man is not infinite. Sooner or later his limitations are reached. That lesson, however, was one which the Emperor had still to learn.

What were his reflections in those brief moments while he stood watching, waiting? If some prophet had appeared as of old, lean of body, scant of vesture, with strident voice, fierce gesture, with wild eyes blazing under a mane of tangled hair, and had foretold the consequences of that crossing what anguish inexpressible, what sorrow colossal could have been stopped. But no voice spoke to the man. Whom the gods destroy, they first make mad. Sober, calm, composed, reflective, assured, confident, certain? Ah, yes, but for all this, that man was—mad!

Casting a glance into the heavens where only the brighter stars could be seen in the waning moonlight and the growing dawn, the little man in the grey coat turned back to the others. His mind was made up. The die was cast, again Hellespont, or Granicus, or Alps, or Rubicon, or whatever barred the way, or marked a limit, or committed to a course, was to be crossed. And the issue? That was in the hands of God. Was there a God? Did He look down out of that silver sky between those silent stars? Were there in the Great Hands of the Almighty balance and sword? To what side would that balance decline, for whose cause would the sword be lifted?

He on the hill that night had said that God was invariably on the side of the strongest battalion. Was that the Gospel? Was it so writ in history, "that power charged with the promulgation of the judgements of God on the pride of men"? Would it prove true then and there? Will the greatest of men and the strongest of battalions win then? The proposition could be tested and its accuracy determined better then and there than any other place and time in that history.

The signal was to be given at that hour and at that moment for which the world had waited with bated breath and beating heart. As early as the winter before from the confines of the vast Empire over which he held sway, and from its allied and tributary states, men had been marching for that purpose. The farm of the tiller of the soil, the machinery of the manufacturer, the counter of the merchant, the desks of the schoolmaster, the ranks of the labourers had been robbed of their youth for that hour. For that moment thousands of horses, hundreds of cannon, tons of provisions and ammunition and equipment had been assembled. For that hour six hundred thousand men

20

had been concentrated within the space of a few miles on either side of this central point a few miles from the town of Kowno on the banks of the Niemen. Every road in Europe south of that river and west of the wild Carpathians had resounded for months with the tramp of armed men, with the beating of the hoofs of the cavalry, with the creaking and groaning of heavily laden wagons, with the rattle and crash of moving artillery. The hour had struck, the time was at hand, the advance must begin.

Overhead light clouds suddenly gathered, fleecy, wraith-like, impalpable, barely seen against the greying sky. Driven onward by the light wind of the night they suddenly concentrated and then spread abroad again until they seemed to cover the vast extent of the heavens with nebulous wings. Were they the upbearing pinions of the bright Harbinger of Victory or the overshadowing wings of Azrael, the Angel of Death? As men looked curiously or carelessly, the wind blew more swiftly, the clouds vanished into thin air and once more the stars shone on undimmed—with what presage?

The Emperor turned, his voice rang sharply, perhaps more sharply than he realised in the tense moment, for the men about him started as if shocked when they heard it.

"Is the King of Naples here?" he asked.

"Here, Sire, and at your service," exclaimed a gay voice with a touch of laughter and a trace of reckless bravado in its notes.

As he spoke a tall, distinguished man, seen more clearly because his uniform was white and elaborately laced with gold, so much so that it would have been ridiculous were it not for some tremendous quality in the man himself that stilled laughter and quieted derision, stepped forward, and saluted the Emperor, his hand to his white-plumed head gear.

"Murat," said Napoleon, speaking familiarly to his friend, "where is your cavalry?"

"Yonder, Sire," said the great horseman, pointing into the valley.

"Are they ready?"

"I have been with them within the hour. Montbrun, Nansouty, Grouchy, with forty thousand sabres behind them are all at your command."

"*Bien!* To you the honour of leading," said the little man slowly, taking a snuff box from his pocket and helping himself to a pinch. "Do you command one of your divisions to pass over on each pontoon bridge, yourself with the centre, with your horse artillery in the rear of each division. Deploy on the other side, search the country thoroughly."

"Very good, Sire," returned the paladin of swordsmen, smiling in fierce satisfaction that at last the war had begun.

"The Prince d'Eckmuhl?" continued the Emperor, raising his voice.

"I am here, your Majesty."

"Davout, you will support the King of Naples with your veteran infantry, Ney, you and Oudinot on the left flank and the rest in order as appointed. Now, gentlemen, to your places and forward. *En Avanti!*"

Murat already on his horse faced the assemblage and lifted his hand. There was no mistaking his meaning or purpose.

Vive l'Empereur" burst from a thousand throats. *Vive l'Empereur!"* cried the soldiers of the headquarter detachment in their turn.

"*Vive l'Empereur!*" roared out the fifty thousand men of the Imperial Guard old and new, camped behind the hill and already awake and prepared for the advance.

As the great roar rose above the hills, the men in the forest glades, restlessly moving beneath their "stiff flags straining in the night wind cold" paused to catch the meaning, and then slowly, softly at first, but extending, deepening, growing louder and louder, until the earth throbbed with it, the sky rang with it, from the peoples and tongues and nations came the great cry, the delirious acclaim, the defiance to Russia, the Voice of the Power of the World, the assurance of that blind, limitless devotion to the sway of this one man, which turned his common soldiers into heroes, his heroes into *paladins* and himself into a *demi*-god.

VIVE L'EMPEREUR!

O Caesar, Morituri te Salutamus

BOOK 1
THE ADVANCE

CHAPTER 1

The Emperor is Angry

The stout, short man in the grey coat standing in the great hall of the old palace at Wilna, was plainly perturbed. His ivory pale face was set in a stern almost angry expression und his massive brow was deeply furrowed. Back of him a little group of *aides-de-camp* and court officials, whose brilliant uniforms, glistening with gold lace and rich with varied colour, only served to accentuate the severe plainness of their chieftain's dress, waited expectantly. They had learned by experience that nothing was gained by breaking in upon the rage of the lion.

He stood with his legs slightly apart, tapping his high and brightly varnished riding boots with his riding whip. The time was well within the beginning of summer, but there had been a heavy rain the night before and in that high latitude the air without was cool and there was a corresponding chill within the vast room of the old royal castle of the by-gone Princes of Lithuania which the huge log fire crackling and blazing in the cavernous fireplace at the far end of the apartment did not entirely dispel; hence the familiar grey overcoat, and the three cornered hat he wore. Sentries were posted at the various doors, tall, stalwart, veteran grenadiers of the Imperial Guard, blue-coated, white-legged, bearskin-topped soldiers who had followed him into every country of Europe and fought for him upon a hundred fields. Outside was heard a confused medley of great noises, the rattle of artillery wagons, the clatter of horses, the jingle of equipment, swords, bits, chains; a mixture of human voices, French predominating above a bass of every language spoken in Europe apparently.

On the other side of the dominant figure stood a deputation of the nobles of the country, dark skinned, black haired Lithuanians and Poles, stem, proud and obstinate in appearance; bearing themselves with more independence, indeed, than had been expressed by the allied, confederated and subjected monarchs of Europe at Dresden a month ago before this new and terrible Lord of the World. The richness of the apparel of some proclaimed their high rank and material prosperity, but there were two or three who were half naked and in rags. The outward appearance and condition of these last affected not at all their manner and bearing.

The echoes of their complaints were still in the air. They had come there to demand protection for their families, their people and their houses, against the fearful outrages taking place in the wake of the invading army. The land was already filled with deserters, masterless men, who, grouping themselves together under some bolder spirit, plundered the territory of the allies as if it were the country of their most bitter enemies. No highway was safe and scarcely any by-way was overlooked by these abandoned and ruthless marauders. The naked Poles in the company had actually been stopped and despoiled of everything they had almost at the very gates of Wilna. The country between there and Kowno was fast being turned into a desert.

There was still a third group in the great hall. Some distance to one side of the Lithuanian nobles stood a handsome, white haired old man in the rich uniform of a general in the Russian army but without a sword. By his side a young French officer was posted with a drawn sword and the two were surrounded by a squad of grenadiers. The Russian was a prisoner of war apparently. Between him and the group of Poles and Lithuanians glances of hatred and contempt were exchanged as often as any one turned his eyes away from the Emperor. The Russian was a very old man, too old for active service, evidently, although he still sported proudly, not to say defiantly, the uniform of his exalted rank.

The silence was suddenly broken by the one person who had the right and privilege of breaking it.

"Montbrun, Jomini, Gérard, here one of you!" he said sharply without looking around.

From the ranks of the staff three men started forward precipitately. It was not well to delay when the lion roared a call.

"You, Gérard," said the Emperor, as the three stopped before him, and saluted, "where is the Prince de Wagram?"

"Receiving a deputation of the nobles of Wilna, Sire," answered Gérard.

"Find him," said the Emperor, "bid him attend me here."

"Very good, Sire."

"And at once," continued Napoleon, as the young officer turned to obey his master's command. "Gentlemen," he went on, facing the deputation and speaking with ever increasing emphasis, "you have justice in your complaint. The condition of affairs is monstrous. It shall be looked into and shall be stopped immediately, if I have to hang every wandering vagabond between here and the Niemen. You have my word that I will not have my faithful Lithuanians and my devoted Poles plundered in this way. I am sure no French soldier is guilty of such excesses and all these other nations that make up my Empire shall learn my will. As for you. Prince, though you are a Russian and an enemy," he turned abruptly to the old man on the other side, "you shall learn the magnanimity of Napoleon. You shall have that protection in which your rank and your merits entitle you. I war not against old men or women and children."

At that moment the door was opened and a stout, heavy-set man in the rich uniform of a Marshal of France, his breast blazing with glittering decorations, advanced hastily and stopped before the Emperor.

"You sent for me. Sire," he began nervously.

"Yes," said Napoleon, assuming an even more haughty and dignified manner and throwing into his voice all the harshness and severity of which he was capable, and as there was no man who could be more sweet, more gracious, more pleasant on occasion, so there was no man who could exhibit the reverse of these qualities at his will "Here, *monsieur*," he continued in a voice of thunder, "is a deputation of the nobles of Lithuania and of Poland who complain, and with justice, of the frightful excesses and ravages of the soldiers in the rear of our armies. This must be put a stop to and I look to you to do it."

"But, Sire," began Berthier, "such excesses are always more or less inevitable in an army composed of so many nationalities as ours, and indeed in any army."

"I tell you I will not have it," returned the Emperor passionately; "these nationalities shall be made to feel the force of my arm and the power of my will as do my faithful Frenchmen. Suspend General Bournon who is supposed to have command of the troops between Wilna and the Niemen. That brigade of Dutch who appear to have gone off in a body and are murdering and plundering, who commands it?"

"General Shempfenk, Sire."

"Cashier him, suppress the brigade, disgrace it in the face of the army, attach its units to other brigades commanded by men who can keep order, and publish an order that whosoever fails to keep his command together and bring it here intact shall be broken before those he does bring in. These scoundrels disgrace my Empire."

"It shall be done. Sire."

"At once," said Napoleon.

"Immediately, Sire."

"And send couriers in every direction with copies of the order, publish it at Wilna, send copies to the commandants at Tilsit, Kowno, Grodno, and have it read to every body of troops marching to join us. Gentlemen!" continued the little man, emphatically, "you have heard my orders to the Prince de Wagram. They will be carried out if we have to use half the army to punish the other half. You are satisfied?"

"We will be, Sire," answered one bolder than the rest," when the orders have been carried out."

"You doubt my intention, *messieurs?*" asked Napoleon, black as thunder again.

"By no means," answered one more pacifically minded than the others, "and we hope that the orders you have given will effect their purpose."

"And when," said the Emperor coldly, "has my will failed to be done in Europe?"

Without waiting for an answer, he turned to the Russian.

"Have I your permission to withdraw, Sire?" interposed Berthier. "The order should be prepared at once, and—"

"Wait. This is Prince Muravieff, an old soldier of Suvoroff's days. He and his daughter and his granddaughter are alone in their *château* of Wilkomir on the banks of the Vilia a score of miles east of Kowno. His daughter is ill, an invalid, and cannot be moved. Most of his retainers have deserted him. He is in peril of his life and his *château* may have been burned over the heads of his children since his departure. He has come to me to ask for my protection and although he is an enemy and his son is a general in the Emperor Alexander's service, he has not asked in vain. Was there not a regiment of light horse left at Kowno to bring despatches and convoy treasure for the payment of the Guard?"

"Yes, Sire."

"Who commands it?"

"Lieutenant Colonel Maurice, Sire."

"Umph—one of the best cavalrymen in my army."

"Yes, Sire."

"Send an order for him to stop at Wilkomir on his way to Wilna. He ought to be ready to start now."

"He should perhaps be leaving Kowno the day after tomorrow. Sire."

"Very good, tell him to stop at Wilkomir and make sure of its safety. Authorise him to leave a detachment of trusted men with an officer to guard it until these disorders are put down and the way behind us is as safe as the way before us is perilous."

"Very good. Sire, have you any further orders?"

"None. Stay, send the Prince Muravieff back to Wilkomir with an officer and a suitable escort. Are you satisfied. Prince?"

"More than satisfied, your Majesty," replied the old Prince, bowing low. "You make war like Napoleon and you temper justice with mercy as an Emperor should. Our master, the Czar Alexander, whom God save, shall not fail to hear of this."

"You are an old man. General," said Napoleon. He glanced out of the window at the darkening sky. "Night will be upon us in an hour. Will you accept the hospitality of my quarters and soldier's fare for the night? I shall be honoured. You can take up your journey in the morning."

"But my women and the *château*—"

"A courier will start at once, eh, Berthier?"

"Immediately, Sire."

"They would far outstrip you, Prince. You could gain nothing by starting now."

"I bow to your Majesty's command," said the Russian.

"Le Grand," said the Emperor, turning and addressing the young officer who stood guard over the Prince, "return *Monsieur le Prince* his sword. See that he is comfortably quartered tonight and have a place set for him at my table."

"Yes, Sire."

"Gentlemen, the audience is over. I trust you shall have no cause to complain of the army again. Goodnight."

The Lithuanians bowed low and withdrew in the wake of Berthier who had hastened away to prepare the necessary orders.

CHAPTER 2

The Light Cavalry Marches

The public square of Kowno was completely filled by a regiment of Hussars, Light Horse, belonging to the Imperial Guard. On a broad street leading away from the square a baggage train, whose small size gave no indication of its great value, was drawn up. It was early in the morning of a bright, cloudless, perfect day. An old officer stood on the steps of the town hall and by his side a younger man clad in the brilliant uniform of the regiment.

"You have the despatches and the treasure?"

"All safe, General"

"Very good. You are to carry one and convoy the other to Wilna without delay. The treasure you are to turn over to the Prince de Wagram, the despatches you are to deliver to the Emperor in person."

"I understand."

"There is not an enemy between here and Wilna, of course, but the country is filled with deserters. They may band themselves together if they learn of the treasure you nave under guard and attempt to despoil you of it."

The young man laughed.

"An army corps composed of deserters and thieves and vagabonds could not wrest anything from my hard riding swordsmen."

"Probably not," said the old soldier, smiling in turn, "but beware of too great confidence."

"You may trust me, General."

"I know that. Yet it is not often that so young a man commands the finest regiment of Light Horse in the Imperial Guard—that is to say, in the army. Goodbye."

"*Au revoir, Mon Général,*" said the young man lightly, saluting and turning away.

Descending the few steps he sprang gracefully to the back of his big black horse, and, followed by his staff, clattered to the head of the regiment, drew his sword and shouted an order. The trumpets blared. The order was repeated, the lines broke into columns and the regiment marched away, the precious baggage wagons in the midst. The populace of Kowno had been surfeited with military spectacles, but there was something in this regiment of picked men and picked horses that differentiated it from the rest of the troops and they broke into cheers as the colonel at the head of his eight hundred rode through the streets and started on his journey. The regiment had chafed viciously at being left behind for the lonesome, tiresome and unexciting escort duty when the rest of the army advanced, but there had been no battle yet and as they realised that they would be in time to take part in the great events which invariably followed the advances of Napoleon, their good humour returned with the order to march.

The road led through a great forest of pine trees which cast somewhat melancholy shadows across their path. There was no need to ask the direction, for the road itself was a thing of horror. Although there had been no battle and therefore no cause for panic, certainly none for withdrawal, it was as if they were riding over the line of retreat of a broken and defeated army.

Abandoned baggage wagons, pillaged, and such of their contents as were not acceptable to their robbers strewn in the road, lay on every hand. The sweetness of the air was polluted by the stench from many dead horses and here and there dead men. Guns, that matchless artillery of the French army, had been abandoned, broken *caissons* full of useless ammunition lay about. Not only on the road but so far as the eye could see under the trees similar spectacles were presented. The trail was blazed with debris, usually only to be seen after a great defeat, a rout, a disaster.

As the regiment advanced a turn of the road would bring it in sight of a band of perhaps fifty or one hundred soldiers, their different nationalities proclaimed by the varieties of their uniform. These rascals invariably took to their heels at the sight of the light horsemen. On either side in the forest could be seen flitting through the trees other masterless deserters. And yet a fortnight had not elapsed since that great army had set forth! What did it mean? What could it mean?

The brow of the young officer was knitted, his lips were compressed. He said finally to the major who was riding by his side.

29

"I would to God the Emperor would give me permission to shoot or hang a few of these wretched deserters, Beaubien. Things could not be worse if we had been overwhelmingly defeated and our army annihilated."

"No," answered Beaubien, the major who was also the lieutenant colonel's intimate friend and comrade of many campaigns. "In all my soldiering I have never seen the like of this."

"Nor I."

"But that we know differently I could swear that we had been defeated."

"But that is impossible! Pass the word," continued the lieutenant colonel, "that if any man of this regiment leaves the ranks without permission he is to be shot instantly by the nearest officer. I will bring this regiment to Wilna intact or leave its bodies on the road!"

The major turned to the adjutant, repeating the harsh order in so loud a voice that those at the head of the column heard it plainly and in a minute that young officer galloped back along the flank, repeating what had been said to every troop commander in succession. Many of these men had followed their lieutenant colonel long enough to know that what he said he would do and that for all his slight, gay, somewhat careless appearance, he was a man of iron resolution and nerve. There was no straggling, therefore, and the regiment moved on over the road until an open space, freer from dead horses and abandoned equipment then usual lay before them. It was noon. Orders were given for the troops to dismount, unsaddle their horses and prepare their noon meal. This regiment carried its provisions with it and fires were soon crackling and blazing while the experienced veterans made ready their simple but wholesome meal.

Just after dinner was over, down the road from the West, a young officer, followed by a dozen troopers, came at a gallop. So soon as he entered the open, he drew rein, sought out the situation of the commander and his staff and at once approached him.

"Lieutenant Colonel Maurice?" he said, dismounting and saluting.

"The same, sir."

"Orders for you, sir."

He drew forth a packet and handed it to the officer who received it, holding it unopened in his hand.

"The health of the Emperor?" he began.

"Was never better."

"The army?"

"The army is in good spirits. Colonel, but—"

"But what?"

"It is hungry."

"Already!"

"Already. There is nothing to eat except what we brought with us. We expected to live off the country, and—"

"And the country?"

"Look at it, forests of pine and fields of green rye."

"I see."

"Horses die by the hundreds, men desert by the thousands."

"I have noticed that also."

"I am carrying orders to the commandants of the various posts along the road to shoot or hang without mercy men who leave the army and cannot give an account of themselves. The Emperor is determined to put a stop to this desertion and pillage."

"It is too late to put a stop to much of it," returned the lieutenant colonel. "We have passed house after house, including some large *châteaux* which have been burned and wrecked. Indeed, the whole way looks as if a beaten army had made use of it."

"You will find the same conditions obtain the farther you go. By the way, there is another order which may interest you."

"And what is that?"

"Any officer in command of troops who arrives at headquarters without his troops, or without a considerable proportion of them, is to be broken before the whole army and reduced to the ranks."

"The Light Horse of the Guard is not affected by an order of that kind," said the lieutenant colonel proudly.

"No, I suppose not," said the officer. "Well, I must proceed."

"Will you not join our meal? It is practically over but we can get you something."

"Thank you, no. We broke our fast from our haversacks on the road. You have your orders?"

"Yes."

"And I have your permission to go on?"

"Most certainly."

The officer saluted, sprang to his hone, spoke to his men and galloped down the road toward Kowno, over which the light horse had just come. The lieutenant colonel broke the seal of the packet, opened the document and read it over carefully.

31

Lieutenant Colonel Maurice, Commanding, etc.:

You are to proceed to the *château* of Wilkomir which lies somewhere south-eastward of the main road between Kowno and Wilna on the banks of the Vilia. You are to make sure the safety of the inhabitants thereof, if necessary leaving a guard with orders to protect it from pillage until such time as it may be withdrawn. Should you come across any troops pillaging, robbing or firing you are to deal with them summarily in accordance with your judgment so far as it is possible for you to do so without imperilling your convoy. Lastly, you are to bring to headquarters all deserters of whatsoever rank or nationality you can secure.

    By the command of his Imperial Majesty,

    (Signed)   Berthier, Prince de Wagram. Chief of Staff.

With a word the lieutenant colonel summoned the major, the adjutant and one or two other officers. He read the order to them and asked if any of them knew the location of the *château* of Wilkomir. No one knew, of course. They were all French and all utterly strange to the country. They had not come across a single native, noble or peasant, that morning. How to find the place was a puzzle.

"The Emperor evidently lays great stress upon our carrying out his orders," said the lieutenant colonel. "That stream that we passed a mile back must have been the Vilia on one bank of which the *château* should lie if it has not been burned before this. The trend of the road has been south-eastward but hardly enough in that direction, I should say, to reach the *château*. Beaubien!"

"Sir."

"I leave you in command of the regiment. You are to march slowly on the road toward Wilna and at four o'clock are to encamp for the night. Captain Grosjean will take one troop and explore the Vilia to the left. Let him search both banks thoroughly and if he finds the *château* he is to notify you and you are to notify me."

"And where will you be, sir," asked Major Beaubien.

"I will take another troop and explore the Vilia to the right. You heard the order about the cashiering of an officer who fails to bring his command to Wilna?"

"I did, sir."

"You will see that our lines are strictly guarded and patrolled by some of the veterans who can be depended upon, with orders to shoot every man who attempts to cross them in either direction."

"Very good, sir."

"If we find the *château* soon we should rejoin you before dark. If not, you may expect us in the morning without fail. You are not to march until we have joined you or until you have definite word from me."

"I understand, sir."

"Very good then; assemble the regiment, give me the first troop, Captain Grosjean the second and we will begin the search. Captain, the place is called Wilkomir. It is a large *château*, I take it. If you should find it, detail a lieutenant and a half platoon to protect and hold it against all comers until further orders and then report to Major Beaubien with the rest of your troop without delay. You will, of course, do everything in your power to reassure the inmates of the *château* and to treat them with the courtesy they merit as friends or *protégés* of the Emperor."

"Very good, sir."

"Come, my braves," said the lieutenant colonel, putting himself at the head of the troop which he had designated should accompany him and leading the way into the forest which extended far to the right of them.

CHAPTER 3

An Interrupted Reverie

It was late in the evening. The troop of light horsemen under the direct command of Lieutenant Colonel Maurice had scouted along both banks of the Vilia and had found nothing. Yet not exactly nothing, for even in the recess of the forest they came across the shattered remains of the Grand Army and were confronted by the same evidences of the demoralisation as abounded on the road. Here and there a peasant's hut still stood either because it had escaped the notice of the pillagers and marauders on account of its being buried in the forest or possibly because it was too poor and too humble to tempt them.

One or two ruined country houses were seen but nothing that resembled the Château Wilkomir. One or two of the inhabitants of the country were routed out of their secret hiding places by the soldiers but they either could or would tell nothing and as none of the horsemen spoke Russian except the lieutenant colonel and he but badly, and as none of the peasants spoke any French at all, the attempt to get anything out of them was given up in despair.

The desire to cover as much ground as possible had caused Lieutenant Colonel Maurice to scatter his forces widely, instructing them if they found nothing to return to the main body by nightfall. Therefore, he found himself at about five o'clock in the evening on the third of July, 1812, alone on the banks of the Vilia in the great pine forests of Lithuania and Poland. After separating from his men he had wandered away to the south-westward through the trees.

Although it was summer, the air was cool and pleasant. The great pines cast soft shadows, hastening the decline of the day. The carpet of pine needles, the product of centuries, deadened the foot falls of his horse. The reins hung carelessly upon the neck of the animal, which pursued his own way indeed, his absorbed rider being plunged in deep thought.

The Grand Army of Napoleon was between him and any possible enemy, that is any possible Russian enemy—for the deserters he had an honest soldier's supreme contempt—and there was no particular demand upon Lieutenant Colonel Maurice's instincts or aptitudes as a soldier. His thoughts were not of war, therefore.

Blessed with an ample patrimony, which had been carefully conserved through a long infancy by prudent administration, and having been fortunate enough to win the approbation and favour of his Emperor and idol during the Napoleonic wars, and having enjoyed substantial proofs of that favour in rich booty, the thoughts of Lieutenant Colonel Maurice were not about money, therefore.

There is left, with the elimination of these possibilities, but one other subject which could properly engage the attention of so young, so successful and so handsome a soldier,—women; or to escape from the general to the particular, a woman.

Lieutenant Colonel Maurice had loved madly and often. There was a catholicity about the campaigns of the Great Emperor which enforced upon his followers an acquaintance with many peoples of many climes. Lieutenant Colonel Maurice in rapid succession had fallen victim to the voluptuous sweetness of Italy, the fiery temperament of Spain, the languid grace of Portugal, the flaxen-haired stolidity of Prussia, the dark beauty of Austro-Hungary, to say nothing of the vivaciousness and sparkle of the women of his own native land; but never before had he been so hard hit as at present. He swore it in his heart and he above all others should know.

In the first place, he had at last found his exact opposite. Lieutenant Colonel Maurice was a man rather under than over the medium height, spare, not to say slender in proportion, but well knit as to frame and intensely vigorous. His eyes, now so thoughtfully turned inward, were of a deep blue colour and very bright, his hair was curly and reddish-gold in hue. Typically French in disposition and temperament, he was not at all so in appearance. Colour came and went easily in his bronzed cheek and his movements were quick and alert, his bearing brave and dashing.

The lady who at present engaged, and as he fondly believed would forever engage his affections, was tall, almost as tall as Lieutenant Colonel Maurice. Her hair was as black as the raven's wing, her eyes likewise. Her face was pale, colourless, her movement slow and stately, her temper calm and equable. When he met her first at Dresden a month before, where he was in attendance upon the Emperor, who was receiving the kings and potentates of Europe, he had fairly flung himself at her feet. The first sight of her had struck him as if with a bullet.

Lieutenant Colonel Maurice carried within his spare frame one or two bullets which had found comfortable lodgement there and which the surgeons had concluded not to disturb and in addition there were various scars on different portions of his anatomy where the swords of the enemy had bitten deep into his flesh. This is not saying that Lieutenant Colonel Maurice was not an expert swordsman, able to protect himself with that gentleman's weapon. Not at all, for he was rated as the best swordsman in the light cavalry of the Guard and that meant the best swordsman in the army, for the light horsemen were supposed to be as superior to the other horsemen as the Guard to the other corps. But what would you? The impetuosity of the young officer frequently plunged him in the midst of myriads of foes against whom his single arm could effect nothing.

So when the sight of Princess Idona Muravieff at Monsieur le Marechal Poniatovski's ball produced upon him, as he had said to his confidentially devoted major, a shock like a bullet, it must be conceded that he knew what he was talking about. Gunshot wounds are not pleasant, however, and that was the difference between this latest wound and those inflicted by lethal weapons.

As usual in a charge, disregardful of the consequences to himself. Lieutenant Colonel Maurice had fairly hurled himself at the feet of Princess Idona, or rather at her heart, but as a cavalry charge is blocked by a hollow square of veteran soldiers, so he had been rebuffed. Perhaps rebuffed is not the best word, for the Princess Muravieff had received his advances, but with discouraging equanimity. His most ardent protestations were met with indifference, real or assumed, but effectual. When orders came to advance and the lieutenant colonel had to tear himself away, he could not flatter himself that he had effected by all his daring manoeuvres, the least lodgement in that lady's heart.

Now this was a new and unpleasant experience for Lieutenant Colonel Maurice. His wealth, his good looks, the favour of the Emperor, which he so evidently enjoyed, had made his career one of conquest. He had known instinctively how to adapt himself to the requirements feminine of every nation. Confronted with this indifference, his passion grew until he decided that at last he saw his fate before him, that his eternal happiness depended upon the winning of the lady as his wife—an indication, that, of the seriousness of the present situation since matrimony had never before entered the mind of the gay young lieutenant colonel. He had loved his freedom as a soldier of the light horse of the great Empire too well to consider donning the fetters of matrimony, but now—well a month had elapsed since he had first seen her and he still thought of her. In fact, it was because he was absorbed in dreams of her that he had wandered so far away from the troop that afternoon, wishing to be alone beneath the pines which somehow recalled her image to him in their somewhat sombre majesty.

He did not realise, wrapped in these thoughts, how far he had wandered or where he was. He had caused inquiry to be made at Dresden after his departure, and had learned that the Princess Muravieff had gone from the city a few days after the army left it. He really knew very little about her. Her father was a general in the Russian army, her brother was a colonel in Alexander's guard. Her grandfather. Prince Muravieff, was a superannuated Russian general who had fought under Suvoroff against Napoleon when he was General Bonaparte years before; but he had long since retired. None of her family had been with her at Dresden. She had come over from Warsaw apparently to attend the festivities consequent upon the presence of the great Emperor, with some Polish relations of hers.

Of course the sympathy of the men of her family was all Russian but Princess Muravieff's mother had been a Pole and so far as he could tell she was entirely Polish in her aspirations and affections. She cherished passionate hopes and dreams of a reunited and independent Poland, springing like Minerva from the head of Jove, through the will of the great Emperor.

It was an odd situation that he should love a Russian woman, he felt, and yet her predilection for the French warranted that, if any warrant were needed. And no matter what she was, he loved her. He had made it a rule in life to beat the men of the enemy in the field and conquer the women in the drawing room. It was a rule by which one could obtain all that was desired and he had meant to follow it in this case. His orders and her departure had changed everything and jet his first orders had been most agreeable to him. He had been left at Kowno with instructions to wait for certain treasure and for certain papers. He had learned vaguely that the Muravieff *château* was somewhere across the Vilia beyond Kowno and he had hoped that he might, by some happy fortune, catch sight of the Princess if she returned to her home as she had intimated, but she must have gone there some other way, for he had not seen her.

Now he was ordered to the front. The army was about to plunge into the heart of Russia. What portion of it would come back? Would he be among the number? No one could say. Certainly there would be hard marching and desperate fighting. It was most unsatisfactory, his situation, and he was correspondingly sad. He did not even know where to write to her.

How much further he would have wandered in the growing twilight cannot be said, for his reveries were interrupted by three things that came to him simultaneously, the deep bay of a wolf-hound, the sharp crack of a fire arm and the piercing *crescendo* of a woman's scream.

CHAPTER 4

A Friend in the Forest

A few seconds later, having spurred his horse fiercely on the instant, Lieutenant Colonel Maurice topped the crest of the low hill and saw before him a woman, a dead dog and four live ones.

It is an insult for which apologies are due to have included the living and the dead in the same category, for the dead was one of the most magnificent animals of his race, and the living were among the most despicable of theirs.

The living wore uniforms, the uniforms of the Grand Army, the yellow of Spain, the blue of Prussia, the green of Bavaria, while one was a renegade Frenchman. The Frenchman held in his hand a smoking pistol with which he had just shot the great wolf hound which had sprung to the defence of its mistress. At the first attack muscles of steel, shrouded in perishable flesh, had matched themselves, as they had often done before, against lethal weapons held by a steady hand and guided by a ruthless heart. They had come off second best. The dog, blood covered, lay on the ground at the feet of its struggling mistress.

As women go, this one was tall and striking in an age when height and strength were not considered as the ideal feminine qualities. The Spaniard and the Prussian had the woman by the arms, and she was struggling violently with them. The Frenchman looked on with an amused, cynical interest, the Bavarian, more stolid, stood indifferently by. A common passion, base, but in these four, greater than nobler feelings, had made them forget their various nationalities and differences; their antagonisms were laid aside in the presence of beauty and booty, love of woman and love of plunder, as easily as they had deserted their colours and had fled from their duty.

Lieutenant Colonel Maurice, tried and experienced soldier as

39

he was, had that trait which old soldiers possess supremely, of being able to act instinctively in an emergency. His regiment of Hussars was armed with heavy carbines or short muskets for this particular campaign, which in effect changed them into mounted infantry on occasion, very much to the disgust of the dashing light horsemen but the lieutenant colonel carried no such weapon. There were two heavy pistols in the holsters before him, however, and these would serve.

Lieutenant Colonel Maurice was one of the best shots in an emergency in the French army, intent upon their efforts, the four plunderers had not observed his swift and sudden approach. Checking his horse abruptly, he leaned forward and seized a pistol from his right hand holster. Taking quick aim, with the daring of his race, he fired at the man holding the woman on the right. It would have been easier, safer, it would have involved less risk to the woman if he had fired at one of the men looking on, but that was not Lieutenant Colonel Maurice's way. He was confident of his skill and with justice as the event determined. The missile sped toward its mark, the Spaniard released his clutch on the woman's arm and collapsed, a bullet through his heart.

Before the group realised what was toward, the other pistol was out and man number two, the Prussian to the left, received the second bullet. This was a more dangerous and difficult shot than the first, for the woman naturally recoiled from the fallen Spaniard and she was closer to her other assailant, but once again the eye of the Hussar proved true, and the Prussian was sent to his account.

The newcomer was so confident of success that he did not pause to see this second assailant loose his grasp on the woman, throw up his hands, stagger, reel and fall, for unsheathing his sword, he put spurs to his horse again and dashed boldly at the other two. The Frenchman retained some of his presence of mind, for whipping out a second pistol he fired point blank at the oncoming horseman. The next instant, with a neat thrust, the Hussar drove his sword through the renegade's throat.

This took some little time. The dull witted Bavarian who had stood petrified, finding himself the sole survivor of the nefarious quartette, suddenly discovered that he had no stomach for further encounter. He turned and fled through the trees. If the country had been open it would have been a matter of little difficulty for Lieutenant Colonel Maurice to have ridden him down, or if he had had another weapon to have shot him as he ran, but as it was, with the blind instinct of the hunted, the Bavarian plunged among the thickest trees and made good his escape.

Reining in his panting horse, Lieutenant Colonel Maurice flung his leg across his saddle and slipped lightly to the ground. Sheathing his sword and adjusting his scarlet dolman edged with white fur which had become somewhat disarranged in the hurry of the conflict, he turned to the woman who had staggered back against a tree and watched in silence the progress of the sharp affair. He raised his hand to his *shako*, or busby, with its scarlet plume and its gold trappings to make a military salute and then as he got a full fair view of the lady for the first time he tore off his fur headgear and swept the ground with it, bowing low before her.

"Princess Muravieff!" he said softly but with great excitement, "what happy fortune—"

"Colonel Maurice," said the Princess, extending her hand, "you have done me a service which I can never repay."

"*Mademoiselle*," said the Lieutenant Colonel, taking her hand and bowing over it, with all the grace of the ancient regime—which was not particularly in evidence among the soldiers of Napoleon's army, by the way—"the service is nothing. It was a happiness, a positive pleasure for me to mete out punishment to those treacherous scoundrels. I have only one regret."

"And what is that, *monsieur?*"

"That one of them disgraced the uniform of France."

"Well, sir," said the Princess, "you have more than atoned for that disgrace."

"It was nothing," protested the hussar, "I should have been more happy to have rescued you from a thousand than from four."

"And my gratitude is forever yours. If I could only repay—"

"If the service had been worth it, *mademoiselle*," interrupted the soldier, "payment could be made far in excess of the highest estimate you could possibly put upon it."

"And with what?"

"With yourself, *mademoiselle*."

It was a bold age, and quick love making was the rule. The Princess Muravieff apparently took little offence at this hasty declaration.

"I am a Princess of Lithuania," she said, smiling somewhat haughtily.

"Exactly, but I am young and with the favour of the Emperor all things are possible. In a few more years, I may be a—"

"What, *monsieur?*"

"A Marshal of France, the peer of kings."

"And even then, do you—"

"No, *mademoiselle*, not your peer; he lives not upon this earth, I do believe, for you are above all—"

She put out her hand protestingly.

"In my heart," he said.

"*Monsieur le Colonel*, you told me all of this at Dresden. You remember those evenings and—"

"Am I likely to forget them?"

"No, I believe not, and I have had the noblest evidence of your remembrance of—me, this night."

"What I told you in Dresden, *mademoiselle*, I would tell you in the face of the whole army, I would tell you in heaven itself, if I were lucky enough to follow you there, I—"

But the way in which the young Light Horseman uttered these words was somewhat lacking in the fire and passion which should have accompanied them. During the latter part of the conversation, Princess Muravieff had carefully looked away from the hussar. The faltering accents of the young officer suddenly disturbed her. She turned her head and stared him full in the face. What she saw there was not reassuring.

Princess Muravieff was pale herself. She enjoyed that exquisite pallor of the cold lands, as clear as the air in the sunshine after snow. But she noted a different kind of paleness on the face of the young officer before her. He had stood erect at first, holding the bridle of his horse. He suddenly turned, put out his arm and grasped the horn of the saddle, leaning heavily against the horse. He was deathly white, the colour receded from his lips.

"*Monsieur!*" exclaimed the woman in surprise, "what is the matter?"

"I believe one of the rascals—" he thrust his hand under the red *dolman* and put it against the green and gold tunic that he wore,— "has—hit—me."

"You are wounded," she cried in alarm, "why did you not tell me?"

"I had—more important things—to tell you."

"How foolish," said the woman approaching him closer.

"The wound—in my heart," faltered the man, "made me—forget the—other."

"Colonel Maurice!" exclaimed the Princess, stretching out her hands to him.

But Lieutenant Colonel Maurice was now well nigh past any further continuance of the conversation.

"I love you," he murmured faintly; "it is happiness—to die—at your—"

He did not finish the sentence in words but in action, for his hand relaxed its grasp on the saddle horn, the horse stepped aside and the man slid gently and somehow gracefully down to the ground at the woman's feet. He lay there whiter than ever, absolutely still.

The Princess Muravieff had not lived in the half primitive wilds of Poland without developing qualities of courage, self-reliance and ability to grapple with emergencies. She did not hesitate a moment. She dropped to her knees beside the young man, unbuckled the strap which held the *dolman* and threw it back. With skilful hands, which showed that she was accustomed to the intricacies of uniforms, she unbuttoned the blood stained tunic and opened it in turn; then she tore open the young officer's shirt, noting unconsciously as she did so the fineness of his linen, and bared his left shoulder.

The bullet had struck him in that shoulder; the wound was an ugly one but not necessarily dangerous. His quixotic indifference to it had caused him to faint from loss of blood. Princess Muravieff was not without experience in gunshot wounds. In that country physicians and surgeons were few and far between and the women, especially those of the higher classes, possessed some knowledge and skill in surgery. The Princess Muravieff, her father and grandfather, and farther back than she could recall, had been soldiers and she had seen wounds before. She did not faint or scream or wring her hands. She acted promptly and well. From her petticoat she tore long strips of white cloth and with these she tightly and skilfully bound up the wound. Lieutenant Colonel Maurice, gracefully and graciously lying unconscious the while.

He had whispered in her ear at the last of the Emperor's balls at Dresden that her touch would awaken the dead. As she worked over him, she thought of it whimsically enough now because her touch did not serve to recall even the fainting, much less the dead. The flow of blood fortunately stopped by her skilful bandaging. Princess Muravieff rose to her feet and looked about her.

The well trained horse had stopped after he had moved away a few steps and now stood waiting. He had been wounded himself and had galloped over many a battlefield before, during and after the conflict when there had been many wounded. What thoughts were passing through his equine brain no one could tell. He was a thoroughbred, however, and recognised others of the class. The Princess stepped toward him quietly and extended her hand. The horse looked at her intelligently and made no effort to avoid her.

On the back of the saddle were two small saddle which she divined she would find what she needed, buckled the straps, rummaged the contents and drew forth a small silver mounted flask. She it, smelt it, tasted it and then satisfied as to its contents, kneeling down, she lifted the head of the soldier and put it to his lips. There was no water nearby and afterward with her hand she put a little of the ardent liquor on his forehead. In a few moments she had the satisfaction of seeing her patient open his eyes.

She was still supporting his head in her arms, she was still bending over him, her face very close to his and the blue eyes of the Light Horseman stared directly her own dusky orbs. No words passed between them for a moment.

"I have died," at last said Lieutenant Colonel Maurice softly, "at least this is heaven and you are an angel."

"Recall yourself, *monsieur*," said the Princess rather severely, at the same time depositing his head gently ground, "this is Lithuania, not heaven, and I am your grateful friend, Idona Muravieff."

"It is the same," said the lieutenant colonel faintly, following her movements with eager gaze.

"You remember what has happened?"

"I remember nothing but that I see you."

"Nonsense, my dear Colonel. I was attacked, you saved me and you were wounded."

"I believe I do remember some trifling hurt which I had forgot while I stood before you until this cursed loss of blood, *mademoiselle*,—I begrudge every drop of that blood that bled away."

"And why?" asked the Princess, more and more deeply interested in spite of herself in this wooer who had become certainly somewhat faint but who was equally certainly still pursuing.

"Because each drop belongs to you."

Although this was very lovely to hear and she could have listened to it indefinitely, the Princess had a practical side to her nature.

"*Monsieur*," she said, "if we pass much more time in conversing, the night will be upon us."

44

"Night," said the lieutenant colonel more strongly, "night and the stars?"

"Of course."

"The one star to which my gaze turns is—"

"I see that I must settle the matter myself," said the woman decidedly. "Do you think if I gave you another draught from your own flask that you could rise and mount your horse?"

"If you will give me your hand, *mademoiselle*," said Lieutenant Colonel Maurice, "you could lift me to any heights."

"You told me in Dresden," returned the woman, smiling, "that my touch would raise the dead."

"And I told you truly."

"On the contrary," returned the Princess, "when I bound up your wounds after you had fainted, it did not even recall you to your senses."

"It was joy at your touch, *mademoiselle*. My feelings were too great to be sustained by this poor human frame."

It was quite evident that Lieutenant Colonel Maurice was growing stronger. Feeling that the scene, delightful, though utterly impractical, must be put an end to, Princess Muravieff knelt down once more and proffered the lieutenant colonel his flask.

"If you would again lift me up," he said artfully; whereat she stooped, slipped her arm under his head and shoulders and drew him up to a sitting position. For a moment he dared to let his head rest against her bosom. "Would," he whispered, "that this moment might continue forever."

"Drink, *monsieur*," said the woman imperatively, whereupon the soldier straightened himself and took a long draught from his flask, handed it back to her and declared himself ready for her further command.

"The Château Wilkomir, where we live, lies through the trees half a mile yonder. If you could mount your horse we could reach it easily. If not, I must leave you here while I go for help."

"I will try. I am confident with your help I can do anything," returned the soldier.

By a great effort, he managed to stagger to his feet; and with a still greater effort, in which she assisted him valiantly, he got Into the saddle. He swayed there and was forced to sustain himself by clinging to the leather. The Princess drew the reins from the horse's neck, took them In her own hands, stationed herself by his head and together

45

they moved off. Lieutenant Colonel Maurice wanted to talk upon the way but the Princess Muravieff, with a truer appreciation of his powers, refused to converse and insisted that he observe the same silence. The horse walked slowly but the way was soon traversed. Presently the great old weather-beaten walls of the *château* or castle of Wilkomir came into view in the midst of an ample clearing.

The two walked through the great gateway in the wall enclosing the *château* and the next moment were surrounded by a handful of servants and retainers of the house, who had come just in time, for Lieutenant Colonel Maurice, at the very end of his resources, collapsed gently in the saddle and would have fallen to the ground but for the rescuing hands of *mademoiselle*, assisted by those whom she designated for the task.

They carried the lieutenant colonel quickly into the house, upstairs and into one of the great bed rooms where they undressed him and made him as comfortable as possible. When he was safely in bed the Princess Idona and one Stepan, her old *major domo*, the only male person of importance left in the house in the absence of old Prince Muravieff, who had gone two days before to Wilna to see the Emperor, came to visit the young officer, and although he protested violently, the Princess insisted upon bathing and redressing his wound with the capable assistance of Stepan.

When it was all over, the bullet which had lodged under the skin of his back had been extracted, and he had been made as comfortable as possible, they bade him good night.

"Don't go," he pleaded beseechingly. "Don't leave me alone; it is jet early in the evening, and I have so much to say to you, *mademoiselle*."

"What you have to do now," said the Princess severely, "is to go to sleep and give your—"

"And do you think, *mademoiselle*, that I could sleep under the same roof with you?"

The Princess laughed.

"You have often told me that you dreamed of me. Here is an opportunity."

"There is some happiness in that," said the young Light Horseman.

"I give you full leave to—"

"To what, *mademoiselle*—"

"Dream about me the night long if you wish."

There was a mute entreaty in the eyes of the soldier and the Princess knew what he would ask before she left him. She extended her hand to him and bent over him. The soldier seized that hand, resisting the temptation to draw her to him, a temptation the force of which she could not understand, and pressed her hand to his lips. Was he delirious or did he fancy that she left it there a moment, that she drew it away reluctantly?

"You will have a good night's sleep—"

"And happy dreams," he interrupted.

"Vassily, one of the house servants, will sleep outside your door and within call and in the morning—"

"I shall see you again?"

"Of a surety," she answered, smiling at him as she disappeared through the door.

The care with which his wound had been treated, the skill with which it had been washed and the deftness with which Stepan, the old servant, and the Princess had extracted the bullet and the cooling draught which he had been given, acted well on the strong constitution and clean healthy body of the young hussar. For a little while he thought of his regiment, wondering what his command would think of his absence, how they would search for him, how he would get word to them on the morrow, and then for a long time he thought of her. He could feel the light touch of her hand on his breast, he could recall the moment when his head lay upon her bosom, when her strong young arm encircled his shoulder, when she drew her hand slowly across his lips. He could close his eyes and see her pale face with its midnight crown of hair, its fathomless eyes, its scarlet lips, bending over him, and by and by he fell into a quiet sleep without a single solitary vestige of a dream.

CHAPTER 5

A Princess With a Will

Lieutenant Colonel Maurice felt so much better in the morning that he insisted upon getting up and dressing. His insistence was met by a positive refusal on the part of old Stepan, who came himself to tender his services and assistance. The result was a clash of wills between the Frenchman and Russian within the *château* which bade fair to be as serious and as determined as the clash of armies on the plains without, but by the simple expedient of causing the lieutenant colonel's uniform to be removed from the room by the servant Vassily, the Russian *major domo* succeeded in his purpose. His stolidity under the reproaches of the soldier was masterly. Nothing that Lieutenant Colonel Maurice could say or do moved him. It was not until his experienced eye saw that the young man was working himself up into a fever that he even condescended to argue the question with him at all. His principal argument was that he, Stepan, was not executing his own will but the will of his mistress, the Princess Idona, and about that there could be no question.

"It is on her account alone," said the soldier savagely, "that I wish to arise, you blockhead," he continued in his imperfect Russian, of which fortunately or unfortunately, Stepan could not make a great deal, no more in fact than the lieutenant colonel could make out of Stepan's very indifferent French. "I have a regiment some miles back on the road yonder. The men will be frantic with anxiety to know what has become of me. I must rejoin them presently. I can only stay here a little while and I must see your mistress as often and as long as possible. I must take advantage of my opportunity, man! I do not know when I shall see her again. Can you not understand?"

"It is the will of the Princess," repeated the imperturbable Russian, "that you remain quietly in bed today."

"If I had a weapon," returned the lieutenant colonel savagely, "I would pistol you where you stand. If you do not order my uniform to be brought back immediately, it will go hard with you. If it were not that I might meet my lady in the halls, I would go in search of it as I am, but—"

"It is the will of the Princess that you remain quietly in bed today," once more said Stepan stolidly as before, resting upon that command as upon a rock.

"And it is my will that I get up, stupid," roared the infuriated officer. "Don't you see that you are throwing me into a fever, and—"

"You are throwing yourself into a fever, *monsieur*," said a low voice from the doorway.

The lieutenant colonel turned his head, and to his great pleasure and equal astonishment, there stood *mademoiselle*, quiet, composed as ever, and yet was it fancy on his part, with a brighter sparkle in her eyes and just a faint tinge of rose, natural rose beyond doubt, in her pale cheek. Stepan was a stolid man but he was by no means stupid. He did not deserve the abuse which the Light Horseman had hurled at his head on that score and he was quick witted enough to notice that the Princess Idona had put on one of her most becoming gowns, having discarded the simple and ordinary dress she wore when attending her invalid mother while at the *château*. Well, it was no concern of Stepan's how his mistress dressed. Since she had come he troubled himself no further with the direction of the affair and with a grave bow, unnoticed by his mistress, he promptly withdrew,

"You are throwing yourself into a fever," repeated the Princess, coming into the room, walking over to the bed and gently and with a sort of detached professional air, laying her cool white hand, perfect in shape though perhaps a thought too large for the prevalent taste of the day, upon his flushed forehead.

Lieutenant Colonel Maurice caught that hand in both of his and pressed it as if he would imprint it upon his brain as her image was already imprinted upon his heart.

"*Mademoiselle*," he exclaimed, "the thought that I should not see you caused my agitation. I did not dream that of your kindness you would deign to visit me here."

"You think then," began the Princess, her modesty taking alarm as she quickly drew her hand away, "that I am unmaidenly in—"

"No, no," protested the lieutenant colonel, catching the passing fingers before it was too late and holding them in a clasp that well substantiated his claim that he was much better. "I meant nothing that is inconsistent with the love I bear you."

"Talking of love so early in the morning?" said the Princess, looking down at him gravely, half critically, half in wonderment.

"There is no time to lose, *mademoiselle*; I am a soldier; I have to go away the minute I am able to ride my horse—today, it may be. I must tell you of my heart while I can, for I know not when the opportunity will be vouchsafed me again."

"Your experiences then," said Mademoiselle Muravieff reflectively, "have taught you the necessity of prompt action, even in the affairs of the heart."

"Experiences!" protested the lieutenant colonel; "I have had none. Love affairs, perhaps; what would you of a soldier, *mademoiselle*? But the minute I saw you in Dresden I knew, and only then, that I had a heart."

"They all say that," commented the lady in a matter-of-fact tone.

"All! Who says that to you?" cried the soldier, quick to take jealous alarm.

"If you were as sophisticated as I and as experienced as I, *monsieur*, in affairs of the heart," replied the Princess with gentle raillery, "you would know that I mean all those who make love. But in your innocence—"

"You are laughing at me, *mademoiselle*."

"Should I laugh at innocence, *monsieur*?"

"Ah, Princess," protested the lieutenant colonel, I tell you the truth. I had often fancied when I had succumbed to the attractions of some fair enemy that I loved, but now—" He stopped and stared up at her as if he could find no words to convey his passion. She thought as she looked down upon him that he made a very attractive picture, with his flushed face, his fair hair, his blue eyes, his dainty and audacious curly moustache. "*Mademoiselle*, I am routed, defeated, at your mercy," he resumed after a long pause.

"Since I have made such a conquest, and so easily—"

"So easily, *mademoiselle*! You underrate your fascination, your beauty, your charm, your—"

"Let us not discuss that now, *monsieur*."

"But I want to discuss it."

"But I do not, and as you have given me the supreme command, I impose upon you the necessity of continuing in bed until you have given yourself some chance to recover the loss of blood and your wound to heal."

"But, Princess—"

"I know what you would say; your regiment, your duty—"

"Of course," interrupted the lieutenant colonel, "those must all be attended to, but it is you I want. I cannot lie here alone all day in the same house with you, under the same roof, breathing the same air you breathe, without seeing you; truly you ought not to ask it, I—"

"I will give you just as much of my society as the duties of my position, the care of my invalid mother permit."

"May heaven bless you for those words. Is it possible that you care—a little—for this poor soldier?"

"Everything is possible—"

"*Mademoiselle!*"

"But all possible things are not probable, *monsieur*. It is a lonely life we lead here. Any stranger is a welcome diversion."

"Call me not a stranger, dear Princess."

"And when this particular stranger has laid me under everlasting obligations, the least I can do is to make the hours of his illness, got in my service, pass pleasantly."

"*Mademoiselle* is pleased to be sarcastic with her most unworthy admirer and servant."

"Not at all, *monsieur*, my will is the best in the world."

"And the strongest, it seems, too, *mademoiselle*, since mine must bend to it, I who obey no orders but from my general and my Emperor."

"And do you rate me below them?"

"Princess, so high above them that to me you are as beloved as—"

"As what, *monsieur?*"

"As France," answered the soldier softly.

"I am a Russian by name," said the Princess, "but my mother was a Pole. My father, my brother, my—"she stopped a moment and resumed in a somewhat altered voice, "my friends are with the Russian army, but I am more Polish than Russian; my heart is here in the forests of my native land. I love France and the Emperor, for they promise us freedom, so that I can understand what you say and appreciate the compliment when you put me in the same category as your beloved land."

"It shall be my hope and dream to localise your admiration for my country, *mademoiselle*, upon one of her devoted people."

"And it will be a vain dream," said the Princess, speaking more seriously; "I am meant for another fate."

"But not of your choosing?"

"Does any woman choose her own fate, *monsieur*? But enough of this. To show you my good will, I have asked Father Vygia, who has more skill at surgery than I possess, to come and dress your wound."

"*Mademoiselle!*"

"He will do you good service." the lieutenant colonel shook his head.

"There is more healing in the touch of that white hand than in all the medicines in the world, *mademoiselle*."

The Princess laughed, yet there was nothing that irked him in that laugh. The soldier had observed women often and closely and he knew well that what he had been saying was not distasteful to this woman.

"You can tell that to Father Vygia," she said, "for here he is."

"Good morning, my son," said a venerable priest of the Greek Church as he stepped within the room. "My daughter, are you here?" he asked in some slight surprise.

"I could hardly do otherwise," said the Princess, drawing herself up, a note of haughtiness in her voice, "since my authority alone has served to keep the patient quiet until your arrival."

"Umph!" said the shrewd old ecclesiastic meaningly, "I did not know that the presence of a charming young woman was quieting to a French soldier. How is that, my son?"

"It ill becomes me to contradict the Princess," answered the soldier; "you see how calm I am, venerable father."

"Just so," said the priest, laying his hand on the other's wrist, and feeling his pulse; "ha, a very excited pulse, indeed."

"Temperamentally so, I assure you," said the lieutenant colonel eagerly.

"I have no doubt of that either," returned Father Vygia, "and this morning subject to unusual stimulus. Will her highness the Princess kindly withdraw and leave me with my patient?"

"I was but waiting for your arrival, good father, to relinquish my charge."

"But you will come back when the good father has finished with me?" burst out the lieutenant colonel impetuously.

"I shall return later in the morning at which time I hope to find you more composed."

"You will find me in a state of fever and agitation, *mademoiselle*, if your return should be long delayed," he cried after the vanishing figure of the Princess.

"Now, my son," said the priest, "let us have a look at the wound. I am sorry that I was not in the *château* last evening when you came. I have no doubt I could have done much more for you than old Stepan or the Princess, although they have doubtless the best wills in the world. Umph," he continued after he had unloosened the bandages and inspected the pierced shoulder; "not a bad wound, a nice clean bullet hole right through the fleshy part of the left shoulder; just missed an artery and by great luck no bones broken. Your vigour and the cleanliness of your body prove you to be an honourable soldier, sir."

"Father Vygia," returned the lieutenant colonel, "I have always held it necessary that a soldier's life to be efficient should be sweet and clean. I do not claim to be better than my comrades but I have had no fancy for the low amours of the ordinary wearer of a uniform."

"I see," said Father Vygia, looking carefully at the young man, and then, drawing a bolt at a venture he quoted, "*Noblesse oblige?*"

"Exactly," said the Frenchman.

"And you are Lieutenant Colonel Maurice; but your ancestors bore some other name in old France, I venture," said the priest with great discrimination.

The lieutenant colonel stared anxiously at the ecclesiastic.

"Have no fear," said Father Vygia; "I have seen many of the nobles of old France and I think I can recognise another when I see one. Your secret is safe so far as I am concerned. Now for your wound again. It has been probed as well as dressed?"

"Yes, last night."

"Who guided the probe?"

"*Mademoiselle.*"

"Ah, she is a rare woman."

"Rare indeed, good father, and I—"

"My son," said the priest emphatically, seeing at once how the land lay and thinking a friendly warning would not be amiss, "she is the daughter of a Russian Prince of wealth and station, the hereditary enemy of France, and to add to these disabilities, she is promised to another."

"Promises," said the Frenchman, "are nothing where love is concerned."

53

"I have not heard that she is in love with you, however, *monsieur*."

"No, not yet," said the Hussar confidently.

The priest laughed and busied himself with redressing the wound which was indeed not serious and in excellent condition. If the lieutenant colonel had not been so quixotic in his devotion, if he had had it attended to at once, he would not have fainted from loss of blood at the feet of his adored. However, perhaps he was not regretful at having done so.

"With care in two or three days you can ride to the front."

"Two or three days!" exclaimed the soldier. "Make no mistake, if my own feelings were consulted I could stay here a thousand years and be happy but I am a soldier, my regiment, the First Light Horse of the Imperial Guard is encamped on the road to the north of here. We are convoying treasure and despatches to the Emperor at Wilna. They must be seeking me now and I must leave at once."

"The Princess has given orders that unless I authorise it, you are not to leave the bed today."

"But you will not order—"

I certainly will."

But my regiment?"

Trusty messengers will be despatched to seek it and convey your will to its commander."

"But, good father—"

"My son, it is so ordered."

"Does the Princess rule everywhere?"

"Have you not found that she does?"

"In truth I have, in my heart at least, but—"

Do not excite yourself further," said the old priest; "I will send you something for breakfast and I will charge myself with the despatch of any message to your command and perhaps I may let you go tomorrow. It is useless to argue," he continued, checking the young officer's speech, "yet I know your impatience and can sympathise with it. In younger days, when I was of the world, I, too, was a soldier. Now what message shall I deliver to your command?"

"Tell Major Beaubien that I am here wounded and in good hands. Ask him to break camp and march hither. I take it we can get to Wilna from here as well and as speedily as by the way we were to follow."

"You can, and perhaps even more quickly than the other way, though the by-road is more suited to a detachment than to an army."

"Good, and you will send the order at once since I needs must stay here?"

"It shall be done Immediately, and your command should be here by nightfall If all goes well."

"And you will ask the Princess to come to me soon?"

"It is not meet that a Princess of Russia should visit the bedside of an enemy, especially when the enemy is a young man, and in love and—is as gallant and interesting as you appear to be, my son," smiled the old man for whom the soldier had already conceived an immense liking.

"But I have got my wound in the Princess' service," returned the lieutenant colonel, smiling in turn; "will not that Incline the Princess to grant me this great favour?"

"That might make a difference," said the priest; "we shall have to leave It to her." And with that half-way assurance the baffled young light horseman had perforce to be content.

Chapter 6

An Ardent Wooing

Lieutenant Colonel Maurice passed through a day of varying emotions. Waiting and longing during the morning for her arrival until he had almost reached the depth of despair, his eyes were at last gladdened and his heart uplifted to the seventh heaven by a visit from the Princess Idona. He had scarcely begun to bask in the radiance of the happiness which he drew from that young lady when she completely eclipsed the sun of his affections by withdrawal. She kept that up at intervals during the day. Whenever the young hussar became too bold, outspoken and ardent in his declarations, a convenient summons which he more than suspected had been prearranged by the lady, called her from his room.

On the whole, however, he enjoyed a good deal of her society and the piquancy of the situation no less than the elusiveness of the young woman greatly increased the attraction and in the end the progress of his love-making almost contented him. Father Vygia also visited him at intervals between the appearances of his lady and through him the Lieutenant Colonel had sent a written order to Major Beaubien, and the lieutenant in command of the battalion and bivouac on the Kowno Road. After he had left the troop, the lieutenant colonel had wandered aimlessly for some miles through the forest and, if the truth be told, he had been so engrossed and preoccupied that he had taken no account of the distance he had travelled or of the direction his unguided horse had taken. He was not able to give a very definite idea of the location of the battalion but the servant who took the order was one of the most intelligent of the retainers of Wilkomir and he declared to Father Vygia that he had little doubt but that he would be able to find it eventually.

On reflection, the lieutenant colonel had ordered his major to bring the whole command to Wilkomir in order that he might make its protection secure and leave it in charge of the guard provided for by the Emperor's order. The regiment should arrive by nightfall if all went well. The Emperor's order would give him an excuse for delay until the next day; and the day after that, whatever happened, it would be necessary for him to depart. His wound, which was healing rapidly, and which, except for the amount of blood which he had so foolishly allowed himself to lose, was not very serious and would hardly keep him out of the saddle any longer.

Toward evening, indeed, at his earnest entreaty, he received permission to rise and don his uniform. Although Father Vygia advised against it, the lady, whose imperious sway extended even over the old priest, graciously granted his request. His uniform had been carefully cleaned where it had been blood-stained and the bullet holes in his clothes had been darned by the fair hands of the Princess herself, who for all her exalted rank and position was, as has been observed, an intensely practical and capable young person—the ideal wife for a soldier he thought as he examined his clothes and noted her handiwork.

In the great hall of the castle, a blazing fire of logs in the huge stone fireplace diffused a gentle warmth throughout the vast room. Although summer was already upon them, the nights were still somewhat cold and there was a threat of rain in the air which made the heat of the fire most agreeable. The architecture of the castle was rude in the extreme yet the background of massive stone wall, the heavy carved furniture, the rough floor covered with fur robes, skins of the great Russian Bear, and the high, dark, beamed ceiling which the candles lighted in soft obscurity, made an admirable setting for the Princess Idona.

Prince Muravieff, her father, was immensely wealthy in his own right, to say nothing of being the heir of the great estates of his father, the old Prince, and he had allowed his daughter to indulge her fancy. She was clad in some sort of tissue of silver, made after the alluring fashion of the Empire—which then as now set the standard in dress—tightly girdled beneath and over the breast. Her magnificent gown was bordered with fur as white as the fabric itself. Her arms and neck were bare and a circle of pearls not more pure than the delicate skin of the Princess encircled her neck.

From the centre of this collar depended a single pearl of great price, whose softness seemed to melt into that of the delicate bosom upon which it reposed. On her head, twined in her dark hair a band or fillet of diamonds glistened like small stars set in ebony. And the wavering rose light of the fire added rich and variable touches of warmth and colour to this lovely, this enchanting, this noble vision.

Lieutenant Colonel Maurice told himself that he had never seen anything so magnificently beautiful as this woman who stood before him on a great bear skin rug by the side of the fireplace as the red glow of the flames played over her regal person. It must be admitted that Lieutenant Colonel Maurice's judgment of women was apt to be influenced by the one who was nearest, but in this instance it could not be denied that he told the whole truth.

He had dined alone in his room and when he had received word that the Princess would receive him, he had come down stairs on the arm of Stepan. He stopped the instant he saw her and his look of spontaneous surprise was the greatest compliment the Princess had ever received in her life. Never before had she dressed herself this way for one man. The dress had been prepared for the great court functions and she had worn it on several occasions in Dresden. She had been but one among many there, and although she easily outshone the many, still in a certain sense they detracted from her glory. Now he saw her alone, beautiful, dressed in the latest and most approved fashion, which by the way, became her tall, somewhat slender figure perfectly, and with a background whose very simplicity and rough, stern plainness seemed the better to bring into relief her every grace and charm.

No wonder the lieutenant colonel stopped and stared, no wonder that the desire to possess her for his own that he had cherished since he first met her in Dresden became an obsession with him then and there. Unconsciously he matched all other women in the world with this one and lightly threw the rest into the discard. Thenceforth, it was to be the Princess Idona and no other until the end of time. At last he loved and loved forever.

In her turn, the lady returned the stare of the soldier. In his turn, he was not unfit to be the companion piece to such a picture as she presented. The regiment had just started on its campaign and the lieutenant colonel's uniform and equipment were all brand new. In fact, that was true of even the veterans. Everything from the red-plumed busby on his head to the half boots on his feet had been especially provided for this campaign. The titular colonel of his regiment, the First Hussars of the Imperial Guard was the Empress Maria Louisa herself and nothing that the taste and wealth of the war office could supply under the Emperor's personal direction, was lacking to the brilliance and magnificence of his uniform.

Lieutenant Colonel Maurice wore varnished half boots. His well turned legs were encased in tight-fitting riding trousers of spotless white. His green shell jacket or tunic was brightly frogged with gold. His sword, curved like a Mameluke's scimitar, reposed in a scabbard of polished silver. Its hilt, a whim of his own, was studded with diamonds. His bright scarlet *dolman*, caught across his breast with a strap of spotless white leather and a gold buckle, was bordered with fur as white as that upon the Princess' gown. His sword belt was chased with gold, and jewels, another whim of his, sparkled in its buckle.

Ordinarily in his right hand he would have carried his *shako*, or busby, of black glossy fur with its scarlet plume or pompon, and its trappings of gold cord, while his left hand would have rested on his sword hilt, but that left hand, was, in a measure, out of commission, and old Stepan, who made an admirable foil, carried the lieutenant colonel's headgear. His right hand, however, rested against his sword belt in the proper and approved fashion.

When he wore his *shako* he had perhaps a more military air, but rising above that mass of colour, his bright face, paler than usual on account of his wound but with a touch of colour in his cheeks brought there by her presence, his blue eyes, his fair, closely curling hair and that little upturned moustache perhaps looked more attractive than when he was crowned by his war gear. He was all colour, red, green, scarlet, gold, silver; she was all white, dead white. The ordinary relations were thus reversed, the male of the sex was the gayer of the two.

The Princess, therefore, gazed at him with deep interest and a like admiration. Neither broke the silence for a little space. Each found the other strangely fascinating if the truth were to be told. The lieutenant colonel raised his right hand to his head as a soldier salutes his emperor, and disengaging himself from old Stepan, who, on a sign from his mistress, withdrew, he advanced slowly toward her across the long room.

"*Mademoiselle*," he said after a most profound bow before her, "you should have prepared me for this."

"For what, *monsieur*?"

"For the sight of you."

"Have you not seen me several times in Dresden, and yesterday and today—"

"I never saw you like this," returned the hussar, "and in my weakened state, I can scarcely sustain the shock."

"Shock, *monsieur!*"

"Yes, Princess, I who have confronted the eagle glance of the Emperor without blenching, I who have looked into the red mouths of the smoking cannon, I who have faced the gleam of the bayonet and the flash of the sword, I am not equal to this, I protest."

He lifted his hand to his face and shaded his eyes as if gazing at the sun. Although the words were extreme, yet there was something in the way in which they were uttered that carried conviction to the heart of the lady. Could it be that she welcomed that conviction?

"I do not understand," she said, understanding quite well but desiring to hear more.

"You are too beautiful. It ought not to be given to mortals, beauty like yours. It fills me with despair."

"That is a sad effect to be produced by what you say, if it be as you say and I cannot understand why," continued the Princess softly.

"It makes me despair. Princess, because no man can merit it. I see no way on earth to be worthy of it, even if I were—"

"Marshal of France?" smiled the lady.

"The Emperor himself, *mademoiselle*; and therefore while I drink it in, while it gives me life, while it plunges me into an abyss of unfathomable happiness and joy to look upon it, nevertheless it breaks my heart."

"The gentlemen of France," said the Princess, laughing, "are delightful in their extravagances."

"*Mademoiselle* is always general in her compliments," said the hussar reproachfully; "if she would only be particular."

"*Monsieur* is particular enough for both of us and how can I believe him?"

"Believe me," cried the lieutenant colonel earnestly. "Mademoiselle, I swear to it."

"And by what do you swear?"

"By everything that I hold sacred, by the memory of my mother, by my belief in God—"

"Does anyone believe in God in France, nowadays, *monsieur*—"

"Some of the old—" the lieutenant colonel checked himself, "some of us still acknowledge Him, Princess," he said quietly, "and by my belief in Him, by my admiration for the Emperor, by—" he hesitated.

"By what?"

"By France itself," he continued with deep feeling. "I have never seen anything like you. There is no other woman in the world. I love you, I am dying with despair."

"And should not one who loves France as you do, find among her daughters—"

"*Mademoiselle*," said the lieutenant colonel, "beauty is of no country, charm is of all lands. If I won you, you would be mine and as I am for France so, too, would you be."

"*Monsieur*," said the Princess gravely, and the Light Horseman did not fail to note that her colour was higher, the rise and fall of her bosom more rapid and there was a little tremor in that voice usually so steady and calm. "*Monsieur*, Father Vygia—"

"Why speak of priests when we are together? Let us talk of nothing but you."

But the Princess shook her head.

"Father Vygia has told you that I am betrothed to another," she insisted.

"But you are not married to him, Princess?"

"Not yet."

"If you were betrothed to every noble in Russia it would matter nothing to me so long as you are free to be wooed."

"But I am not free to be wooed, being betrothed."

"Well then, so long as I am free to woo."

"And are there no fetters to your freedom?"

"None."

"Not another woman?"

"None."

"Think again."

"I can think of nothing but you."

"But answer me."

"None, I swear to you on my word of honour as a soldier."

"And you have never loved? "

"What the world calls love a million times, but never what I call love until I saw you."

"And you tell me this in spite of the fact that I am promised to someone else?"

"*Mademoiselle*, if you were promised to every Prince in Russia, I tell you, it would matter nothing to me."

"But I am not promised to any Prince in Russia, or to any Russian, in fact."

"Well, be he Pole or Lithuanian or—"

"Neither to a Pole nor to a Lithuanian."

"To whom then?"

"To one of your own people."

"Give me his name," cried the lieutenant colonel, "let me know who it is and I will hunt him throughout the entire army and when I have found him the fortunes of war shall decide whether he or I—"

"You cannot do that, because—"

"*Mademoiselle*, do you love this man to whom you have been betrothed?"

"I—"For the first time the Princess faltered. "How dare you question me, *monsieur*," she broke out imperiously; "I know of no right—"

"This is a matter of life and death," pleaded the lieutenant colonel; "I fight for a woman's heart and know no rules nor am I bound by any restrictions in my effort to win it. Do you love this man?" he asked with a firmness that more than equalled her own.

"*Monsieur*, I cannot tell," she said at last, her glance falling, her eyes avoiding his own for the first time.

"That answer is a sure sign that you do not," he commented joyously. "A woman like you made to love and be loved—*Mon Dieu*, could I but awaken in those slumbering eyes of yours passion like that which shines in my own, if in that cold heart I could start the fire that burns in my breast, you would know whether you loved or not."

"But I respect, I admire, I esteem—"

The lieutenant colonel snapped his fingers whereat the Princess drew back.

"Pardon me if I seem disrespectful or ungracious, *mademoiselle*; one respects, admires, a friend, a relative, but a lover never. Ah, if you could but feel!" The Light Horseman stepped closer to the Princess and seized her hand with a grasp which hurt her but she made no effort to draw away.

"*Monsieur*," she said faintly, "what would you?"

"I would everything, *mademoiselle*, but I shall do nothing but this—"

He lifted her hand to his lips and kissed it passionately; his touch on that cool hand almost scorched it.

"Credit me with sincerity at least," he faltered as he released her and his hand sought the table. He leaned upon it, his face very white. "I regret to confess it," he said, "but I—my weakness—"

"Sit down, *monsieur*, sit down," cried the Princess, quickly moving closer to him. She even took him by the shoulders and gently compelled him to seat himself in a great chair.

She herself remained standing perhaps with some faint thought that she could thus look down upon him and in that way assert once more a mastery which she had felt herself gradually losing.

"It would be magnificent," she said softly, "to experience what you say you feel—"

"What I say I feel!" he quoted. "Princess, look at me, do you not see the truth?" continued the young officer, staring at her, and as if attracted by a magnet the eyes of the Princess sought his own and her searching look plunged through the fierce, passionate blue of his glance as if to discover through those windows of the soul its inmost secret.

Their eyes clashed like two swords for a moment and this time the glance of the Princess fell.

"You do me great honour, *monsieur*," she said simply, at last convinced.

"It is myself that I honour," he replied, "love like mine ennobles, it would make a king out of the veriest clod. Had I nothing behind me but what I have won with my sword my love would lift me almost to your level, or as near to it as mere man could be raised."

"And, are the Maurices of an ancient family in France?"

"Of the most ancient, *mademoiselle*."

"I do not recall that name among the nobility of that land."

"Princess," said the hussar gravely, "a man fights under any name, he loves under but one. If I should be so fortunate as to win your heart I would tell you—"

"Tell me nothing, *monsieur*," said the Princess, "I repeat, I am formally betrothed to a gentleman of France—"

"But against your will!"

"With my own consent and with the approval, indeed or at the urgency of my father and grandfather. My troth is plighted, my word is pledged, I must keep it."

"And who is this gentleman of France?"

"His name is—but no, I cannot tell you."

"Cannot?"

"Will not, if that please you better."

"At least tell me where your word was given. Was it in Dresden?"

"No."

"Have you by any chance been in Paris?"

63

"I never saw your native land."

"Where then?"

"Here at Wilkomir, if you must know."

"But it is impossible that any officer or soldier of the Grand Army should have stopped at Wilkomir—it is out of the way—it is—Was it one of Marshal Ney's corps?"

"Sir," said the Princess, not averse to continuing playing with the emotions of this ardent lover, a thought too confident and assured for her taste possibly, "the man to whom I am plighted is an officer in the Imperial Guard."

"I know every officer of rank in the Imperial Guard or at least I can find out their names. I shall go to them one by one until—"

"The Imperial Guard of Russia," said the Princess.

"*Mon Dieu!*" exclaimed the light horseman, "a Frenchman in arms against France, against Poland?"

The Princess bowed.

"And who is he, what is his name?"

The Princess shook her head.

"I cannot tell you his name."

"Are you afraid for him, *mademoiselle?*"

"I do not know," answered the Princess softly; "he is a noble of old France, of a family which would never acknowledge Napoleon."

"There are some," returned the Light Horseman, "and one at least, I know. But France has never been greater than under the Emperor. You have seen the Emperor, you know—"

"I know his fascination—"

"*Mademoiselle!*"

"Have no fear, *monsieur*, not the fascination of which you think. I am a Pole and for Poland—"

"I understand," interrupted the lieutenant colonel.

"The Emperor is nothing to me personally except the possible deliverer of my people, the restorer of our destroyed liberties, who can establish the ancient kingdom of Poland."

"I hope and believe it may be so, *mademoiselle*, but the establishment of the Kingdom of Poland or of anything else is to me second to the establishment of my position in your heart."

"But I have not said that you had any position there, *monsieur.*"

"Nor do I yet claim to have such a position, but I shall make it and first I must—" he hesitated.

"What?"

"Eliminate my rival."

"That may prove a harder task than you anticipate. Colonel Maurice."

"No task which presents a possibility of winning you is too hard for a soldier of France. The fortunes of war will bring me in contact with the Emperor Alexander's guard. That is certain. When we have taken it, I will go over them rank by rank until I find the man—"

"And then?"

"Then I shall call him out and kill him," was the composed and assured answer of the determined lieutenant colonel.

The Princess smiled slightly.

"Think you I cannot do it?" he asked, seeing the doubt.

"I am sure that you cannot,"

"*Mademoiselle*, I will search for him if I have to go through the entire army of Russia. A thought strikes me," he continued, "would you save his life?"

"Certainly, if it were endangered."

"Because you care for him?"

"I would not have him killed because he is so blind as to love me," she replied evasively.

"Then give me authority to say to him that you have broken your plighted troth and when I find him he shall go free," was the magnificently assured answer of the hussar.

"He might care to fight his own battles," said the Princess gravely.

"And you will not marry him?"

"In any case I will not marry him until the war is over."

"And I may hope?"

"I am not a dispenser of hope, *monsieur*," was the smiling, somewhat equivocal answer.

"*Mademoiselle*, Princess," cried the delighted officer, "you make me very happy."

CHAPTER 7

The Battle on the Stair

On the whole, Lieutenant Colonel Maurice was rather more than
satisfied with the progress of his latest and most desperate love affair.
To one of his enthusiastic temperament the fact that the Princess Idona was plighted to another did not induce a great amount of concern;
indeed, had she even been married the fact that her husband was to
be found in the ranks of the enemy and that by the rules of war it was
his duty to kill him as such, if possible, without regard to any personal
feelings, would have ameliorated even that condition. In spite of his
humility before the Princess, which was by no means feigned, the natural assurance of the Light Horseman made him confident of success.
Indeed, he had never failed in anything that he had attempted as yet.
His star in its smaller orbit shone as brightly as that of the Emperor in
its greater circle; the one was confident of the conquest of Russia, the
other was confident of the conquest of this Russian.

Father Vygia came for a final visit after the faithful Stepan had
assisted the lieutenant colonel to prepare for bed and examined and
redressed the wound. It was doing famously. There was no evidence
of infection and it bade fair to heal rapidly and save for the care with
which he must necessarily carry himself, and the resulting inconven-
ience, the young soldier did not give it a thought.

The only cloud upon his happiness was his impending departure
on the morrow. Although he was a devoted lover, he was also a thorough soldier and he knew exactly how far and how long he would
be warranted in delaying his departure by his wound. The regiment
would certainly reach the *château* in the morning, indeed the troops
should have reached it that night had they hurried, and he would be
left without further excuse to stay with his lady. Well, the campaign
would be soon over, the Emperor's tremendous battle strokes were

invariably delivered quickly, the Russians would soon be brought to bay and annihilated, and before the summer was ended he would be back again at Wilkomir, and then—

He had ascertained that the Princess' room was in the same corridor as his own, indeed that it was at the head of the great flight of stairs a short distance away from his door, and before he said his prayers—he was one of the few soldiers of the French army who said prayers, by the way. Perhaps if more of them had followed that estimable Russian custom, it would have been better for that army—he wafted a kiss in her direction, registered his vows anew and like a good soldier went right to sleep.

Princess Idona was more wakeful. Under her rather cold exterior she concealed a passionate heart which on occasion could beat with all the intensity of feeling popularly supposed to be characteristic of those sisters of hers of warmer climes. It had been with great difficulty that she had commanded herself before such swift, tempestuous wooing as she had been subjected to that night. As she said, she had been plighted to a Frenchman of noble birth and ancient lineage and exalted station, an *émigré*, who had taken service with the Russians influenced by bitter hatred of the usurping Emperor. But she made no pretence at loving him. Indeed, after that interview with the lieutenant colonel she began to understand what love was, and she found it an experience as delightful as it was novel.

From the wreck of the family fortunes, her betrothed had been able to save enough to put him in possession of considerable means, a sufficient income at least fairly to support his rank and station. She had met this gentleman on occasions and had liked him. There had been no one else by whom her affections had been engaged and when he had made formal proposal for her hand she had made no great objection. Indeed a refusal would have been fruitless and unavailing when her father and grandfather had once accepted this gentleman as her promised husband. Nor had she made any objection to the formal betrothal which had taken place in due course.

Indeed, the marriage was not at all disadvantageous, for should Napoleon ever be disposed of, the throne of France and her kings restored, as the wife of the Marquis who had sought her hand, she would share in her husband's glory and his position would be a great one, indeed. He was a gallant gentleman, too, and if she had only loved him, all would have been well.

She had remained fairly contented in the situation, *faute de mieux*, until the advent of the young Hussar. It has been seen how he fell in love with her at first sight and how with the reckless, impetuous gallantry of his race, he had made no concealment whatever of his affections. He had seen her but a few times, yet on each time he had wooed her and had persisted in his suit with bold disregard for conventionality or anything else. He had saved her life and honour in the woods of Wilkomir two days before. He had actually almost bled to death because he thought nothing of his wound when he had the privilege of addressing her. He had risen from a bed of pain, and she was woman enough to magnify that pain, simply to talk to her. He had scarcely said a single word in her presence that was not a direct declaration of his passion coupled with a determination to win her.

It was highly unusual and unconventional and had been altogether charming. The Princess was vexed at herself because she had been so profoundly influenced by this man. A scion of one of the oldest and proudest houses of Russia and of a family equally ancient and exalted in Poland, she asked herself how she could ever condescend even to consider a nameless young Frenchman—who appeared to have made his position by force of arms alone—not merely as a lover but as a husband. And that she did so consider Lieutenant Colonel Maurice was evidence to her how deep and sincere an emotion he had awakened in her heart.

He had kissed her hand with passionate abandonment. She saw herself in his arms and imagined that kiss upon her lips. A wave of colour flooded her face, her heart rose until it almost choked her. While he lay at her feet and afterward when she had succoured him, his head had rested upon her bosom, over her heart. How that heart beat and throbbed now! She could not get the picture out of her mind. She lay awake for long hours, while her protesting lover was sound asleep, thinking about these things and other things. She remembered the intoxication that had stolen over her when he had taken her in his arms and they had danced the Varsovianna, the old Polish dance of her forebears at Prince Poniatowski's ball at Dresden.

What was there in the blue eyes, the bright hair, the smiling ruddy face, of this *debonair*, youthful soldier of fortune, this modern knight-errant, that so stirred her to the depths of her being? How long could the iceberg remain intact if moved next to a volcano? What sudden fires were those that suffused her cheeks with colour and caused her breath to come quicker? How far away was that betrothed in the Russian army, how different was her feeling toward him!

The time flew by unheeded for the Princess, being filled with these and similar reflections, until by and by she sank into an uneasy slumber, a slumber from which there came a rude awakening.

The night was very still, the only sound was that caused by the gentle breeze sweeping the tops of the lofty pines. It was very dark under the trees. In the open ground around the *château* the faint light from the stars would have disclosed, had there been a watcher, a number of dark figures, breaking through the forest glades without a sound and approaching the low wall. The great gate was barred; he whose duty it was to guard it was sound asleep. They found the sentry at his post the next morning with his throat cut.

Disdaining the gate, the crowding figures in the starlight, which was reflected here and there upon points of steel, noiselessly surmounted the walls, filled the great courtyard, clambered up the steps of the terrace and assembled before the great door and the long windows on either side. They tried the door gently—it was locked.

They had expected that, for they had brought with them and put it over the wall with some difficulty, a tree trunk from the forest. A score of them seized it and drew back, others clustered around the long windows on either side. There were perhaps one hundred of them on the terrace by this time. There was a whispered consultation between the several groups and finally one who appeared to be the leader, self-constituted or otherwise, gave the signal in German.

The next moment the log was hurled against the great door. The windows were shuttered and barred and the men began to beat upon them with butts of guns. On the instant the quiet house was filled with crashing sound. Neither the windows nor the door gave way at once, but the attack was repeated upon them. They were strained, however, and it was evident that a continuance of the terrific assault would soon break them in. The men outside broke into polyglot yells and cheers. The thundering of the timbers and the guns against the crashing wood was succeeded by shouts and cries of women within.

The battering sound was so tremendous that it penetrated to every part of the *château* and every inmate was aroused on the instant. Although his sleep had been the soundest. Lieutenant Colonel Maurice was the first to awaken and like a practiced soldier, he had awakened with all his faculties at his command. Vassily, the servant, slept in the room with him. The Lieutenant Colonel sprang to his feet, caught the trembling man by the arm.

"Lights," he said, "quick, for your life!"

The coals were still aglow in the fireplace. The man seized a candle and lighted it. While he was engaged in this the soldier had dragged on his trousers with his free hand and the trembling fingers of the servant assisted him with his boots and sword. He flung over his shirt, his fur-trimmed *dolman*, drew his sword, thrust both his heavy horse-pistols into his belt. Then he darted out of the room.

The noise was tremendous. It was plain that whoever was without was assaulting the front of the house. The lieutenant colonel ran down the corridor toward the head of the steps. Instinctively he stopped before the door of the room occupied by the Princess. As he did so, with a final tremendous crash, the great iron-studded hall door gave way. Wrenched from its hinges and badly shattered, it fell inward, and over it poured a yelling, howling, shouting multitude. Torches were kindled and the hall was soon filled with light. Some of the unfortunate servants were caught and dragged into the midst of the ravenous mob. The men fought stoutly and inflicted some damage but they were too few in numbers to do much. They were soon struck down. The women were seized roughly and held prisoners for the moment. The whole lower floor was instantly in possession of the assailants who ran recklessly through all the rooms that opened off the great hall, seeking for booty and plunder.

As the Lieutenant Colonel stood at the head of the stairs, sword in hand, the door to the left opened. He glanced aside to meet the Princess. She had thrust her feet into slippers and had thrown about her shoulders over her night robe a long fur-trimmed cloak. Her hair, dressed for the night, hung in long braids, one in front, the other behind her shoulders. She held a lighted candle in one hand and in the other clasped the cloak across her bosom.

"What has happened?"

"Deserters from the army have entered the *château*, they have killed the servants and seized the women. But fear nothing, I will protect you."

"What can you do?"

"One question. Is there any other way to this floor except by these stairs?"

"None."

"Very good, I will keep them from getting to you long enough for you—"

"Long enough for what?"

"For you to die."

70

"You mean—"

"You must not fall into their hands. I distinguish their uniforms, Dutch, Spanish, German, Italian and, God forgive them. Frenchmen, scum of the army."

"But I am a Princess."

"To them you would only be a helpless woman. You must not fall alive into their hands."

"I shall not."

"Have you a weapon?"

"This was my father's room," answered the Princess quickly, "on the bureau is a case of pistols."

"Are they loaded, charged, ready?"

"They are always ready."

"Do you know how to use them?"

"I do."

"Reserve one for yourself and give me the other."

The Princess stepped back and in a moment returned with a handsomely polished, silver mounted wooden box which she opened and presented to the soldier. He looked at the pistols carefully and handed one back to her.

"Now return to your room, lock and bolt the door. When I am silent, you will know that as I would have lived for you I have died for you."

"*Monsieur*," said the Princess, coming closer to him, "I know. Come within and—"

"They must be checked here. Meanwhile, as I am about to die—"

His eyes finished the sentence.

Moved by an ungovernable impulse the Princess advanced to his side and swayed closer to him. His left arm was more or less helpless. For a moment, he forgot the necessity of watching the stairs. He turned and with his right arm swept the soft, unresisting form to his breast. His lips sought hers and she did not turn away or draw back from them. It was as the salute of the gladiator, about to die, to Caesar. How he could have torn himself away from the enchanting contact he could not have told, had not a harsh voice broken on his ear.

"*Gott in Himmel!* Billing and cooing in the presence of death!"

To release the Princess and whirl about was the work of an instant. Before the voice was silent, the lieutenant colonel was in position again. A heavily bearded Prussian was coming up the stairs, laughing viciously. He had a torch in his left hand and held a musket in his right.

"In the presence of death!" cried the lieutenant colonel. "You speak rightly. You have seen that which it is not permitted you to look upon."

His pistol was out and before he had finished the sentence, two shots rang through the hall, the first that had been fired. The Prussian, awkwardly presenting his gun, had missed and the bullet whistled harmlessly between the man and the woman at the head of the stairs. He had no second chance for on the instant he tumbled backward and rolled down the steps with a pistol bullet in his brain.

"How could I allow a witness to that kiss to live, *mademoiselle?*" said the lieutenant colonel coolly.

In the look of gratitude and admiration which the princess shot at him, the soldier received his full reward.

"You must lock yourself within your room," he added quickly; "they will be upon me in a moment."

"No," said the Princess firmly, "I cannot, will not close the door."

"At least stand back out of danger and watch me. Your presence will be an inspiration to me and when I fall there will be time—"

The Princess nodded.

"May God protect you," she whispered.

There was time for no more. The two shots had been succeeded by a few moments of paralysed silence. The men ransacking the various rooms ran back to the hall and assembled there in groups at the foot of the great staircase. It so happened that he who had been shot had been the leader of the enterprise, the chief villain of the motley band of desperate stragglers which had assembled for the purpose of plunder. They were without leadership for a moment but there were bold spirits among them and two or three stepped from the crowd and advanced toward the stair.

They gazed up the long incline. At the top they saw a slender figure all in white. The lieutenant colonel had thrown aside his *dolman*; it inconvenienced him. He had shifted his sword to his left hand, the point was resting on the ground and his hand could hold the hilt without bringing any great strain upon his wound. The light from the torches below was reflected from the bright blade. They could not see the right hand of the soldier which held a second heavy horse-pistol, nor that he had laid the one just discharged on the stone railing at the head of the stairs convenient to his hand.

"Who are you?" growled out the boldest of those at the foot of the stairs.

"Lieutenant Colonel Maurice of the First Light Cavalry, Hussars of the Imperial Guard, a soldier of France and at your service, Gentlemen," said the man at the head of the stairs, softly, the very gentleness of the reply masking the irony it contained.

"We are not fighting soldiers of France," roared one.

"Come down, *Monsieur le Colonel*, and you shall have your share of the plunder," urged another.

"Join us, and the pick of the women shall be yours," cried another.

"I have no desire to associate with deserters, with thieves, with violators of women, you dogs," answered the lieutenant colonel smoothly, growing quieter in the certainty of action as was his wont.

Instantly the hall below was filled with shouts and angry cries. Moved by a common impulse the mob surged toward the stairs and those in front were forced up part of the way. Any further words of the soldier were lost in the tumult. Quick as before he raised the heavy weapon and taking instant aim, at the nearest man, fired point-blank down into the mass. The heavy bullet tore through one man's chest, broke the arm of a second and glancing, buried itself in the body of a third.

The advance stopped on the instant. Turning the pistol in his hand, he hurled it with tremendous force and astonishingly accurate aim into the faces of the checked mob. He seized the other pistol which had been discharged and flung it after the first. Those in front were now quite willing to go back, but those in the rear were still pressing forward and as they had the advantage in numbers they all began slowly to mount the stairs.

They must be stopped at all hazards. Seizing the last pistol, the hussar emptied it into the faces of the marauders and flung the weapon after the bullet.

"Come on," he shouted and actually darted a few steps down the stairs.

Those in front sought to escape. Swift thrusts accounted for two of them, and stopped them for a moment, but there were too many and they were too determined. Lieutenant Colonel Maurice saw that he had failed. He had slain or seriously wounded half a dozen men but he could not check the slow upward movement. Thrusting at the nearest man, he drove the blade into his throat. Then he dexterously withdrew his sword and ran back to the head of the steps.

The Princess, utterly disregarding herself and her grave peril in her admiration and excitement had stepped out into the hallway and had stared at the conflict below her.

"For God's sake, get back," cried the soldier, and although it gave him excruciating pain, he even thrust her back with his left arm.

The next moment a shower of bullets swept the stairs. Two of them grazed the soldier and staggered him, but none of them wounded him vitally or even seriously.

"It is the end," he cried; "I can do no more. I love you. Shut the door." He turned and faced the men on the stairs. "Come on, you dogs," he continued, "and see how a soldier of France can die!"

And then something happened. Two arms closed about him and before he could struggle he found himself dragged backward across a threshold. A heavy door was slammed and he was in the Princess' bedchamber! She had leaped forward, and taking him by surprise, actually, by a sudden superhuman accession of strength, had dragged him within her chamber.

"I would not have you die there," she whispered, panting.

The next moment the hall was filled with shouts and cries as the mob mounted the stairs and began pounding upon the locked door.

Chapter 8

A Surprising Declaration by the Princess

Fortunately the door was a stout one. The quick-eyed lieutenant colonel saw at a glance, so soon as she had flung it shut and shot the heavy bolts, that it would stand a deal of battering with such means as the assailants had at hand before it gave way at the top and bottom. There were slots for a bar across the middle too, and seeing it leaning against the wall he picked it up and dropped it in its place. Like everything in the castle, the door was of a rude and primitive construction, roughly hewn, but immensely strong. Of course, in the end it would be forced, but for the moment they were safe from assault.

Before he said anything the soldier looked toward the nearest window. The windows were shuttered and barred but if they had not been they were so high from the ground that it would be difficult to force them from without. There was no other exit from the room, therefore, while it was a refuge, it was also a prison.

"*Mademoiselle*," said the lieutenant colonel, turning to the excited, nervous woman, her heart throbbing, her breast heaving, her pulses beating, "you have saved my life."

"And paid my debt," she panted out.

"You owed me nothing," he replied firmly, "and—but as I live!" he cried in a tone of dismay which neither their desperate position, nor the fierceness of their enemies nor any pain however acute would have extorted from him, "you are wounded!"

He had at that instant discovered that her forearm, loosely covered by the long, flowing sleeve of her night robe, was covered with blood.

"It is nothing," she said faintly, but with a little shudder of horror or pain nevertheless.

"Let me see it," he continued and without waiting for her permission, he seized her hand, lifted her arm tenderly, flung back the sleeve and discovered that a bullet, one of those fired at him as he stood in the hall, had grazed the flesh of her forearm when she had so recklessly exposed herself to danger to draw him within the room. If he had been familiar with Shakespeare he might have declared that it was neither so deep as a well nor so wide as a church door, but that it would certainly serve to awaken all his passionate pity and solicitude. And he had seen hundreds of soldiers killed, wounded, frightfully mangled and torn to pieces without feeling or expressing so much concern as over this petty scratch, for it was scarcely more than that! As it was, he stared at it with infinite tenderness and concern, after heaving a great sigh of relief to find it no worse than it was. Nor could she or any woman be indifferent to that manifestation) of deep feeling, as genuine as it was spontaneous.

"It must be attended to at once," he said; "thank God, the flesh is not pierced and the arm is not broken."

He stepped to the bed, tore a long strip from the sheet, came back, tenderly wiped away the blood and rapidly and skilfully bound up the arm. He did not notice as he did so that where he had held them, the bandages had been stained with blood other than her own. The Princess' quick eye took in that detail.

"You are bleeding also," she exclaimed.

"Yes, I believe so," said the soldier carelessly, "but it is nothing. A mere graze, not to be compared to yours."

"Let me see it."

"We have not time for that now. Give yourself no uneasiness. I have been wounded in that way dozens of times."

"But—" she continued insistently.

"It is a happiness. See, our blood has mingled. No more about it. We must decide upon our course."

"Fate has decided for us, *monsieur*," said the Princess, "there is no escape from the room save by the door."

"You forget the windows."

"It is probably thirty feet to the ground which slopes away on that side, and beneath it is an ancient moat, fifteen feet more. We are lost."

"I will not have it so. I was not born to die in a trap like this," said the soldier.

He stamped his foot imperatively and then rushed to the bed, tore the upper sheet from the heap of covering and then the lower. They were made of stout linen and would bear their weight. He knotted the two together skilfully and did the same with the blanket and with the heavy silken coverlet that was over all. Alas, the improvised rope was not more than twenty feet long, the knots taking up so much of the length.

By leaning out of the window he could perhaps make it twenty-five feet long. That meant a fifteen or twenty-foot drop for the Princess to the bottom of the moat. It was dangerous, impossible, yet he decided that it must be tried. The battering of the door had continued all this time and the conversation had been carried on under difficulties. The bolts and bars still held and this, too, in spite of the fact that the marauders had tried to blow them loose by firing through the door with their muskets and pistols. The hussar had carefully kept himself and the Princess out of range the while.

"You are not going to try to descend by means of that?" she asked incredulously.

"No, I intend to lower you."

"And you?"

"I shall stay here and keep them away from the window that you may escape."

"I will not go," said the Princess.

"You must."

The two looked at each other for a moment, fiercely combative. It was the man who won. He seized her firmly and moved her toward the window, drew the bolts and threw open the shutter.

"Too late!" triumphantly cried the Princess, looking out.

Indeed the possibility of such an escape had been foreseen. A group of the marauding soldiers had assembled on the other side of the moat. The two within could scarcely discern those without in the darkness but so soon as the soldier and the woman appeared against the light in the opening, a volley of musket shots rang out. To draw the Princess back from the window was the work of a second.

"Are you safe?" cried the hussar.

"Unharmed, and you—"

"Not touched."

"What is left now?"

"Death," answered the soldier grimly. "Well, if it has to, let it come. I had thought it might be on the field of battle but it is happiness that even though here in this ignominious trap, it is for you."

"And we can die together," said the Princess proudly and yet with a note of tenderness in her voice which it was needless and in fact impossible to deny now.

"Tell me," whispered the man coming very close to her, "under other circumstances could you have loved me?"

"Yes," answered the woman simply.

"I die happy," said the hussar, turning toward the door.

Its panels had been splintered by the tremendous battering and firing that had been kept up on it but the main fabric of the door still held. There was a moment of silence outside, the first cessation of the tumult since the two had sought refuge in the room. The silence was followed by the sound of scurrying of feet, quick whispers and then all was still again. That stillness was more ominous than the noise.

"What is it?" whispered the Princess, coming closer to the Light Horseman.

"I do not know; some mischief is afoot," he said as he made a step nearer the door but the Princess held him back."

"Keep away from the door," she said, "I fear—"

The next instant the room was shaken by a terrific detonation. The door was shivered into pieces. As it fell away a dense volume of smoke poured into the room. The men outside, making a bomb out of the powder from their cartridges, had blown up the door. Fortunately, the heavy bar across the middle still remained in place and as the eager as-sailants made a leap through the smoke for the entrance they brought up against it fair and square.

The door had so fallen as not completely to uncover the entrance. There was not much more room than for one, or at the most two men to pass. The practiced eye of the hussar took in the situation. Shaking himself free of the Princess, he rushed toward the entrance just as the oncoming mass hurled itself against the heavy bar. With his sword he thrust and thrust and thrust, shouting madly and incoherently at the top of his voice. The attack for the moment had failed. Three men, two of them lying in front of the entrance, one hanging over the bar, had been killed by the unerring swordsmanship of the soldier. He shouted in exultation.

In their excitement, the men outside had not thought to reload their pieces. Now, however, seeing the difficulty, they fell back, dropped the butts of their guns to the floor, and recognising the sound, the lieutenant colonel saw that the last hope was gone.

"I die," he said; "remember that I love you and do not fail in your last shot."

"I will wait until I see you fall and then I will follow you," answered the Princess, undaunted, her hand raising the weapon.

The loading of the pieces, an operation requiring some little time then, was about completed; another second or two and all would have been over. At that moment, just as the first man presented himself at the opening, gun in hand, a series of wild shouts, of "Hourra, Hourra!" broke upon the momentary silence that supervened. These peculiar and terrifying shouts and screams were accompanied by the thundering of hoofs of countless horses, and the rattling detonation of muskets and pistols.

"*Cossacks!*" cried the Princess, recognising their shrill cries. "We are saved."

From the hall below and from the courtyard came the sound of a fierce short battle, following the suspense. The men outside the door stood still. If these newcomers were *Cossacks*, and the house were surrounded, they would be caught in a trap, they would be lost!

"*Sauve qui peut,*" cried the nearest man, turning and leaping down the stairs.

The rest stood irresolute for a second: It was the woman who gave the fillip to their wavering determination. Before the lieutenant colonel could stop her she appeared in the doorway. She fired her last pistol full in the face of the nearest man. The rest turned and fled incontinently.

The Princess dropped the smoking weapon. She had seen the man collapse and the thought that she had killed him appalled her. She clapped her hands to her face, turned back and staggered helpless, sick, faint, with the reaction of the fearful moments through which they had just passed. Dropping the sword which he had used so skilfully and for which he had no present use, the lieutenant colonel caught her with his right arm and held her close, whispering into her distracted and almost unhearing ear, words of passionate tenderness and devotion.

Her mantle had fallen away and as he drew her to him he kissed her bended head with all the fervour of his race and time. Unutterably weary, with a languid, faint feeling, she allowed herself to be supported and caressed, scarcely knowing what was toward.

Meanwhile, it was quite evident what had happened. A wandering party of *Cossacks* raiding the rear of Napoleon's army to cut off stragglers, had fortunately come upon those renegades and deserters who were attempting to master the *château* of Wilkomir. They were saved. Time enough to go down the stairs and investigate the matter presently. Time enough to explain the presence of the soldiers later. Now the lieutenant colonel thought only of the woman, white clad, yielding, whom he clasped to his heart and kissed while he whispered in her ear his passion. Such a moment might never come again. He must enjoy it while he could. They had passed, as it were, through death together and this—this was a foretaste of heaven.

There was a jingle of swords in the courtyard, hurried steps in the hall below and a huge, black bearded man, followed by many others hastily mounted the stairs. As in a dream the two within the room heard, though they scarcely comprehended. The fierce eyes of the *Cossacks* stared in surprise in the direction of the two clasped figures.

"What's here?" cried the first arrival in guttural Russian.

The two figures separated.

"This," said the soldier, stepping forward, "is the Princess Idona Muravieff."

"Princess," said the *Cossack*, who could evidently understand French and could speak it passably well, "I salute you. I am glad that we were in time to rescue you from these ruffians, and you, sir, that speak French, who are you?"

"Lieutenant Colonel Maurice of the First Light Horse of the Imperial Guard."

"A French soldier?"

"I have that honour."

"I am Michael Ostrolenko, colonel and kinsman of the Grand Hetman Platoff. This is a regiment of his *Cossacks*. I am sorry for it but your hour has come." He slowly raised his hand and presented a huge pistol at the Light Horseman. "I have sworn to kill the French whenever I find them in Holy Russia, and—"

"No," shrieked the Princess, flinging herself in front of the soldier.

"Stand aside, Princess," said Maurice instantly; "if I were in his place I should do the same, he but does his duty. Bear testimony, at least, *mademoiselle*, that a French soldier is not afraid to die."

He stepped aside quickly but again the Princess was too alert for him. This time she sprang in front of Ostrolenko.

"He saved my life," she cried. "He fought for me in the forest, on the stairs, in this room, I—I cannot have him shot."

"Were he your lover, *madame*," said the *Cossack* roughly, "he is a

Frenchman and—"

    "He is more than my lover," said the woman desperately.

    "What mean you?"

    "He is my—my husband!"

CHAPTER 9

The Strangest Marriage

The lower jaw of the big *Cossack* dropped as did his pistol arm. He stared in bewilderment mingled with doubt at the Princess. She herself was scarcely less appalled by her words than Ostrolenko. On the spur of the moment she had seized upon the only possible method that occurred to her to save the life of the man who had already suffered so much for her and not until she had uttered the fateful words did she perceive into what abysses they plunged her. As usual it was the soldier who recovered himself first.

He, too, had been surprised and shocked beyond measure by her bold declaration. His first impulse had been to dispute it but his second and better thought was to carry out the deception if possible. To do him justice, he saw in her declaration only the effort of a brave and magnanimous woman to shield a man who had struggled so successfully to protect her. It was he who broke the silence. Although he was unarmed and slight in comparison, he sprang in front of the *Cossack*.

"Do you doubt it?" he cried fiercely.

"Doubt it," roared Ostrolenko, recovering himself after a spring backward and glad to face a man with whom he could deal more easily than with a woman, "of course I doubt it. A Princess Muravieff marry a vagabond French soldier!"

"My family is as old and as noble as any in Russia," cried the lieutenant colonel.

"It is some trick to save a—lover," proceeded the *Cossack*, apparently thinking it no derogation from the dignity of the Princess Muravieff to have a lover, although to have married him would have been condescension indeed.

"If you will oblige me with the return of my sword," said the hussar very low and quiet but fairly bursting with rage at the vile insinuation of the big Russian, "or even one of your clumsy *Cossack* weapons, I will condescend to drive that insult to this lady down your throat with its blade!"

"Fight you with a sword?" laughed the *Cossack* brutally—he seized him by the shoulder as he spoke and made as if to shake him. "I could break you with my naked fist, boy! "

To spring backward, jerk himself free and strike the *Cossack* a fierce blow upon the face as he did so, was the work of a second. But the lieutenant colonel was almost at the end of his strength. This violent effort was the last that was possible to him. The wound in his shoulder had opened and it was bleeding again. The strain of the last half hour had been terrific upon a wounded man. He was as pale as death but undauntedly, praying vainly for a weapon, he faced the Russian, who with a roar like a savage bear, made at him. It was again the Princess who interposed.

"Would you strike a wounded man? I tell you, had it not been for this French soldier I had been killed or worse. Thrice he has saved my life. He is my husband. If you harm him you incur the anger of the Muravieff's and not even the Grand Hetman shall protect you from our vengeance. Of the *Czar* himself will I require your blood."

"Princess," said the lieutenant colonel faintly yet with determination, "imperil yourself no further. Let the wretch spend his wrath upon me. You have done what you can. Let him have his way."

There was something in the bearing and manner of the Princess which awed the *Cossack*. He turned his glance from her to the young hussar and hesitated.

"Are you married to this lady?" he asked suddenly at last.

"I swear," returned the lieutenant colonel instantly and without a moment's hesitation, "that I am,"

"And you swear to it, too?" continued Ostrolenko to the Princess.

"*Madame,*—" sharply began the lieutenant colonel.

It was one thing for him to lie like a gentleman to protect her but quite another thing to force her to take an oath to protect him. But once having embarked upon this sea of trouble, the Princess felt impelled to pursue her course to the end, regardless of what might be demanded of her.

"I do," she said firmly, cutting short the protest of the hussar.

If Lieutenant Colonel Maurice had loved her before, imagine the worship he gave her now. In the face of such assurance, the *Cossack* had no further ground for doubt yet that he was not satisfied was quite evident. He scratched his tousled head and pondered deeply.

"*Madame,*" said the lieutenant colonel faintly, at last, "with your permission I must sit down again."

The Princess sprang to his side, her arm went about his shoulder as it had before, and she supported him to a great chair which stood at hand.

"Here," said Ostrolenko, drawing from his pocket a flask of fiery vodka, "I don't want you to die or faint on our hands yet. Drink this."

He proffered it to the lieutenant colonel but it was the Princess who took it, drew its stopper and gave it to the hussar. A long draught of it put some temporary strength into his body at least. He handed it back and the *Cossack* advanced to take it. Then the three stared at one another, the soldier in spite of the pain of his wound, sitting upright in the great chair. The Princess stood close by his side, her arm with its reddened bandage resting protectingly on his shoulder, her white gown falling to her feet one of which was bare, for she had lost her slipper in the exciting events that had transpired. At any other time, under any other circumstances, she would have died of mortification, but now greater issues that outweighed even the claims of modesty, were to be decided. She was bound to save the man that she—well, she only admitted in her mind that he was the man who had saved her honour and her life. Her heart, had it spoken, would have told a different story.

"I tell you frankly," said the *Cossack*, addressing her in Russian and speaking so rapidly that the soldier could not follow him, "I doubt what you say. It is inconceivable; and yet perhaps the presence of this man in your bedchamber at this hour of the night, half dressed as he is and you in your night clothes may better be explained by a wedding than in any other way."

The colour flamed in the face of the Princess at this insult and yet having acclaimed the soldier as her husband there was nothing she could say in resentment. We have a priest with us," continued the invader, I shall summon him hither and you shall remarry this man. If you are already married there will be no harm, if you are not—" he paused and laughed sneeringly, "the Prince Muravieff will thank me that I have saved the honour of his house."

"What says he?" asked the lieutenant colonel, who had listened without being able to catch more than a word here and there.

"Do you speak English?" asked the Princess brokenly in that tongue.

"Yes, a little," answered the other, glancing quickly at the *Cossack* and correctly inferring from his blank look that he did not understand English, so the Princess continued in that language.

"He has a priest here and means to marry us."

"To marry you would be the dearest wish of my heart but I cannot force you to give me your hand in this way. You have made a brave effort to save me. It is enough. I will declare the truth, and—"

"I forbid you to speak," said the Princess quickly. "Do you think that having begun this work I will leave it half-finished? Sir," she turned to the *Cossack* colonel, "I am ready."

"Summon Father Ivan," roared Ostrolenko who had watched them keenly, puzzled by and suspicious of the strange speech they had employed.

The call went echoing down the stairs, through the hall, and presently a bearded *Cossack*, wearing some of the garments of a priest under his military cloak shuffled into the room. He did not come alone, for he was followed by Father Vygia. This ecclesiastic had been made prisoner by those who had first attacked the *château* and had but a moment before been released through the effort of his brother priest. He was, of course, in the proper dress of his order,

"I sent for you, Father Ivan," said Ostrolenko harshly, "to marry this Frenchman to the Princess Muravieff."

"By all that is sacred!" exclaimed Father Vygia in amazement.

"And who is this?" interrupted the *Cossack*.

"The household priest," answered Father Ivan,

"And I suppose it was you who married this couple," said Ostrolenko sneeringly.

"I—"

"For the honour of the family and to save a life devoted to me, imperilled in my service, I told this *Cossack* who rescued us from the robbers that this man was my husband," said the woman quickly.

Father Vygia gave vent to a sharp exclamation but otherwise controlled himself.

"On your allegiance, I charge you. Tell him it is so," continued the Princess imperatively.

Instantly divining the situation and heroically falling in with his mistress' idea, Father Vygia, who was not only a priest but a devoted and faithful attendant of le Muravieff family, nodded his head although no one could guess what the effort cost him.

"Speak," thundered the *Cossack*.

"I married them," the old man forced himself to say I a faint whisper at last.

"You wear a cross," said Ostrolenko. "Upon that cross do you swear to the truth of what you say?"

The priest's hands sought his pectoral cross, his fingers closed around it. He lifted it high, his mouth opened.

"I—I—" he faltered, shooting a desperate glance of entreaty at the Princess, for the demand shocked his very soul, the effort was greater than he could make. He could not bring himself to perjury even for her.

"Enough," interrupted the lieutenant colonel, rising to his feet, "I—"

"Be silent," cried the Princess, forcing him down into the chair again. "You have your priest here, Colonel Ostrolenko; Father Vygia has told you but if you still doubt, the—the ceremony can be repeated."

"But if they have been already married," said Father Ivan.

Ostrolenko laughed harshly.

"I will be played with no longer. Do you Father Ivan marry them instantly. Father Vygia has refused to swear upon the cross that they are married. You can proceed without hesitation. If not the young man dies before you all and if, as I believe, the woman has lied to me—"

"What then?" asked the lieutenant colonel, determining upon a final and desperate effort to prevent this mad marriage.

"The lady will follow her *paramour* and everyone here. Dead men tell no tales, the *château* will be given to pillage and we will blame it on the enemy."

There was a deep silence in the room. It was the woman who broke it.

"You see," said the Princess in English, "it is for me again that you do it."

"So be it," was the answer as the lieutenant colonel struggled to his feet, took the hand of the Princess and faced the humble priest, who had drawn his service book from his pocket and was nervously fumbling its pages.

Surely never before was a wedding solemnised under such circumstances. The *Cossack* priest was old and ill-educated, but he could go through the ritual well enough. When the time came for a ring, the

Hussar drew from his neck a little circlet of gold suspended there by a fine gold chain. He broke the chain and extended the ring toward the Princess. The woman hesitated and looked toward him with a jealous flash in her eyes. The *Cossack* colonel had not noticed before that she wore no ring.

"It was my mother's," he whispered, understanding her question, "a woman so noble and so beautiful that even you can wear it without hesitation."

That was not the only singular thing about the ceremony, for when he was asked to give his name it was not as Lieutenant Colonel Maurice that he was married but as the Count Maurice de Vivonne.

"Vivonne!" exclaimed Father Vyygia, who had watched everything with the greatest interest, as the count gave his name, "do I hear aright?"

"That is my name, gentlemen," said the lieutenant colonel simply; "one fights under any name, one marries under his own."

"It is fate," murmured Father Vygia softly.

The Princess had started abruptly when she had heard the name of her lover and husband. He had noted that involuntary movement at the instant but there had been no time for explanations.

"It is done now," laughed Ostrolenko when the closing benediction had been said; "and when he hears about this midnight rendezvous in which we surprised the lovers the Prince will thank me. Father Ivan, draw up a writing and we will all sign it as witnesses."

"As to the thanks of the Prince Muravieff," said Father Vygia, grimly, "it seems to me that Russia will not be wide enough to afford you asylum from his wrath when he hears what you have done."

"Is that," said Lieutenant Colonel Maurice, rising to his feet from the chair into which he had sunk wearily after the final blessing, "meant as a reflection upon my fitness to be the husband of this lady, reverend sir?"

"By no means," answered Father Vygia, "I recognised your quality when I first saw you. I am not surprised to find you bear so ancient and noble a name. Are you by chance related to the Marquis de Vivonne?"

"I am his brother. I am the younger son of the house."

"There is no likeness."

"None; he is as dark as I am fair, but why these questions?"

"To satisfy the curiosity of an aged priest, if you will. As for you, sir," he continued, turning to the *Cossack*, who seemed now not quite so happy in his exploit, "Prince Muravieff had other designs for his daughter; she was betrothed to an officer in the Imperial Guard of our Master the *Czar*, whom God preserve. I am very much mistaken if his anger be not swift and terrible when he hears of this outrage."

"The lady herself said that she was married and you confirmed it," swaggeringly began Ostrolenko.

"That will avail nothing to excuse you," said the priest; "you made her a wife."

"And I can make her a widow as easily," said the *Cossack*, who began to see his brutal jest in another light.

He raised his pistol as he spoke.

"I have already had more happiness than I merit, in that this lady for a moment has borne my name," said the hussar, rising to his feet and opening his arms. "If it will make her position easier, kill me."

"And is all this to go for nothing?" asked the Princess swiftly. "You gave your word that my husband should go free."

"I will keep it," said Ostrolenko in a spirit of bravado. "If the Prince Muravieff does not thank me for this I suppose I must even sustain his anger as best I can."

He thrust his pistol back into his belt. At this moment one of his officers burst into the room in great excitement.

"A regiment of French Light Horse with four guns is coming down the road. There must be a thousand of them. Prince Muravieff is with them. They are coming here."

Ostrolenko acted with extraordinary celerity and decision.

"Clear the house of our men," he shouted; "let them get to their horses and gallop back to the Vilia to the ford where we crossed before. There is not a moment to be lost."

"Here is the writing," said Father Ivan, tendering a paper to his colonel.

"Your marriage lines," cried the *Cossack*, handing it to her. "Make my compliments to your noble grandfather the Prince who comes, strangely enough, under French escort and tell him what I have done for the honour of his family. Stay, the paper must be witnessed." He stepped to the desk and scrawled his name at the bottom of the paper. "Should he be in doubt as to who has thus served him, or should he be inclined to forget, this will remind him. I regret that his presence with the French prevents my telling him this face to face," and with a rude bow he turned from the room.

The lieutenant colonel had reached the end of his endurance. He rose to his feet, made a step in the direction of the Princess and collapsed again. Father Vygia and the Princess carried him to the great bed, laid him upon it, and the old priest began redressing his wound, the Princess hovering near with water and bandages. Through an open window came the faint notes of a bugle.

"A French trumpet," said the lieutenant colonel faintly, "my regiment. *Madame*, you are saved from your troubles at last."

CHAPTER 10

The Prince and the Princess Decide

With a great clatter of horses, the rumble of wheels, punctuated by sharp orders and jingling of steel weapons, the First Light Horse of the Imperial Guard, the Empress' own, filed through the gates and came to a halt in front of the great paved courtyard surrounding the *château* which was quite big enough to contain them all. With the four-gun battery attached to the regiment for the expedition, was a light travelling carriage from which descended an aged officer in the uniform of a Russian general. Although it was not yet sunrise, it was hard upon it and there was sufficient light to enable the officers to see the devastation and damage which had been wrought by the first assailants. The splintered shutters, the gaping doorway, the corpses of the men in the various uniforms of the Grand Army lying on the terrace with here and there a dead Cossack, all told a portentous story—already too sadly familiar to everyone.

Turning over the command of the regiment to his senior subordinate, Major Beaubien dismounted from his horse and approached the Russian general. The Prince Muravieff was a soldier and he did not lose command of himself in spite of the shock at what he saw but it was only by a great effort that he retained his self-control. Major Beaubien had heard the positive orders his lieutenant colonel had received and when he fell in with him he realised that Prince Muravieff was under the special favour of the Emperor. He was deference, itself, therefore, and he promptly offered the old man his arm and the two gentlemen, followed by a couple of young subalterns whom the major had summoned by a wave of the hand, slowly mounted the steps, the younger suiting his pace to the faltering footsteps of the older.

"There has been hot work here," said Major Beaubien.

"These uniforms, they are the deserters of your army," answered the Russian.

"I recognise them, curse them," said the officer bitterly, "the black-guards—"

"And there are *Cossacks*, too. There has been an engagement," continued the Russian.

"Yes, evidently; I pray God that we may be in time."

The little quartet stepped over the bodies which blocked the door. The practiced eye of both the old and young soldier noted the means by which entrance had been effected as they passed within the hall. A fire was blazing on the hearth. Wantonly the marauders had pitched furniture, books, pictures, anything that had come to hand, into the huge fireplace and the light from the fiercely blazing fire sufficiently illuminated the vast room which otherwise would have been quite dark, since the day had not yet broken outside, and since most of the windows were still closely shuttered.

There were a score of corpses in the hall, lying in every position, and the foot of the stairs was cumbered with them. Most of them were soldiers of the Grand Army but there were a few *Cossacks* also which showed that the deserters had at least made some attempt to sell their lives dearly. Here and there a half-dressed Russian in the livery of the household lay amid the soldiers, stiffened in the agonies of death. Doors were flung open, furniture overturned and every evidence of the short but fierce pillage was apparent. There did not appear to be a living soul in the room. Those who had only been wounded had been finished off with the brutal ferocity of the conquerors.

"Good God! "exclaimed the old general, "my daughter, my grand-daughter!"

At that moment a figure, blood stained and gory, appeared in a distant doorway. By clutching at the hangings old Stepan, who had been badly wounded and left for dead, managed to hold himself erect.

"Stepan," cried the Prince.

"At the master's service," faltered the old man, struggling with his weakness.

"What has happened to my daughter, my granddaughter?"

"I cannot say. We were assaulted by soldiers. I ought, I was struck down. The last I saw they were mounting the stairs. I know no more—" He lost his grip on the hangings and would have fallen but one of the young soldiers caught him and eased him to the floor. "The French officer," he added faintly—

"Yes," cried Beaubien. "Lieutenant Colonel Maurice."

"He was keeping the stairs."

"Do you stay with him, Fleury," said Beaubien to the young officer; "do what you can for him. For the rest, Prince, we must mount the stairs, and prepare yourself for—"

"I am ready for anything," said the Prince firmly, as the three turned toward the stairs.

The stairway was in a horrible condition, covered with blood and weapons and bits of flesh and clothing. No one had had time or inclination to clear it of the men who had fallen upon the stairs and there were a number of bodies upon it. The last comers had simply ruthlessly trampled over them. The smell of blood and powder was in the air which was still dim with smoke. It was a scene indescribable. The passionate hatreds of the struggle were evidenced everywhere. And there was not a sound to be heard. A stillness like death was over all. As they slowly mounted the stairs, the younger again suiting their pace to the older, Beaubien stooped down and picked up a heavy silver mounted horse-pistol. A glance enabled him to identify it.

"This belonged to the brave Maurice," he said with deep emotion; "let us go on."

They had almost reached the head of the stairs when a man suddenly came out of an open doorway to the right.

"Vygia!" cried the Prince, "my daughter?"

"I am going to her," said the old priest.

"My granddaughter," continued the Prince.

"She is here."

"My Colonel?" asked Beaubien, in his turn as they surmounted the last step.

"Yonder," said Vygia, pointing to the door, "wounded, but all right."

"Beaubien," came a faint voice from out of the room.

"What does he in my daughter's bedchamber?" whispered the old Prince half to himself as he and Beaubien entered the apartment.

They found it in a state of great confusion and disorder, although no great damage had been done save to the shattered door. The Princess Idona met them between the bed and the entrance. She had found her missing slipper and she had resumed the heavy cloak which she had had time to button and girdle about her waist. Her hair was still unbound, the sleeve of her night-robe was torn and bloody, her half-bared arm was thrust through the slit in the cloak and was still covered with the bandage.

"Good God, Idona!" exclaimed the Prince. "What has happened? You are wounded!"

"I had been dead," said the Princess, coming nearer to her grandfather and laying her hand upon his shoulder, while the arm of the old man went around her waist, "were it not for this gentleman here."

She pointed to the disordered bed upon which the Hussar still lay. As she did so, the young man sat up, struggled to his feet and saluted the Prince.

"And who is this?" asked the Prince.

"My Colonel!" exclaimed the major joyfully.

"My name," said the young man, "is Maurice, I command the First Light Cavalry—"

"And what do you here, sir, in my grandchild's room on that bed at this hour of the night?" asked the Prince, frowning.

"I might answer you in a dozen ways, *monseigneur*," said the young officer, reaching for the head of the bed to steady himself by means of its support, "but know, sir, that I have at least one right to be here which not even you can—"

"And what is that, *monsieur*?"

"This lady," said the hussar, inclining his head toward the Princess who stood pale and frightened by the side of her grandfather, "is—"

"Is what?" thundered the Prince. "Good God, sir, you do not dare to asperse—"

"Is my wife, sir."

For a moment there was a dead silence. The announcement seemed to petrify the old Russian.

"My friend, my Colonel," said Beaubien, "you know not what you say, you are wounded, you are fevered, you—"

"I am entirely in possession of my faculties, my good Beaubien," returned the lieutenant colonel. "I know exactly what I say. This lady is my wife. None has a better right here than I."

"Idona," said the Prince, turning to his granddaughter, "what is the meaning of this folly—is he mad?"

"No," said the Princess, slowly yet firmly, "he speaks the truth, he is my husband."

"Prince," cried Father Vygia, coming into the room, "your daughter—"

"Do not interrupt us," said the Prince.

"But she is dead, stabbed to the heart with a bayonet."

"My concern," said the old man with terrible calmness, "is with

93

the living; and since this disgrace has fallen upon us, I can find it in my heart to be glad that the poor sufferer has gone to her rest. This is your doing, sir," he continued, turning to the young soldier.

"You spoke a word which in any other man I would not suffer," said the lieutenant colonel haughtily.

"What is that?"

"'Disgrace.' Know, sir, that the Princess Idona is incapable of disgracing your name."

"But she married you. Father Vygia," continued the Russian, "on your allegiance, did you assist in this sacrilege?"

"Your Highness," said Father Vygia, "I—"

"A plain answer, yes or no. Did you marry them?"

"No."

"And then what is all this, a trick?"

"They were married by a *Cossack* priest. Father Ivan they called him," and then Father Vygia stopped, turned and took from the table a paper. "Here," he said, presenting it, "is the notice of it, duly signed and witnessed."

The old Prince took it as in a dream and glanced at it mechanically, apparently without seeing it.

"And why," he said to the Princess, "being betrothed to another, a great noble of old France, honoured by the friendship of the *Czar*, serving with your father in his armies, did you condescend to this nameless soldier of fortune?"

"It was to save his life," answered the Princess.

"And what is the life of one soldier of France to you? Did you wish to do this monstrous thing, break your plighted troth, shame and disgrace me and your father, and bring dreadful degradation upon the house?"

"This officer," said the Princess eagerly, checking her enraged husband, "had saved my life, my honour, everything, not once but again and again."

"I do not understand."

"Listen. The day before yesterday when I was walking in the forest four men fell upon me. They shot Boris, my great wolfhound, and then seized me. This soldier happened to be riding through the woods seeking the *château* of Wilkomir by the Emperor's order."

The old Prince nodded.

"Go on."

"He fell upon these four like a storm, three of them he killed and

94

the fourth fled. In the encounter he had received a shot in the shoulder. He stood and talked to me without mentioning his wound until he fainted at my feet."

"And why was he such a fool?"

"Because I loved her," said the lieutenant colonel promptly.

"And when had you seen her?"

"At Dresden; and to see her was to love her."

"She was there against my better judgement, but proceed," said the Prince, turning again to his granddaughter.

"I could do no less than bring him here. Father Vygia and I dressed his wound. He had fainted from loss of blood. It was not dangerous, no bones were broken. He would be able to leave with two days' rest. In the morning orders were despatched to his regiment to come here. They should have been here last night."

"I did not receive your order until late last night," interposed Beaubien. "The man who carried it had several narrow escapes from being killed by the nameless scoundrels with which these woods are filled. I broke camp immediately."

"You are acquitted of all blame," said Maurice promptly; "I knew when you did not come as well as I know now that it was not because you were negligent. Besides, you got here in time for me."

"But not for me," said the Prince.

"In the middle of the night, I know not what time, but it was after midnight," resumed the Princess, "we were awakened by a terrific thundering on the door. Wounded though he was, Lieutenant Colonel Maurice rose, dressed himself in part and came out here and stopped at the head of the stairs. The marauders effected an entrance."

"I did not stop at the head of the steps," said the lieutenant colonel quickly, "because of any fear to go down and fight the rascals but to protect *mademoiselle*."

"I see," said the Prince, nodding. "I do not doubt your courage."

"Thank you."

"Presently," continued the Princess, "they came up the stairs. Lieutenant Colonel Maurice kept them back to give me time to die rather than fall into their hands. There was a battle on the stair, he killed a number of them with sword and pistol. The rest began to fire on him. I seized him where he stood and dragged him within my chamber."

"And you got that wound then?" asked the Prince.

"Yes."

"What happened thereafter?"

"The officer knotted the bed linen together to make a rope to lower me to the ground but our escape that way was stopped by some of the band. They blew up the door and tried to get into the room. Lieutenant Colonel Maurice fought them off again to enable me to die. I had raised the pistol to kill myself only waiting until he himself had been cut down, when a party of *Cossacks*, raiding the rear of the French army came upon the scene. The robbers broke and fled in every direction. We were left alone. Before I could get out the leader of the *Cossacks* and others burst into the room. They saw Lieutenant Colonel Maurice, they recognised him as a Frenchman and they were about to kill him before my face. I begged for his life but in vain. He had laid me under heavy obligation. I could not see him die. On the spur of the moment, I declared that he was my husband."

"Is that all?"

"I would not have accepted such a sacrifice," interposed the lieutenant colonel, "but—"

"No," answered the woman, "for the *Cossack* told me if I had lied to him that he would kill me with—"

"With what?"

"With my—my—"

The Princess could not pronounce the word.

"He was pleased to call me her—her lover," said the Frenchman.

The Prince could not fail to understand the meaning of that. He asked cruelly,

"And were you, sir?"

"No, no!" cried the Princess.

"In the sense in which you mean," burst out the lieutenant colonel, "no. And let me tell you, sir, that in the question there is an insult to *madame*, my wife. Do not presume upon your grey hairs and new relationship too far. I am not the most patient man in the army of France."

"Proceed," said the old man to the Princess, grimly ignoring both threat and threatener.

"He summoned Father Vygia, and asked him if he had married us."

"And what said he?"

"For the life of the Princess, for the life of the soldier, and for the honour of the family, I said 'yes,'" answered the old cleric.

"You false priest," cried the Russian furiously.

"He could do no other," continued the Princess, "but when he asked the good father to swear upon his cross—"

"I faltered," said Father Vygia, "and yet perhaps I should have—"

"Go on," said the Prince, imperiously.

It was astonishing how he had shaken off the disabilities of age and stood before them with something of that old fire and firmness which he had exhibited so conspicuously on so many great battle fields of the past.

"He summoned his chaplain, a *Cossack* priest who rode with them, Father Ivan—"

"Was he a priest?"

"Undoubtedly," answered Father Vygia.

"And he forced this priest to marry us," continued the Princess.

"And were you unwilling?" asked the old man.

"No. Matters had come to such a pass that there was nothing left but to go through with what we had started."

"I was quite willing to die for the Princess, then and there," said the lieutenant colonel quietly. "I might truthfully say and without boasting that I had shown my willingness over and over again, but her life was threatened also. Nor could I be sure, I being dead and the Princess without a protector, that they would stop at her life and therefore, I consented, but reluctantly; and yet, sir, I give my word that to be the husband of the Princess is the very height of my ambition and the desire of my heart."

"The marriage was soon over. Father Ivan wrote out this certificate at my desk," said the Princess. "Father Vygia threatened the *Cossack* with your wrath. He said you would thank him for preserving the—the honour of our house. At that instant one of his officers apprised him of the approach of the French. He ordered his men to horse and away, but took time to sign his name as witness to my marriage paper and—"

"Is this the paper?" asked the old man.

"Yes."

He stepped toward the window. It was lighter now. The sun was just rising above the horizon and its rays streamed through the open window.

"'Michael Ostrolenko,'" read the Prince; "I shall remember that name," he said grimly. He looked again at the document. "What's this!" he cried in astonishment, "you said your name was Maurice, but here I read de Vivonne!"

"I am the Comte de Vivonne, *monseigneur*."

97

"Born so or created by your Emperor?"

"Born so and of a family of France whose history may be traced back through thirty generations."

"Have you a brother?"

"I have."

"The head of the family?"

"Yes, saving my old father, the Duc de Vivonne. My brother is the Marquis de Vivonne."

"Where is he?"

"He does not think as I. He is an *émigré*, Since I have followed the fortunes of Napoleon, he and the rest have had nothing to do with me. I know not his whereabouts. But why do you ask?"

Father Vygia laid his hand upon the arm of the Prince. The old man looked at the priest, read something in his eyes and nodded.

"It is of no consequence, the name is familiar to me, that is all," said the Prince indifferently. "What is to be done now?"

"Prince Muravieff," said the lieutenant colonel, "my duty calls me to my Emperor, I can delay no longer."

"The army advances the day after tomorrow," said Beaubien, "an intercepted courier yesterday afternoon bade us hasten."

"I must go and leave my wife in your charge."

"Princess Muravieff—" began the Prince.

"Pardon, *Monsieur le Prince*," interrupted the Light Horseman, "*Madame la Comtesse de Vivonne, s'il vous plait.*"

But the Russian paid no attention to the interruption.

"You have been thoughtless, imprudent, blameable, my child," went on the inflexible old man, "but perhaps there may be excuse. This gentleman rendered you great service. Perhaps you were obliged to preserve his life at the sacrifice of your future, against your plighted troth and to the shame of your father and of me but it must go no further. You have effected your purpose. I do not know whether I can have this marriage annulled, but at least I can try."

"Prince!" began the lieutenant colonel sharply.

"Monsieur le Comte de Vivonne, is, I am sure, too much of a gentleman to strive to bind a generous woman who has sacrificed her freedom for his life," said the veteran noble composedly.

The young hussar stopped as if thunderstruck.

"Madame la Comtesse de Vivonne," continued the Prince, "to give her the title to which she is entitled lawfully, is betrothed to a brave and gallant gentleman of France, so faithful to his rightful king that he fights against this usurper in the Imperial Guard of our beloved Czar Alexander, whom God preserve. She entered into this engagement freely and of her own accord and with the approval of those whom she loves. It cannot be lightly set aside, *monsieur.*"

"But she is mine—my wife!"

"When I present the circumstances to the *Czar*, and to the Metropolitan of our Holy Orthodox Church, I am sure that the marriage will be annulled, *Madame* will be free, and you, sir, will be without the encumbrance of a wife."

"But, *Monsieur le Prince*, I tell you that I love your granddaughter, that to marry her is the dearest wish of my heart. I can show you proofs of my nobility. My family is as old and as honourable, if not so exalted as your own. I am not a penniless adventurer, a soldier of fortune. I have enjoyed the favour of the Emperor and by his bounty I have been able to buy back the ancient domains of our house. I am able to give my wife every comfort and luxury that she may desire. If I satisfy you on these points, may not the marriage stand?"

"It cannot stand; it was entered into for a purpose and that purpose has been accomplished. It was entered into in an emergency and that emergency no longer exists. We Muravieffs keep our words. The man to whom she is betrothed has a prior and a greater claim upon her."

"Count Maurice saved my life," said the Princess falteringly.

"And you have saved his. The account is squared. Argue no more, *monsieur*, what I have said, I have said. You must go away, the marriage must be annulled. You must forget what has been."

"I cannot."

"Monsieur de Vivonne, I have taken you for what you say you are, a gentleman. I have appealed to you not to bind the woman whom chance and her own bounty have placed in your power. As you are a gentleman, release her. Trouble her no more, go out of her life."

"You do not know what you ask," said the hussar hoarsely.

"I both know what I ask and of whom I ask it," said the old Russian earnestly. "Come, I believe your story, I see that whatever your name you are a man of honour and to that honour I know I shall not appeal in vain. Were circumstances other than they are, perhaps I should have consented to your suit, but now it is impossible."

"*Madame*," said the hussar, turning toward the Princess, "your grandfather appeals to my honour as a soldier of France. He says that you proclaimed me your husband simply to save my life. That is true, is it not?"

"Yes, *monsieur*," faltered the Princess.

"Of course you do not and you could not love me?"

There was a deadly silence after this direct question. The blue eyes of the young soldier searched the face of the woman he had wedded. Her glance fell before his. She stretched out her hand toward the old Prince.

"Take me away," she murmured; "I have been tried beyond endurance; I can bear no more."

"Remember your plighted word," whispered her grandfather in her ear. "Answer this man; tell him to go. By the memory of your dead mother yonder, sacrificed while you and he—murdered by his people. For the honour of our house, I beg you to speak."

The Princess lifted her head. She was deathly pale again. She stared straight at the young soldier.

"No, *monsieur*," she said very low and falteringly, "I—I do not—love you."

"And this other to whom you are betrothed, you—you love him?"

"Yes," said the miserable Princess, feeling the hand of the old Prince tighten upon her arm.

"But last night you said—"

The Princess shook her head.

"*Monsieur*," she began piteously, "I am tried beyond my strength. I can no more. You saved my life. I have paid the debt. Have pity upon me. Will you not go and leave me?"

The hussar bowed low before her.

"Your wish is my command, *madame*; that you have honoured me by bearing my name for so brief a time is more than I could ever have hoped or deserved. The influence of the Prince will doubtless serve to have this marriage annulled and yet it may not be necessary. We are engaged in war with your people. Doubtless I can find opportunities to die in the service of France and thus insure your freedom. Remember me as one who serves you, loves you and worships you as he serves and loves and worships his God and his native land."

"I shall never forget you," faltered the Princess, extending her hand.

The young soldier bent low over it and kissed it reverently, devotedly. Then he straightened himself up.

"Beaubien," he said, reaching out his hand—

The major caught it and supported the trembling figure of his officer with his arms.

"You have the orders, to you the command. I am incapable of anything further."

"Can you ride a horse, *monsieur?*"

"I fear not."

"My travelling carriage is at your service," said the Prince as the two officers, followed by the young subaltern, stepped toward the door. "You have acted like a gentleman and a man of honour," he continued; "would that I could have come to some other decision. My hand, *monsieur.*"

The hussar touched it with his own.

"It is *madame* who deserves the credit," he said, "for it is she who has decided."

Father Vygia raised his hand, his lips broke into prayer and his fingers cut the air in the sign of the cross. The old Prince had his hand up also, but it was to his forehead in salute, as the three Frenchmen walked from the room without a backward look or moment's hesitation. They went down the stairs, through the hall and out on the terrace before the regiment. A spontaneous cheer went up from the men as they saw once more the figure of their gallant commander in the arms of Major Beaubien and in that cheer the cry of a broken-hearted woman in the room above was unheard and unheeded by anyone except the grim old soldier who for the honour of his family had wrought this undoing.

"Maurice, Maurice, my husband. It is not true. I lied to you; I love you; come back to me!"

101

CHAPTER 11

The Red Cossacks Anger
the Emperor

The army, decidedly not so numerous as when it crossed the Niemen, and indeed considerably fewer in numbers than when it left
Wilna, plodded along the great old Smolensk-Moscow Road, If it
had diminished in numbers and material, its spirit perhaps was rather
better on the whole than when it had first set foot upon Russian soil.
Skirmishes and engagements in which it had been uniformly successful had taken place frequently. One or two of these encounters with
the retreating Russians had risen to the dignity of battles. The temper of the army had been tried and tested. As usual, it was not found
wanting.

The thinning out by desertion and abandonment of the columns
had more or less ceased. Those who were inclined to go had gone
long since. They were the weaker, poorer, meaner moiety; it was the
better half that was left with the eagles. Vast quantities of unnecessary
baggage had been abandoned in the advance. The weaker physically
had succumbed to the strain. Probably Napoleon himself had never
led a tougher, more vigorous, more determined body of men than
those who tramped along the ancient highway, their faces set toward
Moscow, their prayer that the ever-retreating Russians would only
stop long enough to get a beating by the way.

Russia had sustained defeat in every engagement; none of the encounters had been at all decisive, however, and their resistance did not
seem to be losing in stubbornness nor was the army breaking or dis-
integrating under the relentless pursuit and the hard strokes and fine
thrusts of the Emperor. On the contrary, as it went backward, backward, backward, it seemed to gather strength and coherency as if it had

been welded by massive blows into a well-compacted, homogeneous organisation, the capabilities of which could only be guessed at.

On either flank of the French and Allied Army, frequently cutting across its rear, hovered swarms of ferocious Cossack horsemen. The word of Platoff, the Grand Hetman, had gone forth and from the steppes of the Ukraine and the banks of the Don the wild horsemen had rallied to their *"bunchuck"* standards in countless numbers. It was an easy matter for the French to beat off the Cossacks if they could ever catch them. Whenever they were brought to bay they showed themselves utterly unequal to hard fighting, but the trouble was to force them to fight. Mounted on the swift ponies of the steppes, loosely coherent, accustomed to shift for themselves, knowing the country thoroughly, an organisation of several thousand could dissolve into its component units almost before the eyes of the French in a way that defied pursuit; and they had a faculty of assembling so soon as the almost useless pursuit was given over, and once again menacing the flanks in force.

Their presence was the source of the utmost irritation to the Grand Army. One reason why desertions at that stage of the game were exceptional was because stragglers were inevitably cut off and these Cossacks showed no mercy. Prisoners were cumbersome to such mobile troops and a dead Frenchman was better than a live one from a Tartar's point of view. Baggage trains, unless heavily guarded by strong detachments, were equally at the mercy of these raiders. Matters had grown so bad that the Emperor, riding at the head of his Guard, having just received news of an unusually bold and successful raid upon the baggage trains of the Fourth Corps, the Italians under the Viceroy Eugene de Beauharnais, summoned to his side the commander of the first regiment of light cavalry who happened to be marching that day at the head of the Guard and was, therefore, the most available for the service.

The young Light Horseman, so soon as he had received word from the aide of the wishes of the Emperor, spurred his splendid black horse into a gallop and, riding around the general staff, presented himself before his Imperial commander. The contrast between the black thoroughbred of the Hussar and the white horse of the Emperor was not greater than the contrast between the two men. Even the difference in their uniforms emphasised this distinction.

The Emperor wore his usual green coat, buttoned over the breast; only the grand cross of the Legion of Honour diversified the plainness of the uniform. The day was hot and the famous grey cloak had been laid aside. The familiar three-cornered black hat covered his brow, now frowning and portentous enough. As usual, the Hussar was a blaze of colour. Napoleon's face was pale, although not yet unhealthily so, while the cheeks of the Hussar were fairly red with the heat, the excitement of the sudden summons and the quick gallop to the Emperor.

No man stood in the presence of the Emperor unmoved. The hussar was not a tall man as men go, being scarcely more than of the middle height; Napoleon was a very short man. Physically the Marshals and other officers of the staff over-towered him head and shoulders, yet they all seemed and even looked smaller in the presence of the little Corsican. Maurice, whom nothing apparently could abash, used to say that he felt himself to be about shoulder-high to the Emperor when his majesty looked upon him and yet such was the enkindling quality of that look that, although he felt but shoulder-high to the Emperor, when in his presence, so soon as he had received a commission, the mere fact that he had sustained the glance of the Emperor and had been given a command endowed him with a giant's strength in execution. Few men indeed could look upon Napoleon then without at least thinking, "*Vive l'Empereur!*"

The hussar, as was noticed, was a perfect horseman. To check his steed, fling him back on his haunches and sweep the air with his curved blade in a graceful salute was the work of a moment. The Emperor was susceptible to beauty and dash and brilliance. The Olympian brows smoothed a little; the mobile lips, which would have been the despair of Phidias, broke into a light smile.

"Lieutenant Colonel Maurice."

"Sire?"

"Is it your command that marches at the head of my Guard today?"

"This day, Sire, it has the honour of being nearest the Emperor."

"Good," returned Napoleon. "Are you in mood for an undertaking?"

"If it be in your service and that of France,"

"In my service and in the service of my army, therefore, in the service of my France," said the Emperor, promptly identifying himself with France as was natural, whereat the lieutenant colonel bowed low over the saddle.

"Whatever the command may be, I and the riders of her Imperial Majesty's Light Horse are happy to undertake it," answered the cavalryman.

"That is the spirit, gentlemen," said Napoleon, glancing back at the group surrounding him, "which should animate all my soldiers."

"And, Your Majesty," said a deep-voiced, heavily set, bold-looking, redheaded man of gigantic frame, "that same spirit is by no means confined to the Light Horse of your Guard."

"I know that, my dear Duc," said Napoleon, laying his hand affectionately on the gold-laced arm of the Marshal who had spoken, who happened that day to be visiting headquarters. "The enterprise which I have in mind for you. Lieutenant Colonel Maurice, does not involve so much hard fighting as it does *finesse*."

"We are better. Sire, in striking your enemies than we are in strategy."

"And why is that?"

"We are accustomed to leaving that to the master strategist of the world, Sire."

"And you do well," said the Emperor, who was not too big to be pleased with such a statement; "nevertheless, having been so long with the army, you should have learned something."

"I trust. Your Majesty, that the opportunities I have enjoyed in your service have not been entirely wasted."

"We shall see. You have heard of the Red *Cossacks*?"

"Who in the army has not, Sire?" answered the lieutenant colonel, a dark look dimming the brightness of his countenance.

Now every man in that army knew the Red *Cossacks* by this time. They were a band, a regiment it might be safe to call them, or possibly better a brigade who wore red sashes about their waists and red feathers in their caps. They were distinguished for their daring. Of all the raiders of the Russian army, they were the boldest and the most successful. Detachment after detachment had been cut up; train after train had been pillaged. The few survivors in each instance had a tale to tell of the red-girdled, red-plumed horsemen that indicated their quality. The experienced officers and men who had met them and had survived their onslaught estimated their number as little less than three thousand. Latterly they had been accompanied by a contingent of the regular light cavalry of the Russian army and a battery of four guns. In short, from being an irregular body of horse they had been compounded, welded, organised into a light brigade, almost as mobile as the *Cossacks* alone and infinitely more dangerous. Their leadership had been brilliant also.

There was scarcely a corps or division of the Grand Army which had not some score to pay against these men. Flanking columns on either side of the line of march had sought for them while in pursuance of their regular duties but they had never been brought to bay and several light detachments venturing upon further and harder pursuit had been cut to pieces.

"Has your regiment suffered at their hands?" asked the Emperor, noting the alteration in the young officer's demeanour.

"Yes, Sire," was the prompt reply. "We ran across three of my hussars dead by the side of the road, a young officer and two men. They had been sent with a message from the Prince de Wagram to the Prince d'Eckmuhl in the van. They were returning evidently after the delivery of their message and were passing along the left flank of the army; they were set upon and—"

"How were they killed?"

"With sabre cuts and lance thrusts."

"And who did it?"

"By the side of one of them was a blood-stained *Cossack* cap, and—"

"Yes?"

"With a red feather in it."

"Good!" said the Emperor irrelevantly. "Your men know this?"

"Every one of them and they have sworn if they get permission—"

"I see. I give you permission to go after the Red *Cossacks* and bring them to an engagement, *monsieur*, and to annihilate them. As to following them long, our good French horses cannot compete with those *Cossack* ponies in endurance. A long pursuit is not to be thought of; besides, we are approaching Moscow and I shall probably need you and every other of my soldiers, for I do not think that Kutusof can in honour permit me to enter the *Czar's* ancient capital without making an attempt to defend it. Besides, we are pressing hard upon his heels and we must bring him to an engagement. If I could have caught him before, if my plans had been carried out in accordance with my direction, the war would have been over long since. You understand?" continued the Emperor after this rather long speech the effect of which upon his staff he keenly noted. "Your regiment is detached for the purpose of bringing this Red *Cossack* brigade to action and to put it out of their power to give us any more annoyance. Yesterday part of the baggage train of the corps of the Viceroy of Italy was seized. My own personal baggage was attacked this morning within a mile of this very division of my Guard and only by the greatest difficulty were the assailants beaten off. In fact, the escort was cut to pieces and but for the opportune arrival of some of Marshal Poniatowski's Poles I should have had to beg hospitality of the army for a place to sleep and something to eat for tonight. How many men have you in your regiment now?"

"Six hundred, Sire,"

"So many as that?"

"That was the morning report given me today."

"And can it be depended upon?"

"Absolutely."

"Lieutenant Colonel Maurice," said the Emperor, "you are a model officer. I believe there is no regiment in the army which can show so large a proportion of its strength ready for duty. How many had you when you crossed the Niemen?"

"Eight hundred, Sire."

"And you have lost but two hundred?"

"And some of those can be accounted for."

"How?"

"By your orders. Major Beaubien, who was in command at the time, left a detachment of an officer and forty men at the—*château* of Wilkomir. They were to be relieved from Kowno and were instructed to join us on the march. I look for them every day."

"And the rest that you lost?"

"A few were left behind ill at Smolensk and one hundred were buried on the field there. Your Majesty."

"But the stragglers?"

"None of my men has straggled from the columns, they are too devoted to—" the lieutenant colonel checked himself just in time,— "to Your Majesty," he said. "And they all know that I would shoot with my own hand any man who abandoned his Eagle."

"Lieutenant Colonel Maurice," said the Emperor, "I am pleased with you. Come back from this expedition successful and you shall have the star of brigadier general. I rely entirely upon your judgement and skill. I will also supplement your force—"

"With six hundred such men so devoted to Your Majesty," returned the hussar promptly, "I could do anything, go anywhere, in spite of all the *Cossacks* in Russia."

The Emperor laughed and taking their cue from him the whole staff burst into a joyous uproar. Uncertain for the moment whether he was being laughed at or not, the lieutenant colonel suddenly presented his sword and glared about him.

"We are pleased," said the Emperor quickly, "at such spirit, *monsieur*, and we laugh because we are happy to find it in the young soldiers of France. Is it not so, gentlemen? "

"Upon my word. Your Majesty," cried the red-headed Marshal, who had previously spoken, "if you are tired of this brave Maurice, give him to me."

"You want everything. Marshal," answered the Emperor in high good humour, "This is a favour, however, for which you ask in vain. It is with no desire to discredit the accuracy of your statement or the justice of your judgment, my dear Colonel," continued the Emperor, "that I think it well to place under your command a larger force for so important an undertaking and I will leave to your own selection the troops who are to second your hussars. Now, what shall they be? Meanwhile, gentlemen, let us ride on. The men will have enjoyed the little halt but it is not well to protract it too long. Colonel Maurice, you may ride on my left hand. Come, *messieurs, en avant.*"

The Light Horseman had been thinking deeply and quickly.

"I have decided," he said at last, "upon my auxiliaries."

"Yes?"

"I should like to have a battalion of light infantry and a light battery of four guns."

Napoleon looked at him searchingly. He was astonished at such a request. The Marshal on the right interrupted him quickly.

"You ask for foot soldiers and guns to chase these horsemen! *Monsieur*, you are mad!"

"Saving the Emperor's presence," returned the Light Horseman, bristling, "I beg to assure *Monsieur le Maréchal* that I was never more sober and I hope more sane, in my life."

"And yet," said the Emperor, smiling, for he rather enjoyed seeing these flashes of conflict between his officers, and he was not at all averse to the sight of a simple lieutenant colonel of horse, although he had the advantage of being in the Imperial Guard, so stoutly standing up to one of the greatest Marshals of the Empire, the one who was to come out of this campaign with the most fame, more than any other man in the Grand Army, or indeed in the world. "Yet," he continued, "the Marshal's surprise is but natural. Who would think that a soldier—"

"Your Majesty," returned the Light Horseman, "I am glad to explain my plan to a soldier at once so daring and experienced as the Duc d'Elchingen."

"Upon my word," laughed the duke, and he had a tremendous laugh, "so you think I need lessoning in the art of war from a lieutenant colonel of light horse?"

He was in a very good humour about it, almost contemptuously so. The face of the hussar flushed at that. He matched himself with a Marshal without hesitation and indeed, such were the chances of the campaign that long before he reached the age of that Marshal, he himself might carry a *baton*. It was the Emperor who intervened.

"I am an older soldier and it may be even a better than you, Michael," he said gently to the Marshal, "and yet I have never hesitated to learn from the humblest grenadier of the Guard anything—" he smiled and when he smiled he was irresistible—"anything that he might be able to teach me, that is," he added.

"Proceed, proceed, *monsieur*, explain to us how with artillery and infantry you expect to catch these famous *Cossacks* who surpass in speed and mobility the best of our cavalry," began Marshal Ney in a more moderate tone as he acknowledged the Emperor's reproof with a low bow over his saddle.

"The Emperor, whose word is law," said the hussar, "has said and none can dispute him that we cannot cope with these *Cossacks* in speed. If happily I am to succeed—"

"If you are to succeed, *monsieur*," interrupted the Emperor sharply.

"Pardon, since I am to succeed. Your Majesty."

"That is better."

"I must do it by strategy. I must lay a trap for these gentry."

"Oho," said Napoleon.

"And you propose to bait the trap with a regiment of infantry?" said the Marshal, seeing a great light.

"Exactly, Your Grace," returned the soldier.

"And with the guns?"

"I shall complete the annihilation of the detachment when we get them into the ambush which I shall lay for them."

"Quite so; the young man has the right idea, Duke," said the Emperor; "you shall have your regiment and your light battery."

"And may I have an imitation convoy, also, Sire?"

"Go back along the road," said Napoleon grimly, "and pick up all the abandoned wagons you require."

"And horses to draw them?"

"We have none to give you. You can—"

"I can dismount some of my troops, conceal them in the wagons and use their horses for the convoy."

"Lieutenant Colonel Maurice," said the Emperor approvingly, "as you said, your service with the army and especially your tour of duty in my Guard has not been without profit to you."

The lieutenant colonel blushed like a girl.

"Prince," said the Emperor, turning to another Marshal who rode quietly at the head of the staff a few paces in the rear of the Emperor, "you might as well get ready that order appointing Lieutenant Colonel Maurice to the command of the next vacant brigade."

Berthier smiled and nodded.

"It shall be ready when the gallant lieutenant colonel has earned it, Sire," he returned phlegmatically.

"Nothing," said Napoleon, "ever stirs my good Berthier out of the calm which befits the chief of the general staff. Marshal Ney, suppose you give this young man a regiment. I do not care to detail any of the Imperial Guard."

"With the greatest of pleasure," said the Marshal; "I am about to join my corps and I will detach a regiment of regular dare-devils to follow the leadership of this gallant young man. I will have it await your arrival on the right flank. I presume that your expedition will take you forward, *monsieur?*"

"Yes," answered Napoleon for the hussar, "from what I am able to learn, the Red *Cossacks* should be on our right flank covered by those woods yonder."

The army was marching through a vast plain but upon the far horizon to the southward heavy woods extended for miles.

"And the battery of guns, Sire."

"Will you see to that also, Marshal?"

"Certainly," was the hearty answer; "it is the kind of adventure that I would like to undertake myself and the whole corps would enjoy it."

"But it is hardly a command for a Marshal of France," said Napoleon.

The Marshal saluted and followed by members of his own staff, he galloped past the columns marching ahead and was soon out of sight.

"You understand," said Napoleon emphatically, "this command

must be brought to an engagement and it must be wiped out. I have heard a rumour that it is commanded by a Russian officer of rank belonging to the Czar Alexander's Guard and that the *Cossacks* are supported by a detachment of regular cavalry of the Guard with guns also. In fact, it is due to this leadership, doubtless, and this support, that they have accomplished so much and it is probably because of this support and this leadership that you may have a chance to bring them to bay."

"I will earn that promised star, Sire," said the young man, confidently, "or I will have no need of shoulder straps."

"Good," said Napoleon, "and good luck to you!"

CHAPTER 12

Trailing the Red Cossacks

Owing to the wide distance that separated the several columns of the Grand Army, it was not until late in the afternoon that the various detachments were assembled which made up the expedition under the command of Lieutenant Colonel Maurice, to continue to give him the name by which he was known in the army. The dramatic events of his sojourn at the *château* of Wilkomir were only a month behind. No one in the army knew anything about his adventures there except Major Beaubien, his subordinate, his confident and his friend. The young subaltern, who had witnessed the whole thing, had been detailed to remain behind on guard at the *château* and of course could tell nothing.

Although his heart had broken at his renunciation by his wife, somehow or other, the wound in his shoulder mended and after the first great overwhelm of grief and despair, the natural buoyancy and spirit of the young hussar reasserted itself. He began to make plans, to cherish hopes, to dream dreams. In spite of her own words, he was confident that in her heart of hearts, the woman who had been so dramatically made his wife under such thrilling circumstances, loved him enough to be willing to fulfil that role eventually in spite of her repudiation.

He dwelt upon the conversations and happenings of the three brief days in every leisure moment. He was confident that she did not love the French officer in the *Czar's* army to whom she was betrothed. It was only a quixotic notion of honour involved in keeping her word, at the urging of the stern old Prince, which had caused her to speak to him as she had. The impartial and dispassionate Beaubien, younger but more phlegmatic than his superior, was nevertheless, of the same opinion; and the two discussed the affair with ardour whenever opportunity served.

Sooner or later, the retreating Russian army would be brought to bay and the battle would be joined. No one in the Grand Army doubted the issue of that event and Lieutenant Colonel Maurice declared in his heart that he would be very unfortunate as well as very stupid if he did not find out thereafter, from the prisoners, the name of the officer to whom his wife had been betrothed. This was the comforting and consoling thought of the young light horseman. When he found him?—well! in a situation like that in which his own right arm atnd shining blade would play the larger part. Lieutenant Colonel Maurice was absolutely confident that there could be but one end. Woe to that renegade Frenchman when he caught him!

Of course, there was the appeal to the *Czar* and the Metropolitan of the Holy Orthodox Church to be feared, but it so happened that since the day the Hussar left Wilkomir to join the Grand Army at Wilna, the army had been between the Emperor Alexander and Prince Muravieff and it did not seem possible to the lovelorn Frenchman that a message could have reached the Russian Emperor as yet. And even if the appeal had been delivered to that Sovereign, in the confusion and anxiety of the campaign, the *Czar* could hardly be expected to give the matter the attention it merited. Nor could the young soldier see how, even if he wanted to act, the *Czar* could reply to that petition at once.

On the other hand, if the Emperor Napoleon could only deliver the battle he so ardently longed for and if the lieutenant colonel could only be given a few months' time to prosecute his inquiries, he trusted that he could eliminate the gentleman whose betrothal cut so sharply athwart his own prospects for happiness. In that case, he did not despair of inducing the Prince, her grandfather, and the Prince, her father, to let the marriage stand.

He had gone away with despair in his heart, thinking that the only legitimate ambition left for him had been for a sure and speedy death; but he had changed his view point in that particular, not sufficiently, however, to cause him to hesitate in attacking anything or anybody or to jeopard his life on the high places of the field whenever he had a chance in quite the old reckless, light horseman way.

Naturally he was eager to win distinction. The more distinguished he became, the higher the rank he attained, the more glory he acquired, the more adequate a companion he would be for the lovely Princess and the more likely his claim to be considered. He did not even hesitate to think of the Emperor Napoleon ultimately as a possible pleader in his behalf after the war was over, especially should he continue to merit the favour of his beloved idol, of which he had received so many substantial proofs.

He had thought it wise not to allow any inkling of his rank and name to get about. When he had been cut off by his family upon his decision, as a mere boy, to follow the fortunes of General Bonaparte, some years before, he had enlisted in the army, in the cavalry, as a private soldier. His daring and gallantry on a hundred fields had won him his promotion.

Napoleon was always glad to rally to his Eagles the ancient nobility of France. It would no doubt have made his position more secure, and it would have been of immense advantage to the lieutenant colonel if the Emperor had known that he was the Comte de Vivonne and the only representative of that ancient family in France, but the lieutenant colonel believed in winning whatever was coming to him in the future as in the past, by his own unaided efforts.

He rejoiced, therefore, in this present command, which gave him a degree of independence and for the first time in this campaign an opportunity to show that he was something more than a *beau sabreur* and gallant horseman. It should go hard with him if he did not earn that promotion to the command of that brigade and once advanced that far, he might have some hope of becoming a General of Division. He was so confident of success that he actually saw himself already in the gorgeous uniform of that last-named officer.

The regiment of infantry which had reported to him from Marshal Ney's division which had been recruited in Paris some years before, was originally one thousand strong, but it had been reduced in one way or another to a force of about two hundred and fifty; but they were two hundred and fifty of the hardest bitten, toughest, most reckless souled, somewhat insubordinate veterans in the second corps. They were ready for anything and it so happened that they had a particular grudge against these Red *Cossacks*, because while doing escort duty a few days ago, they had been severely handled by these same desperate horsemen.

The light battery of four six-pound guns was the best and the most efficient in Marshal's Ney's corps. The great Ney did nothing by halves. He had been attracted to the young man in spite of his somewhat defiant air, he knew the dangerous nature of the work that had been cut out for him, he wanted to see him succeed, therefore, he sent him the best he had.

When the regiment of light horse and the battery and the regiment of infantry were assembled it was with deep satisfaction that the lieutenant colonel looked them over. There were an even thousand of them, exactly enough for his idea and to make the affair interesting. More would have frightened away the *Cossacks* but even if they caught sight of his entire force they might not refrain from attacking it on account of its numbers. He did not intend that they should catch sight of his entire command if he could possibly prevent it, but if fortune were against him, the smallness of the expedition might tempt so daring and successful a body as the Red *Cossacks* and their dashing leader to try an issue. If the reward for success would be certain and adequate, so would the censure and mortification at failure be in proportion and the lieutenant colonel did not mean to fail by taking too many men and frightening away the enemy.

While he had been waiting for the battery and the infantry to join him he had caused a large collection of abandoned baggage wagons and other vehicles of all sorts to be made by his regiment. The baggage wagons had been already emptied of their contents but the canvas coverings were drawn over frames and empty boxes so that to a casual inspection they looked as if heavily loaded. The regiment of hussars went about this merrily enough, their beloved officer having explained to them what he was detailed to do and part of his plan, but when it came to dismounting from their horses and stowing themselves away in the wagons while the horses were attached to the huge, apparently heavy baggage train, they demurred. A hussar off his horse was like a sailor on one or a fish out of water.

Discipline was not the strongest point of Napoleon's army, especially the older soldiers were allowed a great deal of liberty. So long as the troops kept themselves in good trim, remained in their ranks atnd could be depended upon in action, other things were frequently winked at. But the lieutenant colonel had different ideas. He was still imbued with some of the autocratic spirit of his ancestry. He was a strict disciplinarian and the natural grumbling of the hussars did not rise very loud or go very far.

It was nightfall before all these preparations had been made. The troops had been lucky enough to come upon two wagons in which there were several overlooked barrels of hard bread and one or two casks of light wine. How they had ever escaped destruction when the wagons were abandoned and subsequently pillaged was a mystery, but there they were and hard bread and light wine were a welcome relief from the rations they carried with them. The lieutenant colonel was delighted. He knew that nothing is more healthful to a soldier than to be well fed and he let them eat and drink their full before he called them to attention.

It was almost dark, therefore, when the command was ready to move. The last attack of the Red *Cossacks* had been reported on the rear of the baggage train following the Guard, the largest and most important section of the army. It was easier for the news of the attack to go back along the line than forward and Lieutenant Colonel Maurice reasoned that probably this ferocious band of raiders would turn toward the uninformed van rather than the expectant rear. Indeed careful inquiry along the officers of the detachment which had sustained the last attack confirmed that conclusion.

There had been some pursuit of the raiders by a detachment of *cuirassiers* of the Guard but these heavily armed and armoured horsemen had no chance whatever of overtaking the light, mobile *Cossacks*. They had noted the direction of their flight, however, and in short, everything pointed that they had gone toward Moscow,

South of the road on which the army marched and parallel to it several miles away another road had been opened. The lieutenant colonel decided to make for that road. Loading the infantry and the dismounted hussars into the wagons and selecting the stoutest horses of the command for the purpose of drawing the wagons, the whole command moved off to the right at as rapid a pace as possible.

The distance between the two roads was soon traversed. The country was open and rolling and as the flankers of the army had been thrown out for several miles on either side, they saw no signs of an enemy. It was quite dark when they reached the road. They struck it where it happened to make a sharp turn to the southward to escape a deep ravine cut by a considerable brook. The road builders had been too lazy to bridge it and it was evident that the road would follow its banks until an easy crossing and a practicable ford would be found. This took the command farther into a forest which grew denser and heavier as they progressed until finally they were surrounded on all sides by an extensive and almost impassable woodland.

Flinging out a platoon far in advance and covering and protecting the flanks by the same means, the lieutenant colonel pushed his command on through the greater part of the night. Just before dawn they came to a clearing. They crossed the creek at a good ford. A few feet from the other bank they entered upon a tree-less plain. They could see the opening only indistinctly in the darkness but it appeared to extend several miles to the southward. They had struck the clearing at the north end. The edge of the trees made an arc of a circle of which the road, plunging into the forest on the other side of the clearing, was the chord. From one side of the forest to the other was here not more than a quarter of a mile. The clearing, the end of which they could by no means discern, was in the shape of an ellipse whose sides were lost in the distance to the south, and they were cutting across the top of it. The advantages of such a place for his purpose were instantly appreciated by the young commander.

No very vigilant or extensive pursuit of the Red *Cossacks* had been attempted by the Grand Army. Such pursuit would, as a rule, have resulted in nothing but the disintegration of the Grand Army, and the horses and men worn out by it would effect nothing. The army would be frittered away in such processes. The *Cossacks*, therefore, so he reasoned, thinking they had little to fear would proceed in a leisurely manner along this road, the only practicable way through the vast extent of territory and they would probably bivouac for the night and be ready to make another onfall upon some part of the long line of the Grand Army early in the morning.

Indications, plain enough to a soldier, had confirmed the shrewd guesses of the lieutenant colonel and he and his officers were convinced that a very considerable body of horse had preceded them but a short time on the road. So far as could be determined, there had been no alarm yet given of the approach of this French expedition. The hussar had pushed his command forward at a very great pace, he had spared neither horses nor men. If his guesses were right, and he knew that successful warfare was largely a matter of good guesswork, he ought to be in the vicinity of the enemy.

A whispered consultation between Major Beaubien, his second in command, Major Goujon, the hard-bitten veteran in command of the regiment of Infantry and Captain Champfert of the battery found them all agreed upon that point. Beaubien and Champfert were for a night surprise or an early morning dash upon the camp which they felt sure could not be far away. But Goujon sagely pointed out that in such a case, the force would be deprived of the use of the infantry, in which conclusion the young commander concurred.

"*Messieurs*," he said, "it would be very fine to fall upon them while they are asleep provided they were there and provided we could get near them before they awakened. But even in that case, unless they were bivouacked in some open, we would be at our usual disadvantage in attacking them. They would scatter and while we could break up the band temporarily, we could not annihilate it. The Emperor expects us to teach these bold robbers a lesson. These Red *Cossacks* are the bravest and most successful of the many detachments which are making life a weariness to the convoys of the Grand Army. If we cut them to pieces it would be a lesson to all the rest, and we must kill or capture its commanders. The Emperor was most emphatic that we should get the men who are at the head of these attacks and responsible for them. You know in his philosophy, the general is much, the soldier little. I think I have a better plan than those you have suggested and this is it."

CHAPTER 13

The Red Cossacks Pay a Call

Deep in the midst of the forest glade, in a little clearing six or eight acres in extent, where there stood a humble peasant's farmhouse with a few low adjoining outbuildings, something like two thousand men were sleeping. The night was pleasant, the breeze was warm and agreeable. The sleeping men were of a hardy race. Wrapped in their great coats, with their saddles for pillows and their horse blankets beneath them, they lay quite comfortably upon the dry grass in the clearing. On one side the ponies of the command were grouped and picketed. In the house, from which the poor peasant and his family had been rudely dispossessed, the higher officers got what rest they could.

Although no one in the command had the least fear of attack, he who had the ordering of events was evidently an experienced soldier who neglected no precaution. Guards and patrols were flung back on the road over which they had come and forward on the road over which they expected to move in the morning. The officer himself saw that vigilant watch was kept, for he inspected the nearer patrols personally from time to time.

They had made a long hard march after the sharp skirmishing of the day before and they were very tired when they reached the place of bivouac. The men had slept soundly and the subordinate officers also. The commander himself would have enjoyed an opportunity for much-needed rest but an uneasy sense of danger possessed him, a sense such as veteran soldiers some times experience without being able to assign any exact reason for it. He laughed at himself for his fears, and yet they so far governed his action as to keep him on the alert. His judgment told him that there was no danger to be apprehended and he was rather mortified, though naturally relieved, when dawn approached with- out a sign of an enemy or attack.

Returning to the clearing after a last inspection of the outposts, he surveyed the sky through the tree tops and seeing that it was already grey with the coming light, he decided that it was time to awaken the men, let them get their breakfast and sally out again in search of the adventures he so thoroughly enjoyed.

The light was sufficient to show to any observer that the commander was not a *Cossack*. Indeed, he wore the rich green and white uniform, without the metal *cuirass*, of a dragoon in the Imperial Guard of the *Czar*. He was a slender, well-knit young man of medium height whose every gesture betokened confidence of success, backed by assurance of position. Dismounting from his horse, which he had left with his orderly, a trooper in the uniform of the same cavalry, he made his way over the sleeping *Cossacks* to the hut, the door of which he flung open. In good Russian but with a distinct French accent, he summoned the occupants of the house and then he turned to meet the officer of the night guard who came running at the sound of his voice, and bade him awaken the detachment. The officer was just about to transmit the order to a trumpeter who appeared from behind the house, sleepily rubbing his eyes, when the rapid galloping of a horse on the hard road was distinctly heard. At a signal from the commander, the officer of the guard stopped the trumpeter before he had blown a note.

"We will see what this messenger from the front, who is evidently in a hurry, has to say before we make a sound," he said in explanation.

By this time, the other officers, including one or two of the Imperial guardsmen, but mostly huge bearded *Cossacks* had come crowding through the door of the hut.

"If you will ride with me. *Messieurs*," said the commander, mounting and indicating their horses to the others, "I think from the haste of yonder rider that we shall have news."

The rapid hoof beats on the hard road were much nearer now. The group turned and followed the alert Frenchman. It was growing lighter and by the time the commander had mounted his horse, the others had followed his example, and all had reached the road, the messenger had arrived. Recognising the commander, he reined in his horse.

"A message for the Colonel," he said, saluting in his rough way.

"What is it?"

"Lieutenant Chekoff—" began the messenger.

"Yes, the commander of the patrol—"

"He says a French wagon convoy with a few horsemen is coming through the wood."

The officer laughed.

"Fortune, not content with favouring us in attack seems actually to present us with opportunities, even to force them upon us. Awaken your regiments, gentlemen, but quietly. Get the men to horse at once and we will investigate this convoy and prepare for it a warm, if not a particularly pleasant welcome. You, Verlinski," he turned to one of the Russian officers of the Guard, "assemble my own troop and follow me down the road. You, Ostrolenko, bring the *Cossacks* up after us but silently, silently. We don't want to frighten away our prey before we are ready to seize it. You understand?"

Both officers apparently comprehended the not difficult instructions of the colonel and followed presently by about a detachment of one hundred troopers of the Imperial Guard which had been given to him for his personal escort when he had asked and had received this *Cossack* command with a roving commission, he moved down the road. The *Cossacks* were accustomed to night work and they knew perfectly well how to go about their business without any unnecessary confusion.

At the summons they sprang to their feet, seized their saddles, ran to their horses and presently fell into such order as they were accustomed to maintain. A light battery of four guns was limbered up, although necessarily with more noise than was made by the *Cossacks*. This was a detachment of regular Russian artillery, and the whole party under the lead of Colonel Ostrolenko moved quickly down the road in the wake of the commander. The guards and the patrols had been called in and almost before the astonished peasant realised it, his farm was emptied of its unwelcome visitors.

The French officer in command soon joined the advance patrol but the subaltern in charge had little to add to his first message. A picket which he had flung far down the road just before break of day had observed the head of what appeared to be a long wagon-train, lightly guarded, slowly advancing through an open space in the forest half a mile away. Without discovering their presence, the men of the picket had retraced their steps and told what they had seen. Sending one messenger back to the bivouac, the *Cossack* officer had despatched a swarm of scouts to get complete information and as he talked with his commander some of his men came back, brimful of news and bursting with excitement.

They reported that the wagon train was French—of course, everybody knew that—and that it included some twenty or thirty wagons apparently heavily loaded, presumably of great value, and that it was guarded by a detachment of infantry, not more than two hundred in number.

"It is strange," said the commanding officer, "that a wagon-train should be found on the new road, so far from the French army."

"Might it not be due to the fact," said Ostrolenko, leader of the Cossacks and second in command of the whole detachment, "that it may have come from the south, from Schwarzenberg's Austrians, through Minsk or thereabouts and is now seeking to join the Grand Army?"

"It is a possible explanation, of course. How did the horses look?" the commander continued, turning to the scout.

"It was too dark to see clearly, but they went slowly and seemed tired. Vassily here speaks the French language. We were near enough to hear the soldiers talk."

"And what did they say?"

"Your Excellency, they were cursing themselves and their bad fortune and their long journey."

"You see," said Ostrolenko, "they have come from the south."

"Well, no matter whether they have come from the south or not, we will relieve them of their charge, and—" the commander stopped again. "By the way," he resumed after a moment's thought and including the whole of the scouting party in his glance as he spoke, "did any of you see anything of any other force?"

"We saw nothing but the infantry. They appeared to be just about breaking camp. Fires were burning and the horses were not yet hitched to some of the rear wagons."

"Very good," said the officer, "we will find our breakfast in those wagons. Gentlemen, I depend upon the Red *Cossacks* to live up to their name."

"What is your plan, sir?" asked Ostrolenko.

"The simplest possible. We will go silently down the road—you say they are still in the clearing?"

The head of the scouts nodded.

"They were there half an hour ago, Excellency."

"Good. We will ride slowly down the road until we come within sight of them, and then gallop upon them. Ostrolenko, you with your regiment will defile to the right, Major Ruitzka with his to the left. I, with the guard will fill the gap between you. The battery will remain on the road with the guns unlimbered ready to sweep the clearing if it should be necessary. We can easily divide if we find they fight us more stoutly than we expect, and a few shots from those guns will probably take the fight out of them. Do you understand?"

"Perfectly, sir," came from the several commanders of the different branches of the service.

"Then forward."

By this time, the whole detachment was close up, Ostrolenko's men following hard upon the regular Russian cavalry with the regiment of Ruitzka immediately next, while the artillery brought up the rear. Still leading, with the men of the squadron, the commander trotted rapidly down the road. It was a broad highway, left in an unfinished condition on account of the war which had been suddenly thrust upon the Russians, but it was sufficiently cleared to make the going easy and it had been generously planned so that there was room for the troop of cavalry to ride abreast.

The sun was not yet up but it was very much lighter when the commander caught sight through the trees of the wagon train he was about to attack. It occurred to him the moment he saw it that the wagon train was still in much the same condition and situation as it had been when it had been first reported by the scouts. Only two or three of the wagons had horses hitched to them and were ready to move. The rest seemed to be in a state of disorder. The noise coming from the camp had been heard quite a distance back on the road, in fact, it had whetted the appetites of the *Cossacks* for prey. It was this noise, the commander surmised, which had prevented the French from noting their approach until that moment. French soldiers, apparently in various stages of undress were now shouting and running about like a lot of ants disturbed in their hill. Horses were plunging and rearing and altogether the scene was one of great confusion.

It was evident since the alarm had been given that the French were trying to hitch up and move away. The young commanding officer observing them from the edge of the clearing while the Cossacks in his rear defiled to the right and left *en masse*, so far as the trees permitted them, for their rush, decided that the commander of the escort must be a very sorry fellow indeed to permit such confusion, not to say chaos, as abounded. And yet there was something about it which rather tended to give him pause. It hardly seemed possible that good soldiers could get into such a wretched tangle and veteran troops were usually detailed to protect valuable convoy such as this seemed to be. Could it be possible that things were not so bad yonder in the clearing as they appeared, and if so, for what reason?

Again, after a second inspection, he noticed that although the wagons seemingly lay in every direction, yet really with a few movements they could be flung into a half circle which would prove a formidable obstacle to a cavalry charge. The commander had about made up his mind that before flinging his men on this apparently helpless prey, he would investigate further, when Ostrolenko precipitated the conflict. His men with *Cossack* yells, sifted through the trees into the clearing, there, not more than five or six hundred yards across.

This manoeuvre started the attack at once and forestalled the precautionary methods the Frenchman had deemed it wise to take. Promising to deal with Ostrolenko later for his breach of discipline, and realising that since the attack had begun it was better to deliver it with all his force, the commander shouted an order or two, the bugles blew and the whole Red *Cossack* brigade came forward at a gallop.

CHAPTER 14

The Springing of the Trap

The commander was not going so quickly that he was unable to observe that there was an instant cessation of the noise and confusion. He also saw two or three wagons to which horses were attached, jerked violently into place and that which had seemed like a confused line of wagons suddenly assumed the shape of a half circle. The men within the half circle stopped their aimless running about and formed some sort of an irregular line. Things had a decidedly different complexion, yet the wagon guard seemed few in number and although the work would be harder than he had anticipated and there would undoubtedly be many empty saddles, there was no reason why the Russians could not ride down the detachment. Although, as the flanks rested in the trees, to circle them would be difficult, they could at least break into the half circle and sweep the road.

Motioning to Ostrolenko to go ahead therefore, the commander started all his horsemen for the wagons. From some voice came a sharp word of command. Instantly a swift volley fired apparently between the wagons or from under the wheels, burst out upon the grey air of the morning. Horses and men in every direction, from the enclosing circle of the *Cossacks* went smashing down to the ground. For the moment the advance was checked, but as the smoke of the discharge blew away, the keen eyes among the assailants observed the escort of the wagon train actually abandoning a position which, judging from the first volley, they might have held for some time if not for all time. In short, every Frenchman in sight was running madly toward the forest in the rear of the wagons.

Although they had been so fiercely and disastrously received, the sight of the retreating Frenchmen put new spirit into the *Cossacks*. It caused the heart of the commander of the detachment to sink a little. A Frenchman himself, knowing well the temper of his nation, he could not conceive how anyone with the least bit of soldierly instinct, at the head of such a body of troops would abandon so defensible a position after inflicting such a loss from a single volley. Yet there was now nothing to do but to press on. He would not have sought entrance into such a quarrel, but once in, it had to be pursued to the end.

The next instant the Russians were among the wagons. They were not ranked so closely as to prevent their being penetrated. One or two were jerked aside and the enclosure was soon filled with men and horses, leaping over the tongues and forcing their way between narrow openings.

The Red *Cossacks* were better disciplined than any other detachment of these rough raiders and riders in the Russian service and one of the cardinal rules which had been enforced at the point of the pistol—and indeed many a *Cossack* had been shot before the others learned to obey it—was that there should be no pillaging, no dismounting from their horses even, except upon order. They had been so uniformly successful that into their dull minds had come the conclusion that their future success depended upon their obedience. The Franco-Russian officer over them had given them so many opportunities and had carried them safely through so many adventures that they were gorged with plunder, satiated with success, intoxicated with admiration for their commander; therefore those within the enclosure remained on their horses, handling their swords and pistols, some of them waving aloft lances of which they had possessed themselves from some slaughtered Polish Cavalry, and all of them yelling like mad.

In a charge even the best troops get out of hand and the irregular line of wagons was surrounded by crowds of men. The conquest had been so easy that the forebodings of the experienced officer in command had been increased rather than diminished by the facility by which the train had been seized. Rising in his stirrups, he was mounted on a huge horse, he stared about him. No sound came from the forest into which the French had retreated. Surely even cowards with so fair a mark and with the advantage of the protection of the trees which grew thick on either side of the road, would have sent a shot or two into the immense target presented by the crowding horsemen. He could not understand it. However, he acted promptly.

"Major Ruitzka," he shouted, "take your command or so much of it as you can get, and advance down the road to the other side of the clearing. Fling your men out as skirmishers through the forest. There is something suspicious about this ominous quiet."

"Yes, Excellency," answered Ruitzka, shouting to his men to follow and making ready to carry out his orders.

"Ostrolenko?"

"Here, Excellency," roared the big Russian.

"Draw your men outside these wagons and off to the right yonder, right back of the edge of the clearing." He turned to one of the subordinate officers, "Tell the battery to unlimber and train on this wagon enclosure. The rest of you follow me."

As the confused detachments began to move off in accordance with their directions something happened. From the upper end of the clearing there came the sharp crack of a musket. This was succeeded by a smashing volley from the woods in the rear of the wagon train. Ruitzka's men had just reached the edge of the woodland. The colonel had just given the order for his column to deploy but it was still huddled together in some confusion. Two hundred muskets were fired at point-blank range right into the face and flank of the regiment, doing frightful execution. Major Ruitzka, shouting and storming at the head of the line, was the first one to fall. The French were not cowards after all, flashed into the mind of the commander, and there was a little pride in his heart as the knowledge came home to him; but he was soon occupied himself.

From the woods in rear of the other detachment, for every horseman had instinctively turned toward the smashing up of Ruitzka's regiment, came another volley in the back of Ostrolenko's *Cossacks*. A third volley smote them in the face from the wagons themselves. There was a moment of indecision. The commander saw it all. The wagon train was a trap, it was filled with soldiers, there were other soldiers in the woods to the right and left. Off to the southward the way was yet clear. They must retreat that way, but before they retreated there was one thing that could be done. Turning toward the battery he made a motion to it to open fire.

The artilleryman in command of the battery had realised the situation as well and as quickly as anyone on the field. He was ready to fire and catching the wave of his superior's sword, he shouted an order, but before a single piece was discharged a cross fire of artillery was hurled upon the battery from concealed guns on both sides of the road across the clearing. Three pieces went down in inextricable ruin. The fourth piece, more fortunate than the rest, until a second discharge, escaped.

The gunner applied the match to it, the shot struck the body of one of the wagons, lifted it into the air, swept it over upon its side and killed several of the dismounted cavalrymen within.

The practiced eye of the Franco-Russian perceived at once that his battery was out of action. The enemy in all arms of the service, were in greater force than he had imagined. Well, the way to the south was still open. Putting himself at the head of the troops he started down the clearing. But the *Cossacks* were now panic-struck and completely out of hand. Ruitzka's command came crowding back from the edge and intermingled with Ostrolenko's regiment and the Russian cavalry coming their way. From the wagons another volley was poured at point-blank range into the mass. Some of the raiders broke for the left, charging for the road, now blocked up with the dismantled guns. They were overtaken by a second discharge from the French artillery which had had time to reload.

By this time the Red *Cossacks* were in a state of frenzy. Seeing that the way to the south was still open, by a sort of instinct they wheeled their horses, struck spurs into them and started that way. They had scarcely gone a rod when from out of the forest on either side came galloping squadrons of French cavalry. At the same time the infantry broke from the woods and ran back to the wagons which would afford them protection from the *Cossack* sabres and lances and began a scattered and irregular but deadly and practically continuous firing. The Russian detachment had plunged into the trap which had closed around it in vice-like grip. The *Cossacks* were not used to such a reception, they were not made for such hard close in fighting. In mad terror they reined in their horses one moment, swerved to the right or left the next, advanced or retreated in the next, while from all around them bullets were hurled upon them.

The dismounted troopers in the wagons gave their places to Goujon's veteran infantry and Beaubien's squadrons, which had held the upper part of the clearing, came charging down on the back of the *Cossacks*. The guns on the right, having now completely put out of action the Russian artillery, advanced to the edge of the woodland and, served with extraordinary precision, hurled ball after ball into the *Cossacks* while the hussars to the southward with the lieutenant colonel at the head, pressed home the charge.

Captain Grosjean, who had commanded the detachment of dismounted hussars which had retreated after the first fire, now remounted his men on their horses, catching stray *Cossack* ponies to supply the mounts which had been killed and led his detachment of perhaps fifty or sixty men to the edge of the clearing and surveyed the field before precipitating it into the conflict. He was a veteran soldier and knew that often even a small reserve thrown in at the critical moment decides a battle.

The *Cossacks* were now completely demoralised; the Frenchmen butchered them almost like sheep. Here and there a few fought desperately, among them a group around Ostrolenko, but the heart had gone out of most of them. Not so the troop of cavalry of the Russian Guard. They had gathered about their leader with discipline and precision and had formed a little column of platoons. The battle was lost, it was not much more than a slaughter now. There was nothing the commander could do to restore it and the best effort he could make was to break through the encircling line which was drawing closer and closer and get away. His men were armed with pistols. Selecting the spot where the chance seemed greatest, for the French were there the thinnest, the commander poured a volley into the line and charged it with furious speed.

The place where the Russian officer struck the French line was near the edge of the forest. The hussars did not give back an inch. A few of them had undischarged weapons and they fired them into the face of the line and then rushed at them and fell on them with their sabres. The line was drawn out very thin at that place, however, and the Russian cavalry slowly battered down the opposition and in another moment they would have won free. In fact, some of the cavalry sifted through the reeling, desperately fighting French soldiers, the Franco-Russian commander, his sword red with blood to the hilt, in the lead.

He could have got away but he checked his horse and turned in his saddle and shouted to his men. The sight of their leader on the other side, reanimated these Russians of the Guard. With new determination, they made another gigantic effort and pushing aside the last resistance, they came crowding after their captain, fancying themselves free. No help could be afforded from any other part of the line. The French were outnumbered two or three to one. Although the first discharge upon the *Cossacks* had gone far toward wiping out that difference, yet they needed all the forces they had at every point.

Lieutenant Colonel Maurice saw his line give way and the Russians drive through the opening. There was nothing he could do to support the line. Every man was busily engaged in fighting. To detach

129

any of his force to close the break would only have opened another and resulted in the escape of a great part of the *Cossacks*. Yet the bold assailants must not be allowed to go free.

By this time the *Cossacks* were thoroughly cowed. Many of them threw down their arms and flung up their hands but the excitement of the Frenchmen was so great that at first no attention was paid to these mute appeals for quarter. The whole field was ringing with shouts and cries, the clash of swords, the flash of pistols, the crack of muskets, the roar of cannon. When the Russian cavalry broke through the only thing Maurice could do was to apply himself to the problem. He swerved his horse about and galloped single-handed toward the Russians.

They saw him coming. They had made good their endeavour, they had broken through the line and there was no doubt in the mind of the soldier in command that they could escape. His heart was hot, however, with rage and shame that he had been trapped and his detachment cut to pieces. He was familiar with the uniforms of the French army and he recognised the oncoming horseman as an officer of rank. His quick eye took in the whole scene. He saw that no troops could be spared to pursue him and he decided that a few moments more or less would not change the situation. They could escape just as well after he had killed this officer as before. The lust of battle was high in his heart and it was heightened by his mortification. He turned, therefore, to meet this oncoming Frenchman.

He was a rare swordsman and had no fear of the encounter. By a common instinct the cavalry of the guard checked their horses in their flight and turned to look. The next moment, the two commanders met at full tilt. The issue was in doubt. Both officers reined in their horses and bending forward, rained blow after blow upon each other. To his astonishment, the Franco-Russian found every thrust parried. He, the finest swordsman in the Russian Imperial Guard, had evidently met a man who was almost if not quite, his equal. The swordplay was swift and terrible. The Russian guardsmen slowly wheeled about and pressed closer to the two figures, hesitating whether to wait or fly. That moment of indecision caused their ruin. Originally about one hundred strong, they had already lost forty and of that number twenty of them at least had gone down in that terrific thrust against the weakened line.

Captain Grosjean had seen it all. That was the place for him and his threescore blades. His men were glad to be on their horses once more.

They had been chafing with all the impatience of French soldiers at their inaction.

"*Mes enfants*," said Grosjean, "these gentlemen are for our steel. Forward, but softly, no cheering. See, their backs are turned."

They scarcely waited for the completion of this characteristic command to dash out from under the trees. One of the guardsmen happened to turn his head and caught sight of them a few feet away but before he could give the alarm he was cut down mid in a moment the little hussar reserve fell upon them. They were slaughtered almost to a man.

The two officers still engaged in their deadly combat, scarcely observed what was toward. Grosjean, after the discharge of his task, spurred his horse to the side of the Russian commander. He had his sword shortened for a thrust when his horse stumbled and he suddenly lurched heavily into the horse of the Russian. The next moment Lieutenant Colonel Maurice beat down his enemy's guard and shattered his blade by a powerful sweep of his own heavier weapon. The Russian officer was helpless. He lifted his silver helmet, tore it from his head and opened his arms for the thrust that Maurice was about to deliver.

CHAPTER 15

The Emperor's Disppleasure

The arm of the Frenchman shot out, the point of his blade had already cut into the coat of the Russian when his thrust was suddenly, halted. A look of surprise and horror spread over his face. The officer's life was spared. Others of the French were not so minded, however, for the remainder of Grosjean's squadron crowded around the two ready to kill their unarmed enemy. Just in time Lieutenant Colonel Maurice awakened to action. With a swift blow he swept aside two swords that were aimed at the Franco-Russian's heart. With fierce words, he bade Grosjean lead his men against the *Cossacks*, who seeing that no quarter was given were renewing the fighting with the courage of despair, and the French were having a difficult time to hold them.

"I'll take care of this officer," said the lieutenant colonel imperiously; "into the fight with you all."

The two were presently left alone.

"*Monsieur*," said the leader of the Russians, "I am your prisoner it seems."

"No," returned the lieutenant colonel.

"I do not understand."

With that the lieutenant colonel tore off his *shako* and lifted his head.

"Maurice!" cried the Russian commander.

"Philippe!" was the prompt exclamation of the utterly amazed Light Horseman. "Good God! With your helmet and chin strap and that thick beard *à la Russe*, I did not recognise you. I had almost killed my brother."

"It would have been fitting," returned the Marquis Philippe de Vivonne coldly; "you are a regicide already, striking at the ancient kings of France in the train of this Corsican usurper. If you had buried your

132

steel in my heart it would only have been on a par with your other conduct."

"My brother," began the lieutenant colonel.

"Strike home," interrupted the elder, "as head of the family here, I command it. I would rather die than have seen this day."

"No," returned the Frenchman resolutely, lifting his sword and sending it blood stained as it was, into the scabbard with a crash. "I fight for France, for the greatest man who has ever led her armies but I cannot fight against you. You are free. I could say something in that I found you under the banner of Russia fighting against your countrymen, but I am silent. I have no reproaches to utter, may God decide between us. Farewell."

He turned his horse sharply as he spoke, struck spurs in it and galloped off toward the fighting, leaving his brother alone, staring after his rapidly moving figure. The next moment, having gathered the bridle reins in his hands again, he bent low over the saddle and galloped across the clearing, escaping easily the pursuit of some straggling hussars while he was fortunate enough not to be hit by any discharges from the infantry before he disappeared in the forest.

By this time, the battle was over. The surviving *Cossacks* threw down their arms and again implored mercy. The lieutenant colonel himself stopped the slaughter. The *Cossacks* were driven together in a mass and surrounded by the infantry. The guns of the battery were brought up so as to control them and then Maurice took stock of his command.

He had gone into the fight with six hundred cavalry, two hundred infantry and nearly as many artillerists,—close on to a thousand men. One hundred of his horsemen had been killed or severely wounded, the wounded numbering about a score. Twenty-five infantrymen had been cut down, of whom seventeen were dead. Not more than half-a-dozen artillerymen had been hurt. Of the surviving infantrymen and cavalrymen a great number had received slight wounds, but they would be quite able to keep the saddle. There were, therefore, fit for duty over eight hundred Frenchmen.

The slaughter among the *Cossacks* had been frightful. There were about fifteen hundred dead or hopelessly wounded to which must be added about one hundred of the Light Cavalry of the Guard. Most of the *Cossack* officers were killed. Ostrolenko lay on the ground severely hurt. The little field had all the characteristics of a desperate battle-ground; shattered cannon, broken wagons, dead and dying men, screaming horses, the smell of blood and powder. It was terrific. Beaubien had come through unscathed as had the Lieutenant Colonel. Champfert of the artillery had an arm broken by a pistol shot and Captain Grosjean had added a new sabre cut to the collection which he had amassed in many battles, this one on his cheek. A few other officers had fallen but the whole command was in a surprisingly efficient shape. They were flushed with victory. Such shouts and cheers rang over the field as they took in the extent of their conquest as served to waken the quiet woodland in every direction.

"You have done well," said the lieutenant colonel, as he got his troops in some kind of order; "the Emperor will be pleased with you, I am sure. Now we must get away as soon as possible."

"What shall be done with these wagons?" asked Beaubien.

"Put those of our wounded men who are unable to ride a horse or walk afoot in the best of them and abandon the rest. There are hundreds of *Cossack* ponies here which can be used to draw those we need. And be quick about it. We are on the extreme flank of the Grand Army and for all we know a division of Russian infantry or cavalry may be marching toward us now, so we must hasten away."

"And the Russians?"

"Let them be formed into companies, heavily guarded and marched with us."

"And the Russian wounded?"

"We can't take them back with us. Leave them here with some of their own men to look after them. It is the best we can do," said the lieutenant colonel indifferently. War was a ruthless business and that was the way they made it in those days. "They are in their own country, doubtless some ne will succour them," he went on. "Who was the commander of these Russians?"

"He was a Frenchman," said Beaubien, "an officer in the Imperial Guard, so I have learned from the prisoners."

"Yes," answered the lieutenant colonel.

"And his name—"

"My dear Beaubien," said Maurice, laying his hand on the other's shoulder, "I know his name, do you manage to forget it."

"I understand," said Beaubien; "I thought you had him yonder—"

"He escaped me. Who is the surviving officer of these *Cossacks*?"

"A certain Colonel Ostrolenko—"

"Ostrolenko!" cried the lieutenant colonel, his face flaming, "the villain, where is he?"

His hand instinctively sought his sword as he spoke.

"Release your sword, *Mon Colonel*" said Beaubien, "he is desperately wounded. He lies over there,"

"Beaubien, do you take charge for the time being. Marshal the troops in accordance with my order while I interview this man. Let the men breakfast from their haversacks, and just as soon as they have had a bite to eat and something to drink, we will move out."

"Very good, sir," said Beaubien, saluting while his superior rode off.

Ostrolenko, covered with wounds, lay on the ground, his head pillowed on his saddle. He was conscious and when he recognised the face and figure of the lieutenant colonel, a spasm of fear swept over his face.

"You villain, you dog! "cried the Frenchman, "I can pay you now for the insults and indignities you heaped upon the Princess Muravieff."

"For Christ's sake," cried the *Cossack*, "I am helpless, wounded, would you—"

"I was wounded and she was helpless," hissed the lieutenant colonel, "when you—"

"But you ought to be grateful to me," interposed the Russian desperately.

"Grateful!"

"Yes, for I made her your wife."

"My wife—"

"Did you not wish it?"

The Light Horseman stopped, fairly paralysed by the overwhelming audacity of the man.

"My name is on your wedding certificate. It may be that I am the only surviving witness; you may need my testimony some day," continued the *Cossack* imploringly.

"I would kill you where you lie," said the Frenchman, "in spite of what you say, were you not helpless and wounded. As it is," he turned away, "you may have what remains of your wretched life. For her sake, I spare you."

"You will not regret it," said the other, but Maurice did not wait to hear it.

He stopped, however, and gave some directions about the *Cossack*, for some of the French came back and made him more comfortable. There was a surgeon attached to the regiment and he stopped his attentions to the French for a moment to bind up the wounds of the *Cossack* colonel. After all the French officer reflected, for whatever reason it might be, by whatever method it might have been, it was due to Ostrolenko that the Princess Muravieff had become his wife and the bold plea of the villain had somehow tickled his fancy. Presently he turned and came back to his side.

"I have decided to spare your life," he said; "I have even caused my surgeon to leave my men for a little while to do what he can for you. You did make her my wife after all. No, I want no thanks. Half a dozen lives like yours cannot pay for such a gift as that."

He turned away, mounted his horse and the men by this time having partaken of a breakfast, the unfed *Cossacks* looking hungrily and vainly on, the little command moved up the road, intending to take the next open plain to the left whereby they could rejoin the main body.

It was evening when the lieutenant colonel, riding at the head of his column came in sight of the Grand Army. It had encamped for the night, fires were burning up and down the lines and except for the guards surrounding the troops, the army was taking its ease and cooking its supper.

Of course the approach of such a cavalcade as the column marching across the plain had long since been observed. A company of light horsemen had been sent out to beat them up. From this company, the lieutenant colonel had despatched two riders to apprise the Emperor of his return. Guided by the rest, the expedition with its prisoners slowly made its way to the place where the Emperor's tent had been pitched for the night.

Napoleon, who had not yet dismounted, sat on his white horse in front of his camp, surrounded by his staff and several of his marshals whom he had called for consultation about the next day's march. Back of these were grouped the staff officers of these marshals, couriers were coming and going and the whole scene was one of picturesque brilliancy. Lieutenant Colonel Maurice at the head of his column rode slowly forward. The soldiers of the army rent the air with enthusiastic cheers. The prisoners were easy to see; the red feathers in their caps and the red girdles around their waists clearly distinguished them. And all the army knew that the dreaded scourge had at last met defeat.

Arriving within a short distance of the Emperor, the lieutenant colonel gave command to halt. The ranks came to a stop, another order rang out and instantly the air was filled with flashing swords and enthusiastic acclaim. Napoleon acknowledged the salute, his eyes sparkling, a slight smile on his usually impassive face.

"Dismount, *General* Maurice," he said, emphasising the title, when he could be heard above the tumult.

He saw at once that the expedition had been a success. His eyes took in the number of prisoners, whom he judged to be about fifteen hundred. No man ever had such a wonderful faculty as he for estimating the strength of bodies of men, from a regiment to an army. He knew that the lieutenant colonel had triumphed and he took this public way of bestowing his reward upon him. As he gave command to Maurice the Emperor flung his leg over the saddle, and slipped slowly and somewhat heavily to the ground; an example which was, of course, immediately followed by all his staff and guests.

His face flushing with pleasure, but with a strange misgiving in his heart, Maurice promptly dismounted from his horse according to order, sheathed his sword, and advancing rapidly toward the little group, stopped and saluted.

"It is unnecessary to ask you if you have succeeded," began the Emperor.

"Sire," returned the lieutenant colonel, "your commands have been carried out. The Red *Cossacks* as a band have been annihilated and those that survive, save the seriously wounded, I have the honour of presenting to you. They are yonder."

"Good," said the Emperor "Berthier?"

"Sire?"

"That order gazetting Lieutenant Colonel Maurice as General of a Brigade?"

"I have it ready here," said Berthier, nodding to one of his subordinates. The latter produced an official paper, gave it to the marshal, who in turn handed it to the Emperor. "It lacks only your signature, Sire," continued the Prince of Wagram.

"Give me a pen," said the Emperor, unfolding the paper.

"Your pardon, Sire," interrupted the lieutenant colonel, "but—"

"But what?" asked Napoleon in great surprise.

"Before Your Majesty signs that paper, I have a report to make."

"Report," said the astonished Emperor, "there is report enough in those red-feathered gentry, and did you not say that all but these were either severely wounded or killed?"

"All but one, sire."

"Ha! And who was that one?"

"The commander of the detachment."

"And did he escape? Well," continued the Emperor, good-naturedly, not giving the lieutenant colonel time to answer, "that, of course, is unfortunate, but at least you have deprived him of his command and it often happens that one man manages to get away. He had no following left him, I take it?"

"There may have been a few stragglers who got off in the woods, but the Red *Cossacks* are utterly wiped out."

"I wish you had caught him, but your good fortune has been so amazing, that you deserve the commission even without him."

One of the officers now tendered the Emperor a fresh quill and an ink bottle, another held up a portfolio upon which Napoleon laid the paper and dipped the pen in the ink.

"Sire," persisted the lieutenant colonel, biting his lips, very pale but resolute, "the commander-in-chief of the Red *Cossacks* did not escape."

Napoleon paused, pen in hand.

"What did you say?"

"I engaged him in single combat, disarmed him and was about to kill him but I let him go free."

"Free!" cried Napoleon, dropping the pen to the ground. "What do you mean, *monsieur*? I gave you positive orders—"

"Yes, Sire."

"And how could you disobey them, you a soldier of my Guard—"

Poor Maurice could only stare helplessly.

"You must have had some powerful reason for your action, *monsieur*," said the Emperor severely.

"He was a Frenchman, Your Majesty."

"A renegade Frenchman in the service of the *Czar*, my enemy! Did I hear you aright, young sir?"

"Alas, yes, Sire."

"More reason for inflicting punishment upon the traitor," said the Emperor severely; "you had him in your power and you let him go. Why? Weigh well your answer, *monsieur*," continued the Emperor, with increasing gravity and sternness, as Maurice moistened his lips and strove to speak, "he who pardons a traitor is himself—"

"Your Majesty," burst out the Lieutenant Colonel, "he was my brother!"

"Your brother?"

The Light Horseman bowed his head.

"Umph!" said the Emperor. "What is his name?"

"Vivonne," returned the soldier.

"But you are Maurice?"

"I am the Comte Maurice de Vivonne, at your service."

"And your brother? "

"My elder brother, the Marquis de Vivonne."

"I seem to remember the name. With what is it connected? Is there not a Duc de Vivonne plotting against the throne?"

"My father, doubtless."

"Ha, and you?"

"Have I not always shown myself a true soldier, devoted to France and to Your Majesty?"

"Yes, yes. I have heard of these Vivonnes. He is without doubt one of the most dangerous men in the Russian army. Yet exactly what he has done escapes me. Well for you that it does, *monsieur*," continued the Emperor thoughtfully.

"But I could not kill him, Sire."

"No, perhaps not, although in becoming the sworn enemy of myself and France he should cease to be your brother, but you should have captured him and brought him to me."

"To be executed by you as a traitor. Sire."

"Silence," cried the Emperor, his face flushing. "Do you assume to question me, *monsieur*? By heavens, I have had men shot for less than that."

"I knew that I would incur your displeasure. Your Majesty."

"And why did you tell me? If you had kept silent—"

"I could not in honour accept a reward which I knew that when you knew all you would withhold," said the lieutenant colonel.

This sentiment does you honour, *monsieur*," said the Emperor slowly, "but you have been guilty of a grave offence and a serious breach of discipline in that you spared an enemy whom I had directed you to kill or to capture. You merit no promotion. As I have said I have had men shot for less and more reduced to the ranks, but one reason why I hesitate to inflict one or the other punishment upon you, Monsieur le Comte de Vivonne—"

"Will Your Majesty permit me?"

"Speak, but no plea."

"I have none to make. Sire. Will Your Majesty continue to know me only as Maurice in whatever rank Your Majesty may be pleased to place me? "

"Yet you are the Comte de Vivonne?"

"Yes, Sire, but it was as Maurice that I entered your service, it was as Maurice that I fought in your battles, it was as Maurice that I earned your favour and it is as Maurice that I would remain until the end of the chapter."

"Be it so," said the Emperor, "for the success of your expedition, which has been brilliant, I inflict no further punishment upon you, save to remove you from the Imperial Guard and attach you to some other command."

"Your Majesty," spoke out big Marshal Ney at this juncture.

"What is it, Duke?" said the Emperor.

"Give him to me. I love soldiers like that. He has done what no one else in the army could do, break up that damnable band. He is a strategist and a tactician as well as a fighter. My corps is sadly deficient in cavalry. I will make good use of him if Your Majesty—"

"Very good," said the Emperor, tearing up the order appointing Maurice brigadier general and throwing the pieces to the ground, "you and your command are attached to the corps of Marshal Ney; as for the rest, now that you have been properly punished, I hope that you may some time again justify my confidence and my clemency."

"May I add one word. Sire?" asked the lieutenant colonel.

"Yes, but be brief," said the Emperor.

"Young man," interrupted Marshal Ney, "if you object to entering my command—"

"Next to the Imperial Guard," said the Light Horseman quickly, "it is the command of all others, without prejudice to these gallant gentlemen, that I would have sought."

"Good," said Ney, "that is settled then."

"My men. Your Majesty, they will feel keenly their dismissal from your Guard, they have done nobly, they—"

"Summon your officers," said the Emperor.

The officers had gathered in front of the hussars and had heard all that had passed. Their indignation was great against the Emperor and their affection for their lieutenant colonel was consequently heightened. They came forward, led by Beaubien.

"Gentlemen," said Napoleon, "you have doubtless heard our conversation. Lieutenant Colonel Maurice is detached to Marshal Ney's corps. He is of the opinion that you gentlemen may prefer to remain in my Guard. In such case, the command would fall upon you, sir. Your name is—"

"Beaubien, at your service, Sire."

"Well, what say you?"

"For myself. Sire," returned Beaubien, and it took immense bold-ness for him to say this,—"I will follow my colonel as I have followed him for many years. The regiment, I am persuaded, is of the same mind."

"Good," said the Emperor, smiling again; he seemed to have re-covered his good humour as quickly as he had lost it, and some of the sharper observers of the scene were quite sure that the Emperor's displeasure was assumed for the occasion and to produce the effect that he desired. "I like to see troops devoted to their leaders, regi-ments follow their commanders. It may be that by bearing yourselves gallantly in the forthcoming battle, you may regain my favour and be once more given your place about my person. You will make a report in writing," he continued, "to the Prince of Wagram; the prisoners will be attended to by the proper officers. *Au revoir*, gentlemen."

"I am glad," said Marshal Ney heartily, flinging his arm over the young man's shoulders, "to have in my command a man of your stamp, Maurice, and it will not be my fault if I do not give you opportunity enough to enable you to win back the favour of the Emperor, who is perhaps after all, not so angry with you as he seems. For myself, if it had been my brother—" yet he lowered his voice so as to be sure the Emperor did not hear, "I would have done just the same!"

CHAPTER 16

Borodino

At two o'clock on the morning of September the seventh, the Emperor retired after having completed all his preparations for the contest to begin at daybreak. He was in great need of rest but in spite of his fatigue and his serious indisposition—he was suffering from a terrible cold and a painful sore throat—he found himself unable to sleep. Summoning Berthier to his tent he talked with him for some three hours during which the two men again went over the plans and possibilities of the battle pending. The Russian retreat had come to an end at last. The Russians, under the command of one-eyed, old Kutusoff, had been driven back just as far as they intended to go without fighting. Moscow, holy Moscow, the sacred capital of ancient Russia lay a few leagues in their rear, they would not yield that city without a struggle. One great battle, at least must be fought for its preservation. From the highest to the lowest, every man in the Russian army was anxious to measure strength with Napoleon.

The fighting of the day before about the village of Schevardino protected by a formidable earthwork, which had been at last captured by the French, had been of the most sanguinary description. The redoubt had finally been taken by assault, the gallant regiment that had penetrated it had almost been cut to pieces by the heroic defenders before they themselves were all killed. When what remained of that regiment had been paraded late that evening before the Emperor, he noticed how few were in the ranks and riding to the colonel he asked where was the other battalion.

"In the redoubt, Sire," was the proud reply.

Truly they were there and they did not come out save in the arms of their comrades. Eight thousand Russians and half as many Frenchmen lay dead and still unburied back of the position where the Emperor's tent had been pitched.

At five o'clock in the morning, the Emperor dismissed his chief of staff and flinging himself down on his camp bed got a little rest. The Emperor was a sick man. As has been noted, he was the victim of a severe cold which rendered it almost impossible for him to speak above a whisper and which tended to numb and paralyse his other faculties. Shortly before six o'clock he arose, mounted his horse and rode out to a little hillock in front of his tent before Schevardino to take a last look at the Russian position.

Directly in front of the Emperor, perhaps a mile and a half away, rose a series of low hills. On the left of his position and perhaps about as far from him as were the hills ran a little river, or brook, called the Kolotsa. This river roughly paralleled the new Moscow-Smolensk road until it approached the foot of the range of hills mentioned, when it turned to the north-east and at a distance of some two miles from the turn fell into a larger stream, called the Moskowa, The angle made by the brook and the road at the crossing was at least one hundred and twenty degrees.

To the right of the Emperor, southward that is, for as he faced the Russian army, he was looking directly east, ran another highway from Moscow to Smolensk, called the old road. Fronting the Emperor between these two roads here about two miles apart, on the crest of the range of hills, the left wing of the Russian army was posted. The right wing of the same army was drawn up far to the northward on the hills before which the Kolotsa flowed northeastwardly. The extreme Russian right rested on and was protected by the Moskowa. The hills back of the Kolotsa on the Russian right were much higher and more formidable than the gentler slopes between the two roads where the Russian left lay. The Russian position on the right was almost Impregnable, therefore their left was more open to assault.

Just where the Kolotsa crossed the road was the insignificant village of Borodino. Above the village and a quarter of a mile to the right, or the south of it, upon the most commanding of these hills, the Russians had built an enclosed bastioned redoubt or fort of large size, upon which they had mounted twenty-one heavy guns. This work was In the very centre of the Russian position and about at the apex of the very obtuse angle formed by the right and left wings. Recognising the comparative weakness of his left wing, Kutusoff had also erected three other smaller redoubts a mile south of the great fort; two In front on the very edge of the slope and one higher and further back, commanding the others. These redoubts were not completely enclosed, they were rude earthworks open in the rear, technically termed filches, or arrow-heads, or they perhaps might be called redans. They were only hastily thrown up entrenchments behind which men could fight with some protection to their great advantage.

The ground at the foot of the slope on the top of which the Russian lines were drawn, was covered with brushwood with here and there some groves of trees. The extreme left of the Russian line got what protection it could from a thick woodland through which the old Moscow-Smolensk road meandered. In many places hard-working pioneers had cut down the trees, leaving the trunks to fall as they would, forming what was known to the soldiers as slashing, almost impenetrable by horse or artillery and even extremely difficult for infantry.

There were one hundred and twenty thousand men in the Russian army and half a thousand guns. They were planted in every possible position on the crest of the slope. The Grand Army of the Emperor had been reduced by daily fighting, by appalling desertion, by continued straggling and by sickness until it just about equalled in men, horses and guns the Russian strength. Naturally, however, the thinning-out process had resulted in the survival of the fittest. The cream of the Grand Army was present with the colours. In the same way and for many of the same causes, the Russian army had been sifted, though in much less degree, and save for the detachment of ten thousand Moscow militia, Kutusoff's command was justly representative of the manhood and valour and devotion of the Slavs.

The Russian left could easily have been turned by the French army and doubtless Napoleon would have merely amused Kutusoff by a heavy demonstration on his front while he attempted one of those tremendous flanking movements for which he, no less than the great Frederick, was famous; but in that case, Kutusoff might have extricated himself from the dangerous turning movement and his army might have drawn further back and would have been as formidable as ever. A battle and a victory were absolutely necessary and essential to the French cause and for two hundred leagues of terrible pursuit Napoleon had been endeavouring to force that battle. He could not, even if he would, have declined with honour and no successful manoeuvring would have much advantaged him if it did not result in action. The bold challenge of the old Russian warrior must be met by fighting.

The Emperor quickly perceived that the Russian left was the

proper object of his attack. With the Viceroy Eugene de Beauharnais and Grouchy's cavalry division containing the Russian right, he determined at the same time upon assaulting both Borodino and the great redoubt which was the Russian centre while with Poniatowski on his extreme right on the old road, he would strive to turn the Russian left. Meanwhile Davout and Ney would assault the arrowhead protections and the Russian left centre. In other words, he would pierce the centre, turn the left and then crush it, leaving the right to take care of itself until he was ready to deal with it—a truly Napoleonic conception, indeed.

His troops were all up and in hand when at six o'clock in the morning he gave signal for advance. The half-fed French soldiers were hungry, although they had become used to that, and they were sleepy and tired, for their preparations for the attack had caused them to be on their feet most of the night; but in spite of these disadvantages, not an army on this planet has ever fought with higher courage or more persistent determination than these men displayed on that famous day. On the other hand, the Russians had enjoyed several days of rest, their commissary arrangements were excellent, they had been well fed and were now established in a position of their own choosing and of great defensive strength. However these advantages may be reckoned in their favour, it must be admitted that the stubborn Slavs made full use of them, for the French and allies found them entirely worthy of their own terrific valour and magnificent reputation. No armies have ever deserved more praise from their rulers and countrymen than these two.

It had been raining for several days during the week before but for two days the sun had shone, the roads were dry, there was no dust and nothing that could imperil or render difficult any manoeuvre that might be attempted. In modern warfare, men fight in their old clothes with the colours of their uniforms carefully chosen to render them inconspicuous individually and indistinct even en masse. At that time men had not learned the value of this practice. Therefore, every Frenchman had been ordered to put on his best uniform and make his bravest showing as if on parade. Accordingly, the different regiments and detachments blazed with colour and light as they moved to take their final places under the eye of the Emperor, whom they saluted with their customary enthusiasm.

It is a singular fact that all through this campaign, advance, battle, retreat, summer or winter, dust or rain, sleet or snow, no matter what the conditions or what the disaster or what the demand, the men never lost their enthusiasm for their great and beloved captain. When they could say nothing else, their lips, freezing or burning, bursting or bloodless, could still manage to acclaim him in the old familiar way—*Vive l'Empereur!*

"Your wound is a severe one," said a surgeon to a dying grenadier. "I do not know what I shall find as I probe it."

"If you cut as deep as my heart you will find the Emperor," was the whispered answer of the indomitable soldier.

The morning was misty but as the Emperor watched the masses of men rapidly taking their appointed stations, the sun rose over the hills back of the Russians, showing plainly as *en silhouette* their massed lines and gleaming on the polished barrels of their hundreds of cannon. For the rest, they all looked solidly black against the morning light.

"It is the sun of Austerlitz," whispered Napoleon to one of the attendants, smiling.

But it was the sun of Austerlitz misted in clouds!

Back of the infantry of Davout and Ney which had already moved forward were the cavalry divisions of King Murat; Montbrun, most gallant of horsemen on the left and Nansouty and Latour-Maubourg with the corps of Junot in the second line. Off to the right the column of Poniatowski could with difficulty be seen forcing its way slowly through the woods. In rear of Napoleon were massed the flower of the army, the old and the new Guard in reserve. From the woods on the French right, into which Poniatowski had plunged, to the Kolotsa on the left were ranked the corps of Davout and Ney accompanied by their guns, the horses restlessly chafing under the tight reins of their drivers.

Near at hand stood the massed battalions of Marshal Junot. On the other side of the river on the right flank could be seen the Eagles of the Viceroy's division. The troops before Napoleon were in that position which in military science is known as "*Écheloned* by the Right"; Davout was thrust far forward. Drawn back from him was the corps of Ney like the second step in a flight of human stairs and farther back and a little to one side was the Cavalry and then the Corps of Junot. In rear of Napoleon's position before Schevardino were drawn up the closed ranks of the Imperial Guard, the *corps d'élite* of the army.

A heavy detachment of the artillery of the Guard had been advanced to engage the Russian guns and cover the attack of the infantry. The slope of the hill was not so steep nor was its elevation so

146

great as to render it impossible or even difficult to use the French guns effectively. The echo of that first shot had scarcely died away when the whole hill and plain before the Emperor was covered with sound and smoke, under cover of which the French advance began, slowly at first and then more rapidly. The divisions of Marshal Davout commanded by the veteran Friant, the brave Dessaix, the hard-fighting Compans, moved forward and fell terribly on the Russian left.

The underbrush and groups of trees were first cleared of detachments of the enemy who, however, held their positions to the last and mostly died fighting, selling their lives dearly. So soon as Davout finally gained the crest of the hill, Marshal Ney was sent forward. By nine o'clock the whole line was engaged and the fighting was of the most tremendous character. The Russian guns swept the hills with terrific effect. The plunging fire of the French artillery was also horribly disastrous. The Russian reserves had crowded too close to the front and many of the cuirassiers and infantrymen of the Imperial Guard, obstinately refusing to withdraw, were cut down by bullet after bullet. Poniatowski and his Poles struggled forward desperately, driving the Russian skirmishers ahead of them through the thick woods and well-nigh impenetrable slashing, but in spite of all that he could do he could not for a long time come up on the extreme Russian left, which unturned as yet, still held on.

By nine o'clock in the morning the three arrow-heads had been taken and retaken. Davout had been wounded but had insisted upon remaining at the front. Ney, Junot, Compans, Dessaix, Friant, and many other gallant officers had gone to the front of their commands and by their personal presence on the battle line had reanimated their veterans to charge and countercharge, to successful assaults, to desperately fierce defences, until the ground about the arrow-heads was carpeted with the dead and dying of both armies. The undergrowth had been mown down by the storm of fire and the trees cut to pieces by musket bullets.

On the far left, Eugene, not contenting himself with demonstrating and threatening the Russian right, had captured Borodino at the point of the bayonet. Ney, thereupon, made desperate efforts to rush the main hill and capture the great redoubt. Murat, leaving his cavalry still chafing impatiently, had ridden to the front line to take part in the struggle in person, while Junot had moved his fresh divisions to support his brother marshals. Meanwhile, the Russians, withdrawing men from their now unthreatened right, ruthlessly hurled division after division upon the French. The great redoubt, which was blazing like a volcano from its guns and the small arms of its heroic defenders, still stood, the key to the Russian position. Thrown out of the arrowheads, at last, the Russians rallied and took up a new position back of a little ravine in front of the smoking ruins of the burning village of Semenovski and continued to fight as gallantly and with as much determination as if they had lost nothing.

It was somewhat after ten o'clock in the morning when Poniatowski's guns, firing heavily on the right, announced that he had at last got to the extreme left flank of the Russians. Although General Prince Bagration, the commander of the Russian left, used all his efforts and the advantages of his position—for the little Georgian was almost as great a fighter as Ney himself—and had flung in every last man, he was unable to dislodge Poniatowski from the left and at this very crisis of his battle this Russian commander was mortally wounded, whereat the Russian left at last, but slowly, began to give back before the French and the Poles.

The sight of the slow but unmistakable withdrawal of these troops reanimated the French with new courage and fresh ardour and zeal. Again led by Ney, Murat and Davout in person, with the generals of division and brigade in front, the French fell on the dogged, slowly retreating Russians and at last drove them through the smouldering embers of the village of Semenovski. The French, however, try as they might, could not break through the Russian line, which although it gave back, swinging on the central redoubt as a great pivot, still held in spite of all that could be done by the assailants. Napoleon's veterans had never in twenty years met with such determined resistance.

Emerging from the woods at last, Poniatowski joined hands with Davout, and Napoleon, observing a gap between Davout and Ney, flung in the remainder of Junot's corps. Eugene, the Viceroy, was still hammering away on the redoubt. He had actually succeeded in forcing an entrance into it at one time, only to be driven out by the Russians. By this time, all the Russian divisions, or practically all, from the right had been withdrawn and sent in to aid the hard-pressed left. For a space of two miles, therefore, the struggle was a hard one, a hand-to-hand combat of the most appalling description.

Over one hundred thousand men on each side fired in each other's faces, rushed at each other with bayonets, and sometimes disdaining weapons, grappled each other with naked hands. Captains, colonels, generals, marshals, mingled with private soldiers in one titanic, awful conflict, the like of which had been seen perhaps in no battle since ancient Roman times when most of the fighting was of necessity of the hand- to-hand variety.

The smoke-overhung field was covered with shattered cannon, with dying horses, with ruined caissons, with the bodies of the dead and of the wounded, all ruthlessly trampled underfoot by the living fighting over them. The grassy slopes had been cut to pieces by the hoofs of the horses, the wheels of the guns, the bullets of the weapons, and the feet of hundreds of men. The earth was wet with blood. A strange, horrible red mud, compounded of dust and human life, clung to the feet of the combatants who slipped, struggled and fell into it. The air was filled with the groans of the dying, the shrieks of the wounded, with curses of despair in every language of Europe.

Yells of rage burst from the throats of the fighters and words of command, like appeals for pity, went unheeded in the mad tumult caused by the deep, thunderous, rolling roar of the great guns, the continuous crackling staccato of the small arms, and, most horrible of all, the screams of maddened, wounded horses. And everywhere was the acrid smell of burning powder and the sickening odour of blood. And everywhere men, wounded and dying or unhurt, would have given anything for a draught of water.

The horses on either side charged and recharged the fighters. Old Friant, "the model of all warlike virtues," was struck down. His division had scarcely time to form two squares connected by a line of artillery before the Russian *cuirassiers* were hurled upon them *en masse*. But Murat threw himself into the principal square and under his eye it held.

"Soldiers of France and of Friant," cried the King of Naples, "you are heroes."

"Long live Murat," came the thundering answer.

The Russian left had at last been driven back until it ran almost at a right angle to its former position. The great redoubt from being the centre had become almost the extreme Russian right. The Russian line was now a great salient thrust forward to the huge fort with the French and allies hemming it in on both sides. It was past noon by this time and the redoubt had not yet been taken. The two armies on the Russian left at last drew sullenly apart for a space, utterly exhausted by the awful exertions of the day. They separated, as it were, by mutual consent and yet halted within easy musket-shot range, firing volley after volley point-blank at each other, the cannon with their deeper roar punctuating the rattling of the smaller arms. And the hard-working captains on both sides sought at this time to straighten out and re-form their entangled lines and mixed commands.

If the redoubt could only be taken, the centre of the Russian army would be pierced, the Russian left, what remained of it, that is, might be annihilated, and the Russian right driven back against the Moskowa and cut to pieces or forced to lay down its arms. Ney, Murat and Eugene, who had been doing terrific fighting, brought up three fresh French divisions, those of Morand, Broussier and Gérard, which had not yet suffered as the other divisions and made another sustained and desperate effort to force the position so tenaciously held by Doctoroff, Ostermann and Raeffski. Their commands were soon mingled together in a perfectly inextricable mass of desperate soldiers and only the heroic personal examples of their generals and their own indomitable fighting spirit kept them in action.

Again and again the great redoubt was assaulted. As before, Ku-tusoff flung into it his freshest and bravest men and brought to their support others of his tired but tenacious fighters. A division main-tained it, two divisions supported it, three divisions attacked it, Ney on the right, Eugene on the left. It was Murat, the King of Naples, who finally brought about its downfall by one of the most amazing feats which the French cavalry or any other cavalry ever achieved. Galloping to the head of Montbrun's splendid division of heavy horse, he bade them ride round the Russian flank, fall on the Russian lines and get in the rear of the great redoubt. Then he raced to the divi-sions of Nansouty and Latour-Maubourg and told them to support Montbrun's charge.

The horsemen, whose ardour had been inflamed by a period of enforced idleness, for, after taking part brilliantly in the earlier assaults, they had been drawn off and re-formed, leaped forward at the word of command. Their gallant leader, his sword upraised, dashed across the intervening ground and, without drawing rein or checking the speed of his horse, breasted the gentle slope, passed by the flank of one of the struggling French divisions, which opened to give him freedom to charge, and fell on the Russian line extended outside of the great redoubt to the left.

Under cover of a terrific discharge of cannon and muskets, the Russian infantry endeavoured to form a square to meet the onslaught of these five thousand sabres of Montbrun's *cuirassiers*. The French were too quick for them and before the slow-moving Russians could order their ranks, the gleaming horsemen burst out of the smoke and fell upon them. They were beaten to pieces. Raeffski, their commander, was killed. Montbrun might have turned to his left and crushed the Russian right, but his orders were to take the great redoubt. Once before, French cavalry had actually captured ships of war frozen in an icebound harbour. That remarkable exploit was as nothing to this that followed.

Turning to their right, therefore, the great body of horsemen made for the redoubt. The Russian Imperial Guard, still in reserve, hurried forward, its cannon opened on the great mass of horsemen. The brave Montbrun went down, cut in two by a cannon ball. His own men, unable to stop their rush, galloped over his dismembered body. His second in command, the gallant young Caulaincourt, the young brother of the Grand Chamberlain of the Emperor, spurred to the front to take his dead leader's place. The assault was not checked for a moment, although bullets fairly swept away the front rank, crashing like glass in the bosoms of men and the breasts of horses, so that they went down as if struck by lightning. Leaping their horses over this rampart of dead and dying comrades, the great rush of battle-mad *cuirassiers* swept roaring on.

Now they were in the rear of the great redoubt. Disdaining the fire of the Russian division posted to cover the rear, Caulaincourt actually led his men into the fort. Some of the garrison had faced about and he was shot from his horse in the very entrance, but again the impetus of the charge was so great it could not be denied and instantly the great redoubt was filled with horsemen. In its narrow confines a conflict unparalleled raged. No Russian thought of surrender. They turned some of them to fight the horsemen while others still held the bastions and manned the guns.

At this moment Ney and Eugene delivered their final charge on the redoubt. Again the leaden hail buried itself in the flesh of men; ranks, platoons, companies, regiments, went down but the attack was pressed home. Slowly the wave of men mounted the slope and paused a moment in the face of the last frightful volley and then fell inward like an avalanche of flesh and blood and steel.

The redoubt was taken! The Russian line was completely broken. Standing on the apex of the highest bastion as the smoke of the battle blew away, Marshal Ney, covered with blood and dust and powder stains, who had fought so terribly, who had horse after horse shot under him, who had led charge after charge in person, saw the Russians slowly drawing backward. They retreated in good order, taking their guns with them, save those that had been mounted on the redans and the redoubt. At this mass of Russians as a target, salvo after salvo, volley after volley was hurled by the French.

CHAPTER 17

The Emperor Hesitates and is Lost

Hard by the great Marshal, who that day won his new title, Prince of the Moskowa—for so the French called the battle—stood Lieutenant Colonel Maurice who had acted as *aide* to Ney on that day, who had participated in the fighting and who had never left his great leader's side save to bring up fresh troops, to carry an order or to rally a wavering command.

"Maurice!" cried the redheaded fighter in a great voice, "ride back to the Emperor and ask him to send us his Guard. We have the great redoubt; the Russians are retreating. If he puts in the reserve we can crush them and tear them to pieces. Tell him that the Viceroy is pressing forward on the left, that Davout and Junot and I are pushing the centre back; the Pole is on the extreme left flank. One more thrust and the day is gained. Hurry. You understand?"

Maurice nodded. He turned and ran down the hill. Both he and the Marshal were on foot. In the last assault they had scrambled up the redoubt on foot like common soldiers. There were thousands of masterless cavalry horses running wildly about, many wounded and screaming horribly. Catching the first unwounded one that came to hand, the lieutenant colonel swung himself into the saddle and galloped madly backward.

The whole slope of the hill was covered with dead bodies. The Light Horseman stopped for nothing. He could not pick his way. This was war and the individual must suffer if he stood in the way of the good of the mass. He himself saw the great opportunity as well as the Marshal. Murat, who had galloped up, saw it also; Eugene saw it; Junot saw it as well as Davout. Every Marshal had despatched an officer to the Emperor with a similar message, Maurice had seen all this and as he raced recklessly down the hill he determined that the man who

153

had befriended him and who had been, above all others, the lion of the field, should not be deprived by any prior messenger of the glory of the suggestion which he never doubted would be heeded.

He drove his poor horse like one possessed. The few miles between the Emperor and the redoubt were soon covered. Napoleon, telescope in hand, was standing where he had been all day, surrounded by his staff. Back of him were the closed ranks of the Imperial Guard. Reining his horse in with a jerk that fairly threw him on his haunches, the hussar sprang to the ground and saluted. He was so black with powder and dust and blood and red mud as to be almost unrecognisable.

"Sire!" he cried, his eyes flashing out of his grimed face.

"What news from the front?"

"Marshal Ney," shouted the young man hoarsely, "begs you to send forward your Guard. The great redoubt is at last taken; the Russians are retreating; Poniatowski—" in his excitement he forgot titles—"is on their extreme left; Davout, Junot, the King and Prince Eugene are pressing them. If you will only send forward the Guard, Sire, they will be undone!"

He had scarcely begun speaking before another horseman dashed up and listened.

"The same plea from Marshal Davout," cried he, as the hussar paused.

"A like request from the Viceroy, Your Majesty," cried a third arrival

"And from Marshal Junot," shouted a fourth.

"Send in the Guard, Sire, at the request of the King of Naples," panted out a last messenger.

Napoleon looked round at the bronzed faces of his last reserve, the picked soldiers of his great army. The Old Guard and the Young Guard were drawn up side by side, the first division of the Young Guard on the left, the first division of the Old Guard on the right. He could see the gleam of their eyes, the nervous movements of their moustaches, the concentrated expression of their faces. They were crazy to be put in. One of the Young Guard on the left completely lost control of himself and shouted without rebuke from older veterans and officers.

"Forward! Forward!"

And yet at that supreme moment Napoleon hesitated! Ney, Murat, Davout and Eugene waited and waited in vain for the Emperor's command to get their shattered divisions ready to go forward in support of that advance of the as yet untouched divisions of the Guard for which they looked and prayed. But Napoleon hesitated. His usually pale, composed, marble face was red with blood. He was strangely excited, nervous, apparently feverish, but no word came from his lips.

Some strange lethargy had possessed the Emperor throughout the hours of hard fighting. If he had been the Bonaparte of other days, he would have been forward himself at the front of the battle long before and with his unequalled, tactical eye he would have seen clearly the necessity of what now he took on hearsay and with suspicion.

The Emperor hesitated, the Emperor waited. The Emperor spoke no word. Above and beyond the battle roared. About him there was a ghastly silence. Although he was a young soldier, yet charged with the intensity of the great fighting Marshal, Maurice at last ventured to break the silence.

"The Guard, Sire; give us the Guard," he said hoarsely.

"For God's sake, Your Majesty, put in your command," came from another.

"We can ruin the Russian army, if you will give us the Guard, Sire," said a third desperately, while a murmur rose from all about.

"Claparède," said the Emperor at last to the general commanding the first division of the Young Guard, "advance with your division. Bessières, gentlemen, we will—"

But the wished-for order was never finished. By evil chance at that very juncture from the rear division of the Viceroy's force across the Kolotsa a courier came riding furiously.

Cavalry," he shouted breathlessly, "are moving from the Russian left. They have fallen upon the rear of Delzons' division. General Delzons has formed his command into a hollow square, Sire, and General Grouchy's cavalry is about to engage the enemy's horse."

That was the last despairing effort of the Russian Marshal. He had directed Ouvaroff with the *cuirassiers* from the Imperial Guard, his last reserve, and the Grand Hetman with his *Cossacks*, to make a diversion on the French left and it succeeded. Napoleon watched that attack seen far off on the northern horizon beyond the Kolotsa. What did it portend? Was Ney, carried away by his passion for fighting, mistaken? Seeing only what was in front of him, did he and the other Marshals realise a possible danger to the rear and the left of his army? The Guard was his last reserve. If they were flung into the battle it would leave nothing else for that day or for any other day.

"Your Majesty," said Bessières, giving the needed fillip to the again wavering decision, "remember that you are seven hundred leagues from Paris and this is your last reserve."

Bessières had earned his Marshal's *baton* by gallant service on many a hard-fought field, but nothing that he had done or would do could make up for that bad advice in that decisive hour. Napoleon shut his glass with a snap.

"Claparède, go you to the left to the aid of Delzons and Grouchy," he said; "we will keep the rest here."

"But, Your Majesty!" cried Maurice.

"Sire, Sire," broke out the other staff officers, picked and chosen men all, as they surged toward him.

"Gentlemen," said the Emperor severely, "be silent. You forget yourselves. I myself will go forward to survey the field. I do not like that attack on the left. Marshal Bessières is wise in his caution to me. I thank him."

By this time Claparède's division was obliquing to the left on the run. Napoleon signalled his staff officers and rode rapidly forward, passed the division and mounted the hill. An hour or more had been wasted; an hour or more had been lost. When he reached the great re-doubt, a little after five in the afternoon, the Russians had withdrawn to another ridge of hills and had formed behind another ravine. They were in plain sight; they seemed to be in no great disorder; they were stubbornly and resolutely taking another formidable position.

The golden opportunity was gone. Claparède's division arrived at Delzons' position too late to be of any service. Nor was it needed after all. Ouvaroff had withdrawn. It was useless to try to assault the Russian position with the shattered, decimated and battered troops already on the field. Their only possible chance lay in the Guard, which, cursing and groaning in disappointment and rage, stood to its arms back of the battle. The Marshals gathered around their great chief to protest as forcibly as they dared, in great bitterness of heart at his failure to comply with their pleas.

The hesitation of the Emperor had lost the advantage of the posi-tion. The Russians had been driven from their first lines and forced back, but they had not been defeated. The Emperor Alexander still had an army in being and so long as be bad an army in being he would not listen to Napoleon. There the Russians stood as grimly threaten-ing as ever; the position they had taken was scarcely less strong than the one of which they had been dispossessed. Indeed, that Russian army had actually been concentrated, hammered into concentration in the field.

One thing Napoleon did. He brought up every gun and massed them and then poured such a decimating fire upon them, to which somehow they found themselves unable to reply effectively, as carried death and destruction to the Russian ranks.

"Since they are still anxious for it," said the Emperor with the cruel jocosity of the battlefield, "let them have it."

The Russians, in spite of this concentrated fire from four hundred massed guns, persisted in remaining in their massed lines until night closed the contest.

Forty thousand Frenchmen and allies lay dead or wounded on that field, a testimony of their valour that is inexpressible, and fifty thousand Russians lay mingled with them, evidence of their courage as great as the other. And fifty generals, thirty French and twenty Russian, had fallen with their men. No such slaughter had ever been sustained by contending armies since the fabulous exploits of captains and soldiers of pre-Christian times.

The French army was hungry, thirsty, weary still. It was incapable of energetic pursuit. Napoleon expected to renew the battle on the morrow, but the next morning the Russians had gone. The horrible retreat of the Grand Army really began the day after that battle, though for a little space the army advanced and for a little space seemed to enjoy some fruits of that hollow victory.

A week after that battle the French mounted that eminence called "The Hill of Salvation" outside of the capital and from that "*coign* of vantage" surveyed the minarets and domes and towers of the churches, convents and palaces, including the Kremlin itself, which lay before them, enclosed by huge grey walls. There was the last capital in Europe into which they were to force their way. It seemed to the eighty-odd thousand left to bear arms, and the twenty or thirty thousand wounded or sick men, that their salvation lay within those ramparts in that abandoned town. No wonder as they saw the gold domes of the Byzantine architecture of the semi-Oriental City set in the far northland, shining in the bright, warm September sunlight, they broke into shouts of "Moscow! Moscow!"

They were as happy, as triumphant, as relieved, as satisfied, as those ten thousand Greeks under Xenophon with their cry of "*Thalatta, Thalatta!*" when at last they saw the sea.

BOOK 3
THE RETREAT

CHAPTER 18

The Wrecking of the Army

It had been whispered after Eylau years before. It had been talked about with bated breath after Essling and Aspern on the Danube. Now it was a fact accomplished. Retreat! The Emperor Alexander would not negotiate with the Emperor Napoleon. His army, that same army that had been withdrawn from Borodino, would not fight. The citizens of his capital city would not remain within its walls; even their dwellings had ceased to afford shelter for the army which had seized Moscow, for those dwellings were not. The French brought the sword, the Russians applied the torch and between the two Moscow had disappeared. What the fire had spared, and that was but little, the French had ruined. Although they had entered it with good intentions, before they left it the wreck of the city had been given over to pillage.

There had come into it perhaps eighty or ninety thousand strong, comparatively well men with thirty thousand sick and wounded, many of whom had recovered during their long sojourn in the city. A few reinforcements had also arrived, so there marched through Moscow's smoking, smouldering streets and out of the now futile gates in its now useless walls one hundred and twenty thousand arms-bearing men. There were left behind to the tender mercies of the Russians— and the Russians were really merciful and they were tender to those left behind in Moscow—some twelve hundred too desperately ill to be moved. Their despair at being abandoned was pitiful, yet had they known it, fate was far more kind to them than to those who set out in retreat.

In the wake of the army followed some fifty thousand stragglers, non-combatants, camp followers, including numbers of women of all nationalities, among whom were many French women who had formerly lived in Moscow but who did not dare now to remain behind.

Every vehicle of any sort that had survived the flames in the city and every farm wagon or cart that could be procured for miles around had been loaded with plunder of every description. And every gun which the Emperor carried into Moscow he carried out with him. Napoleon would give up anything rather than his artillery and his Eagles.

The divisions of the several army corps had been reorganised so far as was possible. Dead generals had been replaced. Everything that an imperious will and a furious energy, together with a wide experience, could suggest had been suggested and ordered, but means had been lacking to carry out most of the suggestions. Napoleon had led armies for twenty years and he had always led them victoriously. They were not accustomed to anything else and they did not take to their present situation easily. They were not good losers, as we would say.

It was late in October, but the weather had held beautifully fine during the six weeks' sojourn in the capital. The army was not badly off except for two things, food and drink. They had ammunition in plenty, muskets more than they could use, cannon more than they could drag away. They were loaded with plunder of all sorts. It was not an uncommon thing to see men sitting around a camp fire on the most costly and delicate furniture, their shoulders draped with furs that were fit only for royalty, eating stringy horse meat off gold and silver plate! The army had the Midas touch. It could almost make the precious metals, but with all its rich plunder it could not buy or make the simple, daily bread of life. There was none to be had.

The instant that the army moved out. Marshal Kutusoff had moved also. Napoleon had determined to strike south-westward toward Minsk, but Kutusoff had intercepted him and a deadly battle at Malo-yaroslavets had forced him to retrace his steps and return as he had come, *via* Smolensk and Wilna toward the Niemen. Once again the army had passed over the battlefield of Borodino, now ghastly with the bleaching and horrible remnants of forty thousand dead bodies! Impossible as it may seem, one or two who had been wounded on that day still survived. In the great Convent of Kolotskoi which had been used as a hospital there remained a number of wretched sufferers. These were loaded on wagons, by order of the Emperor, but before the next village was reached most of them had been abandoned, tumbled out to die by the wayside by the drivers.

There have been retreats and retreats. Generally a retreat is a disaster, but all the previous retreats in the world perhaps did not equal this one as a disaster. The trail over which they advanced was blazed with the debris, the *dejecta membra* of the Grand Army. They could see at what fearful cost their advance had been made, how great a sacrifice of men, horses, arms and equipment had been involved in their march forward when everything was favourable. They did not dare to look back and see what a wake of ruin they were leaving on their return journey.

The mortality among the horses was frightful. As one of the officers said, "Horses have no patriotism; they have to be fed!" There was nothing with which to feed them. The Emperor would not hear of the abandonment of a single gun. Army baggage wagons might go, the private wagons and carriages of the officers might go, the horses of the cavalry might go, but the guns and the ammunition must be hauled away. Lean, hungry skeletons, at which even Rosinante would have blushed, tugged despairfully in the traces attached to cannon and *caisson*.

There was fighting all the time. Clouds of *Cossacks* hovered on either flank just out of gunshot range. The slow pursuit of the Russian army, which always kept just out of touch, forced on the weary French. Save for the miscellaneous garments they had been able to pillage, the men were wretchedly clothed. They had advanced with summer uniforms and they still had them on. They were worn to rags. The man who possessed a pair of good shoes was the envy of his comrades and he had to sleep lightly lest they should be torn off his feet by some barefoot soldier.

There was little straggling in that army. What there was was involuntary. Everybody kept closed up, or tried to. To drop behind the rear guard meant death. The peasants, returning to their homes in the wake of the passing army, came out of their hiding-places and with bitter, ruthless ferocity wreaked their vengeance upon the hapless Frenchmen who fell into their hands. The tortures of these unfortunates were beyond expression. Some of them were actually buried alive, the peasants counting their efforts praiseworthy and esteeming themselves as fulfilling their duty and the highest dictum of patriotism and devotion.

The nights were growing intensely colder; the sun at midday was burning hot. There had been no rain and the roads were soon cut to pieces and ground into clouds of dust. The stragglers, the unarmed, the camp followers, suffered the most and yet their number did not seem to decrease. Why? The daily loss was more than made up by accessions of men too weak to carry a gun, who left their colours and merged into this vast mob of wretched humanity. Davout was charged with the defence of the rear and right well did that cool, calm, determined soldier perform that duty. So fighting, reeling, staggering, choking, dying, the lean men and the leaner horses slowly struggled westward.

And then the weather changed. Winter came with a suddenness and a severity for which their long immunity had ill prepared them. The temperature fell, the sky grew black with clouds, the wild, cold north wind swept down over the illimitable plains, driving before it the snow and the sleet. Still the army struggled on, still hungry and growing hungrier, still weak and growing weaker, still cold and now freezing beneath the bitter sky. Woe to the wounded, woe to the sick, woe to the helpless, now! Even the Russians, prepared for, protected from and inured to such conditions as they were, suffered horribly. It was not only the pursued that succumbed to angry nature but the pursuers, though in much less proportion.

To the *Cossacks* were joined a new enemy. At every bivouac the fearsome *Cossack "Hourra!"* was mingled with the awful howl of the Russian wolf and by day to this sound was added the harsh and repulsive croak of raven and vulture. The Russian army pressed closer now. Some strange obsession in the mind of old Marshal Kutusoff, who, it appeared, would rather build a bridge for a flying enemy than seize and crush him, alone kept the French from being overwhelmed.

Yet there were battles and skirmishes all the time. The French might starve, they might freeze, but while they lived they could and they would fight. Snarling they turned at bay again and again. Strung out in a long line upon a single road, not once but often, the van would wait until the main body had joined it and they in turn until the rear guard, spitting fire and destruction, had come up.

Smolensk was entered in mid-November by an army of madmen—mad from hunger. There were provisions there sufficient for a reasonable supply for all, but no man could restrain that frenzied army. The magazines were pillaged by the first comers. The lucky men gorged themselves with food, drank themselves into insensibility and wasted riotously what they did not use. The late arrivals got little, the camp followers nothing. Ah, the wretchedness of those camp followers! Life, with its operations, went on among them. Travail pains seized poor women and by the wayside babes were born only to die. Since there was neither food nor drink nor shelter it was necessary to move on without delay. Forty thousand men and nearly as many camp followers staggered out of Smolensk, leaving wounded and sick behind.

At this time and thereafter the rear guard was given to Michael Ney. And this was the order of march: First came the Guard, now worn down from forty thousand to six thousand men. The Emperor might better have put them into the fighting at Borodino when he had the chance. As it was, they had been frittered away, accomplishing nothing, never even having fired a shot in the whole campaign. In the middle of the Guard marched the Emperor oftentimes on foot. The cavalry had practically disbanded. There was scarcely a trooper left with a horse. A few squadrons were composed of officers. Colonels acted as captains, brigadier-generals as majors, generals of divisions as colonels and marshals of France as *chefs-de-brigade*. Gun after gun had been left behind to fall into the power of the enemy. Private baggage had gone; there were still wagonloads of ammunition which were dragged forward somehow, because without ammunition even the miserable remnant of the army would be instantly cut to pieces. It was only the terrific, Homeric, heroic courage that the survivors manifested that kept them from being cut to pieces anyway.

So long as they could handle a gun these Frenchmen would fight. Other virtues were lost. A terrible selfishness pervaded the ranks. The wounded or disabled generally appealed for assistance in vain, and yet on occasion there was manifested here and there self-sacrifice and devotion which reached the sublime. Mothers, dying, lifted up their children, vainly perhaps for a while, but presently some haggard, grimy grenadier would stoop over and pick up the baby, wrap it in his own great coat and press on. In the end baby and soldier would both die, but the man had done what he could.

The cold grew more and more intense. Sometimes in the forests there was wood in plenty, but it was green and they had no way of chopping down the trees. The pitiful fires of the night bivouacs were kept up by gleanings from the forest. In the early morning the pursuing *Cossacks* would often come upon French encampments with the men arranged like the spokes of a wheel. Around the hub, which was always a dead fire, would lie fifty Frenchmen. All the Frenchmen would be dead, frozen to death.

Here and there wretched houses stood. The *Cossacks*, approaching cautiously, would find them filled with dead and dying men. If a weary man stopped for rest, his hand or his foot or his face would be apt to freeze and sometimes when he struggled to his feet to resume his march, the frozen member would break off and throw him to the ice to die. Rivers which had been crossed easily on the advance now proved almost impassable. Creeks like the Vop flowing through deep ravines could not be passed at all until a bridge of human beings, horses and guns had made a sort of horrible causeway over which the survivors ruthlessly tramped.

Sometimes the French made prisoners. Once they trapped a *Cossack* detachment of two thousand. They forced them off their ponies, stripped them of every article of clothing they wore, dressed themselves in the garments of their captives, and then drove them along naked until they died. And the *Cossacks* and the Russians retaliated in kind. The suffering was horrible. If captured French soldiers, stragglers or women had anything that was worth wearing, that would help to keep out the cold, it was taken away ruthlessly. The trail was blazed with naked bodies as white, as cold as the snow on which they lay.

On the sixteenth of November the Emperor reached the little village of Krasnoi with the corps of Junot and Poniatowski and the Guard. He had with him scarcely fifteen thousand men able to bear arms. After him came the corps of Eugene and Davout and last of all the rear guard of Ney. Speed was the most imperative necessity. From the south the army of Tchichagoff was pressing up to fall upon the left flank and cut off his retreat. There was no force to oppose him. The Austrians under Schwarzenberg, half-hearted in their devotion to France, had retired and left the way open.

To the north, Wittgenstein, with an overwhelming force, was striving to overwhelm Victor and fall upon the right flank. The road westward led across the Beresina at Borisoff. If Tchichagoff or Wittgenstein, or both, could seize that river the remains of the Grand Army would be ground to pieces between them and the pursuing Russians under Kutusoff and Miloradovitch.

Awakening on the morning of the seventeenth of November, at the village of Krasnoi after a few hours of sleep, the Emperor was met by the information that Miloradovitch, who was called the Murat of the Russian army, threatened to interpose between the Guard and the commands of Eugene, Davout and Ney. No man can ever impugn the battle courage of Napoleon. From the day he enlisted the "Battery of the Fearless" at Toulon, from the time he had seized the battle flag with his own hand and had advanced over the bridge of Arcola at the head of his grenadiers in the face of a storm of shot, he had freely exposed his person to the chances of battle. "Bah," said he to one who remonstrated with him on one day in this retreat, about the dangers of his position, "the cannon balls have been flying about our legs for twenty years!" But never in his career did he show a more splendid courage, a more resolute devotion, a more complete, entire, absolute consecration of himself to his soldiers than he did on that morning.

The Russians were coming up fast; he had the choice of two courses. He could stay and fight for his men or he could press on with his guard and what men he had with him, leaving Eugene, Davout and Ney to their fate. He knew that, though these three brilliant fighters were outnumbered three to one, before the battle which would bring about their annihilation was over the Russians would be in no condition for further pursuit and that he and his Guard and the troops with him could proceed on their way with a much better chance of ultimate escape. What did he? He remained and offered battle—the lion at bay.

The Emperor has been accused of abandoning his army at Smorgoni a month later but he has enough to bear without that unjust reproach. Reasons of the highest importance rendered it absolutely necessary for him to return to France, yet he postponed his departure until there was absolutely nothing more that he could do in Russia. And he shared all the hardships of the troops, marching with them, starving with them, freezing with them, constantly watching over them, planning for them and animating and reanimating them with his presence and his words.

His actions on this day at Krasnoi ought to put a stop forever to any charge of betrayal or abandonment, for there is nothing more splendid in the whole range of military history than his decision to stay and brave it out. He drew up his little force of fifteen thousand men and attacked eighty thousand Russians who menaced him. By a series of brilliant and skilful manoeuvres, flashes of the original Napoleonic conceptions of strategy and tactics, he so manoeuvred his little force as to deceive the Russians, as to crowd them back and hold them in check and open the road so that the troops of Eugene and Davout finally effected a junction with him.

The lion stood at bay with all the brave, fierce determination and courage that made him a lion. The Russians, chary still of an encounter with the great Napoleon, gave way before him, certainly a triumph of mind over matter.

The operation was as successful as it was brilliant except in one particular. Marshal Ney did not come up. Too late the Russians perceived how they had been imposed upon, what a sorry part they had played. In solid masses they reoccupied their former positions and interposed between Ney and the Emperor. Napoleon had done his best for his favourite Marshal. He had done more than any human man perhaps who lived before, then, or thereafter, could have done. There was no help for it. He must at last go on and leave Ney to his fate.

How he felt about it can be seen from a remark that he made.

"I have three hundred millions in gold in my war treasury in France. I would give it all," he said, "for a sight of Marshal Ney."

To sacrifice the rear guard for the sake of the army had become necessary. With sad countenance and sadder heart. Napoleon gave the order to march. The rear guard was abandoned.

CHAPTER 19

Ney and the Rear Guard

And what of that rear guard? Out from the ashes of Smolensk amid dull detonations of exploded mines destroying what was left of the town, marched the third corps, that of Marshal Ney; six thousand men able to bear arms, as many invalids and stragglers, twelve guns and two hundred cavalrymen riding on wrecks of horses. That was all that was left of the corps that had numbered forty thousand men, six thousand horses and one hundred guns when they crossed the Niemen. The proportion of officers among the survivors was very great, not because the officers neglected the men to care for themselves, for they did not, but because the officers were, as a rule, in a better condition physically and better understood how to care for themselves than the men. Worth, without any disparagement to the others, almost the whole army corps, was the Marshal himself.

With unfailing cheerfulness, with undaunted courage, with indomitable resolution, with unfaltering heart, this great soldier led his men, inspiring them with his own magnanimity of soul. He did not know what had happened on the road near Krasnoi. He did not know that the Russians had at last closed about Napoleon. He did not know of the heroic attempt the Emperor had made to fight them off and hold them back until the last straggling soldier had rejoined the Grand Army. He did not know of the partial success and the partial failure. He did not know that Miloradovitch, a soldier not unworthy to measure swords even with the great Marshal Ney was drawn up across the road down which he was advancing and that his little force was marching blindly into the whole Russian army in position.

The day was cold but there had been a slight rise in temperature and a heavy mist-like fog turning into snow covered the land. The Marshal, riding in the advance, suddenly discovered a dark line stretching across the road in front of him and disappearing into obscurity on either side.

"Maurice," said the Marshal, checking his horse and peering intently ahead through the mist and snow with his fierce grey eyes, "what do you make of that?"

The Hussar in turn shaded his eyes with his hand and stared long and intently ahead.

"I see movements, sir," he answered at last; "they are men!"

"And you, de Feyzenzac," said the Marshal, turning to another young *aide*.

"Men, undoubtedly," answered the other.

General Ricard's division had been recently incorporated with Ney's command and the general, as the officers halted, slowly rode forward.

"What is it?" he asked as he came within speaking distance.

"Look yonder," answered the Marshal.

"Umph," said the general who was a veteran soldier; "a line of men evidently. I don't at all like the looks of it."

"Nor I," answered the Marshal; "they may be Marshal Davout's men, however."

"Not they," answered Maurice who was unusually keen eyed, and who had been staring hard at the Russians, "we have not a corps, division or brigade in the army uniformed like that." He pointed with his hand. "They are all alike, they have great coats on, they are warm."

"I can see a Russian flag," said the Marshal, "you are right."

"They are dismounted," said General Ricard.

"Therefore, they cannot be *Cossacks*," added the Marshal, "they have not seen us yet, evidently. The wind and the snow are blowing in their faces which is fortunate."

"What do you intend to do, sir, if I may ask?" asked the general.

"What is there to do," answered the Marshal, "except break through them? This is the only road by which we can join the army. They do not seem to be in very great force."

"Very well," said General Ricard, his eye lighting.

"Your division seems to be in the best shape of any in my command," continued Ney, "so I assign you the lead."

The French had halted in a little depression in the road behind a ridge which would almost have hidden them even had the weather not been so thick. The Marshal and his little staff had ridden to the top of the ridge but they were a small group and the mist and the snow

167

concealed them. It did not appear that they had been noticed. The Russian lines were moving slowly back and forth. What they were doing was not to be discovered on account of the thick weather. The Marshal looked back at the white, snow-covered, ghost-like ranks of his own tatterdemalions.

"We can manoeuvre yonder," he said, "without being noticed. I will attack with your division in line, General Ricard, the rest of the corps in two columns on either flank and the guns can go into action on this ridge, a battery on either side. They will open fire and concentrate on the middle of the road. General Henin, you will look after our artillery, sir. The troops will move down the road at double quick. We will smash the centre and if we do that the line will give way probably in all directions and let us through. The guns can limber up the moment the men strike the Russian lines and follow us."

"And the stragglers, sir?" asked de Feyzenzac.

"They must follow through as best they can. Put the wagons containing the wounded and the ammunition in the middle of the square. We can't leave the guns anyway."

"And the cavalry, sir?" asked Maurice.

The Marshal smiled and looked back at the little huddle of horsemen perhaps two hundred in number, on terribly gaunt, starved steeds. Maurice, however, took quiet issue at that smile.

"Sir," he said proudly, "you will find the cavalry more than anxious to do its part."

"My dear boy," said the Marshal, laying his gloved hand on the other's shoulder, "I know that. It may be that we won't find that line so easy as it seems. The Russians may be in greater force than we imagine."

"And it is just possible," said General Ricard, "that it may be a trap. We have had *Cossacks* about us, flitting on either flank for two days. They may know how few we are and how helpless."

"Exactly," said the Marshal, to whom these possibilities had presented themselves, "I have thought of all those things, therefore, I will constitute the cavalry as our reserve."

Maurice opened his mouth to protest but the Marshal silenced him with a look and a wave of his hand.

"My orders, *monsieur*," he said briefly, "you will hold yourself in readiness for a command from me in the rear of the guns. I may have to sacrifice you at the last moment to save the rest, for whatever happens we shall not lay down our arms."

Maurice saluted and bowed.

"Now, gentlemen," continued the Marshal to his ragged little staff, "to your posts. We will advance until we are discovered, and then we will give them a volley and then smash into them, for France and the Emperor!"

"*Vive l'Empereur!*" came like a ghostly whisper from the cracked, drawn lips of the dauntless little assemblage.

The officers saluted and rode down the hill. There was soon movement in the ranks, not the old time celerity or movement, but movement that was slow and painful, and yet that was in obedience to orders and indicated drill and discipline. Slowly Ricard's division, numbering less than a thousand men, was drawn up in their ranks, its centre on the road which was here very broad, in fact, they had just come out of a stretch of woodland into a smooth, level country. There were no fences, the snow was frozen hard and a whole army could have manoeuvred there without difficulty.

On either side were ranged two thousand men in close columns in half company front. Between these columns were the ammunition wagons and a few wretched vehicles containing the more severely wounded. On the rear of the attacking column the dejected, disorderly mass of fugitives pressed close. The twelve six–pound guns were divided into two batteries of six guns each. Slowly and painfully the broken horses tugged the guns and caissons past the flanks of the column and up the slope. The *caissons* were dropped beneath the crest and the guns were hauled to the crest and unlimbered. Back of all the cavalry was drawn up. A gallop for half a mile at top speed would have probably resulted in the death of every horse. They were good for a short dash, however.

Leaving an under-officer in command, Maurice rode to the top of the hill in the rear of the guns whence he could see operations. The Marshal had stayed where he had at first stopped. The officers came up one by one and reported that all was ready. One swift glance forward, one long glance backward and Ney gave the order to advance.

Slowly the tired troops took up the march. All but the veterans had perished and as soon as they broke over the hill and caught sight of the enemy, they knew exactly what was before them, what they were expected to do and how they were expected to do it.

"My children," said the Marshal, drawing to the side of the road a little as the head of the column approached him, "the winter may beat us but not the Russians. Let us show them that a French soldier is never so dangerous as when he is at bay. For France and the Emperor, forward!"

A veteran in the column croaked out a hoarse, "*Vive l'Empereur!*" and the cry was taken up by the devoted six thousand. It was not the full-voiced, lusty, hearty, splendid, magnificent cheer of other days; it was harsh, it was low, it was broken, it was disconnected. The voice of the whole six thousand would scarcely have carried one hundred yards, yet it was the same salute and perhaps rarely had it meant more than when it fell from the lips of those men in the midst of the snow. This salute to their leader who was miles ahead, and although they knew it not, had been compelled to leave them to work out their own destiny!

Such was the powerful impression that the little man in the grey coat had made upon his soldiers that, in spite of all they had suffered, in spite of the fact that fight as they would, struggle as they might, there was but one end to be expected; ay, in spite of the fact that he had gone, his spirit was still with them. They could close their eyes to the deadly monotony of the grey and white of the ice and snow and see the immobile faced, silent, stubborn, tremendous figure plodding along the frozen road in the midst of his men. "*Vive l'Empereur*" the old war cry that had carried such consternation to the enemies of Napoleon. Those Russian soldiers yonder in the road did not hear that ghostly acclaim, the wind blew in the wrong direction.

The column advanced slowly. It was not capable of much more but it was not necessary to put forth their last ounce of strength in the charge yet. The movements of everybody were deliberate because of weakness. The column cleared the brow of the hill with the stragglers hard upon its heels. A detachment had been thrown back to keep those stragglers from bursting into the square. There was left a little open space into which the guns could go when they had done their work.

The Marshal turned to the veteran artillerist, who was in command, and nodded his head. Instantly the twelve guns of the battery were discharged. The concussion was deafening yet the noise did not ring clear and sharp but dull, heavy, muffled. Only expert gunners were left and every single bullet tore through the Russian lines. The French were near enough now. The Marshal struck spurs into his jaded horse and followed by his escort galloped at a charge, shouting and waving his sword. They could hear his great voice above the dying echoes of the guns. The front rank of the French column suddenly blazed out with musket fire and the next moment, slowly still and with nothing to compare to the speed with which they once would have hurled themselves upon the enemy, the French ran forward shouting. The excitement of the battle put a little strength into their exhausted bodies. The fighting warmed them a little. They forgot their hunger.

The Russians had been taken by surprise. They were quite aware that the French were approaching, indeed they had made every preparation to meet them. Columns on either flank were all ready to surround them. They had been fully advised of the movements of the French ever since Marshal Ney had left Smolensk. They had expected to round them up and capture them almost without firing a shot. They did not understand the temper of these Frenchmen. It so happened that Marshal Ney had done the one thing that would save his command—he had attacked boldly.

As the sharp volley died away, the French hurled themselves on the Russian line but by this time the forty Russian guns had also awakened to action. Out of the mist and the fog leaped lances of flame and above the cheers of the combatants came the roar of the Russian cannon, the rattle of the Russian volleys. But the French were not to be denied. They struck that line like a thunderbolt, and crumpled it to pieces. Marshal Ney, with the instincts of a born fighter, wheeled the columns that were supporting his line to the right and left and they tore a great hole in the Russian line. It began to give back.

Amid this confusion, the French guns which had been placed upon the right and left of the road poured shot after shot into the quivering Russian ranks. It was the last service those guns were to do and right well they did it. The Russian line was in retreat everywhere. Ney, for a moment, riding on the right flank, thought he had broken through and could get away, but Miloradovitch who commanded was not yet done for by any means. The open space in front filled with Frenchmen pressing resolutely on, was suddenly black with horsemen. It was with the utmost difficulty that the French formed square and met the swift charge of the cuirassiers of the Imperial Guard. The charge was beaten off but the retreating Russian line was rallied, halted and reformed. The Russian guns which had been dragged to the rear were unlimbered and fire was opened again.

By this time, the Marshal discovered that he was assaulting with his six thousand a whole Russian army, at least there were thirty thousand men in front of him and no one could tell how many others. Unless he was to be cut to pieces, he must retreat and retreat at once. The ridge

171

over which he had come was a better place for defence than the open. He gave the order and after two or three smashing volleys, the French began their retrograde march, firing and firing as they drew back. Ney was a master at that sort of fighting—of every sort, in fact—but he had practised that manoeuvre for long days in this very campaign.

The Russians did not recover immediately. Pursuit was attempted by the horse and they might have broken the French and driven them into complete rout but for the action of Maurice posted on the ridge. He could see all that was happening and he knew just the right moment to go in. They gave way before his onslaught and Ney finally reached the ridge. He deployed his columns and from his guns and muskets opened a steady fire on the slowly advancing Russians. Every man in the regiments expected death. To retreat was impossible, to advance was impossible. If they separated and sought escape by detachments the *Cossacks* would cut them to pieces. There was nothing for them to do but stay there on that ridge and die. Well, they were willing to die and while the Russians hesitated they made ready for it.

The Marshal and his *aides* on foot walked up and down the line, the Marshal talking to his men as a father talks to his children. They had a little respite and they improved it by rectifying the lines, stripping the bodies of the dead so far as they could of their clothing, their guns and their cartridges and taking the weapons and ammunition from those too badly wounded to use them. Some of the bravest among the stragglers who were huddled in the rear came forward and were given muskets and cartridges. The cannon were planted in front of the line and then everything was done. The Russians, however, most unaccountably delayed their advance.

"I wish I knew," said the Marshal to those around him, "what they are up to."

"I suppose," returned General Ricard, "that they are gradually enveloping our flanks and when they get us completely surrounded they will summon us to surrender."

"My light horsemen," said Maurice, "might be divided and sent to scout either flank."

The Marshal shook his head.

"If they are doing that, we can't prevent them. We will be just throwing you away. We will do better if we all stay together and fight to the bitter end."

"There is a man yonder approaching with a flag, sir," exclaimed young de Feyzenzac suddenly, pointing down the road.

Sure enough a Russian officer on a splendid black horse, attended by a *Cossack* on his pony and carrying a flag of truce, came galloping down the road toward the French line.

"See what he wants, de Feyzenzac. Keep fast your pieces, men," shouted Ney, observing one or two soldiers making preparations to fire, "it is a flag of truce."

De Feyzenzac sprang through the lines and walked down the road, the horseman stopped, saluted, and the two men engaged in brief conversation. The watchers in the French lines saw de Feyzenzac suddenly straighten himself up, then he shook his head vigorously, turned and ran back toward the lines.

"What is it, de Feyzenzac?" asked the Marshal who had approached the front himself.

"We are asked to surrender, sir."

"Does the Russian commander know that I am here?"

"Yes, sir."

"Tell him that a Marshal of France does not surrender," said Ney proudly.

"I have already told him that as from myself, sir," said de Feyzenzac, smiling.

"Repeat it from me also," returned the great Frenchman. He spoke loudly so that all near him could hear and they greeted his splendid remark with shouts and cries of joy and approval. "I might have added," continued the Marshal, as de Feyzenzac trotted down the road to deliver his reply, "that no soldier in my command would surrender either."

"And you would have been right," said General Ricard.

"We are bound to die anyway," said another philosophically, "and we might as well die fighting the Russians as freezing or starving. It's warmer at least."

De Feyzenzac delivered his message and in spite of expostulations turned on his heel, after bidding the flag go back to his own lines, and returned to his commander.

"Well," said the Marshal as de Feyzenzac came back.

"He began to talk to me about the number of his troops but I cut him short and told him we didn't care how many troops he had or who was there. Your message was final."

"And then?"

"He galloped off saying that he would report to his superiors and perhaps bring another message."

"What's the use of all this talk?" growled old General Ricard.

"I see much use in it," said the Marshal, "it is very late, darkness will soon be upon us. If we can hold them off until then we may escape."

"Escape in this ghastly wilderness, in this ice and snow—"

"Patience, my friend," said the great chief, "while we have strength to fight we have strength to march. All is not lost, and—"

"Here he comes again," said de Feyzenzac, who had been following the movements of the stranger.

"Do you meet him as before, and—"

But the Russian envoy was approaching at a rapid gallop, his *Cossack* outrider finding it hard to keep pace with him. Before de Feyzenzac could meet him again, he drew rein almost touching the front of the French line. It was the Marshal himself who greeted him.

"You approach boldly, *monsieur*," he began.

"Marshal Ney will, I am sure, pardon me," returned the newcomer in excellent French, "if I overstep the rules a little. We are anxious to preserve the life of so great and brave a commander."

"More anxious than I am," grimly interposed Ney half to himself.

"I come with special messages from Marshal Prince Kutusoff and from Lieutenant General Miloradovitch."

"What is your message, sir?" asked the Marshal.

"With your permission," returned the Frenchman, "I will dismount and we can talk on more equal terms." He flung his leg over the saddle, leaped to the ground and made a graceful salute to the Marshal, which the latter acknowledged briefly. "The whole Russian army is in front of you, sir," continued the envoy. "Miloradovitch's corps, the one you attacked, is supported by every other corps under the command of Prince Kutusoff. They are anxious to spare the life of so great and brave a Marshal and the brave men that he leads. It is entirely consistent with your honour to lay down your arms before such overwhelming odds."

"Allow me to judge for myself as to what is consistent with my honour, sir," said the Marshal briefly.

"Exactly, *monsieur*," answered the Russian, "therefore, I am empowered to offer you a safe conduct within our lines. You can see for yourself. The Russians are in position and your situation is absolutely helpless. They beg you to surrender, sir."

The Marshal glanced around at the long lean lines on either side of him. A low, hoarse murmur rising to a growl burst from the cracked lips and dry throats of the men. The noise was neither articulate nor definite. It was wordless but none the less understandable on account of that. These men had no wish to preserve their lives, they were with the Marshal entirely in that.

"Return," said the Marshal, smiling, "you have had your answer from the lips of my braves and I only repeat what I said before, a Marshal of France does not surrender to any odds or on any terms, and—"

The silence was broken by a cannon shot on the far right followed by a sharp volley. The Russian officer turned to his horse.

"Stop, *monsieur*," cried the Marshal.

The envoy stared in surprise.

"What mean you?"

"You are a prisoner," said the Marshal.

"I am under a flag of truce."

"Yes, but your army has taken advantage of that flag of truce to fire upon mine. You cannot go back."

The envoy stopped as if thunderstruck. The truth of the Marshal's statement could not be denied.

"Yield your sword, sir," said Ney. "De Feyzenzac, do you take it."

"A prisoner!" shouted the nearest grenadier.

The cry was taken up and two or three men left the ranks.

"We are naked, your Excellency," they cried, "we are freezing, let us have the Russian's coat."

For a moment they crowded around the little group. They wanted to treat this Russian as they had treated their other prisoners, strip him of his clothes, his horse—

"Back in the ranks," thundered Ney furiously.

But these men were not to be mastered by word. Quick as lightning, Maurice flung himself in front of the envoy, sword in one hand, pistol in the other.

"The first man who lays hands on him," he cried, "meets my sword."

"What is he to you?" asked the Marshal, turning upon his officer quickly.

"He is my brother," answered the lieutenant colonel.

CHAPTER 20

The Marshal's Ruse

The soldiers stood petrified. The Marshal turned on them severely and again ordered them back into the ranks. Then he turned to the other two.

"Did I understand you to say, Maurice, that this Russian envoy was your brother?"

"Yes, *Monsieur le Maréchal*"

"A Frenchman?"

The hussar bowed.

"In arms against France?"

"I cannot deny it," answered Maurice.

"Then this is he whose life you spared when you cut up the Red *Cossacks*?"

"The same."

"It grieves me, *monsieur*," said the Marshal, turning to the impassive figure of the envoy, "to see a Frenchman in arms against Frenchmen."

"I fight for my King," returned the other quickly, "you for yours."

"Be it so," said Ney. "We will not quarrel personally though by the laws of war, you are a prisoner, but for your brother's sake—"

"I want no indulgence," interposed the other quickly.

"I will ask your parole," said the Marshal, "and—"

"I decline to give it."

"Be advised, young man," said Ney impressively, "with the best will in the world, remember that I command a pack of ravenous wolves and without that parole it will ultimately be impossible for me to protect you, for they will take your horse, strip you of your warm furs and your clothes and leave you to die. Not even I could prevent it very long."

"Philippe, I beg of you," said Maurice softly, "to give your word."

"Very well," said the Marquis de Vivonne, to the Marshal, "I give my word, sir, to make no attempt to escape until I am exchanged."

"Good," said the Marshal, "I parole you in the custody of your brother."

"And this poor *Cossack* officer," said the Marquis de Vivonne.

"I can scarcely protect him," answered the Marshal. "Let him go. Perhaps he can explain why you are detained, and—"

The Marquis turned and spoke to the *Cossack* colonel, who listened attentively, his eyes brightening. He answered a few words, put spurs to his horse and galloped away. To release him showed the magnanimity of the Marshal, for the *Cossacks* were the deadliest foes, save the winter, with which the French had to contend, more deadly than the wolves themselves on the flanks and the rear of the retreating army.

Ney, rendered desperate, resolved upon another attack, hoping to catch the enemy unprepared. General Razout with the second division in a column of regiments fell upon the Russians, but although the attack was in the nature of a surprise, it was finally repulsed with frightful slaughter. Razout was wounded. In turn, the Russians assaulted the ridge and only by the most desperate and costly fighting were they at last driven back as night fell by the defenders. Ney and his officers as usual fought in the ranks as common soldiers. Indeed the great size and wonderful strength of the Marshal made him especially formidable in the hand-to-hand bayonet fighting that followed the last Russian effort to rush the position.

Six guns were taken, twenty-five hundred of the six thousand were killed or wounded, when to be wounded was equivalent to death. Some of the regiments lost over fifty *per cent* of their fighting force. But as night fell the six thousand made good their final defence against the eighty thousand—a glorious feat of arms indeed! Night found the French bleeding but triumphant. The Russians had had enough of it for the time being.

A night attack would be attended with much more danger and difficulty than an assault by day, especially in such weather and under such odds. Marshal Ney believed that the darkness gave him a chance to outwit his foes. He had said that a Marshal of France did not surrender and he intended to show that he was not to be taken either. Therefore, he ordered the soldiers to gather wood and kindle fires along the crest of the little ridge as if they were making camp for the night.

So soon as the wood began to blaze here and there, the Marshal enjoining the utmost silence upon every one, formed up his shattered command and started them back eastward over the road to Smolensk whence they had just come. Nobody understood what he would be at, they knew that Smolensk was a ruined town which, even if they reached it, would provide no shelter and there would be no food. It seemed to the soldiers that every step they made took them farther from their companions, yet such was their trust in the Marshal that they followed him implicitly, all who could march, that is. The little band was sorely diminished. Of necessity, the most desperately wounded were left to shift for themselves around the fires on the ridge they had defended. As before, every moment witnessed the collapse of some poor straggler in the rear. Maurice's cavalry scouted ahead, although there was not much danger of running into any enemy in that direction.

The invalids who were left behind kept the fires going as best they could because it was their only means of self-preservation and Miloradovitch was completely deceived. When he advanced his troops in the grey dawn of the next morning, he found nothing but dead, dying and helpless men. Most of the wounded had been frozen around the wretched fires.

Marshal Ney had decamped and although he had left a trail of dead bodies which could easily have been followed, the Russians attempted no pursuit. Satisfied that the Marshal would lose himself in the ghastly solitudes they faced about and resumed their march after the main army under Napoleon. But Marshal Ney had no intention of losing his command in the solitudes, either. He divined that by this time Napoleon had crossed the Dnieper and that if he were to join him it would be necessary for him to cross also. He knew further that he would have to pass around one flank or the other of the Russian army.

He rode in silence for a long time plunged in profound thought. At last he turned to Maurice.

"It is not well with us," he said.

"What are you going to do, sir?" returned this favourite officer.

"Get to the other side of the Dnieper."

"Where is the way to it, sir?"

"We shall find out."

"But how, may I ask?"

"You will see."

"But if it be not frozen. If this slight rise in the temperature has already softened the ice," continued the hussar.

"You will find that it will be frozen," returned the Marshal confidently, leading on the weary detachment.

The general advance of the Russians had been from the southward. Ney reasoned that it was more practical to pass about the northern flank, therefore. Accordingly, he left the road about midnight and struck boldly off across the frozen *steppes* through the driving snow followed by his mystified but devoted men. He had no maps, not even a compass, he had no guides, and he knew no landmarks by which to tell the direction. As soon as he left the main road he knew that he would be lost. He did not intend to wander around the *steppes* aimlessly, however.

With Maurice and de Feyzenzac, he rode at the head of the plodding column, growing smaller every moment.

The Marshal kept his keen blue eyes bent straight ahead, striving to pierce through the awful gloom of the snowy night. Presently he checked his horse on the edge of a steep ravine and as he halted and waited the little column came straggling up behind him. No one had the least idea what he was about to do, how he was to do it or what would be the result of this march. It was better to move than to stand still, however, for movement kept the intense cold from penetrating the vitals. To stop was always to die.

The troops came tramping up, broke from column into line and extended along the banks of the ravine. It was so cold that they could scarcely hold their muskets. A naked finger touching the barrel of a gun would freeze to it instantly. In their rags, wretchedly covered as they were, with the wind driving the snow over them, they resembled a long line of scarecrows abandoned to the winter's fierce assault.

Assembled around Ney were the troop of cavalry and such officers as still retained horses. Last of all came the six guns, their horses almost at the end of their strength. The wagons had been abandoned. Ammunition had been served out to the men, all they could carry. There was nothing else to serve, nothing to eat, nothing to drink except melted snow and nothing to melt that with except the human heat in their bodies and there was not much of that.

The Marshal waited until all had come up except the never ending lines of stragglers, stretching interminably across the plains! Then slowly dismounting from his horse and summoning Maurice and de Feyzenzac to follow him, he climbed down the steep bank of the ravine until he reached the bottom. It was covered with snow, of course.

He walked across it toward a place where it made a sharp turn and where the wind had in a measure swept away the snow. Speech was almost impossible in such weather. Neither of the officers who had followed him had said a word. Indeed, walking was extremely difficult and painful and all three of them had trouble in keeping their feet.

Marshal Ney knelt down and with his gloved hand swept away the snow and the other two, in obedience to a gesture, assisted him. Soon he cleared a space. A sheet of ice was visible. The men on the bank watched them breathlessly. With his sword Marshal Ney chipped away at the ice, the others helping him, until quite a piece was broken through and pried out. The Marshal bent down over the opening and he and the two *aides* saw the black water flowing westward! This was their guide.

"All the water in this vicinity flows into the Dnieper," said the Marshal. "Gentlemen," he continued triumphantly as he rose to his feet, "our way lies yonder."

He pointed down the ravine and toward the west.

"That was well thought of," cried Maurice.

"It is an old huntsman's trick I learned in Sarrelouis as a boy," said the Marshal, smiling. "Come, gentlemen, let us return to our soldiers."

In a short time the three were back on the crest of the ravine and the march was once more taken up. They followed the ravine, which, although it twisted and turned, held in the main steadily westward and at daybreak, another dull, grey, snowy, freezing day, they stood on the bank of a much larger stream. It could only be the Dnieper.

The river was frozen. The banks were very steep and how to get the horses down the banks and the men across was a problem. Of course, by scouting along the banks in either direction undoubtedly a practicable crossing would be found but it was almost impossible to think of doing that. The army was so exhausted, it had marched all day, had fought a terrific battle and had thereafter marched all night with nothing to eat and no opportunity to rest. The men were almost crazy. They felt that they must get to the other side and that they must cross it wherever they struck the river. Although their devotion to the Marshal was boundless, it was doubtful if even he could get them to scout on either hand. It would have been more than humanity could endure. Some of the men flung themselves down on the snow, utterly broken as it was and had to be forced to their feet by threats and blows and bayonet thrusts even.

Back of the Marshal and his men stretched the straggling remains of the camp followers as before. Yes, the crossing had to be made there. Whether the ice would prove strong enough to bear the guns was another problem. As they walked back and forth in the growing dawn, waiting the word of command from the Marshal, they heard faint shots in the rear and these shots decided the question. They could come only from a detachment of Russians, probably *Cossacks*. They had to cross there and they had to do it quickly. Indeed, if the *Cossacks* were in force and came upon them in the act of crossing, they would be annihilated.

"Maurice, *Mon Enfant*" said the Marshal slowly, "I am loath to give you the order."

"I understand," said Maurice resolutely, "you want me to take the horse and go back and hold off the Russians attacking us."

"Yes, unless we agree to perish here together on the banks of this river."

"That is not to be thought of," said the lieutenant colonel stoutly, "you have shown us tonight, as never before how valuable you are to France and the Emperor; we will hold them back with our lives."

"*Au revoir*" said the Marshal, extending his hand.

"I am afraid it will be *adieu*, sir," returned the young soldier. "You will see that my brother is well treated?"

"Certainly. And if we cross the guns, I will try to protect your own crossing. If you should escape, there is a bit of woodland over yonder. Do you see it? You will find us in bivouac there. These worn-out men must have rest."

"I understand."

"And if you escape the Emperor shall know. In any case, he shall know."

"Thank you."

"And now you had better go, the firing grows heavier."

There had been but little intercourse between Maurice and his brother. The latter had ridden with the staff, bearing himself somewhat haughtily. Yet he had heard all that had passed between the Marshal and his younger brother and he now drew near.

"You are going back?" he asked quickly.

"It is my duty to drive off these pursuers, if possible."

"But it is madness, you will be—"

"What of that?"

The elder stared out through the snow.

181

"You have twice spared my life," he said; "we had counted you as one dead, but—"

"Would you requite me for what you are pleased to say I have done?"

"Gladly."

"There is a woman in Russia that I love," said the lieutenant colonel. "I don't think I shall come back from this. Will you tell her how I died and say to her that I am glad that she is free?"

"If I live, I will," said the elder brother, extending his hand which the other clasped; "and now her name."

"Idona Muravieff," answered Maurice.

"Muravieff!" cried the elder brother, releasing the younger's hand.

"Colonel Maurice," said the Marshal, "you must hasten or you will be too late."

The lieutenant colonel saluted, mounted his horse, summoned his men and plodded slowly across the *steppes* leaving his elder brother petrified with astonishment in which a great fear was mingled. The Marshal instantly gave the order to descend the bank and attempt the passage.

De Feyzenzac gallantly led the way. Alas, the ice was not yet frozen solid because of the swift current and the sudden rise in temperature. It broke when he was half way over and it was with difficulty that he reached the other side. It was evident that the guns could not pass. They had to be abandoned with every other vehicle. Driving the points of bayonets in the vents of the cannon to spike them, the army attempted the passage. By the direction of the Marshal, the men marched in long files far apart and with several yards between each file.

By this means the ice was not subjected to such a strain as to break it. These got over safely. There were but few horsemen left. Most of them abandoned their horses, a few others whose horses were in fair condition rode them over and among these were the Marquis de Vivonne and the Marshal himself. The last detachment of soldiers, the guns having been drawn as close to the edge as possible, hurled them over the bank and they went crashing down to the river some of them breaking through the ice. At least the Russians would get nothing from them.

Away back on the eastern horizon, the crackling of small arms which had kept up fiercely during the process of crossing died away. Under cover of the protection afforded by a bit of woodland, the attack of the small *Cossack* detachment was at last beaten off by the hundred French horsemen who were still fit for action. The conflict had been a fierce one and the troops that Maurice finally led back to the river numbered scarcely a score and of those some were wounded. A comparatively slight wound sufficed to put a man out of commission in the terrible state of weakness to which they had all been reduced.

As the remaining horsemen came slowly up to the river bank, a scene of horror met their eyes. The stragglers, among whom there were still women and children, refusing to cross as the soldiers had, crowded in great masses on the ice. It broke and precipitated most of them into the torrent. What happened to a few thousands in the crossing of the Dnieper was exactly what happened to many thousands a short time after in the crossing of the Beresina, but the little disaster was sufficiently horrible to those who looked on. The Marshal himself and the hardiest of his officers waded down into the icy river and strove to save here a woman, there an old man, now a wounded soldier, or perhaps a child, frantically uptossed in the arms of some sinking, dying mother.

The passage of the river at that point when Maurice reached it was impossible. He turned his horse and followed by his little band plodded up the bank and a few miles above they managed to get over.

Chapter 21

The Messenger of Despair

It was midday when Maurice now attended by but six horsemen staggered into the camp which true to his promise the Marshal had made in the forest. Huge fires were blazing—this particular woodland, fortunately, abounded in dead trees and much easily cut underbrush—and the exhausted men lay about them, panting like dogs from their efforts. Some of the horses, which had been attached to the guns had been brought over. They were instantly killed and the tough, stringy meat was cooking over the fires. The six thousand men had been reduced to two thousand. Those who had been in the water, de Feyzenzac, the Marshal and the other officers were suffering acutely from the cold in their wet, frozen garments. De Feyzenzac was already in the grip of a high fever.

The weather had changed again, the wind had shifted suddenly to the north and it was growing colder every moment. The fires were not sufficient to raise the temperature appreciably. Men near them burned on one side while they froze on the other. It was almost hopeless to allow them to lie down and sleep after they had eaten their scanty ration of horseflesh, yet it was imperatively necessary. They could not go one more mile without rest. The strongest among them were engaged in keeping the fires blazing. The Marshal himself gathered wood like a common soldier and the other officers followed his example. Even the Marquis de Vivonne, finding his lot cast in with the French, worked like the rest.

He had been rejoiced to receive his brother. Indeed, it had been into his arms that the young hussar had fallen when he slipped from his horse. The Marquis was burning to ask his brother questions, but when he saw his frightful state, he forebore. He found a place for him between two fires. He took off his own magnificent fur coat and wrapped the young man in it. He had preserved a flask of brandy and he gave a small portion of it to the Hussar and then he generously proffered it to the Marshal. Ney hesitated.

"You can take it, sir," said the Marquis, understanding the other's reluctance, "we are fighting a common enemy, the cold, and unless you live to lead us, we shall all die."

Fortunately they were not molested during the long day. The *Cossacks* had not appeared, although the fire and smoke, if kept up long enough would serve to attract them. At nightfall, the Marshal determined to move again. The woodland seemed to extend for miles to the westward and he decided to keep within it because he would be less subject to attack by the wild horsemen of the *steppes*, especially if they came in force, and better able to defend himself there even against sledge or horse artillery. He knew, however, that unless some help came to him his whole force would be lost; unless they found food and drink they could not go on more than another thirty-six hours even if unmolested. If he could get word of his plight to Napoleon he felt sure that the Emperor would send him succour.

At nightfall and before his men were summoned to march, he assembled his little staff about him.

"Someone," he said, "with the best horse, must ride across the country toward Orsha. It is probable, since the Russians are between us and that point, that the Emperor will be found there or Prince Eugene or Marshal Davout. If any of them are there, they must send help to us. We must have wagons, bread, brandy. Without these we are all dead men. It is a forlorn hope, a desperate chance. Who will go?"

There were only three or four of the staff who were able to ride and they all volunteered, even de Feyzenzac, who was almost delirious with fever. The Marshal looked them over.

"You, Maurice," he said at last, "to you the duty. My horse is the best one left. He has carried me faithfully. Take him."

"With your permission, sir," said the Marquis de Vivonne, "my horse is by far the best."

"We have no right to your horse, *monsieur*."

"I give him freely."

"Ah," said the Marshal, "you have the heart of a gentleman. In the name of these poor fellows, I accept your offer. I have no instructions to give you, Maurice. You know our condition, you know our needs. You have a good horse, and indeed, sir, it is a noble animal," said the Marshal, running his hand over the horse and even patting it lovingly

185

with his gloved hand. "You must get through. If you cannot, we are dead men. Perhaps dead men anyway. And if they come too late, tell the Emperor how we died."

"*Vive l'Empereur*" cried old General Ricard, and again the old cry went forth from a battalion of spectres.

"You must take my coat," said the Marquis to his brother, "there is some brandy in the flask still and here is a piece of roasted horse meat which I saved for you."

"I thank you," said the lieutenant colonel, "but what will you do?"

"I will fare just like these brave men here," said the other. "Although I fight on the side of Russia for my rightful King, I am proud of these Frenchmen."

"Would God that you were with us for France," said the younger, as the two walked away from the rest for a little space.

"I do fight for France but in my own way and for a different France. No more of that," he added as the Hussar strove to interrupt him. "You are riding for me, for us all. This morning you thought you were going to your death and you gave me a message to a woman. Now you are going out again and I am left behind, perhaps to die. It may be that you will get through and if you do will you take a message to a woman from me as well?"

"Gladly, is it a woman of France?"

"Of Russia."

"And the message?"

"The love of my heart. Tell her that I died with her name on my lips, her image with me to the last."

"And who is this woman?"

"You know her."

"The Princess Muravieff!"

"Good God, then you are—"

"Her betrothed, and you—"

"Her husband!"

Again it was the Marshal who interrupted.

"If you are to go at all, you must go at once, Maurice," he said, approaching the two brothers.

The hussar saluted, stared long in the face of his brother, climbed slowly to the back of his horse, bent his head westward and went out of the forest.

Twenty-four hours later he saw the camp fires of the army around the village of Orsha. The horrible journey remained in his mind like a hideous nightmare. Once he was surrounded by a band of *Cossacks*. There was something familiar about the face of the leader. It was the man whom Marshal Ney had spared and allowed to go free at Krasnoi. There was gratitude in that *Cossack* colonel's heart and when he learned that the rider came from Marshal Ney he spared his life, drew off his men and actually let him pass !

It had stopped snowing but the temperature had grown much colder. He had long since eaten his scanty piece of horse meat and finished his brandy, sup by sup. His mind was in a singular turmoil. The woman he had married had been betrothed to his brother. That brother had the prior claim, he must give up his wife. If he did not reach the army soon the problem would be solved, his wife would be a widow. The cold grew more and more terrible, the midday sun shone with pitiless brilliance. He was almost blind and nearly frozen, still he plodded on, taking his direction from the sun.

The horse had done nobly. He was almost at the end of his strength, however. Experienced horseman as he was, the hussar had saved the animal as much as possible, but he had driven him ever relentlessly on. The poor brute had been without anything to eat for two days and he was weak from hunger. He was not of the *steppe* pony breed, he was a thoroughbred. Lacking the tremendous endurance of those little *Cossack* ponies, he had a spirit which those little mongrels did not possess. He would go on until he died and in fact did go on until he fell and lay, to freeze and die.

The hussar was so numb with the cold that he scarcely managed to get his feet out of the stirrups and escape falling under the horse. If it had not been for the fur coat that his brother had given him, he would have perished of the cold. His limbs were so weak he could scarcely force them to drag him forward. He thought perhaps it would be better for him to die. He had wild moments in which his stiffened fingers fumbled at the fastenings of the fur coat with a dim idea in his brain that it would be an easy solution of his problem to tear it off and let the cold finish him. Yet his problem was not personal. Back there under the trees, toiling through the snow were his comrades. There was the great Marshal Ney, there was de Feyzenzac, there was General Ricard, there were those soldiers who had shown themselves worthy of such leadership !

No, he must go forward. He tightened his belt and plodded on. The short day drew to a close quickly.

He thought he had lost his way. Clouds came with the evening, he could not see the stars. Some snowflakes drifted down upon him. He wondered how much longer he could stand it. His feet were as heavy as lead, he could scarcely drag them through the snow. Pains as if from a thousand red-hot needles darted through him. The dark night was filled with brilliant coruscating lights which had no existence save in his fevered brain.

By and by he fell. Oh, the comfort of lying prone upon the snow! Drowsiness stole over him. Just in time he recollected that he must not sleep. To sleep would be to die and while it would perhaps be better for him to die, better for his wife, yet he must go on for his comrades. Clenching his teeth, by a titanic effort of will he rose to his feet again and once more plodded on. Sometimes, he was in the forest, sometimes in the open. Suddenly before him rose a low hill. To his distorted vision, it looked like an unscalable mountain. He knew he must surmount it. He realised that he might perhaps get to the top of it, but after that he could do no more. He struggled up the slope, clinging pitifully to the icy trees.

Finally he reached the top. Before him twinkled hundreds of lights on the level plain below. He could hear noises, human voices and the neighing of horses. Some army was there, but what army? It might be Russian, it might be French. What difference, they were men, men with hearts in their bodies. They would give him something to eat, they would let him warm himself at some fire, they would give him something to drink.

If he could get these things, nothing else would matter. They might kill him thereafter.

Once more he staggered forward. A sentry shouted at him, a guard came running. Men seized him, he heard voices addressing him. He managed to gasp out who he was and what he was.

"A messenger," he whispered, "from Marshal Ney. I must see the Emperor."

A flask was held to his lips. Nectar! He drank and the warmth returned to his body. Someone gave him a piece of hard, frozen substance. He tasted it, it was bread. Manna from heaven was never sweeter. He lifted his head and spoke again, hoarsely:

"The Emperor?"

"He is over yonder," said an under officer of the guard, "you say you are from Marshal Ney?"

"Yes, he is back in the woods twenty-four hours behind me. I must see the Emperor."

In spite of the sustaining liquor and the bread at which he gnawed ravenously as he went along, half led, half supported by his comrades, he scarcely realised anything until finally in the midst of a little room he saw the figure of Napoleon. The Emperor's cheeks were pale, but no paler than they had been. His face was grave and there were heavy lines upon it. He was frowning, but otherwise he looked much the same.

Although a huge fire was burning in the fireplace of the principal house in the village which Napoleon had chosen for his own, the room was still cold. The officers with whom the Emperor was surrounded and the Emperor himself wore their great coats. The Emperor was standing directly in front of the fire, with his hands behind his back warming himself when, having passed the guard, Maurice was admitted. Above the rich furs of the great Russian coat, his ghastly haggard face rose, white as death, covered with a ragged growth of blond beard, streaked with dirt. His once gallant busby was a ragged ruin. Shifting his precious piece of bread to his left hand he saluted the Emperor with his right.

"Well sir, well sir," said the Emperor quickly.

"I come from Marshal Ney," answered Maurice, endeavouring to hold himself erect as a soldier should.

"Give him a chair," said the Emperor, "he is almost done for."

Someone dragged forward a chair and the hussar sank into it.

"Wine," said Napoleon, and again from the private store of the Emperor, almost the last of it, they gave him a refreshing draught.

"Now," said the Emperor, "what of Marshal Ney?"

"I left him with his division twenty-four hours away in the woods to the northeast."

"Did he break through Miloradovitch?"

"We tried to, we were driven back, fought off a counter attack, retraced our steps, turned to the northward, crossed the Dnieper—"

"Good," said the Emperor, his eye lighting, "and your message?"

"The Marshal bade me tell you, Sire, that someone must come to meet him with bread and brandy. His men are exhausted, they will starve unless they are succoured."

"How many of them are left?"

"Less than two thousand when I rode on ahead to deliver this message."

"And when did you leave them?"

"Last night, Sire."

"Was the Marshal encamped?"

"He was just about to break camp to move this way."

"Gentlemen," said Napoleon, contemplating the little staff of officers, "shall we allow Marshal Ney and his brave men to die?"

"I will go to his rescue," said a tall, handsome officer of high rank.

"And I," answered another.

"Good," said the Emperor. "Eugene," he continued, addressing the first man, "take your troops and, Davout," he added, turning to the second speaker, "support him with yours. I will hold Orsha with the Guard and the rest even if the whole Russian army comes upon us. Bring back the brave men of the third corps, and Marshal Ney, the bravest of the brave."

"We will do it or die, Sire," answered Eugene.

"Take the horses from the guns and take wagons that you may bring back those who cannot march, divide with them whatever we have. I shall be glad for the return of Marshal Ney, as glad as for the return of a whole army corps. In war," said Napoleon half to himself, "men are nothing, a man is everything."

As the officers mentioned turned to go out with their staffs and muster the troops who were to rescue Ney, Napoleon stepped over to the side of the lieutenant colonel. Maurice was in a state of complete collapse. He sat with his head buried in his hands, oblivious to everything. He had gnawed the last crumb of the little piece of bread. No man noticed him in the excitement of the departure. Napoleon laid his hand upon the young man's shoulder. The latter lifted his head.

"Yes," said the Emperor, "I thought so. It is Maurice; I sent you to Ney in disgrace because you spared your brother in disobedience to my command. Was it not so?"

"Yes, Sire."

"It seems to me that you have redeemed yourself. I have no longer any brigades to which to appoint you. Colonels command companies; generals, regiments; marshals, princes, kings, divisions; but when we get back to France come to me and you shall have it, Maurice." His hand fumbled at one of the buttons of his coat, he detached therefrom a little white ribbon and with his own hands he fastened it upon the ragged uniform that covered the breast of the Hussar. "My own Cross of the Legion of Honour," he said, "you have deserved it."

"Sire, what do you mean!" cried the young man, rising to his feet.

"Sit still," said the Emperor, smiling, while the whole room rang

190

with a hearty acclaim, "*Vive l'Empereur,*" "will it please you to go back into my Guard?"

"In France, yes, Your Majesty, if we ever reach there, but meanwhile, I prefer to stay in the rear guard with Marshal Ney," was the answer, at which the Emperor nodded approvingly.

CHAPTER 22

The Clemency of Napoleon

Twenty-four hours later, and it was a precious twenty-four hours since every moment rendered the conjunction between Tchichagoff and Wittgenstein more certain and the position of the French more precarious—Eugene and Davout reached Orsha with the remnant of the force they had gone out to relieve. It was dusk when the troops halted in the square in front of the house occupied by the Emperor.

Napoleon was out and waiting for them. The returning troops, with indomitable French gaiety, actually sought to give some festal touches to their march past. The Prince and the Marshal had only taken with them their best soldiers, a small squadron of cavalry, one of the best brigades of the old Guard and a division of light infantry with an artillery train of twenty-four light guns; in all perhaps six thousand men. The lines were dressed and ordered as if for formal inspection and the weary, snow-covered troops assumed once more the martial bearing of happier days as they marched in what was to most of them a last review.

There was no band left with the army, indeed no brass instruments could have been played in that cold and the musicians had either gone into the stragglers or entered the ranks. But there were drummers still and the drums rolled lustily at the head of the marching column.

First came the contingent of the Prince Eugene, then the remainder of the corps of Marshal Ney. A good many of the Marshal's men were in the wagons, perhaps one-third of them, the other two-thirds were on foot, as was the Marshal himself with General Ricard and all of his staff. Eugene had offered Ney a horse, indeed he had offered to dismount his cavalry and turn over the horses to Ney's men, but the Marshal had refused. He declared that he would walk with the rest. The rear was brought up by the contingent of Davout. The best of the relieving troops looked horrible enough, but what could one say of Ney and his men! They had been righting their last desperate battle in the forest against the *Cossacks* accompanied by a battery of guns on sledges, when the rescuing party had appeared in the very nick of time to save them from annihilation.

Napoleon had a marvellous faculty for correctly estimating the number of men in a regiment or in a division or in an army, as has been noted. His swift eagle glance took in the small body following the Marshal.

"My God," he said under his breath, "there are less than a thousand of them!"

And indeed the six thousand soldiers and the five thousand stragglers had been reduced to nine hundred soldiers alone—no stragglers! of whom three hundred wounded and broken down were in the wagons. The Marshal saluted as he drew abreast of the Emperor. Napoleon raised his hand.

"Halt the column," he cried in his clear voice.

Instantly the order was repeated. The snow-covered ranks stopped. Eugene and Davout rode to the front.

Sharp commands rang out. The columns wheeled in line facing the Emperor.

"Present arms!" cried the Viceroy.

In an instant with a martial clash the guns of the troopers were brought to the fore. The swords of the officers were bared and the blades flashed aloft in the evening air and swept downward in graceful salute. There was grace even in death in these Frenchmen.

"*Vive l'Empereur!*" roared out an old sergeant suddenly and the whole line burst into acclaim.

He had heard it many times, that Emperor, in many lands, in many climes, from many men, he never grew tired of hearing it either, but never had this impassive war god heard it with such a human throb of the heart as from the lips of those frozen men in that ghastly retreat.

He was responsible for it all. His overwhelming ambition, his mad desire to rule the world, his terrible passion for omnipotence was the cause of their suffering. And sometimes as they struggled along out of sight of him, as they experienced the pangs of hunger, as the awful cold ate into their vitals, as they thought of sunny France, the homeland, of wife, or children, or sweetheart, they cursed him; but let him again appear before them, let them even in the very articles of death, catch a glimpse of that famous grey overcoat hidden except as the wind revealed it under the great fur *pelisse* he wore, and in spite of themselves, the old admiration, the old love, the old enthusiasm, which had made them his irresistible instruments, flashed into life again and if it were with their last breaths, they gave him that imperial salute. *Vive l''Empereur*. His impassivity made no difference, he was Napoleon, they had loved him, they would love him until the end. *Vive l'Empereur*.

The Emperor stepped slowly forward. He passed by the figures of Prince Eugene and Marshal Davout and their staffs, grouped back of them, vouchsafing to them a nod of recognition.

"You have done well," he said, as he slowly advanced toward the centre of the line.

Discipline held that everyone should keep his eyes to the front, but discipline was forgot. The soldiers' glances were drawn from the left and right toward that silent figure, slowly moving, standing out a few paces in front of his staff, still brilliant in spite of all it had gone through.

He stopped opposite Ney, the great Marshal of the fiery red hair and the bright blue-grey eyes, and extended his arms. The Marshal, sheathing his sword, came slowly forward. That proud head was bent and those fierce eyes were dimmed, even the firm lips trembled. The Emperor took him in his arms.

"For you and these brave men," he said as he released him, his hand sweeping out toward the remainder of the third corps, "I would have sacrificed everything, and nothing in this campaign has so filled me with satisfaction as that you and those who are left with you are back in the army again. We have but little, but what remains is at your service. Berthier has made arrangements to feed your men yonder—" he pointed to the left, "my Guard has been taken out of those houses. They are yours. You will find a little bread and wine there and fires. Every surviving officer of the corps, commissioned or non-commissioned, shall have promotion when I have anything to which to promote him. To every private soldier I give a month's pay and the stripes of a non-commissioned officer. And if there are any who especially deserve it, high or low, the cross of the Legion of Honour shall be theirs."

"Your Majesty overwhelms me," said the Marshal, "we would die for our Emperor. Every soldier has been a hero. Maurice—"

"He already wears the grand cross," said the Emperor, pointing back to where Maurice stood with the staff.

"General Ricard, de Feyzenzac—all that are left, all, Sire."

"Good," said Napoleon, "I expected nothing less. I will keep you no longer in the ranks, my children. Get what rest you can tonight. We must move in the morning. The Russians are closing around us again." He turned as if to walk away when he caught sight of the Marquis de Vivonne, standing with Ney's staff officers but a little apart. "Who is that?" he asked, stopping abruptly, "a Russian?"

"No, Sire," answered the Marshal, "a Frenchman."

"In that uniform?"

"He is an officer of the Imperial Guard of the Czar Alexander."

"A traitor to France and to me?"

The Marshal bowed.

"Send him here," continued Napoleon.

In a moment, the Marquis de Vivonne, summoned by a wave of the hand of Marshal Ney, presented himself. Meanwhile, the troops, under orders, broke into companies, were marched away under their sergeants and dismissed, Ney's men going to the quarters cheerfully given up to them by the Guard. Eugene and Davout with their staffs gathered about the Emperor who confronted the Marquis de Vivonne. Ney also remained in place.

"And who are you, sir? "began the Emperor as the Marquis stopped and saluted him with his right hand.

"My name is Philippe de Vivonne," he answered haughtily, "I am the eldest son of the Duc de Vivonne."

"Ha!" exclaimed the Emperor, a little colour creeping into his face, "I have heard that name before—Vivonne—"

"I am happy that you have discovered it," said the Marquis.

"You fight against me, against France. I find you in the ranks of my enemies, wearing a Russian uniform—"

"I regret that to fight against you, General Bon—"

"The Emperor," thundered Marshal Ney, laying his heavy hand on the young man's shoulder.

"Be it so," said the other, "I regret that to fight against your Emperor seems to fight against France, but I stand for my King—"

"For your king—Bah!" interposed the Emperor contemptuously.

The pale face of the Marquis flushed. His hand instinctively sought his left side, but he wore no sword. It had been taken from him when he had been made prisoner.

"Where have I heard your name," said the Emperor, bending his head and knitting his brow,—"Vivonne—Vivonne—you commanded the Red *Cossacks*, I know, but before that—" Suddenly he lifted his head and his hand with it. "I have it now," he cried, his face darkening with anger, "you were with d'Enghien! Upon my life, you plotted and conspired with him against the country."

"I cannot and will not deny it," returned the Marquis firmly.

"It is a pity," said the Emperor coldly. "You have the courage of your race and now you have great need of it."

"I do not understand."

"What was the fate of d'Enghien? "

"You had him murdered, I believe," returned Vivonne, boldly.

"You call it murder? "said Napoleon, his face flushing, then by a great effort he calmed himself and shrugged his shoulders. "Call it what you will, *monsieur*, for the good of France he is dead and for the good of France you shall follow him. Marshal Ney, detail an officer and a squad of men to shoot this traitor out of hand."

"I expected nothing else from the justice of the Emperor," said the young man contemptuously.

"Your Majesty," protested the Marshal, "it is impossible, this man is a prisoner of war."

"Sire," exclaimed another voice.

As Napoleon turned his head, Maurice, his face aflame, presented himself before the Emperor. His hand was fumbling at the white ribbon of the cross on his dingy jacket. He extended it toward the Emperor.

"What do you mean, sir?"

"Sire," said Maurice passionately, "I have loved you, I have fought for you, I would die for you without a murmur, without a word, without regret, gladly even. If you do this thing, I am no longer a soldier of yours. You took me back into favour yesterday, you gave me your own cross, I return it to you. I will break my sword at your feet if you do this thing."

"Are you seeking your brother's fate, audacious boy?" thundered the Emperor, in a tone that would have reduced some of the greatest Marshals to impotence before him, but he was dealing with stern stuff in these Vivonnes.

"Yes, Sire," cried Maurice, "I had rather be dead a thousand times than live to see my Emperor dishonoured."

"You are a fool," said the Marquis coldly, bitterly; "my death would remove an obstacle to your marriage."

"Is this the man to whom that Russian Princess was betrothed?"

asked the Emperor.

"Yes, Sire," answered Maurice.

Napoleon laughed grimly, sardonically, terribly.

"I think," he said to the Hussar, "that I was about to do you a favour by sweeping your rival and my enemy out of your path."

"I would not want that freedom as the result of murder."

"Murder! You speak boldly to your Emperor."

"It is because I love him that I use the term."

"The Marquis de Vivonne is a prisoner of war, Sire," said Marshal Ney quickly. "He came to us under a flag of truce and but for the unwarranted action of the Russian army in firing upon us then, he would not be here. He is entitled to every protection. If you had captured him in the open, you might have done this thing, but my honour now, Sire—"

"Your honour!" said Napoleon. "Am I not the font of honour of my army?"

"Your Majesty," persisted Ney, his face flushing, "you are still all of that, but after we have agonised for you, as we are dying for you, I ask—"

"Let no man plead for me," interposed the Marquis hastily; "let the tyrant and the usurper work his will."

"Your Majesty," said Maurice hotly, "you love the Marshal. It has been told me that you said you had three hundred millions in gold in your treasury and that you would give all to have him safe and sound. It is to this gentleman, whom you would assassinate, that you owe his life."

"What mean you?"

"You were good enough to say that had I not brought the news all would have been lost."

"Sire," said Ney, "it was to Maurice's riding and your prompt action that we owe our lives. Another hour and the swarms of *Cossacks* against whom we were fighting would have cut us to pieces."

"And what had this renegade to do with that?"

"It was his horse and his coat and his flask that enabled me to reach you, Sire," said Maurice quickly.

"And did you take them from him, Ney?"

"He gave them voluntarily."

"What, this enemy of France?"

"I could not see brave men freeze and die—" answered the Marquis.

"And therefore—" began Maurice.

But Napoleon silenced him with a gesture. He bent his brows again and no man ventured to break his reverie. At last he lifted his head.

"*Monsieur*, he who has saved for me Marshal Ney and brought to me even the handful of men that I love, has more than atoned for whatever may be charged against him. The mercy of the Emperor is extended to you. You are free to go your way."

The Marquis stared at him like one possessed.

"Your Majesty—" he began.

"No words," said the Emperor, "no thanks. You have bought your own life in preserving these. Berthier, a safe conduct to him. Let him ride with our army or seek his own without the camp at his pleasure."

Again the Marquis endeavoured to speak. Again Napoleon stopped him.

"Keep away from me," he said harshly, "lest I repent me of my action. Is it well done, Ney?"

"Excellently well, in faith, Sire," cried the great Marshal heartily, "and like my Emperor."

Napoleon turned away and his glance fell upon the straight figure of Maurice.

"Well, sir, and you, what have you to say now?"

He bent his face and stared at the young man with the fierce intensity of his imperial gaze. It was with difficulty that Maurice sustained that look. His pale face flushed, his eyes filled with tears.

"You renounced my service, did you not?" continued the Emperor. "You tendered me the cross with which I decorated you, my own cross—"

"Your Majesty—"

"You would fain break your sword or perhaps run your Emperor through before you did so."

"My God, Sire—"

"You called me—"

But Maurice had sunk to his knees.

"It was because I loved you," he protested, stretching out his arms toward the little figure towering above him, "because your honour is dearer to me than my own, because—"

"Enough," said the Emperor kindly, laying his hand on the other's shoulder, "rise. You have courage rare and high enough to beard your

Emperor and rebuke Napoleon when you thought him wrong. So faithful and brave a friend will be the more terrible to my enemies. I pardon you," he added with imperial magnanimity and clemency.

Somehow or other Maurice got to his feet.

"Is it Your Majesty's will that I surrender the cross?" he choked out brokenly.

When Napoleon did a thing he did it royally and he wanted to impress the Marquis de Vivonne, who stood at one side staring with all his soul at the scene.

"No," answered Napoleon, "if you had not already received it, I would bestow it upon you again."

"*Vive l'Empereur*," whispered the hussar, brokenly.

Napoleon extended his hand, the soldier caught it and bent over it.

"Come to my quarters tonight at eight, I shall have orders for you," he said, turning away.

The group dissolved at once.

"*Monsieur*," said Berthier, as he passed the Marquis, "your safe conduct will be ready for you immediately. Meanwhile, if you will accept my hospitality, you can march with my staff if you wish, although I warn you that you will enjoy but scant fare."

"I thank you, sir," said the Marquis, "my movements are undecided until I have conferred with this gentleman," he pointed to his brother, "meanwhile, I want to assure you that if I get back to the Russian army, not one word of what I have seen or heard will pass my lips."

"I should expect nothing else from a man of honour," said Berthier, turning away, "although there is little that goes on here that is not known to Marshal Kutusoff and your Imperial Master."

"Now," said the Marquis de Vivonne, facing his brother, when they were left alone, "things have to be settled and explained between us."

CHAPTER 23

Brothers in Arms

By the Emperor's orders Maurice had been assigned comfortable quarters in one of the smaller houses of the town. Thither, at the younger's suggestion, the two brothers had repaired after their dismissal by Napoleon. The single room of the hut was small, therefore the fire was better able to raise the temperature almost to a comfortable degree. The two men entered in silence which neither of them cared to break. Throwing off the rich fur *surtout* he wore, Maurice extended it to his brother.

"Your coat," he began rather formally, "it has served me well. Without it I should have by no means reached Orsha."

"Keep it," said the other carelessly.

"I cannot; it has served its purpose and I may not retain it longer."

"As you please, I could find plenty more like it in the Russian army."

"Do you mean to rejoin your command?"

"Certainly. Why should I remain with this beggarly rabble to freeze and starve a moment longer than is necessary," answered the Marquis disdainfully.

"You are my brother," said Maurice, slowly, colour coming into his thin cheeks, "and in my father's absence, the head of the house. Though you have cast me off I have always loved you and yet I cannot allow even you to speak of these brave men in that contemptuous way."

"Is it not the truth ? What else are they, sir, but a collection of scarecrows?"

"This is unworthy of you. They are soldiers, officers, gentlemen."

"Led by a—"

"Stop!" cried the hussar furiously. "You owe your life to the Emperor. I will not hear you say a word against him."

The Marquis shrugged his shoulders indifferently.

"We have other causes for difference. We need not import the Corsican," he resumed.

"Neither will I allow that statement to pass unchallenged. He is of France!"

"Not my France."

"But mine."

"Be it so. There are greater questions for us personally than the discussion of this man."

"Yes," answered the lieutenant colonel.

"And these centre around our curious relationship to Idona Muravieff."

"Pardon me, my brother," said the hussar proudly and with great emphasis, "Idona de Vivonne."

"You did indeed say that you had married her. Is it true or was it a word of madness?"

"It is the solemn truth."

"Impossible; she was betrothed to me."

"Upon my honour, *foi de Vivonne*"

"And when was it?"

"Six months ago."

"Where?"

"At Wilkomir."

"And does the lady love you?" asked the Marquis, suddenly changing his tactics.

"I cannot say."

The Marquis laughed bitterly.

"You appear to be a very confident husband, *monsieur, mon frère*" he said, his lip curling.

"When you hear all you will understand better the reasons for my uncertainty," returned the hussar; "listen!"

Rapidly he related to his brother the details of the great adventure in which he had played so large a part at the *chateau* of Wilkomir. The latter listened with a growing frown but without interruption. Indeed no comment was necessary, for Maurice possessed the art of vivid and picturesque narration, and he missed no facts or incidents worthy of note. His brother naturally gave the greatest attention to the dramatic story. When he came to the command of the old Prince Muravieff and his announcement that the marriage must be annulled, his brow cleared and when with unflinching fidelity the Light Horseman related the story of his renunciation by his new-made wife and the caustic comments of the Emperor, he threw back his head and laughed. It was not until then that he spoke.

"You see," he said triumphantly, "she loves you not. She is betrothed to me. She is a woman worthy of my highest regard. Into what madness she has been betrayed by a sudden desire to requite your services, and save your life, we need not enter. She will keep her word. I have no doubt that already papers have been forwarded to the Czar Alexander and that steps to annul the marriage are being taken, if they have not already been completed. She is your wife in name only and I do not respect your so-called rights. As a man of honour, and I suppose even in the service of your Emperor you have scarcely forfeited all right to that title, you cannot press your claim."

"Philippe," said Maurice hotly, "do not try me too far. I love this woman."

"And I, am I insensible to her appeal, think you?" asked the Marquis with equal fervour.

"You do not love her as I. I have fought for her and she for me. We have faced the enemy side by side. Our blood has mingled. There is no power on earth that can make me yield her up except—"

"Except what?"

"Her own will."

"Well, you had it when she bade you go."

"Yes, and yet I would not be human, the hot blood of the Vivonnes would not flow in my veins, did I not cherish hope in spite of that. I came away with despair in my heart but with a fixed purpose."

"And that was—"

"To hunt out the man to whom my wife—"

"Spare me the title," interposed the Marquis fiercely.

"Until the marriage has been annulled it is her lawful title and I shall continue not only to speak of her but to think of her by that term," retorted the other.

"As you will," said the Marquis, shrugging his shoulder; "titles amount to but little."

"They mean, in this instance, much to me."

"Proceed."

"I had sworn, I said, to hunt down the man and when I had found him to tell him the story and then to kill him."

"And after that?"

"To go back to my wife—"

"With the blood of her betrothed on your hands!"

"That would matter little to me. I would have gone to her gladly and begged her to be my wife in fact as well as in name."

"And would she have welcomed you, do you think, under such circumstances?"

"I know not, but at least it would have been possible for her to have done so without incurring the reproach of having broken her plighted troth. Well, *monsieur*, that was my plan, but now, God help me, I know not what to do."

"And three times," said the Marquis slowly, "you have saved my life. Once when you cut the Red *Cossacks* to pieces—that was splendid soldiership and I confess that, though I was defeated, I was proud of you."

"We have had brilliant teaching."

"Yes, that undoubtedly," admitted the elder brother, "and again," he went on, "when Ney's men would have stripped me, and the last time a moment since before your Emperor."

"And what of that?" asked the Hussar.

"It seems to me," replied the Marquis, "that by the rules of war, my life is yours."

"You don't mean—"

"I mean everything that is implied. Look."

The elder brother stepped forward and seized the Light Horseman's sword, which he had laid with its belt on the table when he had taken off the cloak, and drew the blade swiftly from the scabbard. The latter made no movement to check him.

"Would you kill me with my own sword and make my wife a widow that you might claim her?" asked Maurice quietly. "Well, perhaps it would be best; it would nobly requite—"

"You mistake me," said the Marquis, quickly reversing the weapon and tendering the hilt with a graceful bow to his younger brother. "My life is yours. Three times you have bought it at the risk of your own. You have even incurred the disfavour not once, but twice, of your beloved leader because of me. You have taken my betrothed; you might as well finish."

"My God!" exclaimed the Light Horseman.

"Take your sword, *monsieur*," continued the elder brother, "and pass it through my heart. So shall you regain the favour of your Emperor and perhaps the affections of your wife."

"And do you think me capable," cried the young man hotly, shrinking away from the proffered weapon, "of raising my sword against my own brother, wilfully, knowingly?"

"You have raised your sword against your lawful King, and in my eyes that is a greater crime."

"We have no king but Napoleon!"

"*No king but Caesar!*" quoted the Marquis softly. "So said the traitors who betrayed their Lord."

"Listen," said Maurice impetuously, "you have cast me off. To my father I am as one dead, and but for these chances of war which have thrown us together you would never have seen me again or, having seen me, would have passed me by like the idle wind. No one has ever heard me in my own defence. I am a Frenchman; I love France. Until I met Idona Muravieff it was my only real passion. There was no King, Louis XVI was dead; royalty tumbled as his head fell into the basket of the guillotine. Anarchy, disorder, greed, selfishness—that was the condition of France. Came this man and wrought order out of that chaos. Our enemies pressed us on every side, Austria, England, Prussia, Russia! One by one he fought them back, one by one he brought them to heel. He restored the ancient boundaries of our land. He made it greater than ever before.

"Prosperity, contentment, joy, followed in his train. He ruled France as none in her long line of kings had ever done. The heart of the nation beat in time to his heart. He gave it laws and enforced them. He built cities and roads. We thrilled to his voice, to his presence. There is no robe so splendid as that grey overcoat, no crown so beloved and honoured as that cocked hat he wears. He does things! He is things! I was alone; you had not seen fit to take me with you across the seas. Irresistibly he appealed to me.

"I came to him. I, the Comte de Vivonne, shouldered a musket and fell into the ranks of those who sought to save France from her enemies under his wonderful leadership. But I was not born for the ranks. The pride and prowess of my family were inherent in me as well as in you, and no family edict could deprive me of them. Fortune favoured me. I have risen and risen, and now, although I am not yet twenty-four, I may wear the stars of a General of Brigade, yes, of Division."

"And where is your brigade or your division, my general?" asked the other mockingly. "You do not answer, but I can tell you, back on the road, freezing, starving, dying."

"No, it awaits me in France."

"Provided you both live to reach there."

"I shall live and he shall live."

"Not if Wittgenstein and Tchichagoff and Kutusoff use their advantages. You will never get across the Beresina."

"There are not in Russia," answered the hussar proudly, "men enough or power enough to stop my Emperor and me."

"And to what pitch has the ambition of this man reduced our France?" asked the Marquis, relentlessly pressing his advantage. "Six hundred thousand men crossed the Niemen. Save for those on the extreme left under MacDonald and on the extreme right under Schwarzenberg, all but perhaps sixty thousand starving, dying men have already perished or have been taken by us. It is the glory of Russia that she has put a final stop to the career of this—"

"A check only, not a stop, and it is not the Russian army which has undone us but this Russian winter."

"A check, say you? Where will you replace the men you have lost?"

"While there is a man in France, old or young, grandsire or beardless boy, able to bear a musket, the Emperor will not lack an army."

"Would you rob the cradle and the grave?"

"What of that? We are all his, blindly, passionately, devotedly his. Do you know the watchword of the people?"

"No."

"'Vive l'Empereur,' for France is the Emperor and the Emperor is France. Lay aside that sword, my brother. Not that way can we solve our problem."

"How then?"

"I know not. Oh, that it is you that have tied my hands!" returned Maurice mournfully. "Were it not so, one of us would never leave this room alive; the question would be settled here and now—"

"But as it is—"

"As it is, it is in God's hands."

"And the woman's."

"Truly, and the woman's. You are free," continued the Light Horseman; "go to her. Say what you will to her. I must follow the Emperor, but because I have spared you, and I would scorn to mention it under other circumstances, tell her of this interview. Let her decide and I will abide by her decision. Meanwhile, let us part friends. Marshal Berthier will give you a horse, at my request, the best left us ! The

Russian army is not far away. Your coat is there. Your sword has been lost in the retreat but if you would wear mine, take it and welcome. And when you see my father, tell him that I may be mistaken, yet my ideals, perhaps even he will admit, are not unworthy of our ancient house and honourable name."

"I wish you no ill," said the Marquis slowly; "I am not insensible of what you have done for me, nor do your arguments seem so altogether contemptible in my eyes as they would once have appeared, and yet I cannot be your friend. It is impossible that I should be the friend of anyone who—"

"Not even of your brother—"

"Not even of my brother, in arms against his rightful King."

"I bow to your decision."

"And I will report you fairly to the Princess and she shall make her own choice."

"Gentlemen," said a staff officer, entering the room at that moment, "your pardon—"

"What is it?" asked Maurice sharply, although he was rather glad of the interruption.

"His Majesty the Emperor desires your presence, General Maurice, and as for you, sir—" he turned to the Marquis, "Marshal Berthier, the Prince de Neufchatel, directs me to hand you this safe conduct with his compliments and he begs that you will communicate your decision as to whether you will remain with the army or seek your own lines as soon as you make it. Meanwhile, such hospitality as we can confer is yours. *Au revoir, messieurs.*"

"You will wait here until I return, will you not?" asked Maurice.

"No," answered the Marquis, "I could not bear to enjoy the enforced hospitality of your army a moment longer than is necessary. I go at once."

"So this is farewell then?"

"It is. *Adieu.*"

CHAPTER 24

For the Safety of the Emperor and France

The sentry at the door had evidently received his orders, for as he saluted the approaching officer, he told Maurice to enter without ceremony. The last time the Light Horseman had been in that room it had been filled with members of the staff. On this night the room was empty save for the Emperor himself. The stout, heavy set little man stood before the fire, facing it, one hand behind his back, the other holding a riding whip. Napoleon had laid aside his fur *surtout* and wore the familiar grey overcoat, for it was cold in the room in spite of the large fire blazing in the open fireplace. The Emperor was whistling softly to himself and appeared plunged in deep reverie.

Maurice had entered the room quietly and stood for a moment unobserved. He looked at the man in whose hands were still the destinies of Europe and the world. The Emperor was keeping time to the tune he was whistling by tapping the whip upon the high leather boots he wore, and the young man recognised the air as *"Malbrook s'en-va-t'en-guerre"* which was a favourite tune of the Emperor's apparently since he had been known to whistle it before and was observed to whistle it afterward. He had the habit of whistling or humming that very tune in grave emergencies) also.

Maurice, as he stared at the little man, felt that overwhelming surge of affection toward him which filled the bosom of every French soldier when in his presence. He did not, however, dare to remain silent for more than a few seconds.

"Your Majesty—" he began.

Napoleon wheeled swiftly.

"Ha," he said, "it is you!"

"Yes, Sire, you sent for me."

"And like a good soldier you are here."

"Ready to die for Your Majesty, as ever."

"Although you did return my cross and you did interfere with my plans and you did dispute my words and you did cross my purpose."

"Your Majesty has forgiven me for all these things, I am sure, and you but repeat them to—"

"To make you know the depth of my forgiveness," said the Emperor, smiling. "Well," he continued, stepping nearer and laying his hand on the young man's shoulder—if it had been earlier in the game and the young man had been of less rank, he might have pinched his ear, for that was a habit of his also—"I like men who are fearless. I have made dukes before now and Marshals of France out of men whose chief recommendation to the office was that they were afraid of nothing, not even of me. Now, sir, I have selected you for a difficult and dangerous enterprise."

"The more difficult and the more dangerous, the more gladly do I welcome it," returned the Light Horseman quickly.

"I thought so, and that is why I have chosen you. You know our position. You know that we are losing men by the hundreds daily, that horses, guns, wagons, are all gone and whether we shall ever get out of Russia with what we have left or not, is a grave problem."

"I fear it is, Sire, and yet with Your Majesty to lead—"

"Ah, the men have confidence in me yet," said Napoleon, "and they are right. But I am needed elsewhere—everywhere, in Paris especially. There is perhaps little to be hoped for from this army. My enemies, encouraged by this reverse of fortune—" and that phrase was characteristic of the Emperor's method of speaking and thinking, the greatest disaster of history being to him only a reverse of fortune!— "will undoubtedly take advantage of the opportunity afforded to rise in revolt. Prussia we hold by fear alone, Austria by self-interest merely. Our rule has been one of force. Spring will be the time for them to assemble their forces and strike at me unless I can assemble my force and strike at them first. Therefore, I am needed, frightfully needed in France, but I cannot leave these brave soldiers here yet. I will stay with them until my presence is no longer necessary or until there are none left with whom to stay. Do you understand?"

"I understand, Sire, and your army would die for you."

"Indeed, it is dying for me. I have spoken most frankly to you, young sir, because I wish you to understand. You will, of course, respect my confidence."

"Nothing could wrench from me anything that Your Majesty chooses to confide in me."

"Very well. The situation lies this way. The last obstacle, natural obstacle that is, in the way of our retreat is the Beresina River. Once across it, I think our difficulties, save for the cursed winter, are all over. I have several times fancied that Kutusoff was willing to build a bridge for a flying enemy. I cannot otherwise understand his failure to press us harder."

"Unless it be," interposed the hussar, "that he fears to try conclusions with Your Majesty, even if you are practically alone."

"It may be that. I have beaten him horribly every time we have come in actual battle contact. Perhaps he has not forgot Friedland. But be that as it may, a singular supineness seems to have characterised his pursuit. Had I been in his place——"

"Had you been in his place, Sire, the affair would have ended at Borodino."

"Yes, undoubtedly," returned the other, who took the compliment in an entirely matter-of-fact way, which indeed, the circumstances warranted. "But even Kutusoff cannot restrain the Russians much longer; I have advices that he is being urged all the time to complete our ruin. The crossing of the Beresina will afford him his chance. Help from MacDonald is out of the question. Schwarzenberg has cravenly withdrawn from the south without fighting, and Tchichagoff has free access to the river. To the north the Duc de Belluno is holding back Wittgenstein's army. Wittgenstein is one of the ablest and most energetic of the Russian officers.

"I have no doubt that he is in much greater force than Victor. If he overwhelms that corps he will have a straight, easy way to the river. Loison's fresh division is marching from Wilna to join us on the twenty-sixth or -seventh of November. It has not strength enough to oppose either of these armies, let alone both of them. There are here with me barely fifteen thousand effectives. I must reach the river with them and I plan to cross at Borisoff or Studianka before Tchichagoff gets up and in time to unite with Loison. Victor must fight, crush or elude Wittgenstein at any cost and join us on the same day, the twenty-sixth, or the day after at the latest. Do you understand?"

"Perfectly, Sire."

"The safety of the three armies depends upon that junction. If we arrive separately we shall be beaten in detail and all will be lost. If our arrival be practically simultaneous, we shall be in sufficient numbers to crush Tchichagoff, push back Wittgenstein or cross before he can come upon us, and hold off Kutusoff as circumstances may require. That is clear to you?"

"Entirely clear, Sire."

"Being so, I have chosen you to play an important part in it."

"I hope that I may be worthy of your confidence, Sire."

"To hope is not enough," said the Emperor severely.

"Your reproach is just, Sire, I will be worthy of it."

"That is the better spirit. You are to go to Marshal Victor, the Due de Belluno, with orders, written orders which are of the same purport as those I have just communicated to you. And on no account will you let those orders get into the hands of the enemy. You are to destroy them should you be captured or even be in danger of capture. If they are destroyed and you should yet manage to escape—"

"I shall manage."

"Good, you must.—You can repeat your verbal orders of the same kind. Are you known to Marshal Victor?"

"Well known, Sire."

"No identification papers will be necessary, then. It is well that you should have as few papers as possible. Orders have been prepared—" Napoleon lifted a tiny packet from the mantel above the fire, "they have been reduced to as small a compass as possible so that they may be more easily carried and more readily destroyed."

"I shall swallow them if I am captured, or if there seems to be danger of it," said the hussar.

"That will be the best way. Berthier has orders to give you the best horse left in the army, one of my own, and you are to have an escort of forty men, all officers, who are also to be given the pick of the surviving horses. You understand that the fate of the army rides with you and you are to get through—"

"I shall get through, Sire."

"More than the fate of the army rides with you, for I have determined never to submit to capture by the Russians." Napoleon reached his hand into the closely buttoned grey overcoat he wore over his green uniform coat and drew forth a tiny flask. "There is here," he said, "that which will free me in the end from any threatened capture."

"God forbid," cried the hussar, stepping forward and in his impetuous way he made to take the flask of poison from the Emperor's hand but Napoleon thrust it back into its place.

"I carry it ever about my person," he said, "I shall grace no triumph for the Czar Alexander. Therefore, not only the fate of the army, but the fate of the Empire, the fate of France, the fate of the Emperor, rides with you."

"Your Majesty honours me above all men."

"But I do not honour you lightly. I have chosen you from all the army for this duty."

"It shall be carried out, *foi de Vivonne!*"

"That is it, upon the word of a soldier and a gentleman," said the Emperor. "Well—"

"I am ready to start now, Your Majesty."

"A moment. I have further commands for you."

"And I welcome them."

"The rest will be easy. After you have delivered your message to Victor, you will proceed—"

"To rejoin the army, is it not, Sire, to die by Your Majesty's side?"

The Emperor smiled.

"To live for me. I want you to go on to Veleika, Smorgoni and finally to Wilna. Say to the commanders of the places to have everything ready to receive the remains of the army. Urge them to use every possible endeavour to assemble clothing, shoes, rations, bread. We ought to have thirty thousand men after we cross the Beresina, and if they can get across, as many camp followers. Impress upon them, as only one who has lived through these awful days, can impress upon them, the supreme importance I attach to their efforts in that direction."

"It shall be done, Sire."

"Discipline, save in the Guard and among a few of the better divisions, is nearly at an end. An abundance of supplies of all kinds is the only thing that can restore it. You see?"

"I see it, painfully, Sire."

"It is ill arguing or ordering freezing and starving men. If one hundred thousand rations are not waiting at Wilna, I shall be sorry for the city. The army is horribly worn out."

"Alas, I know it, Sire."

"And another thing. The Duc de Bassano, Maret, is at Wilna. I am anxious that there should be no agents of foreign powers at Wilna. This army is not good to look at now," continued the Emperor meaningly. "As to those who are in the city, they must be got out of the way before we arrive. He might tell them that he is going to Warsaw and that I am, too, and convey them there. We do not wish to be seen by

211

our friends or enemies."

"It shall be done, Sire. Is that all?"

"Not yet. After you leave Wilna," the Emperor smiled for the first time and when he smiled he was the more irresistible, "it seems to me," he said softly, "that the *chateau* of Wilkomir is not far from Wilna. On your way to Kowno, I authorise you to revisit the *chateau*, make inquiries as to the health of the *chatelaine*, present my compliments to Prince Muravieff, and in short, do what you will."

"Your Majesty overwhelms me."

"Your brother, where has he gone?"

"Back to the Russian lines."

"Good, I would not have you forestalled by him. I do not like to have my soldiers beaten even in love, *monsieur*."

"Your Majesty!"

"I am much mistaken," continued the Emperor, "if you do not improve your opportunity to your ultimate advantage."

The hussar smiled.

"It will not be my fault if things do not turn out well, Sire," he said with great satisfaction.

"After Wilkomir carry the same orders to Kowno, if possible, and then," Napoleon stopped and looked earnestly at the young man, "and then, come to me in Paris and you shall receive a command as General of Division and perhaps I may add a patent of my own nobility to your ancient degree, the Marquis de Wilkomir. How will that sound in the ear of the Princess, I wonder?"

"I cannot find words, Sire," faltered the hussar brokenly.

"Never mind words," said the Emperor. "What I want is deeds."

"And you shall have them."

"Now go. Berthier has your orders. You have no preparations to make?"

"All that I possess is on my back."

"You are not much worse off than your Emperor or the rest of the army In that," said Napoleon. "Remember, you must get through."

"The Duc de Belluno himself shall inform you at Borisoff that I have done so, Sire."

CHAPTER 25

The Man and the Snow

The man and the horse were alone in the wilderness. The horse was dying, there was no doubt about that. The man was not in much better case. He had endured greater hardships than the horse which had done so well by him, but because he was a man and not an animal, he was still on his feet. It was a very unsteady footing, however, that he maintained.

Something like despair entered his heart as he stood looking at the prostrate animal, and that in a way measured the depths into which he was plunged, for this was the very first time that he had ever despaired. This man had looked death in the face for months until, in fact, he had grown indifferent to the dread proximity. He had been wounded, starved, frozen, over and over again. Like St. Paul, he had died daily, nay, even hourly, momentarily on that ghastly retreat. He had seen his superiors and his inferiors, his comrades, and equals, drop away one by one. Some of them had been mercifully shot by the enemy, some of them had fallen down by impotent camp fires and had slept silently, and in the end painlessly, into death.

Some of them had been tortured with wounds. Some of them had been drowned in icy rivers. Some of them had starved to death. Some of them had been stripped naked by human wolves and left to freeze. Some of them had been torn to pieces by dogs, wolves of the four-footed class, no less ravenous or savage than their human exemplars. Vultures had gorged themselves upon the dead. Upon this man's brain had been printed an imperishable panorama of horror. It had grown monotonous after a while and he had become accustomed to it. Finally he had faced every danger almost with an indifference from which despair had been absent. He had been sustained by duties to be performed, by devotion to the Emperor.

Many in that army had taken the advice of Job's wife and had cursed God and died, but terrible as is the contrast, few had cursed the Emperor. And this man had been sustained above all by an object to be attained. He, at least, had never given up. Hope in him had not been killed before. Consequently, the feeling of despair as he recognised it, was the more appalling.

The horse had fallen on one of the *steppes*. Back of him and on either side so far as the eye could see rolled away into infinite distance, the snow-covered plain. He and the horse were alone. The main army, what was left of it, had passed far southward and had fought its way across the Beresina, leaving thirty thousand dead on either shore and in the icy bed of that river of death. As usual it had pillaged the store houses that had been prepared for its return in the towns through which it passed. The first comers had gorged themselves with food and drink as before; the later comers made themselves drunk with what was left; but whether fed or hungry, whether drunk or sober, they had continued to die and die and die. The winter, so long delayed, had made up for its tardy arrival by its intensity once it came. It had grown colder and colder and colder.

This man's faculties were numbed. He could scarcely have heard it if it had been within a mile of him, but off to the southward beneath the cold grey horizon, on that ghastly road, reeled the skeletons of the companies, the battalions, the regiments, the divisions, the corps, of the Grand Army, staggering along. The Russians suffering almost as greatly pressed doggedly after them, the dreaded *Cossack "Hourra"* mingled with the long howl of the wolves, the bark of the wild dogs, the harsh croak of the ravens. Again and again, the dauntless band covering the rear, hurriedly formed square, the icy guns blazed fire. The oncoming enemies were beaten back so that march could be taken up again.

Marshal Ney was there. Sometimes, as he plodded along over the steppes, Maurice, seeing his little escort dwindle away until only he himself was left, wished that he was back with the red-headed Marshal, fighting in the ranks like a common soldier, using his gun with the skill of his yeoman days at Sarrelouis. And yet in heart, in soul, in courage, in animation, the great Marshal was in his greatest day then.

Much opportunity was to come to Marshal Ney in later years. His it was to lead thousands once more; his it was to be in the fierce rush and storm of terrible battles; his it was to gain an immortal name, when as the very *paladin* of war he led charge after charge with the

214

most transcendental gallantry against the red- coated stubborn British squares at Waterloo, but he never attained greater heights, he never showed himself a greater man than when he marched and fought, himself the rear guard, the last man of the Grand Army, fending off the Russians, conquering the cold, indomitable, the bravest of the brave !

Yes, Maurice often wished that he was there, for he thought now he would never reach Wilkomir. He did not know the way to it even. Before him half a league away the pine forests began. How black and melancholy those pine trees looked in spite of the snow that covered them, that had drifted about them. He knew the general direction of the *chateau*, he knew that it was hidden in that woodland somewhere, so he had pressed on, doggedly, determinedly on.

His time was his own. He had not failed the Emperor. Every order had been carried out, every message had been delivered. He was free to seek his wife. Abode she still in the great hall of the ancient building? Slept she still in that upper chamber at the head of the stairs which he had held for her, where he and she had fought together against the common foe and where the *Cossack* priest had made them man and wife? Was that grim old grandfather still with her? Had he enjoyed an opportunity to lay his granddaughter's case before those authorities? Was she indeed his wife now, or had that marriage been annulled? Sometimes, when he thought of these things, he laughed; at least the hoarse, croaking sound that came from his cracked and bleeding lips was what passed as laughter. Whether she was his wife or not would be a matter of little importance presently, for the highest probability was that a few hours more would eliminate him from any further consideration.

So despair began to enter his heart and as for the first time he recognised it there he presently came to regard it with a sort of philosophy, for he realised that he must be very far gone indeed if that were his mental and spiritual condition. He had an impulse to lie down and let it end there on the wind-swept, icy plain by the side of his horse—it was a poor animal that had been given to him at his last stop, but the best to be had. The steed, and the man too, had done his best in the Emperor's service as everything and everybody had done on that march.

And the Emperor, where was he? Maurice had picked up enough rumoured news in the towns in which he had stopped to feel that the Emperor was sorely needed in Paris. Napoleon had stayed with his army as long as there was a thing he could do for it. Now the safety of the nation imperatively demanded his presence elsewhere. Maurice divined that he had gone. Well, if he went to the ends of the world, he could not take the imprint of his spirit off the souls of the soldiers, nor obliterate the devotion from their hearts.

Just because it was in him, the Light Horseman lifted his head bravely at last. He would press on. Time enough for death later. Perhaps she had not meant that dismissal, perhaps—He stopped reflecting, he gathered himself together. There was little about the horse or its equipment of value. He wrapped about him the tattered remains of his coat. He drew his belt a hole tighter. He slipped the pistols out of the holsters and thrust them into that belt. He opened his inside pocket and felt the precious flask with a few drops of priceless liquor still in it. He put his raggedly gloved hands to his face a moment in prayer, swept the horizon thereafter with a long look, bent his head and started toward the nearest wall of forest trees.

The morning had been still and clear, but as he plodded on over the hard snow—fortunately it was frozen hard enough to bear him, otherwise, he would have got nowhere in the drifts—the sky became overcast with the threatenings of a storm. The distance was not great between his last halting-place and the wood but of necessity—weakness—he went slowly. His desire and his spirit as well outranked his physical capacity, but his power of endurance had to govern his progress. He had to fight an overwhelming desire to lie down and end it all.

The two great motives of his life were ever present with him. He could close his eyes a moment and see the figure of the Emperor—the little man in the grey coat—on the one hand, and on the other, the snow-clear, ice-pure face of the woman, his wife. How strangely they were juxtaposed in his imagination. One urged him on, the other led him forward. One stood for France, the other for home. Love of country, love of woman—those great passions!

By and by he came to the wood. The trees were small and sparse at first, but as he advanced they grew thicker and larger. When he was well within the confines of the forest, the storm broke. He was glad and thankful that it had delayed until he had reached even that sorry shelter. Out on the open *steppe* he would have been forced to drift before it until he fell and then it would have buried him in shrouds of snow. Here he could make shift to go on.

When he judged it to be about noon, he stopped for rest. Carefully ungloving his hand, he searched the pocket of his coat for a few crumbs of coarse bread, more precious than the dust of diamonds. He lingered over them although he was intensely hungry and he craved to swallow them in one mouthful. Then he took out his flask. It was yet a quarter full. He took one small swallow, once again mastering his craving to drain it and die. He had not dared to sit down lest he should not have the strength to get up.

The crumbs and the drops gave him a little accession of energy. Gathering himself together once more he plodded on. He was blessed with an unerring sense of direction and although the sun was no longer visible, he still held his course steadily enough toward the north-westward. He had a dim idea that somewhere in the forest he would strike the Vilia, on the banks of which he remembered the *chateau* of Wilkomir had been reared, so he staggered on. He had a fine topographical memory and he recalled that the distance from the *chateau* to the edge of the forest had not been very great. Indeed, it had been passed all too rapidly when he rode away from it on that day after his Emperor. He reasoned that of course it would be longer now that he was compelled to go so slowly, but if he kept on long enough he would reach it, and presently he did.

Somewhat late in the afternoon, he came upon what was without doubt a river. The Vilia ran, as he remembered it, between steep banks, as this stream which was frozen solidly. It could be no other. There should have been a road somewhere, a road that led from Wilna to Wilkomir. Where was it? Was it up or down the river? He stood on the steep bank staring into the snowy gulf, trying to determine. It seemed to him that the river where he stood was wider than it had been where he had crossed six months ago in the beginning of summer. It seemed to him also that the *chateau* must lie to the northward.

Again he covered his face with his gloved hands and again he made his prayer and then he turned to the right and went slowly along the bank of the river, still keeping under the trees. The ravine in which the river ran acted as a sort of a draw and the storm and snow swept down it irresistibly. He could not afford to leave the shelter of the trees until he had to cross. The short day was drawing to a close when he came upon a clearing through the trees. He could see nothing underfoot, but evidently a road ran there and the bank had been cut or worn away so that it declined gently down to the river on both sides. This must be the place.

Summoning all his resolution he left the shelter of the trees and plunged down the road to the river bed. He could scarcely stand up against the sweep of the storm. Somehow or other he managed to get across. He could not sustain many more fatigues or stresses of that kind. Indeed, when he reached the shelter on the other side, he could hardly have gone another step.

He leaned against a great tree that sheltered him from the north wind's bitter assault until he recovered his breath and then he staggered blindly on.

How far he went he did not know, but he suddenly saw moving figures ahead of him, he heard a voice crying for help. Someone was in trouble. He could not make out what the trouble was, but he hurried,—at least compared to his other progress, he hurried, although he still moved slowly—to give assistance. Was this the road to Wilkomir? Was he always to meet someone desiring succour there? Could it be the Princess, that dark figure against the tree? No, his heart sank as he recognised it to be a man.

The man had his back against a tree and something bright in his hand. He was surrounded by snarling, leaping figures. As Maurice plodded forward, staring, he heard sounds with which he had become quite familiar—the long howls of famished wolves! They had dogged the army every step until he knew their cry—neither he nor any one there would ever forget it. Many a man, caught alone, had been pulled down by some half-starved pack and here was a man in that situation.

In the presence of danger the faculties of the hussar cleared a little. He stared hard as he staggered forward. There were half-a-dozen of the brutes and they were yelping and snarling and biting at the man. Maurice was too spent to cry out. The traveller had his face turned away from him. Dropping to his knees he drew one of his pistols, rested it upon a low branch that offered its support—he could scarcely have aimed the pistol unaided—and pulled the trigger. The heavy bullet tore through the body of one of the gaunt, starving beasts and buried itself in the brain of a second.

The pack stopped petrified. The sword of the traveller, with which he had been feebly beating back the ravenous animals, dropped to the ground. Maurice got to his feet and went forward vigorously, his second pistol in his hand. He did not aim. Thrusting the muzzle fairly into the jaws of the biggest wolf, he pulled the trigger. The next instant, the survivors, intimidated by the shots and the arrival of the newcomer, snatching the dead bodies of their fellows, dragged them away into the forest and began the meal which they had hoped to make on the traveller. They were soon out of sight.

Maurice stooped, lifted the other's sword and turned to proffer it to him. The man was wrapped in fur. He stood, his back against a tree. His head had fallen forward. He gave no sign of life and but for a low branch that supported him, he would have collapsed to the ground. Maurice thrust the point of the sword into the ice and examined the man more closely. He lifted the fur cap and started back in amazement. For the fourth time, he had saved the life of his brother. There was some meaning to it, there was some purpose. There must be some explanation of God's will in the fact that he had been so often instrumental in preserving the man to whom Idona Muravieff had been betrothed before her marriage.

The Marquis de Vivonne's face was as white as the snow. Maurice looked about him in great perplexity until his glance fell upon a rude sledge, such as the *Cossacks* used for dragging a gun or carrying a load. There was no horse, although some of the harness still was attached to the front of the sledge. There was no food on it, the wolves had torn at it, but there were blankets and pieces of canvas. Maurice reconstructed the scene. His brother had camped for the night and somewhere, somehow, had lost his *Cossack* pony. He had dragged the sledge himself until the wolves caught him. Well, it was a godsend, that sledge. He lifted the form of the Marquis and laid it down on the rough vehicle, he poured what remained in his flask down the almost dying man's throat, he covered him carefully, then gathered the traces in his hand, bent his head and staggered on, dragging after him sledge and its unconscious burden.

There was an enormous fire blazing in the great hall of the *chateau* of Wilkomir. The vast apartment was empty save for one woman who stood before the fire, looking down into the flames. Upstairs, in his own chamber, the body of the old Prince Muravieff, dressed with all the magnificence of a Russian *Boyar* lay awaiting burial. He had died that very day, following his son, her father, who had been killed at the head of the Imperial Guard on that fatal day of Borodino and the Princess was alone—alone in the world and alone in the *chateau* save for Stepan, who had recovered from his wounds and a few others of the house servants, alone in the great *chateau* whence it was impossible to pass without escort and protection.

On the table in the huge hall she had just laid a packet of papers. The last request of her grandfather had bade her at the first moment possible to take those papers to the Czar Alexander and implore him as a final favour to his dying and now dead servitor to comply with his request, a request that had been in the old man's mind ever since the day he had come home and found his granddaughter married; and she had promised to do that. Her eyes turned from the fire and looked at the packet. How easy it would be to step across the great hall, get the papers and drop them into the fire. Who would know? Who could tell?

That man, to whom she was betrothed, where was he? That man to whom she was wedded, where was he? Did either or both of them live or die? Which one of them did she love? Would she fain be wife or maid or widow? Although the great fire filled the room, at least that portion of it where she stood, with pleasant warmth, the Princess shuddered. She lifted from a settle a great wrap of fur and drew it about her.

As she did so there came a feeble knock upon the door. The Princess listened. One of the women of the household, on some errand of her own, came into the room.

"Stop," said the Princess, "do you hear anything?"

"Nothing but the wind screaming about the building, my lady."

"Wait and listen."

"Ay," said the woman at last, "someone knocks at the great door. Who can be abroad on such a night as this?"

"We shall see," answered the Princess. "Send Stepan and Vassily to me at once."

In a few moments the old *major-domo* and the younger attendant entered the room. They bowed low before the Princess.

"There is someone at the front door," she said. "Open it."

"Had we not best make sure before we open the door, my lady?"

"I would not allow even our bitterest enemy to remain without the walls on such a night as this," said the Princess.

Old Stepan, followed by Vassily, turned toward the door. Slowly he lifted the various bars from their sockets, turned the ponderous key and swung open the door. Into the apartment a great gust of snow whirled and the room was filled instantly with chilling cold. Out of the snow-cloud there staggered a ghastly semblance of a man. He bore in his arms a shrouded figure. This new burden bearer turned toward the fire instantly and made a step or two in that direction when his eyes apprehended the Princess. Save for the sable furs she was in white. He had loved her in that dress and she often wore it. Great God, it was she.

"Idona!" broke from his lips hoarsely.

"Maurice—my husband," whispered the woman.

"I have brought you back your betrothed," said the hussar with his last remnant of strength laying the body of the Marquis on a couch before the fire.

CHAPTER 26

The Princess Chooses Again

The Light Horseman was a pitiable looking object. The uniform he had worn the night he had made love to her in that room, he still wore—what was left of it, that is. It was in rags. The scraps of gold braid that still clung to it were black. It had worn through at the elbows and knees, everywhere in fact, and wherever it had worn through it showed the naked flesh, black or red and raw. His boots were in strips, his feet were wrapped with sacking. His busby had gone long since and his head was wrapped about with a dirty piece of blood-stained cloth. He had been wounded in the last skirmish with the *Cossacks*. The horseman's coat was in little better condition than the rest of his uniform. It hung in ribbons from his shoulders and his gloves were a jest. But the diamonds still sparkled in his sword hilt and the gold of his belt buckle still shone in the firelight.

His worn face was covered with a thick growth of ragged and un-trimmed beard, originally blond, but now covered with dirt, powder smoked, blood stained. Naturally a dainty man, he had striven at first to keep himself clean with washes of snow, but latterly even this had been impossible. The moustache which he had worn so gallantly up-curled, drooped now, yet it did not hide the firm line of his lips, and like the diamonds in his sword hilt and the gold in his belt buckle, his eyes still shone with some of the old fire.

It was with the old grace and something of the old gallantry that, having deposited the body of his brother in a great armchair, he drew himself up and bowed before her, having delivered his message. No one would ever know what it had cost him to carry the heavy body of the Marquis from the sledge up the steps to the door and into the room. It was only by an iron effort mentally and physically that he kept himself from trembling and that he held himself erect and apparently undaunted before her. The last time he had come into her presence he had collapsed at her feet and he determined that he would not do it this time, or that if he did, it would be for the last time indeed, for he would be dead.

He was starving and had he not been starving, he would have been dying of thirst. He was suffering from exhaustion so great that it did not seem possible he could sustain it longer, and yet it is evidence of the strength of his affection that for the moment he forgot these things in looking upon her. She was as beautiful as ever, the anxiety and the uncertainty of the past six months fell instantly away from her. A rare colour touched the translucent purity of her cheeks. She was in his eyes as she had been when he had made love to her in the great hall on that never-to-be-forgotten night.

That he was ragged, wounded, haggard, sick, dirty, meant nothing to her, for she loved him and she had him back. Rumours of success and defeat, of triumph and disaster, had reached her, but she had kept largely at home and she knew little of what had really happened.

She had thought of him as dead on some battlefield. No word had come to her from him, of course, and there had been no means by which she could hear any tidings. When it was safe to do so, the detachment that had been left to guard the house had been withdrawn and with the coming of winter she and her old grandfather had been shut off from the world. She had prayed and hoped for him. She had blamed herself a thousand times for having been influenced by the old man to reject the man she really loved, and yet her further promise to her grandfather had been made but the day before!

She was conscious of the papers lying on the table which she was bound in honour to present to the *Czar* at the first opportunity. She had resolved to go through with what the honour of her family seemed to demand, but she knew that her life, despite the fact that her betrothed was a gallant gentleman and loved her truly, would be one of long misery, even hell, to her. Why could it not have been the other way! Now they were both here before her and by the grim irony of fate, the husband, whom she loved, had brought to her the betrothed whom she did not love.

For a moment, her eyes, which had been searching his with passionate devotion and pity—which he had been acute enough to read to the last line—wavered from the Light Horseman's face. His had been a hopeless love. It had been with the greatest self-sacrifice that he had carried his brother into the room but now his heart leaped within his breast in spite of himself. Therefore, it was with a frightful pang that he saw her turn her gaze toward the motionless figure on the sofa. Then she looked back at him inquiringly.

"No," he said hoarsely, "he is not dead. I forced him to drink the last drop from my flask. He wants warmth, food——"

"Stepan," said the woman, "take the Marquis de Vivonne to my father's room upstairs. Do everything that you can for him. Send someone for Father Vygia and bid him spare nothing for his comfort and report to me as soon as may be."

While Stepan and Vassily carried the Marquis upstairs, the woman turned again to the hussar.

"And you, my friend, how are you?" she said. She came nearer to him and laid her hand upon his ragged shoulder and then started back shocked at what the touch revealed. "Why, you are starving!" she cried.

She clapped her hands loudly and as a maid entered the room she gave imperious and quick directions to have food and drink prepared and brought to the room at once. All her woman's heart was touched with the sheer physical wretchedness of the man before her.

"Starving," said the hussar slowly, "yes, for the sight of you. Hungry, thirsty, dying to see you again. I had frozen to death in the dark and the cold, like my comrades, but that your image in my heart kept warmth and light and life there."

It was the old man still. Nothing could overcome his gallantry or wither his passion. It was almost like being made love to by a dead man and yet the woman thrilled to it. She saw, she realised, that in the very articles of death itself his thoughts would be for her.

She did not allow herself the luxury of listening to him now, however. She acted. She seized a great high-backed, thickly cushioned, fur draped chair, thrust it nearer the fire, led him to it, forced him to sit down and sank to her knees before him, looking up at him with swimming eyes while she drew off his ragged gloves, baring those poor, frozen, cracked, bleeding hands upon which she softly laid her lips in pity and tenderness.

"Oh, my love, my love," she murmured, "you were dead and are alive again."

"In faith," said the hussar, giving way before such emotions when nothing else had had the power to wring a cry from him, "I was dead and I am alive again, since I see you once more."

Presently the maid entered the room with food, a bowl of nour-

224

ishing broth, steaming, fragrant, with a flagon of ancient wine and, sight rarer than all, with fine wheaten bread. She set it on a little table before him.

"My lady," said the hussar hoarsely, "I have not seen food and drink like this for months. Would you go away? I would not have you watch me eat. I am afraid that I shall forget that I am a man and spring upon it like a ravenous beast."

His teeth clenched together, his hands locked as he stared at the food and drink, but she shook her head, whereat he fell into a sudden fit of trembling from his great weakness. And then with her own hands she fed him. She broke the bread and gave it to him, she lifted the cup of broth to the bleeding, blackened lips. She gave him of the wine, first touching her own lips to the edge of the silver goblet. She ministered to him as if he had been a child, hovering over him and mothering him with passionate love and tenderness. And amid all the trying circumstances through which he had passed he had never found it harder to play the part of a man and gentleman and control his appetite and his nerves than just then. He had fought against adversity and it had failed to conquer him, but he succumbed to kindness.

He had barely finished his meal and he had sense enough to eat sparingly, and she had wit enough to give him much less than he craved, when old Step an interrupted them. His advent recalled them to the other patient.

"My brother—" said the Light Horseman.

"The Marquis de Vivonne," began the Princess, "how is he?"

"He is conscious, knows where he is and is asking for you, Your Highness," answered the *major-domo.*

"And is he wounded or hurt?"

"Only starved."

"Don't go to him," said Maurice, throwing out his hand as the Princess turned slowly toward the door.

"I must," she said.

"But you are my wife."

"I have not forgotten it."

"And I cannot."

"Well, then, *monsieur*," said the woman, picking up the packet from the table, "know that my grandfather lies dead in his room above us. With his last breath he extorted from me a promise that I would keep my word, that I would present this petition to the *Czar* and that when I had been freed, I would—"

"But he had no right to bind you in that way. You are married. You love me. You tried to deny it once before. You cannot deny it now. I have felt it in your touch, I have seen it in your eyes, I have heard it in your voice. I cannot give you up."

"There is one thing," she said slowly, "that is above love and that is honour, yes, even a woman's honour. I gave my word to the living and to the dead and although it kills me I must keep it."

"Would God that I had died in the ice and snow, would God that I slept with my brave comrades out yonder."

"And where are they, those gallant gentlemen and splendid soldiers?" asked the Princess.

"Gone, gone all. You could walk from Wilna to Moscow on their dead bodies and every river and every brook has been dammed and bridged with men and horses, guns and equipment. Perhaps I, I alone, am left alive."

"And the Emperor?"

"Well enough when I saw him at Orsha and by this time, please God, on his way back to Paris and to France to summon a new army to defend the Empire and himself."

"And the Russians?"

"It is not they who have beaten us but the winter. Great God, the winter!"

"Alas, poor Poland!"

"And have I been preserved through it all only to come back to give you to another, to my brother, whose life four times I have saved? Before God, I cannot do it. He has succumbed at last, I am stronger. I—"

"Monsieur Maurice," said the woman softly, "I pity you as much as I love you and I pity myself in the same way. You talk wildly. It cannot be. *Noblesse oblige!* I must keep my word. Would God it were otherwise. No, do not strive to stop me. Stepan will take you to your old room. There are clothes there, things that you will need. I will see you in the morning. Goodnight. It is not goodbye, just goodnight."

It was a strange trio that met in the great hall of the castle after breakfast the next morning. The storm had ceased and the bright sunlight outside on the snow flooded the world with dazzling brightness. Through the double glass windows every nook and corner of the vast department was flooded with radiance. The bright light showed what had not been revealed the night before, the ravages that her anxiety, uncertainty and misery had wrought in the face of the Princess. She was thinner, paler, there were dark circles under her eyes. She had added another sleepless night to many which she had suffered. Yet the two men who loved her and had seen nothing of noble womankind for months, whose eyes had been filled with pictures of ghastly, terrible horror, thought she had never been so beautiful.

The Princess, declining to sit down, stood by the old mantelpiece close to the fire. The Marquis de Vivonne sat in the chair which his brother had occupied the night before and his brother stood leaning against the table between the two. For the first time in months, the Light Horseman was decently clothed. Stepan and Vassily had worked wonders in his appearance. Food and rest had already began the changes to be wrought by them alone. His face was shaved, there was even an upturn, though a poor one, to his moustache. His hair had been clipped and he had scrubbed and scrubbed and scrubbed until most of the grime had been washed away. He had buckled about the dark blue, fur-trimmed habit of a Russian *Boyar* which had been given him, his sword. His feet luxuriated in new boots, fortunately a trifle too large for him or he could scarcely have drawn them over his frozen members.

With food and drink and proper clothing some of his *gaîté de coeur* came back to him. He had had time to think, not during the night, for in his weariness, after he had bathed and prepared for rest, he had sunk into the sleep of complete and utter exhaustion, but during the morning. The ideas and habits of his ancient line and race had not been lost by years of Republican and Imperial campaigning. It was his duty to defer to the head of the house. Although it killed him, he would do so, and having once made up his mind, he would do so without repining. Time enough for him to give way when he left the Princess forever. So he faced them calmly, brightly, almost smilingly. Whereat the Princess wondered, jealously, almost resentfully.

His brother, habited in his uniform as an officer in the *Czar's* Imperial Guard had received the same attention and he, too, was in much better condition. It was he who began the conversation.

"It is to you," he said slowly to his younger brother, "that I am indebted again for my life. The Princess," he bowed toward her, "has told me how you found me in the forest and brought me in."

"I would have done it for anyone," answered Maurice quickly.

"Doubtless, but it so happened that you did it for me and this is the fourth time, is it not, that you have laid me under such obligation to you?"

The Light Horseman waved his hand as if to say that the matter was not worth discussing.

"There was no obligation," he answered.

"You may be interested to know that I was coming here. Marshal Kutusoff had sent me with a message to Lieutenant General Wittgenstein and after that had given me my liberty to make my way to Wilkomir."

"As my Emperor had sent me to Marshal Victor with a similar permission."

"Doubtless with the same message."

And the two brothers were both soldiers enough to understand the desires of their respective captains, without further questioning or explanation.

"Doubtless," said Maurice.

"I left my escort and with a *Cossack* pony sledge came this way alone. At my last bivouac something frightened my horse away and I was forced to proceed on foot, dragging the sledge after me. I was frightfully hungry and cold. I do not seem to have your hardy constitution, *monsieur*. I was attacked by wolves. I fought them off as best I could but was at the end of my strength when you came. I heard your pistol shots, saw you spring forward, that is all."

"I was lucky enough to drive them away. They were starved and they fell on the bodies of the slain—"

"Instead of upon me," said the Marquis.

"Yes, I suppose so, or upon me," returned the other.

"And then?"

"Then I gave you a few drops of spirits I happened to have in a flask, laid you on the sledge and dragged you here. It was a short distance and not difficult. Then I carried you up the steps. You weigh little. You are quite as thin and as wasted as most of the soldiers of either army, and—the rest you know."

"Exactly. I was coming here," continued the Marquis, "in accordance with the last interview we had at Orsha to tell the Princess all that had happened and to allow her to decide between us."

"You may spare yourself the trouble," said the Light Horseman. "Pardon me, *madame*," he continued to the Princess and as he turned his face toward her he did not see his brother wince at that marital word, "if you will allow me, I will make it easy for you. The Princess married me with noble self-sacrifice to save my life, thinking to require what she was pleased to call some slight service that I had done her. It was nothing which any gentleman would not have done for any woman. When I unworthily sought to bind her to the engagement she had entered upon for such a purpose, her grandfather interfered, and reminded her that her word was pledged to you and told her that he would use his influence with the *Czar* and enlist the *Czar's* influence with the Church, to cause this marriage ceremony to be annulled and indeed it was irregular at best. He bade her choose between us."

"*Messieurs*," exclaimed the Princess, her breast heaving, her colour high.

But the hussar gently checked her.

"I have not yet finished, *madame*. She chose you, my brother, and last night, carried away by her pity, when I besought her to change her decision, she—" He hesitated. By a great effort he had spoken smilingly, almost carelessly, but now in the last crisis, the smile faded away. His face was suddenly set and grim. He did not dare either to look at the Princess or his brother. He stared into the fire. "She chose—you— finally," he added at last.

A little silence fell over the room. It was broken by the Marquis.

"And I, may I ask you a question, Princess?" he began softly. "Did you choose me because—"

"Because I—because—"

"Because you love me and—"

"*Monsieur*," said the woman slowly, "because I had plighted my word to you, because my honour was involved, because my father, my grandfather wished it."

"Yes, that was six months ago, but last night—"

"Because I had promised my grandfather on his deathbed that I would keep my faith, that I would go to the *Czar* with the petition drawn by his own hands and secure the annulment of this marriage that I might—marry—you."

"But you love me, do you not, Princess?"

And again there was silence.

"*Monsieur*," said the Princess tremulously at last, "I keep my word, is not that enough?"

"My God," burst out the hussar, "I can stand no more of this. Do you think I am not made of flesh and blood? Have you forgot that we have the same father and mother, that the same human passion throbs in my breast? Do you think I am made of ice and snow to be tortured further? She chooses you, I give her up, what more do you wish?"

"Nothing more," answered the Marquis with curious quietness.

"Princess, you spoke of a petition. Have you it?"

"It is here," said the Princess, taking it from the table.

"Will you allow me to look at it?"

She handed it to him without a word. It was unsealed. He opened it and read it carefully. For a moment, Maurice thought his brother might throw it into the fire. Certainly even he could see that the Princess did not love the elder brother, that her affections were given to the younger. But the Marquis did nothing of the sort. He carefully re-folded the paper after he had read it and looked again at the Princess.

"His Majesty the *Czar* will be at Smolensk. You have sledges and ponies and men, I presume. Properly equipped we could make the journey in a few days. We could set out tomorrow. You will accompany us to the *Czar*," he said to his brother.

"In God's name, no," cried Maurice.

"Pardon me, but it is necessary. It will facilitate proceedings and enable us more easily to arrive at the desired end if you see His Majesty in person."

"I tell you I cannot and will not do it!"

"But for the sake of the Princess Idona, her happiness and her future," persisted the Marquis relentlessly.

"It is almost more than I can bear," said the younger brother, "but since you put it in that way, I will go with you."

"I pledge you my word and honour," said the Marquis, "that after you have seen my Emperor, you can go on your way—" he hesitated and added one bitter word—"rejoicing."

"You speak with nice precision, sir, 'On my way rejoicing.' Even so. *Madame*, it is for you and your happiness that I do this and pray God that with my brother you may find that which would have been my fondest dream to have assured, if you could have remained, as you are today, my wife."

CHAPTER 27

The Solitary Conquest From Russia

Twice before the Light Horseman had traversed the way between Wilna and Smolensk. Once in the summer, comfortably and easily; once in the winter, desperately, terribly; now in luxuriously equipped sledges, protected from the rigours of the winter by masses of Russian sables, drawn swiftly over the icy *steppes* by hardy Russian ponies, with plenty to eat and drink and every comfort attended to; yet of the three journeys, this was the most miserable. The first time he had gone over it with a broken heart because the Princess, whom he had married had rejected him, the second time, some little hope shone through the misery but on this last occasion his journey was for the purpose of assuring her freedom and there was absolutely no hope in his heart.

There were many roads here and there in this world over which he had travelled that had pleasant associations for him, and there were roads that he had hated because of things that had happened thereon, but he felt perfectly certain that no spot on earth could ever be so abhorrent to him as this stretch of country.

Instead of following the more southerly highway, the little party had struck straight across the country.

The ice and the snow made the going easy in any direction and they had taken almost a bee-line for their destination.

It was late December now. The broken remnants of the Grand Army had by this time crossed the Niemen. Ney throwing his musket upon the ice of the river had crossed last. No Frenchmen were left alive in Russia except prisoners. Save for the dead bodies of the allied nations they met only Russians on the journey. The rank of the Marquis de Vivonne and the passes with which he had armed himself enabled them to proceed without molestation.

Indeed, they were warmly received by the various divisions of the Russian army which they came across and provided them with everything they needed. For the sake of the Marquis, who explained enough of their errand, no one molested or interfered with Maurice. By the tactful provision of the Princess, each of the three travellers had an individual sleigh. Intercourse between them was of the most formal character and as nothing could dispel the terrible restraint that lay upon them all, it was better that their conversation should be as brief and as impersonal as possible.

Travelling that way, the distance was soon traversed. Late one afternoon the sleighs passed through the ruined gates into the ruined town. As it happened, Maurice had been with Ney among the last Frenchmen to leave it, so he was the only member of the Grand Army to come back to it. Fortunately, as it now turned out, their efforts to complete the destruction of the town had not been attended with entire success. A number of buildings were still standing and the largest and best of them had been hastily made ready for the use of the *Czar* who had left St. Petersburg and had followed in the wake of his advancing army.

The Marquis had but to mention his name and rank to the officer of the Imperial Guard and the name and rank of his fair companion to be received with open arms. The three were at once conducted to an ante-chamber, rudely but comfortably furnished and delightfully warm from a great Russian stove. The ante-chamber was filled with officers coming and going, for the *Czar* took a most active interest in the movements of his army and in fact had only been prevented from accompanying it in person by the most urgent protestations of his ministers. Reports were made to him constantly of every movement and every happening; deputations from the towns and various provinces around about were constantly entering and leaving, and altogether the room was filled with animation and life.

There were, however, no women present and the Princess Idona immediately became the centre of observation and attraction. Several of the officers who had the privilege of her acquaintance spoke to her and she was soon surrounded by an interested group. The Marquis de Vivonne stood by her side while young Maurice drew away and watched them with much bitterness in his heart. The Princess herself was most miserable but she was woman enough to allow nothing of that to be seen and by a great effort she responded in kind to the gay advances and bright compliments of those gallant young Russians. It greatly increased the irritation of the Frenchman that she could laugh and be gay at such a time and under such circumstances. It was more than he could understand and almost more than he could bear.

He was glad, therefore, when an equerry came into the room and summoned the three of them into the presence of the *Czar*. In spite of his preoccupation, Maurice looked with the liveliest interest and curiosity at the great antagonist of his Emperor and with a thrill of pride he realised at once that there was no comparison between the two.

He saw before him a tall, shambling, rather ill-made young man, dressed in the uniform of his Guard, with a very slim waist and a very large breast, almost womanish in shape. Nor did his uniform fit his ill-jointed figure. His epaulets were too high and forward, his arms hung loosely in front of him. An expression, at once frivolous, crafty and bold was on his face. One instinctively felt that he was in the presence of a generous, kindly man, whose courage was absolutely unquestioned, but whose other qualities were not equal to this; and a keen observer would have seen back of all a haunting remorse, perhaps for the death of his father at which he had more than connived, and an anxiety and apprehension as to the future of the great controversy with Napoleon into which he had embarked.

They had been great friends, these two Emperors, at least Alexander had been fascinated by the great Corsican who had honoured him with his regard, and he had been blindly, almost passionately devoted to him with the devotion the weaker nature sometimes feels for the stronger. He had been flattered beyond measure at being admitted into an intimacy with the lord of the world which he persuaded himself no one but he shared. Together these two had partitioned creation but Alexander had presently grown tired of the dominating character of Napoleon.

Removed from the influence of his overwhelming personality, the Russian had awakened to the fact that he was playing the subordinate part and the pride of the Romanoffs had induced him to grasp the chance for rupture produced by Napoleon's excessive demands and exactions against England. And now, as is often the case with weaker natures, the former devotion had been turned into an antagonism and a hatred which was almost equal to his previous admiration. Yet he desired to be regarded as the friend of the French people just in proportion as he was the enemy of Napoleon.

Indeed Napoleon's campaigns had brought the people to the fore and one use of his conquests had been to call to the attention of men that the voice of the people was more often than not the voice of

233

God. Absolutism received its most stunning blow from the absolute himself in the twenty years of his imperious and unquestioned rule.

Alexander was particularly well-affected to those Frenchmen—and they were not few in number—who were members of the old *régime* who had joined his army to whom he had given commands in his Guard. He welcomed, therefore, with a spontaneous smile and with the utmost cordiality, the Marquis de Vivonne. He extended his hand to him and then turned to the Princess Idona.

"My lady," he said in a pleasant and agreeable voice, "what good fortune brings you to the court of camp of a Soldier Emperor in the field? Whatever the reason, I welcome it and you. It is long since we have been cheered by such freshness and beauty. And pray tell me how does my old friend, the Prince, your grandfather?"

"Sire," said the Princess, "I thank you for the warmth of your welcome and I bring you the last greetings of my grandfather, the Prince."

"Is he dead?" asked Alexander in shocked tones. "Have those French—"

"He died quite peacefully in his bed, Sire."

"And your father," continued Alexander tenderly, "was killed at the head of my Guard at Borodino. Your brother laid down his life for Russia at Maloyaroslavets. My poor child."

The Princess bowed, not trusting herself to speak at these terrible recollections.

"And you are the last of your race then?"

"The last one, Your Majesty."

"We must not allow it to die out," said Alexander thoughtfully, "the Muravieffs have served us and Russia well. My child, I will myself look to your future. My sister, the Grand Duchess, is here and if you will join her court—"

"It is about the future of the Princess Idona that we have come, Your Majesty," began the Marquis.

"Ah, is it so?" said the Emperor, "and who may this gentleman be?"

"I am General Maurice, Your Majesty," said the Light Horseman, drawing himself up and saluting, "of the French army."

"A Frenchman within our lines and without a uniform!"

"The uniform of my rank I have worn out in the service of France and I was forced to don these clothes given to me by the Princess in default of any other."

"He is in my company, Your Majesty," said the Marquis.

"And what is he to you, Marquis?"

"He is my brother, Sire, my younger brother."

"And to you, Princess?"

It was Maurice who answered for her.

"I have the honour to be the husband of the Princess Idona, Sire."

"What!" exclaimed the *Czar*, "has she presumed in the absence of my consent, being an orphan she is therefore the ward of the Emperor, to marry and to marry an enemy?"

"Stands the case this way, Your Majesty," began the Marquis.

Clearly and dispassionately, he told the story of the strange marriage of his younger brother and the Princess, of the services rendered to the lady by the young Frenchman, of the forced marriage and all that had happened. The Emperor listened like one entranced. He listened without comment or question until the Marquis stopped.

"Princess," he said, "is this true?"

"Absolutely, Your Majesty."

"And you, sir," he turned to the Light Horseman, "you admit the truth of this?"

"Entirely, Sire."

"I know not whether the marriage would stand," said the *Czar*, "but it is the strangest and most romantic tale I have ever heard."

"The marriage is not to stand, Your Majesty," said the Light Horseman.

"What, *monsieur*! do you repudiate the lady?"

"Before God and Your Majesty, no. To claim her as my own would be the dearest wish of my life, but I yield her to my brother."

"Well," said the Emperor, "how can you yield your wife—"

"Sire, at the decisive moment, the Princess repudiated me. At the request of her grandfather, she bade me begone, she declared her intention of keeping her plighted word."

"But how?"

"By an appeal to you to use your Imperial authority and influence with the Metropolitan of the Holy Orthodox Church and procure the annulment of this marriage so that she may marry my brother."

"Umph," said the Emperor slowly, "and is that your wish, Princess?"

"I—" began the Princess, "Your Majesty, I—"

She stopped.

"Take your time, Princess," said the Emperor kindly, "and speak your mind freely."

"I gave my word, Sire," said the Princess, as she drew from the pocket of the coat she was wearing the papers. "Here is the petition which my grandfather prepared setting forth the facts and asking you to have the marriage annulled. I promised on his deathbed that I would present it to you and that I would second his request with my own. I do so. Ask me no more. I cannot bear anything more."

"But I must ask you," said the Emperor, "do you love the Marquis de Vivonne to whom you are betrothed?"

"I—"

"I must insist upon an answer," said the *Czar*.

"I respect him, I esteem him—"

"But do you love him?"

The Princess stared at him in silence.

"I will change the form of my question," said Alexander, "do you love this gentleman the Comte—is it not?—de Vivonne?"

And again the Princess was silent. Yet in spite of herself the expression of her face altered. She shot one swift glance at the Hussar and the Emperor noted it. So did the elder brother.

"Will Your Majesty permit me to decide?" asked the Marquis at this juncture.

"I will at least hear what you have to say," returned the *Czar* kindly.

"Sire, when my brother elected to follow the Emperor Napoleon, my father cursed him and cast him off. I never thought to see him or speak to him again. I hated him as did the rest of my family save my mother. When we met on the field in arms on that day when the Red *Cossacks* were cut to pieces, I could have killed him. Although I do not think him the better swordsman, chance gave him the advantage. He had shortened his sword to strike and I had opened my arms to receive the blow when he recognised me and spared my life."

"Good," said the *Czar*.

"Again at Krasnoi, when my character as envoy was forfeited because Prince Miloradovitch's troops fired on the French while I was under the protection of a white flag, and the half-mad soldiers of Marshal Ney would have stripped me naked, he interposed again."

"Did you know?" asked the *Czar*, turning to the Light Horseman, "that your wife was betrothed to your brother?"

"Not then, Sire."

"And would you have saved him if you had?"

"I can answer that question also, Your Majesty, if you will allow me," continued the Marquis quickly. "My father and I were both with the unfortunate Prince of the House of Condé."

"D'Enghien?"

"Yes, Sire. When he was apprehended and shot we escaped with our lives. The Emperor remembered my connection with his enemy at last when Marshal Ney's corps, what was left of it, joined him at Orsha. He would have had me shot. My brother interposed again. He offered to give back the Grand Cross of the Legion of Honour with which the Emperor had just decorated him. He said he would break his sword and leave his service, if he did not respect my character as envoy and let me go free."

"And the Emperor Napoleon—"

"He was pleased to give me a safe conduct, Sire."

"He bade me keep the cross and nobly gave the Marquis, my brother, his liberty," added Maurice in turn.

"And did you know then?"

"Then I knew, Sire."

"And did you regret the impulse that spared his life?"

"That question I again can answer better than anyone, Your Majesty," interposed the Marquis once more. "My brother was charged with a message to Marshal Victor, I with one to Prince Wittgenstein with both of us free after the delivery of our messages. We met in the woods of Wilkomir. I was attacked by a band of starving wolves. I had lost my horse and was at the end of my strength. It was my brother who drove them off and rescued me. He dragged me to the *chateau*, carried me into the hall—"

"And presented me with my betrothed, Your Majesty," said the Princess.

"It is marvellous," said the Emperor. "He has four times saved your life, then?"

"Yes, Sire, and for that reason, if for none other, I resign all pretensions to the hand of the Princess. If she loved me—"

"Philippe, my brother," cried the Light Horseman.

"Maurice, she is yours, your wife in the sight of God, and God forbid that I should take her away from you. If she loved me, it would be different. I would fight for her until the end, but Your Majesty sees—"

"Marquis de Vivonne," said the Princess, her face aflame, her eyes alight, she stepped closer to him as she spoke—"I never came so near loving you as at this moment."

"You see," said the Marquis, with a certain melancholy dignity, turning toward the *Czar*.

Alexander nodded.

"I see," he said, "a beautiful woman. I see two brave, gallant gentlemen, neither to be outdone in magnanimity by the other. One of them is to go from my presence happy, the other miserable, for I see how you both love the woman, who is worthy of the affections of such men. Yet the misery of the one whose hopes are doomed to disappointment is salved by the consciousness that he has acted like a gentleman and a man of honour and if I may be permitted to say so, he has gained the admiration and receives the highest commendation of his Emperor. Marquis de Vivonne, the *Czar* approves of your course.

"You have done well, sir. General Maurice, if so you are called, although we are in arms against each other, I cannot count you an enemy. You have deserved the Princess and I give her to you. Princess Idona, I take it that the disposition of the problem in this way is in accordance with your own wishes. I would have been happier had you remained in Russia and had your affections fallen upon the Marquis, my trusted friend, but I am glad that your husband is not unworthy of your rank, your birth and your beauty. You have nobly and faithfully carried out the wishes of your grandsire. Give me the petition."

With a slow movement, as if half uncomprehending, though her heart was throbbing at this delightful consummation of which she had not had even the faintest expectation or hope, the Princess extended the paper. The Emperor took it from her.

"As *Czar* of all the Russias I deny this petition," he said, tearing it across. "It is with regret that I say no to my dead friend's request, but the happiness of his granddaughter, which, after all, is what he would most desire, is the paramount consideration. The marriage must stand."

A good deal of the littleness and insignificance of the Emperor disappeared as he drew himself up, quite imperial in his graceful and generous decision.

"Your Majesty," said the Light Horseman, "next to my own Emperor, you will always be highest in my heart and from the bottom of it, I thank you."

"That marriage," said the Emperor, "was a trifle irregular. We will have it celebrated again by my own chaplain. I myself will give away the bride. General Maurice, you are, I believe, save the prisoners, the last Frenchman in Russia. Those who are left alive are now beyond the Niemen. My army will follow them there. If I must have enemies, I am glad that they are of your stamp. You shall be provided with an imperial safe conduct for your wife and yourself to within your own lines. When we meet again, remember me as one who, though he is your Emperor's enemy, and therefore yours, wishes you well and when peace shall come, as come it must please God sooner or later, if I am alive to celebrate it you and the Princess shall ever be welcome at our court."

There is but little left to tell. The marriage was solemnised that very night before the *Czar* and all his court. The Marquis de Vivonne stood by the side of his brother. Though it broke his heart, he declared he would not deny himself the privilege. The Emperor having summoned the Grand Duchess and some of the ladies was very gay that evening, evidently very much pleased with the charming role he had played. The next day found the happy young couple on the way to the Niemen and to France.

A month later the soldier and his bride presented themselves before their own Emperor in Paris. Napoleon was furiously busy. He was recruiting another army to take the place of that which had been lost in Russia. Like the ancient Roman it seemed that he had but to stamp on the ground to bring forth armed men. All over France young and old were assembling, gigantic plans were maturing. The Emperor, with his unrivalled capacity for infinite detail work, was organising armies and making all the preparations for the war which was inevitable in the spring. He had led the nations against Russia and lost and he realised that Russia would lead the nations against him. Would they lose or would he? If he did it would not be because of indifference or supineness or want of effort.

So many experienced officers had died in Russia that every one left was worth his weight in gold and he welcomed Maurice and his bride almost with open arms.

"I made you General of Brigade, or was it of Division?"

"I think Your Majesty indicated that if I got through and discharged my errand I should have a division."

"And well did you discharge that errand. Victor was at Borisoff in time. Disastrous as was the crossing of the Beresina—you have heard?"

"Yes, Sire."

"It would have been impossible but for his corps. You shall have your division in the third corps, the corps of Marshal Ney here and perhaps at the end of the campaign you may be in command of a corps and you may even some day carry the baton of a Marshal of France."

"Speed that day, Sire," said a great voice from a huge man whose red head towered above the Emperor, "I am glad to have Maurice under my command again. I know him."

"And you, *madame*, do you know that saving the Empress, my wife, you are the most precious of women," said the Emperor with a little touch of grave sadness in his voice.

"I do not understand, Sire," said the Princess, looking at him wonderingly.

"You are our only conquest in Russia, the only trophy of a campaign in which more than five hundred thousand men laid down their arms."

The Eagle of the Empire

Contents

Dedication

Dedications have gone out of vogue save with the old fashioned. The ancient idea of an appeal to a patron has been eliminated from modern literature. If a man now inscribes a book to anyone it is that he may associate with his work the names of friends he loves and delights to honour. There is always a certain amount of assurance in any such dedication, the assurance lying in the assumption that there is honour to the recipient in the association with the book. Well, there is no mistaking the purpose anyway.

One of my best friends, and that friendship has been proved in war and peace, at home and abroad, is a Bank! The Bank is like Mercy in more ways than one, but particularly in that it is twice blessed; it is blessed in what it receives, I hope, and in what it gives, I know. From the standpoint of the depositor sometimes it is better to receive than to give. It has been so in my case and I have been able to persuade the Bank to that way of thinking.

Therefore, in grateful acknowledgment of the very present help it has been to me in time of need and in public recognition of many courtesies from its officers and directors, and as some evidence of my deep appreciation of its many kindnesses to me, I dedicate this book to

The Mount Vernon Trust Company
of
Mount Vernon, New York

Preface

The Battle of Waterloo, which was fought just one hundred years ago and with which the story in this book ends, is popularly regarded as one of the decisive battles of the world, particularly with reference to the career of the greatest of all Captains. Personally some study has led me to believe that Bautzen was really the decisive battle of the Napoleonic wars. If the Emperor had there won the overwhelming victory to which his combinations and the fortunes of war entitled him he would still have retained his Empire. Whether he would have been satisfied or not is another question; and anyway as I am practically alone among students and critics in my opinions about Bautzen they can be dismissed. And that he lost that battle was his own fault anyway!

However Napoleon's genius cannot be denied any more than his failure. In this book I have sought to show him at his best and also almost at his worst. For sheer brilliance, military and mental, the campaigning in France in 1814 could not be surpassed. He is there with his raw recruits, his beardless boys, his old guard, his tactical and strategical ability, his furious energy, his headlong celerity and his marvellous power of inspiration; just as he was in Italy when he revolutionized the art of war and electrified the world. Many of these qualities are in evidence in the days before Waterloo, but during the actual battle upon which his fate and the fate of the world turned, the tired, broken, ill man is drowsily nodding before a farmhouse by the road, while Ney, whose superb and headlong courage was not accompanied by any corresponding military ability, wrecks the last grand army.

And there is no more dramatic an incident in all history, I believe, than Napoleon's advance on the Fifth-of-the-line drawn up on the Grenoble Road on the return from Elba.

Nor do the Roman Eagles themselves seem to have made such

romantic appeal or to have won such undying devotion as the Eagles of the Empire.

This story was written just before the outbreak of the present European war and is published while it is in full course. Modern commanders wield forces beside which even the great Army of the Nations that invaded Russia is scarcely more than a detachment, and battles last for days, weeks, even months—Waterloo was decided in an afternoon!—yet war is the same. If there be any difference it simply grows more horrible. The old principles, however, are unchanged, and over the fields upon which Napoleon marched and fought, armies are marching and fighting in practically the same way today. And great Captains are still studying Frederick, Wellington and Bonaparte as they have ever done.

The author modestly hopes that this book may not only entertain by the love story, the tragic yet happily ended romance within its pages—for there is romance here aside from the great Captain and his exploits—but that in a small way it may serve to set forth not so much the brilliance and splendour and glory of war as the horror of it.

We are frightfully fascinated by war, even the most peaceable and peace-loving of us. May this story help to convey to the reader some of the other side of it; the hunger, the cold, the weariness, the suffering, the disaster, the despair of the soldier; as well as the love and the joy and the final happiness of the beautiful Laure and the brave Marteau to say nothing of redoubtable old Bal-Arrêt, the Bullet-Stopper—whose fates were determined on the battlefield amid the clash of arms.

Cyrus Townsend Brady.

The Hemlocks,
Edgecliff Terrace, Park-Hill-On-Hudson.
Yonkers, N.Y.
Epiphany-Tide, 1915.

Prologue

The weatherworn Château d'Aumenier stands in the midst of a noble park of trees forming part of an extensive domain not far to the northwest of the little town of Sézanne, in the once famous county of Champagne, in France. The principal room of the castle is a great hall in the oldest part of the venerable pile which dates back for eight hundred years, or to the tenth century and the times of the famous Count Eudes himself, for whom it was held by one of his greatest vassals.

The vast apartment is filled with rare and interesting mementos of its distinguished owners, including spoils of war and trophies of the chase, acquired in one way or another in the long course of their history, and bespeaking the courage, the power, the ruthlessness, and, sometimes, the unscrupulousness of the hard-hearted, heavy-handed line. Every country in Europe and every age, apparently, has been levied upon to adorn this great hall, with its long mullioned windows, its enormous fireplace, its huge carved stone mantel, its dark oak panelled walls and beamed ceiling. But, the most interesting, the most precious of all the wonderful things therein has a place of honour to itself at the end farthest from the main entrance.

Fixed against this wall is a broken staff, or pole, surmounted by a small metallic figure. The staff is fastened to the wall by clamps of tempered steel which are further secured by delicate locks of skilful and intricate workmanship. The pole is topped by the gilded effigy of an eagle.

In dimensions the eagle is eight inches high, from head to feet, and nine and a half inches wide, from wing tip to wing tip. Heraldically, "*Un Aigle Éployé*" it would be called. That is, an eagle in the act of taking flight—in the vernacular, a "spread eagle." The eagle looks to the

249

left, with its wings half expanded. In its talons it grasps a thunderbolt, as in the old Roman standard. Those who have ever wandered into the Monastery of the Certosa, at Milan, have seen just such an eagle on one of the tombs of the great Visconti family. For, in truth, this emblem has been modelled after that one.

Below the thunderbolt is a tablet of brass, three inches square, on which is a raised number. In this instance, the number is five. The copper of which the eagle is moulded was originally gilded, but in its present battered condition much of the gilt has been worn off, or shot off, and the original material is plainly discernible. If it could be lifted its weight would be found to be about three and a half pounds.

Around the neck of the eagle hangs a wreath of pure gold. There is an inscription on the back of it, which says that the wreath was presented to the regiment by the loyal city of Paris after the wonderful Ulm campaign.

One of the claws of the eagle has been shot away. The gold laurel wreath has also been struck by a bullet, and some of its leaves are gone. The tip of one wing is missing. The head of the eagle, originally proudly and defiantly erect, has been bent backward so that, instead of a level glance, it looks upward, and there is a deep dent in it, as from a blow. And right in the breast gapes a great ragged shot-hole, which pierces the heart of the proud emblem. The eagle has seen service. It has been in action. It bears its honourable wounds. No attempt has been made to repair it.

The staff on which the eagle stands has been broken at about half its length, presumably by a bullet. The shattered, splintered end indicates that the staff is made of oak. It had been painted blue originally. The freshness of the paint has been marred. On one side, a huge slice has been cut out of it as if by a mighty sword stroke. The tough wood is gashed and scarred in various places, and there is a long, dark blur just above the broken part, which looks as if it might be a blood stain.

Below the eagle, and attached to the remainder of the staff for about three-fourths of its length, is what remains of a battle flag. The material of it was originally rich and heavy crimson silk, bordered with gold fringe. It is faded, tattered, shot-torn, bullet-ridden, wind-whipped; parts of it have disappeared. It has been carefully mounted, and is stretched out so as to present its face to the beholder. In dull, defaced letters of gold may be read inscriptions—the imagination piecing out the missing parts. Here is a line that runs as follows:

Napoleon, Empereur des Français, au 5e Infanterie de la Ligne.

And underneath, in smaller and brighter letters, as if a later addition:

Grenadiers du Garde Imperiale.

There has been some sort of device in the middle, but most of it has disappeared. From what remains, one guesses that it was a facsimile of the eagle on the staff-head. There are little tarnished spots of gold here and there. A close observation discloses that they are golden bees. In the corners near the staff, the only ones that are left are golden wreaths in the centre of which may be seen the letter "N".

On the other side of the flag, hidden from the beholder, are a series of names. They have been transcribed upon a silver plate, which is affixed to the wall below the broken staff. They read as follows:

Marengo; Ulm; Austerlitz; Jena; Berlin; Eylau; Friedland; Madrid; Eckmuhl; Wagram; Vienna; Smolensk; Moskowa; Bautzen; Leipsic; Montmirail; Arcis.

Beneath this list is a heavy dash and below all in larger letters, which unlike the rest have been filled with black enamel, is the last word,

WATERLOO.

The eagle, the staff, and the flag are enclosed and protected from careless handling by a heavy glass case, the panes set in steel and silver, and the doors carefully locked to prevent its being stolen away. But its security is not entrusted to these inanimate materials alone. Every hour of the day and night there keeps watch over it an old soldier. He is armed and equipped as if for battle, in the uniform of the old Fifth Regiment of the Line, somehow temporarily incorporated in the Imperial Guard as a supplementary regiment of the Grenadiers thereof. The black gaiters, the white trousers, the blue and scarlet coat, with its crossed belts and brilliant decorations, the lofty bearskin head-dress, are all strangely in keeping with the relic and its surroundings.

Sometimes the soldier—and there are five of them whose sole and only business it is to watch over the flag—paces steadily up and down in front of it, like a sentry on his post. Sometimes he stands before it at parade rest. As to each individual's movements, he suits his fancy. These are old soldiers, indeed, highly privileged, veterans of twenty campaigns, fifty pitched battles, and smaller affairs without number. Their weather-beaten faces are lined and wrinkled, their moustaches are as white as snow.

The guard is always relieved at the appointed intervals with military formality and precision. One soldier, older, taller than the rest, is in command of the other four. From his buttonhole dangles from a white ribbon a little cross of white enamel. Though he shows no insignia of rank higher than that of a Sergeant of the Guard, he has won the proud distinction of the Legion of Honour.

At one stated hour in the day, a tall, handsome, distinguished, middle-aged man, wearing for the occasion the uniform of a colonel in the Imperial Guard, a blood-stained, tarnished, battered, battle-worn uniform, be it observed, comes into the room. He is more often than not attended by a lovely lady of beauty and grace, in spite of her years, who leads with either hand a handsome youth and a beautiful maiden. The four soldiers are always present in full uniform under the command of their sergeant at this hour.

As the officer enters they form line, come to attention, and present arms, a salute he gravely and punctiliously acknowledges. Attendants follow, bearing decanters and glasses; wine for the officer and his family, something stronger for the soldiers. The glasses are filled. With her own fair hands, the lady hands them to the men. When all are ready the officer holds up his glass. The men, stacking arms, do the same. The eyes of all glance upward. Above the eagle and the flag upon a shelf upon the wall stands a marble head, product of Canova's marvellous chisel. It is Napoleon. White it gleams against the dark stone of the old hall. At a nod the soldiers face about, and——

"*Vive l'Empereur*," says the officer quietly.

"*Vive l'Empereur*," in deep and solemn tones repeats the old sergeant.

"*Vive l'Empereur*," comes from the lips of the four soldiers, and even the woman and the young people join in that ancient acclaim.

The great Emperor is dead long since. He sleeps beneath the willows in the low valley in the lonely, far-off, wave-washed islet of St. Helena. But to these men he will never die. It is their blood that is upon that eagle staff. It was in their hands that it received those wounds. While they carried it, flung to the breeze of battle, it was shot-torn and storm-riven. It is a priceless treasure to them all. As they followed it with the ardour and devotion of youth so they now guard it and respect it with the steadier but not less intense consecration of maturity and old age.

The eagle of a vanished empire, the emblem of a fame that is past.

It is as real to them as when into the hands of one of them it was given by the Emperor himself on the Champ de Mars so long ago when he was lord of the world. And so long as they live they will love it, reverence it, guard it, salute it as in the past.

BOOK 1

THE EMPEROR AT BAY

CHAPTER 1

Bearers of Evil Tidings

The Emperor walked nervously up and down the long, low-ceiled apartment, the common room of the public inn at Nogent. Grouped around a long table in the centre of the room several secretaries were busy with orders, reports and dispatches. At one end stood a group of officers of high rank in rich uniforms whose brilliance was shrouded by heavy cloaks falling from their shoulders and gathered about them, for the air was raw and chill, despite a great fire burning in a huge open fireplace. Their cloaks and hats were wet, their boots and trousers splashed with mud, and in general they were travel-stained and weary. They eyed the Emperor, passing and repassing, in gloomy silence mixed with awe. In their bearing no less than in their faces was expressed a certain unwonted fierce resentment, which flamed up and became more evident when the Emperor turned his back in his short, restless march to and fro, but which subsided as suddenly when he had them under observation. By the door was stationed a young officer in the uniform of the Fifth Regiment of the infantry of the line. He stood quietly at attention, and was evidently there on duty.

From time to time officers, orderlies and couriers came into the room, bearing dispatches. These were handed to the young officer and by him passed over to the Emperor. Never since the days of Job had any man perhaps been compelled to welcome such a succession of bearers of evil tidings as Napoleon on that winter night.

The Emperor's face was pale always, but there was an ashy grayness about his pallor in that hour that marked a difference. His face was lined and seamed, not to say haggard. The mask of imperturbability he usually wore was down. He looked old, tired, discouraged. His usual iron self-control and calm had given place to an overwhelming nervousness and incertitude. He waved his hands, he muttered to himself, his mouth twitched awry from time to time as he walked.

"Well, *messieurs*," he began at last, in sharp, rather high-pitched notes—even his voice sounded differently—as he lifted his eyes from perusing the latest dispatch and faced the uneasy group by the fireplace, "you are doubtless anxious to know the news." The Emperor stepped over to the table as he spoke, and gathered up a handful of dispatches and ran over them with his hands. "It is all set forth here: The Germans and the English have shut up Carnot in Antwerp," he continued rapidly, throwing one paper down. "The Bourbons have entered Brussels,"—he threw another letter upon the table—"Belgium, you see, is lost. Bernadotte has taken Denmark. Macdonald is falling back on Épernay, his weak force growing weaker every hour. Yorck, who failed us once before, is hard on his heels with twice, thrice, the number of his men. Sacken is trying to head him off. The King of Naples seeks to save the throne on which I established him by withdrawing from me now—the poor fool! The way to Paris along the Marne is open, and Blücher is marching on the capital with eighty thousand Russians, Prussians and Bavarians. Schwarzenburg with many more is close at hand."

Something like a hollow groan broke from the breasts of the auditors as the fateful dispatches fell one by one from the Emperor's hand. The secretaries stopped writing and stared. The young officer by the door clenched his hands.

"Sire——," said one of the officers, the rich trappings of whose dress indicated that he was a Marshal of France. He began boldly but ended timidly. "Before it is too late——"

Napoleon swung around and fixed his piercing eyes upon him, as his voice died away. The Emperor could easily finish the uncompleted sentence.

"What, you, Mortier!" he exclaimed.

"I, too, Sire," said another marshal more boldly, apparently encouraged by the fact that his brother officer had broken the ice.

"And you, Marmont," cried the Emperor, transfixing him in turn with a reproachful glance.

Both marshals stepped back abashed.

"Besides," said the Emperor gloomily, "it is already too late. I have reserved the best for the last," he said with grim irony. "The courier who has just departed is from Caulaincourt." He lifted the last dispatch, which he had torn open a moment or two since. He shook it in the air, crushed it in his hand, laughed, and those who heard him laugh shuddered.

"What does the Duke of Vicenza say, Sire?" chimed in another marshal.

"It is you, Berthier," said the Emperor. "You, at least, do not advise surrender?"

"Not yet, Sire."

"But when?" asked Napoleon quickly. Without waiting for an answer to his question, he continued: "The allies now graciously offer us—think of it, gentlemen—the limits of 1791."

"Impossible!" cried a big red-headed marshal.

"They demand it, Prince of the Moskowa," answered the Emperor, addressing Marshal Ney.

"But it's incredible, Sire."

"What!" burst out Napoleon passionately. "Shall we leave France less than we found her, after all these victories, after all these conquests, after all these submissions of kings and nations? Shall we go back to the limits of the old monarchy? Never!"

"But, Sire——" began Marshal Maret.

"No more," said the Emperor, turning upon the Duc de Bassano. "Rather death than that. While we have arms we can at least die."

He flashed an imperious look upon the assembly, but no one seemed to respond to his appeal. The Emperor's glance slowly roved about the room. The young captain met his look. Instantly and instinctively his hand went up in salute, his lips framed the familiar phrase:

"*Vive l'Empereur!* Yes, Sire, we can still die for you," he added in a low respectful voice, but with tremendous emphasis nevertheless.

He was a mere youth, apparently. Napoleon looked at him approvingly, although some of the marshals, with clouded brows and indignant words of protest at such an outburst from so young a man, would have reproved him had not their great leader checked them with a gesture.

"Your name, sir," he said shortly to the young officer who had been guilty of such an amazing breach of military decorum.

"Marteau, Sire. Jean Marteau, at the Emperor's service," answered the young soldier nervously, realizing what impropriety he had committed.

"It remains," said the Emperor, looking back at the marshals and their *aides*, "for a beardless boy to set an example of devotion in which Princes and Dukes of the Empire, Marshals of France, heroes of fifty pitched battles, fail."

"We will die for you, Sire, for France, die with arms in our hands, if we had them, and on the field of battle," began impetuous Ney.

"If we don't starve first, Sire," said cautious Berthier gloomily.

"Starve!" exclaimed the Emperor.

"The army is without food," said Marmont bluntly.

"It is half naked and freezing," added Victor.

"Ammunition fails us," joined in Oudinot.

"We have no arms," added Mortier.

"Do you, then, advise that we abandon ourselves to the tender mercies of the allies?" asked Napoleon bitterly.

"*Messieurs*, it is surely better to die hungry and naked and without arms for the Emperor than to consent to his dishonour, which is the dishonour of France," suddenly burst forth the young man at the door.

"How dare you," thundered the usually cool and collected Berthier angrily, "a mere boy, *monsieur*, assume to speak in the presence of the Emperor, to say nothing of these great captains?"

"May my life be forfeit, *Monsieur le Duc*," said the young soldier more boldly, since Napoleon had condoned his first remark, "if I have done wrong in assuring my Emperor that we would still die for him."

"Of what regiment are you?" said Napoleon, waving Berthier of the frowning face into silence.

"I belong to the fifth of the line, Sire."

"He is in my corps, Sire," said Ney. "I have brigaded that veteran regiment with the new recruits of the Young Guard."

"But I have seen service before," said the young captain.

"And I have seen you before," said Napoleon, fixing upon him a penetrating glance.

"Yes, Sire, at the end of the bridge over the Elster at Leipsic. You were watching the men streaming across when the bridge was blown up. I was among the last to cross the bridge."

"Go on," said the Emperor, as the young man paused.

"Your majesty was pleased to say——"

"I recall it all now. I saw you plunge into the river and bring back to shore an Eagle—that of your regiment. You fell at my feet. You should have had the Legion of Honour for it. I promised it to you, did I not?"

"Yes, Sire."

"Why did you not claim it?"

"I was wounded and left for dead; when I got back to France and my regiment I could not add to your anxiety by——"

"Here," said the Emperor, "I still have power to reward faithful servants and bold spirits." He took off his own cross, fastened it on the heaving breast of the amazed young soldier. "Prince," continued the Emperor, turning to Ney.

"Sire?"

"Spare me this young man. I need him on my staff."

"I can ill spare any officer from my weak corps of boys and old men, much less a veteran," the marshal laughed. "One campaign makes us veterans, it seems, nowadays, but you shall have him."

"Berthier," continued Napoleon, "make out the transfer. Give the young man a step up. Let him be Major."

"Very well, Sire," said Berthier, turning to one of the secretaries and giving him directions.

"Meanwhile, what's to be done?" continued Napoleon.

"Tell Caulaincourt to agree to anything," said Maret bluntly.

"I yet live," said Napoleon proudly. "Naked, starving, unarmed, though we may be, I and my soldiers have not forgot our trade. Courage, *messieurs*. All is not yet lost while your Emperor breathes. Here at Nogent, at Montereau and farther back we still have seventy thousand men. With seventy thousand men and Napoleon much may be accomplished. Blücher, it is true, marches on Paris. He counts on the army of Schwarzenberg to contain us. He marches leisurely, with wide intervals between his divisions. What shall prevent us——"

"Your majesty," cried Marmont, his eyes flashing as he divined the Emperor's plan.

He was the quickest witted and most brilliant of the marshals, but by no means the hardest fighter, or the most loyal and devoted subordinate.

"I am worn out," said the Emperor, smiling more kindly upon them. "I have scarcely been out of the saddle—I have scarcely had an hour of sleep since the bloody day of La Rothière. I must have rest. Let none disturb me for two hours. Hold the messenger from the Duke of Vicenza. I will give an answer then."

The Emperor drooped, as he spoke, much of the animation went out of his face and figure. He looked grayer than ever, heavier than ever, older than ever.

"In two hours awaken me," he said.

He stepped toward the door that led to the room reserved for himself, but before he reached it two officers were admitted. Napoleon stopped and looked at them. They saluted him, walked over to Berthier, the Chief of Staff.

"The soldiers are dying of hunger," said the first. "The Commissary General has nothing to give them. He expected a convoy of provisions, but Cossacks, who are reported at Fontainebleau, have captured the train. What shall we do?"

Berthier threw up his hands, and turned to the other officer to hear his report.

"Ten thousand men are without arms, or with arms unserviceable and broken. The supply of powder is low. Where shall we get any more?"

The silence in the room was terrible.

"Sire," said Berthier in a low voice, turning to Napoleon, standing staring, "you hear?" He stretched out his hand in appealing gesture.

The Emperor turned on his heel, without deigning to look or speak.

"Watch the door for two hours," he said to the young officer, crashing to the door behind him. "Awaken me then."

"Gentlemen," said Berthier despairingly to the other officers, "we shall never persuade him. You had better repair to your commands. Some of you must have something to eat. Divide what you have with the less fortunate divisions. Arm and equip the best men. There is a small supply at Nogent, I am told. The others must wait."

"If we could only get at these pigs of Prussians, these dogs of Russians," said Ney, "we could take food and guns and powder from them."

"Doubtless," said Berthier, not caring to argue that point.

He bowed to the officers, as they saluted, and went out of the door muttering and arguing noisily and insubordinately, it must be admitted, and then turned to the table where the secretaries sat. One of them had laid his head down on his arms, stretched out on the table and was fast asleep. The marshal awoke him and dismissed him with most of the rest. From another Berthier took a paper. He examined it, signed it, sealed it, and handed it to the young officer on guard at the door.

"Your commission, *monsieur*," he said. "Once I was young and full of enthusiasm and hope and determination. It is well for France that some of her children still retain those things."

"I thank the Prince de Wagram," said the young officer, bowing low, "and I beg his pardon for having spoken."

"The Emperor has forgiven," said Berthier indifferently. "His abso-
lution covers us all. At least if I fall behind you in those other qualities
of youth I shall not fall behind you in devotion. Come, Maret," continued the grand marshal.

The two worthies turned away and went out. The long room sank
into silence. A soldier came in after a while and replenished the fire,
saluted and passed out. The pen of the busy secretary, the only one left
of the group, ceased scratching on the paper. He, too, sank back in his
chair asleep. The short day faded into twilight and then into darkness.
From outside beyond the courtyard of the inn came confused noises,
indicating moving bodies of men, the rumble of artillery, the clatter
of cavalry, faint words of command. A light snow began to fall. It was
intensely raw and cold. The officer picked up his cloak, wrapped it
around him, and resumed his immobile guard.

CHAPTER 2

The Emperor Dreams

Within a mean room, which had hastily been prepared for his use, upon a camp bed, having cast himself down, fully clothed as he was, lay the worn-out, dispirited, embittered Emperor. He sought sleep in vain. Since Leipsic, with its horrible disaster a few months before, one reverse of fortune had succeeded another. He who had entered every country a conqueror at the head of his armies, whose myriads of soldiers had overrun every land, eating it up with ruthless greed and rapacity, and spreading destruction far and wide, was now at bay. He who had dictated terms of peace in all the capitals of Europe at the head of triumphant legions was now with a small, weak, ill-equipped, unfed army, striving to protect his own capital.

France was receiving the pitiless treatment which she had accorded other lands. With what measure she had meted out, it was being measured back to her again. The cup of trembling, filled with bitterness, was being held to her shrinking lips, and she must perforce drain it to the dregs. After all Napoleon's far-flung campaigns, after all his overwhelming victories, after the vast outpouring of blood and treasure, after all his glory and all his fame, the end was at hand.

The prostrate Emperor stared out through the low window into the gray sky with its drift of snow across the panes. He heard faintly the tumult outside. Disaster, ruin, despair entered his heart. The young conscripts were disheartened by defeat, the steady old veterans were pitifully few in number, thousands of them were in foreign prisons, many more thousands of them were dead. Disease was rife among the youthful recruits, unused to such hard campaigning, as he had summoned to the colours. Without food and without arms, they were beginning to desert their Eagles. The spirit of the marshals and great officers whom he had raised from the dust to affluence and power was waning. They were worn out with much fighting. They wanted peace, almost at any price. He remembered their eager questions when he had joined the army a month ago.

"What reinforcements has your majesty brought?"

"None," he had been compelled to answer.

"What, then, shall we do?" queried one after the other.

"We must try fortune with what we have," he had declared undauntedly.

Well, they had tried fortune. Brienne, where he had been a boy at school, had been the scene of a brilliantly successful action. They had lost no glory at La Rothière afterward—although they gained nothing else—where with thirty thousand men he had beaten back through one long bloody day and night thrice that number, only to have to retreat in the end for the salvation of those who had been left alive. And, to him who had been wont to spend them so indifferently, men had suddenly become precious, since he could get no more. Every dead or wounded man was now unreplaceable, and each loss made his problem harder to solve.

Since those two first battles he had been forced back, step by step, mile by mile, league by league, everywhere; and all his lieutenants likewise. Now Schwarzenberg, with one hundred and thirty thousand men, confronted him on the Seine and the Aube, and Blücher, with eighty thousand men, was marching on Paris by way of the Marne, with only Macdonald and his beaten and dispirited men, not ten thousand in number, to hold the fiery old Prussian field marshal in check.

"How had it all come to this, and why?" the man asked himself, and, with all his greatness and clearness of vision, the reason did not occur to him. For he had only himself to blame for his misfortunes. He was not the man that he had been. For a moment his old spirit had flashed out in the common room of the inn two hours before, but the reaction left him heavy, weary, old, lonely. Physically, he felt unequal to the strain. His human frame was almost worn out. Mere men cannot long usurp the attributes of God. Intoxicated with success, he had grasped at omnipotence, and for a time had seemed to enjoy it, only to fail. The mills of the gods do grind slowly, but they do grind immeasurably small in the end.

What a long, bloody way he had traversed since Toulon, since Arcola, since the bridge at Lodi, since Marengo? Into what far-off lands it had led him: Italy, Egypt, Syria, Spain, Austria, Prussia and the great, white, cold empire of the North. And all the long way paved with corpses—corpses he had regarded with indifference until today.

It was cold in the room, in spite of the fire in the stove. It reminded him of that dreadful retreat. The Emperor covered his face with his hand. No one was there. He could afford to give away. There rose before him in the darkness the face of the wife of his youth, only to be displaced by the nearer woman, the Austrian wife and the little son whom he had so touchingly confided to the National Guard a month ago when he left Paris for the last try with fortune for his empire and his life. Would the allies at last and finally beat him; would Francis Joseph, weak monarch whom he hated, take back his daughter, and with her Napoleon's son, and bring him up in Austria to hate the name of France and his father? The Emperor groaned aloud.

The darkness fell upon the world outside, upon the room within, upon the soul of the great captain approaching the *nadir* of his fortunes, his spirit almost at the breaking point. To him at last came Berthier and Maret. They had the right of entrance. The time for which he had asked had passed. Young Marteau admitted them without question. They entered the room slowly, not relishing their task, yet resolute to discharge their errand. The greater room outside was alight from fire and from lanterns. Enough illumination came through the door into the bedchamber for their purpose—more than enough for the Emperor. He turned his head away, lest they should see what they should see. The two marshals bowed and stood silent.

"Well?" said the Emperor at last, his voice unduly harsh, as if to cover emotion with its roughness, and they noticed that he did not look at them.

"Sire, the courier of the Duke of Vicenza waits for his answer," said Maret.

There was another long pause.

"Will not your majesty give way for the good of the people?" urged Berthier. "Give peace to France, sire. The army is hungry——"

"Am I God, *messieurs*, to feed thousands with a few loaves and fishes?" cried the Emperor bitterly.

"No, Sire. Therefore, authorize the duke to sign the treaty, and——"

"What!" said Napoleon fiercely, sitting up on the bed and facing them. "You would have me sign a treaty like that? Trample under foot my coronation oath? Unheard-of disaster may have snatched from me the promise to renounce my own conquests, but give up those before me, never! Leave France smaller, weaker than I found her! God keep me from such a disgrace. Reply to Caulaincourt, since you wish it, but tell him I reject this treaty. We must have better terms. I prefer to run the uttermost risks of war."

Berthier opened his mouth to speak again, but Napoleon silenced him with word and gesture.

"No more," he said. "Go."

The two marshals bowed and left the room with downcast heads and resentful hearts. As they disappeared Napoleon called after them.

"Send me that boy at the door. Lights," he cried, as the young officer, not waiting for the order to be repeated, promptly entered the inner room and saluted. "The maps on the table, bring them here, and the table, too," commanded the Emperor.

Even as the lights which were placed on the table dispelled the dusk of the room, so something had dispelled the gloom of the great man's soul. For a moment he looked almost young again. The gray pallor left his cheeks. Fire sparkled in his eyes.

"Not yet—not yet," he muttered, spreading the maps upon the table. "We will have one more try with fortune. My star is low on the horizon, but it has not set yet."

"Nor shall it set, Sire, while I and my comrades live," returned Marteau.

"You are right," said the Emperor. "You stand to me for France. Your spirit typifies the spirit of my soldiery, does it not?"

"Theirs is even greater than mine, Sire," was the prompt answer.

"That's well. Do you know the country hereabouts?"

"I was born at Aumenier."

"Let me see," said the Emperor, "the village lies beyond Sézanne?"

"Yes, Sire."

"In an opening in the great woods beyond the marshes of St. Gond," continued the other, studying the map, "there is a *château* there. Are you by any chance of the ancient house of Aumenier?"

"My father was a warden on the estates of the last marquis."

"Good. Do you know that country?"

"I have hunted over every rod of it as a boy, Sire."

"I must have news," said the Emperor, "information, definite tidings. I want to know where Blücher is; where his several army corps are. Can I trust so young a head as yours with great matters?"

"Tortures could not wring from me anything you may confide, your majesty," said the young man resolutely.

"I believe you," said the Emperor, looking at him keenly and reading him like a book. "Look. Before daybreak Marmont marches to Sézanne. The next day after I follow. I shall leave enough men behind the river here to hold back Schwarzenberg, or at least to check him if he advances. With the rest I shall fall on Blücher."

The young man's eyes sparkled. He had been bending over the map. He drew himself up and saluted.

"It is the Emperor at his best," he said.

"You have studied the art of war, young sir?"

"I have read every one of your majesty's campaigns."

"And you see what I would do?"

"Not altogether, but——"

"Fall upon the flank of the unsuspecting Prussian, burst through his line, break his centre, turn to the right or left, beat him in detail, drive him back, relieve Paris, and then——"

"And then, Sire?"

"Come back and do the same thing with Schwarzenberg!"

"Your majesty!" cried the young soldier, as the whole mighty plan was made clear to him.

"Ha! It brightens your eyes and flushes your cheek, does it not? So it will brighten the eyes and flush the cheeks of France. I will show them. In six weeks I will drive them across the Rhine. In another month they shall sue for peace and the Vistula shall be our boundary."

"What does your majesty desire of me?"

"That you go at once. Take with you whomsoever you will. Bring or send me reports. You are educated?"

"I was a student at your majesty's Military College," answered the young man.

"Did you finish there?"

"I finished in your majesty's army last year."

"How old are you?"

"Twenty-two, Sire."

"You belong to the foot, but you can ride?"

"Anything."

"Marshal Berthier will give you horses. I shall be at Sézanne the day after tomorrow night. You will have news for me then?"

"Or be dead, Sire."

"I have no use for dead men. Don't get yourself taken. Any fool can die, or be made prisoner. It is a wise man who can live for me and France."

266

"I shall live," said the young man simply. "Have you any further command, Sire?"

"None."

The hand of Marteau was raised in salute.

"Stop," said the Emperor, as the soldier turned to the door.

"Sire?"

"Come back with news, and let us but escape from this tightening coil, and you shall be a lieutenant colonel in my guard."

"I will do it for love of your majesty alone," cried the soldier, turning away.

It was not nearly dawn before Berthier and Maret, who had been pondering over the dispatch to Caulaincourt, who was fighting the envoys of the allies at the Congress at Chatillon, ventured to intrude upon the Emperor. Having come to his decision, as announced to the young soldier, who had got his horses and his comrade and gone, the Emperor, with that supreme command of himself which few men possessed, had at last got a few hours of rest. He had dressed himself with the assistance of his faithful valet, Constant, who had given him a bath and shaved him, and he now confronted the two astonished marshals with an air serene—even cheerful.

"Dispatches!" he said, as they approached him. "It is a question of a very different matter. Tell Caulaincourt to prolong the negotiations, but to concede nothing, to commit me to nothing. I am going to beat Blücher. If I succeed, the state of affairs will entirely change, and we shall see what we shall see. Tell Marmont to give orders for his corps to march immediately after they get some breakfast. No, they may not wait till morning. Fortune has given the Prussians into my hands. Write to my brother in Paris; tell him that he may expect news from us of the most important character in forty-eight hours. Let the Parisians continue their *misérérés* and their forty-hour-long prayers for the present. We'll soon give them something else to think of."

"But, Sire——" feebly interposed Berthier.

"Do as I tell you," said the Emperor, good-humouredly, "and leave the rest to me." He was in a mood apparently that nothing could dash that morning. "And you will be as much surprised as the Prussians, and I believe that nobody can be more amazed than they will be."

CHAPTER 3

The Army Marches Away

Gallantly on his errand rode young Marteau. Napoleon's order to Berthier, by him transmitted down the line, had secured four of the best horses in the army for his messengers. For young Marteau went not alone. With him rode a tall grenadier of the Imperial Guard, whose original name had been lost, or forgot, in a sobriquet which fitted him perfectly, and which he had richly earned in a long career as a soldier. They called him "Bullet Stopper," "*Balle-Arrêtante,*" the curious compound ran in French, and the soldiers clipped it and condensed it into "*Bal-Arrêt!*"

He used to boast that he had been wounded in every country in Europe and in Asia and Africa as well. He had been hit more times than any soldier high or low in the army. He had distinguished himself by valour, and, but for his humble extraction and meagre education, might have risen to a high command. As it was, he was personally known to the Emperor, and was accounted as one of the favourite soldiers of the army.

He, too, had been a dweller on the Aumenier estates. It was his tales of adventure which had kindled the martial spirit in young Marteau, whom he had known from his birth. A warm friendship subsisted between the young officer and the old soldier, which no difference in rank or station could ever impair. When the Emperor had given him leave to take with him whomsoever he would, his thoughts had at once turned to old Bullet Stopper. The latter had gladly accepted the invitation.

Behold him now, his huge body astride of an enormous horse—for, although the grenadier was a foot-soldier, he could still ride after a fashion—plodding along through the mud and the wet and the cold on the mission which, if successful, would perhaps enable Napoleon to save the army and France, to say nothing of his throne and his family.

Captain Marteau, or Major Marteau, to give him his new title, had said nothing as to the nature of his mission, upon which they had been dispatched, to the humble comrade, the faithful follower who accompanied him. He had only told him that it was difficult, dangerous, and of vital importance, and he had explained to him that his familiarity with the country, as well as a warm-hearted admiration and respect for his shrewdness and skill and courage, had caused his selection. That was enough for the old soldier; dangers, difficulties, were as the breath of life to the veteran. And he was always happy to follow Marteau, in whose career he took an interest almost fatherly.

The weather was frightful. It had snowed and then thawed. The temperature was now just above the freezing point. The rough wind was raw, the fierce winter gale was laden with wet snow. The roads, like all country cross-roads in France, or anywhere else, for that matter, in that day, were a sea of mud. It was well that the pair had brought two extra horses. By changing mounts from time to time they were enabled to spare their beasts and make the greater speed. The Emperor had impressed upon his young *aide* the necessity for getting the information to him at the earliest possible moment. Haste was everything. So they pressed on.

Without waiting for their report, and presuming on his general knowledge of Blücher's character and shrewdly deducing the exact state of affairs Napoleon was already acting as if he possessed absolute and accurate information. The drums were beating the long roll as they rode through the still dark streets of the little town of Nogent. Horses were being harnessed to guns, baggage wagons were being loaded, ammunition *caissons* were being got ready. The troops were assembling out of houses and tents, and coming from around fires, where many of them had passed an unsheltered night.

There was little of the joy, the gaiety, the *élan* of the French soldier, to be seen in the faces of the men thus summoned to the Eagles. They came, indeed, they answered the call, but with black looks and sullen faces and a manner almost despairing. They had fought and fought and fought. They had been beaten back and back and back, and when they had not been fighting they had been retreating. And always they were hungry. And always they were cold.

The enormous armies of Schwarzenberg had been extended on either side. They were constantly threatened with being outflanked.

Most of them were young soldiers, weary and dispirited, and many of them unarmed. Every battle had reduced the stock of good muskets. Many of those still in possession of the troops had been ruined by their unskilful handling.

The supply of regimental officers was utterly inadequate to the demand. The bravest and the best are usually the first to fall; the boldest and most venturesome the most liable to capture. Perhaps, if the Emperor had broken up his guard and distributed the veterans among the raw troops, the effect might have been better, but in that case he would have destroyed his main reliance in his army. No, it was better to keep the guard together at all hazards. It had already been drawn heavily upon for officers for other corps.

War was popularly supposed to be a thing of dashing adventure, of victory, and plunder. It had been all that before. Experience had thrust them all unprepared face to face with the naked reality of defeat, disease, weary marches over awful roads in freezing cold, in drifting snow, or in sodden mire. They had no guns, they had little food, thank God, there was some clothing, such as it was, but even the best uniforms were not calculated to stand such strains as had been imposed upon these.

Only the old guard, staunch, stern, splendid, indomitable, a magnificent body of men, held the army together—they and the cavalry. Murat, peerless horseman, was playing the traitor to save his wretched Neapolitan throne. But Grouchy, Nansouty, Sebastiani and others remained. Conditions were bad in the cavalry, but they were not so bad as they were in the infantry. And Druot of the artillery also kept it together in the retreat. Guns, cannon, were more precious almost than men.

Now early that morning, while it was yet dark, they were called up from their broken sleep to undertake what to them was another purposeless march. Even the Eagles drooped in the hands of their bearers. The soldiers did not know, they could not see. The great high roads that led to Paris were being abandoned; they were plunging into unfathomable morasses; they were being led through dark, gloomy, dreadful woods to the northward. Where? For what purpose? The dumb, wrathful, insubordinate, despairful army indeed moved at the will of its master, but largely because it realized that it could not stay where it was, and largely because it was better to move on and die than to lie down and die. They were at least warmer on the march!

The spirit of the guard and of the subordinate officers, say from the colonels down, was good enough, but the generals and the marshals were sick of fighting. They had had enough of it. They had gained all that they could gain in their world-wide campaigns, in fame, money, titles, estates. They had everything to lose and nothing to win. They wanted rest, an opportunity to enjoy. Some of them were devoted to the Emperor, in fact, all of them were, but their own comfort and self-interest bulked larger and larger before them. They saw nothing but defeat at the end of their endeavours, and they wanted to negotiate peace with such honour as could be had while they were still a force to be reckoned with.

Their unwillingness and mutinous spirit, however, had not yet reached its highest development. That came later, and brought treachery in its train. The awful will of the Emperor still overruled them. Wrathfully, insubordinately, protestingly, they still marched when he gave the word.

The Emperor had been working with that furious concentration which he alone of all men seemed to be able to bring about, and which was one of the secrets of his power. Orders borne by couriers had streamed in all directions over the roads. Napoleon was about to undertake the most daring and marvellous campaign of his whole history. The stimulus of despair, the certainty of ruin unless the advance of the allies could be stayed, had at last awakened his dormant energies, filled his veins with the fire of youth and spring.

With that comprehensive eye which made him the master of battlefields and nations he had forseen everything. Soldiers were coming from Spain. He had given instructions to magnify their number and their strength. He shrewdly surmised that their appearance on the left flank would cause the cautious Schwarzenberg to pause, to withdraw his flankers, to mass to meet them. There would be a halt in the advance. The allies still feared the Emperor. Although much of his prestige was gone, they never made little of Napoleon. He intended to leave some of the best troops to confront Schwarzenberg between Nogent and Montereau, under Victor and Oudinot, hard fighters both, with instructions not to engage in any decisive battle, not to allow themselves to be trapped into that, but to stand on the defensive, to hold the River Seine, to retreat foot by foot, if pressed, to take advantage of every cover, to hold the enemy in check, to contest every foot of the way, to assume a strength which they did not have.

He promised that so soon as he had fallen upon Blücher he would send the news and see that it got to Schwarzenberg and the allied monarchs who were with him. Reverses which he hoped to inflict on the Prussian Field Marshal would increase the Austrian hesitation. The Emperor believed that the pressure by Oudinot and Victor would be effective. They would draw in their columns and concentrate.

After he had finished with Blücher and his army, he intended to retrace his steps and do the same thing with Schwarzenberg. Of course, if he failed with Blücher it was all over. He was the last hope of France—he and his army. If his magnificent dash at the Prussians and Russians was not successful, nothing could delay the end. Napoleon was staking all on the throw, taking the gambler's chance, taking it recklessly, accepting the hazard, but neglecting no means to insure the winning of the game.

The Emperor flung a screen of cavalry in front of Marmont, to patrol every village, to control every farmhouse, to see that no news of his advance came to the unsuspecting old Prussian. And then he himself stayed back in Nogent to see his own orders carried out. He personally inspected every division, as it marched to the front through the waning night, the cheerless dawn, the gray dark day. It cut him to the heart to see his soldiers go so silently and so sullenly. Here and there a regiment did cry: "*Vive l'Empereur*"; here and there a voice sounded it, but in the main the men marched dumbly, doggedly. It was only the old guard that gave him the imperial salute in full voice in the old way.

Nothing indicated to the Emperor more thoroughly the temper of the soldiers than that open indifference. Why, even in Russia, ere their stiffened lips froze into silence, they had breathed out the old acclaim. The Emperor remembered that grenadier who, when told by the surgeon that he feared to probe for a ball that had pierced his breast because he did not know what he would find, "If you probe deep enough to reach my heart," said the soldier with his dying breath, "you will find the Emperor."

Grave-faced and frowning, shivering from time to time in the fierce, raw cold, the Emperor watched the troops march by. Well, the day after tomorrow, if there were any left, they would acclaim him loud enough. The Emperor was cold and cynical. He had never allowed the life of men to stand in the way of his desires, but even his iron nerve, his icy indifference had been shaken. He gave no outward evidence of it, but in his heart he realized more plainly than ever before that when these were gone there were no more. And so, perhaps, his shudder was not altogether due to the cold.

272

Whatever his emotions, he steeled his heart, he made his preparations for the last try with fortune, the last card to be played, the last die to be thrown. What would be the end of it? What would be the result of that final desperate game? The Emperor was a master player—could even his finesse and skill and talent and genius make up for the poor hand that had been dealt him because the pack had been so drawn upon that the good cards had been exhausted, used up, long since?

Did the Emperor realize that even he was not what he had been? Did he comprehend that he was no longer the soldier, the man, of the past? Did he realize that at last he had tried the patience of that fortune he had worshiped, beyond the limit; and that whatever favour might be vouchsafed him would only delay the end?

The boys might march and fight, the old guard might sustain its ancient fame, the genius of the Emperor might flash out in full effulgence once more—and it would make no difference. The stars on their courses fought against Sisera. The doom sentence was written. Postponement he might look forward to, but no final stay of judgment! A few thousand more lives he might throw away, but these late sacrifices would avail nothing. Oh, no; the Emperor's shudder was not altogether due to the cold that winter morning.

CHAPTER 4

Marteau And Bal-Arrêt Ride

Of this young Marteau and old Bullet Stopper, plodding along at the best speed they could get from their horses, knew nothing. The old grenadier was laconic by nature, and his habit of silence had become intensified by his years of subordination and service. The young officer was wrapped in his own thoughts. Knowing, as they did, every foot of the way, the two were able to find short cuts, take advantage of narrow paths over the hills and through the woods, which would have offered no passage to the army, even if they had been aware of it. They reached Sézanne hours before Marmont's advance, long before the cavalry even.

Baiting their horses, and getting a welcome meal at the inn—the town itself had as yet suffered nothing from the ravages of the Cossacks, being too strong for raiding parties—and refusing to answer questions, and paying no attention to wondering looks of the inhabitants, they rode out again. Their way through the marshes of St. Gond was dreadful. If only the weather would change, the ground would freeze, how welcome would be the altered conditions. But the half snow, the half rain, still beat down upon them. Their poor beasts were almost exhausted. They broke the ice of the Grand Morin River to get water for the horses and themselves, and, not daring to kindle a fire, for they were approaching the country occupied by Blücher, they made a scanty meal from their haversacks.

They had found the farmhouses and *châteaux* deserted, evidences of hasty flight and plunder on every side. The *Cossacks* had swept through the land beyond the town. The people who could had fled to Sézanne, or had gone westward hurriedly, to escape the raiders. In the ruined villages and farms they came across many dead bodies of old women, old men and children, with here and there a younger woman whose awful fate filled the old soldier and the young alike with grim and passionate rage.

"Yonder," said Marteau, gloomily pointing westward through the darkness, "lies Aumenier and my father's house."

"And mine," added Bullet-Stopper.

There was no need to express the thought further, to dilate upon it. It had been the Emperor's maxim that war should support war. His armies had lived off the country. The enemy had taken a leaf out of his own book. Even the stupid could not fight forever against Napoleon without learning something. The allies ate up the land, ravaged it, turned it into a desert—*lex talionis!*

Marteau's father still lived, with his younger sister. Old Bullet-Stopper was alone in the world but for his friends. What had happened in that little village yonder? What was going on in the great *château*, so long closed, now finally abandoned by the proud royalist family which had owned it and had owned Marteau and old Bullet-Stopper, and all the rest of the villagers, for that matter, for eight hundred years, or until the revolution had set them free?

Plunged in those gloomy thoughts the young officer involuntarily took a step in the direction of that village.

"On the Emperor's service," said the grenadier sternly, catching his young comrade by the arm. "Later," he continued, "we may go."

"You're right," said Marteau. "Let us move on."

Whether it was because the roads really were in a worse condition because of that fact that they ran through marshy country, or whether it was because the men were worn out and their horses more so, they made the slowest progress of the day. They plodded on determinedly through the night. The two weaker horses of the four finally gave way under the strain. Husbanding the remaining two with the greatest care, the two soldiers, passing through the deserted villages of St. Prix, on the Little Morin, and Baye, finally reached the great highroad which ran through Champaubert, Vauxchamps and Montmirail, toward Paris, and which, owing to a northward bend of the river, crossed the country some leagues to the southward of the Marne.

Day was breaking as they reached the edge of the forest bordering the road, and from a rather high hill had a glimpse of a wide stretch of country before them. Fortunately, while it was still raw and cold, the sun came out and gave them a fair view of a great expanse of rolling and open fields. A scene of great animation was disclosed to them. The road was covered with squadrons of green-coated Russian cavalry, evidently just called to the saddle, and moving eastward at a walk or slow trot. They looked like the advance guard of some important division. There was a low, rolling volume of heavy sound coming from the far north, and in the rising sun they thought they could distinguish in that direction smoke, as from a battlefield. The sound itself was unmistakable to the veteran.

"Cannon!" he said. "Fighting there."

"Yes," answered Marteau. "The Emperor said that the Prussians and Russians were pressing the Duke of Tarentum, Marshal Macdonald."

"But what have we here?" asked old Bal-Arrêt, shading his eyes and peering at the array on the near road.

A division of Russians, coming from a defile to the right, had debouched upon a broad plateau or level upon the edge of which the little village of Champaubert straggled forlornly. The *Cossack* horsemen and the Russian cavalry had cleaned out Champaubert. There were no inhabitants left to welcome the Russian division, except dead ones, who could offer no hospitality.

The division was weary and travel-stained, covered with mud, horses dead beat; the cannon, huge, formless masses of clay, were dragged slowly and painfully forward. It was evident that the commander of the division had doubled his teams, but the heavy guns could scarcely be moved, even by twice the number of horses attached. The poor brutes had no rest, for, as fast as one gun arrived, both teams were unhitched and sent over the road to bring up another. A halt was made on the plateau. It was evident to the experienced eyes of the watchers that a camp was about to be pitched. The two men stared in keen interest, with eyes alight with hatred. What they had seen in the country they had just passed intensified that hatred, and to the natural racial antagonism, fostered by years of war, were now added bitter personal resentments.

"That's one of old Marshal Forward's divisions," said the grenadier, referring to Blücher by his already accepted name, "but what one?"

"Russians, by the look of them," answered Marteau.

"You say well. I have seen those green caps and green overcoats before. Umph," answered Bullet-Stopper, making for him an extraordinarily long speech, "it was colder then than it is now, but we always beat them. At Friedland, at Eylau, at Borodino, aye, even at the Beresina. It was the cold and hunger that beat us. What wouldn't the guard give to be where we are now. Look at them. They are so sure of themselves that they haven't thrown out a picket or sentries."

In fact, neither Blücher nor any of his commanders apprehended any danger whatsoever. That Napoleon would dare to fall on them was unthinkable. That there could be a single French soldier in their vicinity save those under Macdonald, being hard pressed by Yorck, never entered anybody's head.

"What Russians are they, do you think?" asked Marteau of his comrade.

"How should I know?" growled the other. "All Russians are alike to me, and——"

Marteau, however, had heard discussions during the time he had been on duty in Napoleon's headquarters.

"That will be Sacken's corps, unless I am very much mistaken," he said.

"And those up yonder toward Épernay, where the firing comes from?" asked the grenadier.

Marteau shook his head.

"We must find out," was the answer.

"Yes, but how?"

"I don't know."

"There is only one way," continued Bal-Arrêt.

"And that is?"

"To go over there, and——"

"In these uniforms?" observed the young officer. "We should be shot as soon as we should appear, and questioned afterward."

"Yes, if there was anything left to question," growled the grenadier. "The Russians will do some scouting. Perhaps some of them will come here. If so, we will knock them on the head and take their uniforms, wait until nightfall, slip through the lines, find out what we can, and go back and tell the Emperor. It is very simple."

"Quite so," laughed the young officer; "if we can catch two Russians, if their uniforms will fit us, if we can get through, if we can find out, if we can get back. Do you speak Russian, Bal-Arrêt?"

"Not a word."

"Prussian?"

"Enough to pass myself through I guess, and——"

"Hush," said the young man, as three Russians suddenly appeared out of a little ravine on the edge of the wood.

They had come on a foraging expedition, and had been successful, apparently, for, tied to a musket and carried between two of the men was a dead pig. How it had escaped the *Cossack* raiders of the day

277

before was a mystery. They were apparently coming farther into the forest for firewood with which to roast the animal. Perhaps, as the pig was small, and, as they were doubtless hungry, they did not wish their capture to be widely known. At any rate, they came cautiously up a ravine and had not been noticed until their heads rose above it. They saw the two Frenchmen just about as soon as they were seen. The third man, whose arms were free, immediately presented his piece and pulled the trigger. Fortunately it missed fire. If it had gone off it might have attracted the attention of the Russian outposts, investigations would have been instituted, and all chance of passing the lines there would have been over.

At the same time he pulled the trigger he fell like a log. The grenadier, who had thrust into his belt a heavy knife, picked up from some murdered woodsman on the journey, had drawn it, seized it by the blade, and, with a skill born of olden peasant days, had hurled it at the Russian. The blade struck the man fairly in the face, and the sharp weapon plunged into the man to the hilt. He threw up his hands, his gun dropped, he crashed down into the ravine stone dead. The next second the two Frenchmen had seized the two Russians. The latter were taken at a disadvantage. They had retained their clutch on the gun-sling carrying the pig, and, before they realized what was toward—they were slow thinkers both—a pair of hands was clasped around each throat. The Russians were big men, and they struggled hard. A silent, terrible battle was waged under the trees, but, try as they would, the Russians could not get release from the terrible grasp of the Frenchmen. The breath left their bodies, their eyes protruded, their faces turned black.

Marteau suddenly released his prisoner, who dropped heavily to the ground. To bind him with his own breast and gun straps and belt was a work of a few moments. When he had finished he tore a piece of cloth from the coat of the soldier and thrust it into his mouth to gag him. The grenadier had a harder time with his enemy, who was the bigger of the two men, but he, too, mastered him, and presently both prisoners lay helpless, bound and gagged. The two Frenchmen rose and stared at each other, a merry twinkle in the eyes of old Bullet-Stopper, a very puzzled expression in those of the young soldier.

"Well, here's our disguise," said the old soldier.

"Quite so," interposed the officer. "But what shall we do with these two?"

"Nothing simpler. Knock them in the head after we have found out what we can from them, and———"

But Marteau shook his head.

"I can't murder helpless prisoners," he said decisively.

"If you had seen what they did to us in Russia you wouldn't have any hesitation on that score," growled the grenadier. "I had comrades whom they stripped naked and turned loose in the snow. Some of them they buried alive, some they gave to the wolves, some they burned to death. I have no more feeling for them than I have for reptiles or devils."

"I can't do it," said the younger soldier stubbornly. "We must think of some other way."

Old Bullet-Stopper stood frowning, trying to think of some argument by which to overcome these foolish scruples, when an idea came to his friend.

"About half a mile back we passed a deserted house. Let's take them there and leave them. There will probably be ropes or straps. We can bind them. They will be sheltered and perhaps somebody may come along and release them."

"Yes, doubtless somebody will," said the grenadier gravely, thinking that if somebody proved to be a peasant their release would be an eternal one, and glad in the thought. "Very well, you are in command. Give your order."

At Marteau's direction the straps around the feet of the men were loosened, they were compelled to get up; they had been disarmed, of course, and by signs they were made to march in the required direction. Casting a backward glance over the encampment, to see whether the absence of the three had been noticed, and, discerning no excitement of any sort, Marteau followed the grenadier and the two prisoners. Half a mile back in the woods stood the hut. It was a stoutly built structure, of logs and stone. A little clearing lay around it. For a wonder it had not been burned or broken down, although everything had been cleaned out of it by raiders. The door swung idly on its hinges. The two Russians were forced to enter the hut. They were bound with ropes, of which there happened to be some hanging from a nail, the door was closed, huge sticks from a surrounding fence were driven into the ground against it, so that it could not be opened from the inside, and the men were left to their own devices.

As neither Frenchman spoke Russian, and as the Russians understood neither French nor Prussian, conversation was impossible. Everything had to be done by signs.

"I wouldn't give much for their chance, shut up in that house in this wood," said the grenadier, as the two walked away.

"Nor I," answered Marteau. "But at least we haven't killed them."

The two Frenchmen now presented a very different appearance. Before they left the hut they had taken off their own great coats, the bearskin shako of the grenadier, and the high, flat-topped, bell-crowned cap of the line regiment of the officer. In place of these they wore the flat Russian caps and the long Russian overcoats. Bal-Arrêt might serve for a passable Russian, but no one could mistake Marteau for anything but a Frenchman. Still, it had to be chanced.

The two retraced their steps and came to the ravine, where the dead Russian lay. They had no interest in him, save the grenadier's desire to get his knife back. It had served him well, it might be useful again. But they had a great interest in the pig. Their exhausted horses were now useless, and they had thought they would have to kill one to get something to eat. But the pig, albeit he was a lean one, was a treasure indeed.

To advance upon the Russian line in broad daylight would have been madness. Darkness was their only hope. Reaching down into the ravine, the grenadier hoisted the body of the poor pig to his comrade, and the two of them lugged it back far in the woods where it was safe to kindle a fire. With flint and steel and tinder, they soon had a blaze going in the sequestered hollow they had chosen, and the smell of savoury roast presently delighted their fancy. They ate their fill for the first time in weeks be it remarked. If they only had a bottle of the famous wine of the country to wash it down they would have feasted like kings.

"So far," said the grenadier, when he could eat no more, "our expedition has been successful. If those youngsters down at Nogent could only smell this pig there would be no holding them."

"I think it would be well to cook as much of it as we can carry with us. I don't know when we may get any more."

"That is well thought on," agreed the old soldier. "Always provide for the next meal when you can."

"And, with what's left, as we can't be far from the hut, we'll give those two poor Russians something to eat."

"You're too tender-hearted, my lad," said Bullet-Stopper, his face clouded, "ever to be a great soldier, I am afraid."

On an expedition of this kind rank was forgotten, and the humble subordinate again assumed the role of the advisor. Marteau laughed.

"Rather than let them starve I would knock them in the head," he said.

"That's what I wanted to do," growled the other savagely.

When it came to the issue, however, he really did respect the rank of his young friend. Accordingly, pieces of the roast pig were taken to the hut and placed in reach of the prisoners, who were found bound as before and looking very miserable. Yet there was something suspicious in their attitude. The old grenadier turned one of them over and discovered that one had endeavoured to free the other by gnawing at the ropes. Not much progress had been made in the few hours that had elapsed, but still it was evident that the rope would eventually be bitten through and the men freed. He pointed this out to his officer.

"Better finish them now," he said.

But Marteau shook his head.

"It will take them all day and night to get free at that rate; by that time we will be far away, and it will be too late."

"But if they should tell what they have seen?"

"What can they tell? Only that two Frenchmen fell upon them. No, let them be. Set the food on the floor here. If they get hungry they can roll over toward it and eat it."

The gags had been taken out of the mouths of the men. If they did give the alarm there would be none to hear them, save perhaps a French peasant passing that way, and at his hands they would meet short shrift.

Having stuffed their haversacks full of roast pig, they retraced their steps and reached the edge of the clearing. It was noon by this time, so much of the day had been spent in the various undertakings that have been described, but the Russians were still there. Evidently they intended to encamp for the day and rest. Probably it was part of the program. These would move on, presumably on the morrow, and another division of the army would come up and take their places. The firing still continued on the horizon.

Marteau, who had a soldierly instinct, divined that the cavalry, which had long since disappeared to the westward, would try to out-flank Macdonald, perhaps get in his rear, and this Russian division would move up and join Yorck's attacking force. The whole proceeding was leisurely. There was no especial hurry. There was no use tiring out the men and fighting desperate battles when manoeuvring would serve.

The two made a more careful investigation and discovered that trees led across the road about half a mile to the left, and, although the roads were filled with galloping couriers and many straggling men and small commands, yet they decided that by going to the edge of the wood that touched the road and watching their opportunity they could get across unnoticed.

While they stared deliberating a squadron of cavalry, not of *Cossacks*, but of Russian *cuirassiers* left the camp and moved off down the cross-road that led to the south and west—the road, indeed, that led to the Château d'Aumenier. The officer in command rode in front and with him were several civilians, at least, while they were covered with heavy fur cloaks, no uniform was visible, and among the civilians was one unmistakably a woman. A Frenchman always had an eye for a woman. The party was too far away to distinguish features, but the two men noted the air of distinction about the party and the way the woman rode her horse, the deference that appeared to be paid to her, and they wasted no little time in wondering what might be toward. However, no explanation presenting itself to their minds, and, the matter being of no great importance after all, they turned their attention to the business in hand.

Working their way through the trees they reached a little coppice close to the road. They lay down on the ground back of the coppice, wormed their way into it, and waited.

"Here we part," said Marteau. "There are but two of us. We must get all the information we can. I will find out what division this is in front of us, and I will go back along the road to the eastward and ascertain where the other divisions are, and by nightfall I will return to Sézanne to report to the Emperor."

"And what am I to do?" asked the grenadier. "Remain here?"

"You will cross the road and proceed in the direction of the firing. Find out, if you can, how the battle goes, what troops are there, what Marshal Macdonald is doing, and at nightfall retrace your steps and hasten back to Sézanne."

"Where shall I meet you?"

"Let me think," answered Marteau. "I shall first go east and then west, if I can get around that division ahead yonder. Let us take the road to d'Aumenier. I will meet you at the old *château* at ten o'clock, or not later than midnight. There is a by-road over the marsh and through the forest by the bank of the river to Sézanne."

"I know it."

"Very well, then. It is understood?"

Old Bullet-Stopper nodded.

"The road is clear," he said. "Good luck."

The two men rose to their feet, shook hands.

"We had better go separately," said Marteau. "You have the longer distance. You first. I will follow."

The officer watched the old grenadier anxiously. He passed the road safely, ran across the intervening space, and disappeared in a little clump of fruit trees surrounding a deserted farmhouse. The young man waited, listening intently for the sound of a shot or struggle, but he heard nothing. Then he turned, stepped out into the road, saw it was empty for the moment, set his face eastward, and moved across it to see what he could find out beyond.

CHAPTER 5

When the Cossacks Passed

For the first time in years the great hall of the Château d'Aumenier was brightly lighted. The ancient house stood in the midst of a wooded park adjacent to the village, overlooking one of the little lakes whose outlets flowed into the Morin. In former days it had been the scene of much hospitality, and, even after the revolution in the period of the consulate and the early empire, representatives of the ancient house had resided there, albeit quietly and in greatly diminished style. The old Marquis Henri, as uncompromising a royalist soldier as ever lived, had fled to England and had remained there. His younger brother, Robert, compromising his dignity and his principles alike, had finally made his submission to Napoleon and received back the estates, or what had not been sequestrated. But he had lived there quietly, had sought no preferment of the government—even rejecting many offers—and had confined his recognition to as narrow limits as possible. He had married and there had been born to him a daughter, whom he had named after the ancient dames of his honourable house, Laure.

The Count d'Aumenier, living thus retired, had fallen into rather careless habits after the death of his wife, and the little *demoiselle* had been brought up indifferently indeed. Dark, brown-eyed, black-haired, she had given promise of beauty to come. Left to her own devices she had acquired accomplishments most unusual in that day and by no means feminine. She could ride, shoot, swim, run, fence, much better than she could dance the old courtly minuet, or the new and popular waltz, just beginning to make its appearance.

A love of reading and an ancient library in which she had a free range had initiated her into many things which the well-brought-up French girl was not supposed to know, and which, indeed, many of them went to their graves without ever finding out. The count had a well-stored mind, and on occasion he gave the child the benefit of it, while leaving her mainly to her own devices.

Few of the ancient nobility had come back to the neighbourhood. Their original holdings had been portioned out among the new creations of the Imperial Wizard, and with them the count held little intercourse. Laure d'Aumenier had not reached the marriageable age, else some of the newly made gentry would undoubtedly have paid court to her. She found companions among the retainers of her father's estate. The devotion of some of them had survived the passionate hatreds of the revolution and, failing the Marquis, who was the head of the house, they loyally served his brother, and with pride and admiration gave something like feudal worship and devotion to the little lady.

The Marquis, an old man now, had never forgiven his brother, the count, for his compromise with principle and for his recognition of the "usurper," as he was pleased to characterize Napoleon. He had refused even to accept that portion of the greatly diminished revenue of the estate which the younger brother had regularly remitted to the Marquis' bankers in London. The whole amount lay there untouched and accumulating, although, as were many other *émigrés*, the Marquis frequently was hard pressed for the bare necessities of life. With every year, as Bonaparte—for that was the only name by which he thought of him—seemed to be more and more thoroughly established on the throne, the resentment of the Marquis had grown. Latterly he had refused to hold any communication with his brother.

The year before the Battle of the Nations, or just before Napoleon set forth on his ill-fated Russian adventure, Count Robert d'Aumenier died. With an idea of amendment, which showed how his conscience had smitten him for his compromise, he left everything he possessed to his brother, the Marquis, including his daughter, Laure, who had just reached her sixteenth year. With the will was a letter, begging the Marquis to take the young *demoiselle* under his charge, to complete that ill-begun and worse-conducted education, the deficiencies of which the father too late realized, in a manner befitting her station, and to provide for her marriage with a proper portion, as if she had been his own daughter. The Marquis had never married himself, lacking the means to support his rank, and it was probable that he never would marry.

The Marquis was at first minded to refuse the bequest and to disregard the appeal, but an old retainer of the family, none other than Jean

Marteau, the elder, complying with Count Robert's dying wish, had taken the young Countess Laure across the channel, and had quietly left her in her uncle's care, he himself coming back to act as steward or agent for the remaining acres of the shrunken Aumenier domain; for the Marquis, having chosen a course and walked in it for so many years, was not minded even for the sake of being once more the lord of Aumenier to go back to France, since the return involved the recognition of the powers that were.

Old Jean Marteau lived in his modest house between the village and the *château*. And the *château* had been closed for the intervening time. Young Jean Marteau, plodding along the familiar way, after a day full of striking adventure and fraught with important news, instantly noticed the light coming through the half moons in the shutters over the windows of the *château*, as he came around a brow of the hill and overlooked the village, the lake and the castle in the clearing. The village was as dark as the *château* was light.

Marteau was ineffably weary. He had been without sleep for thirty-six hours, he had ridden twenty leagues and walked—Heaven only knew how many miles in addition. He had extricated himself from desperate situations only by his courage, daring, and, in one or two cases, by downright fighting, rendered necessary by his determination to acquire accurate information for the Emperor. He had profited, not only by his instruction in the military school, but by his campaigning, and he now carried in his mind a disposition of the Russian forces which would be of the utmost value to the Emperor.

The need of some rest, however, was absolute. Marmont's troops, starting out at the same time he had taken his departure, would barely have reached Sézanne by this time, so much more slowly did an army move than a single person. The Emperor, who had intimated that he would remain at Nogent until the next day, would scarcely undertake the march before morning. Aumenier lay off to the northwest of Sézanne, distant a few miles. If the young *aide* could find something to eat and get a few hours' sleep, he could be at Sézanne before the Emperor arrived and his information would be ready in the very nick of time. With that thought, after staring hard at the *château* in some little wonderment, he turned aside from the road that led to its entrance and made for the village.

His mother had died the year before; his father and his sister, with one or two attendants, lived alone. There was no noble blood in Marteau's veins, as noble blood is counted, but his family had been followers and dependents of the Aumeniers for as many generations as that family had been domiciled in France. Young Jean Marteau had not only been Laure d'Aumenier's playmate, but he had been her devoted slave as well. To what extent that devotion had possessed him he had not known until returning from the military school he had found her gone.

The intercourse between the young people had been of the frankest and pleasantest character, but, in spite of the sturdy respectability of the family and the new principles of equality born of the revolution, young Marteau realized—and if he had failed to do so his father had enlightened him—that there was no more chance of his becoming a suitor, a welcome suitor, that is, for the hand of Laure d'Aumenier than there was of his becoming a Marshal of France.

Indeed, as in the case of many another soldier, that last was not an impossibility. Men infinitely more humble than he in origin and with less natural ability and greatly inferior education had attained that high degree. If Napoleon lived long enough and the wars continued and he had the opportunity, he, too, might achieve that coveted distinction. But not even that would make him acceptable to Count Robert, no matter what his career had been; and even if Count Robert could have been persuaded the old Marquis Henri would be doubly impossible.

So, on the whole, Jean Marteau had been glad that Laure d'Aumenier had gone out of his life. He resolved to put her out of his heart in the same way, and he plunged with splendid energy into the German campaign of 1813, with its singular alternations of success and failure, of victory and defeat, of glory and shame. He had been lucky enough to win his captain's commission, and now, as a major, with a position on the staff of the Emperor, he could look forward to rapid advancement so long as the Emperor lasted. With the bright optimism of youth, even though affairs were now so utterly hopeless that the wise old marshals despaired, Marteau felt that his foot was on the first rung of the ladder of fame and prosperity, and, in spite of himself, as he had approached his native village, he had begun to dream again, almost to hope.

There was something ominous, however, in the appearance of the village in that dark gray evening hour. There were no barking dogs, no clucking hens, no lowing cattle, no sounds of childish laughter, no sturdy-voiced men or softer-spoken women exchanging greetings. The stables and sheds were strangely silent.

The village was a small one. He turned into it, entered the first house, stumbled over a corpse! The silence was of death. With a beating heart and with a strength he did not know he possessed, he turned aside and ran straight to his father's house.

Standing by itself it was a larger, better and more inviting house than the others. The gate of the surrounding stone wall was battered off the hinges, the front door of the house was open, the garden was trampled. The house had been half destroyed. A dead dog lay in front of the door. He could see all that in the half light. He ran down the path and burst into the wrecked and plundered living room. A few feeble embers still glowed in the broad hearth. From them he lighted a candle standing on the mantel shelf.

The first sight that greeted him was the body of his sister, her torn clothing in frightful disarray, a look of agony and horror upon her white set face under its dishevelled hair. She was stone dead. He knelt down and touched her. She was stone cold, too. He stared at her, a groan bursting from his lips. The groan brought forth another sound. Was it an echo? Lifting the candle, he looked about him. In a far corner lay a huddled human body. He ran to it and bent over it. It was his father. Knowing the house like a book, he ran and fetched some water. There were a few mouthfuls of spirits left in a flask of vodka he had found in the Russian's overcoat. He bathed his father's face, forced a few drops of the strong spirit down his throat, and the old man opened his eyes. In the flickering light he caught sight of the green cap and coat.

"Curse you," he whispered.

"My father!" cried the young officer. "It is I."

"My son!"

"What has happened?"

"The *Cossacks*—I fought for the honour of your sister. Where——" the old man's voice faltered.

"She is dead yonder," answered the son.

"Thank God," came the faint whisper from the father. "Mademoiselle Laure—she—the wagon-train—the castle——"

His voice died away, his eyes closed. Frantically the young man recalled his father to his senses again.

"It's no use," whispered the old man, "a ball in the breast. I am going. What do you here?"

"On the service of the Emperor," answered the young officer. "Father, speak to me!"

"Alas—poor—France," came the words slowly, one by one, and then—silence.

Marteau had seen death too many times not to know it now. He laid the old man's head gently down, he straightened his limbs, he went over to the form of the poor girl. To what horrors she had been subjected—like every other woman in the village—before she died! Like his father, he thanked God that she was dead. He lifted her up tenderly and laid her down on a huge settle by the fireplace. He stood a moment, looking from one to the other. The irreligion of the age had not seized him. He knelt down and made a prayer. Having discharged that duty, he lifted his hands to heaven and his lips moved. Was he invoking a curse upon these enemies? He turned quickly and went out into the night, drawing the door behind him, fastening it as tight as he could.

He forgot that he was hungry, that he was thirsty, that he was tired, that he was cold. For the moment he almost forgot his duty toward his Emperor and France, as he walked rapidly through the trees toward the great house. But as he walked that stern obligation came back to him. His sister was dead, his father murdered. Well, the first *cossack* he came upon should pay. Meanwhile there was his duty. What had his father said?

"The *Cossacks*—the wagon-train—the Countess Laure."

What did it mean? Part of it was plain enough. The *Cossacks* had raided the village, his father had been stricken down defending his daughter, his sister had died. That was easy, but the wagon-train, the castle, the Countess Laure? Could she have come back? Was that the occasion for the lights in the *château*? That body of cavalry that he had seen leaving Sacken's men that morning with the civilians—was she that woman? The mystery would be solved at the *château*. And it was there he had arranged to meet his comrade, anyway.

He stopped and looked back at the devastated village. Already a light was blazing in one of the houses. It would soon be afire. He could do nothing then. The *château* called him. He broke into a run again, heavy-footed and tired out though he was. Around the *château* in the courtyard were dozens of wagons. His experienced glance told him that they were army wagons, containing provisions, arms, ammunition. Some of the covers had been raised to expose the contents. There was not a living man present, and scarcely a living horse.

There had been some sort of a battle evidently, for the wagons were in all sorts of confusion and there were dead men and horses everywhere. He did not stop to examine them save to make sure that the dead men were French, proving that the convoy had come from Paris. He threaded his way among the wagons and finally reached the steps that led to the broad terrace upon which rose the *château*.

The main door was open. There were no soldiers about, which struck him as peculiar, almost terrifying. He went up the steps and across the terrace, and stopped before the building, almost stumbling over the bodies of two men whose uniforms were plainly Russian! He inspected them briefly and stepped toward the door of the entrance hall. It was open but dimly lighted, and the light wavered fitfully. The faint illumination came into the hall from a big broad open door upon the right, giving entrance to what had been the great room. Still keeping within the shadow, he moved carefully and noiselessly into the hall, until he could get a view of the room beyond.

A huge fire was burning in the enormous fireplace. The many tables with which the room had been furnished had been pushed together in the centre, several tall candles pulled from the candelabra and fastened there by their own melted wax stood upon these tables and added their illumination to the fire-light. Several men in uniforms, two of them rough-coated *Cossacks*, and two whose dress showed clearly that they belonged to the Russian Imperial Guard, lay on the floor, bound and helpless. A stout, elderly man, in civilian garb, with a very red face and an angry look, his wig awry, was lashed to a chair. Between two ruffianly looking men, who held her firmly, stood a woman.

There were perhaps two dozen other men in the room, unkempt, savage, brutal, armed with all sorts of nondescript weapons from ancient pistols to fowling pieces, clubs and scythes. They were all in a state of great excitement, shouting and gesturing madly.

The woman standing between the two soldiers was in the full light. So soon as he caught sight of her Marteau recognized her. It was Laure d'Aumenier. She had grown taller and more beautiful than when he had seen her last as a young girl. She had been handled roughly, her clothes were torn, her hair partially unbound. Her captors held her with an iron grasp upon her arms, but she did not flinch or murmur. She held herself as erect and looked as imperious as if she had been on a throne.

CHAPTER 6

Marteau Bargains for the Woman

The sight of her predicament filled the young Frenchman with rage and horror. Drawing his pistol, he strode into the room. What he intended to do, or how he intended to do it was not clear even to him. There stood the woman he loved in the clutch of wretches whose very touch was pollution. He must help her. All duties and intentions gave way to that determination.

A dead silence fell over the room as he entered and the people caught sight of him. He stood staring at the occupants and they returned his stare in good measure. Finally the biggest ruffian, who seemed to be the leader, found his voice and burst out with a savage oath:

"Another Russian! Well, the more the merrier."

He raised a huge horse pistol as he spoke. His words were greeted with jeers and yells from the band. With a flash of inspiration Marteau, realizing into what he had been led, dropped his own weapon and instantly threw up his hands.

"I am French, *messieurs*," he cried loudly as the pistol clattered on the floor at his feet.

"What are you doing in that uniform, then?" roared the leader.

Marteau tore open the heavy green coat, disclosing beneath it his French uniform. He had a second to make up his mind how to answer that pertinent question. He was quite in the dark as to the meaning of the mysterious situation. He opened his mouth and spoke.

"It is quite simple," he began, "I am——"

What should he say? What was he? Were these men for the Emperor or for the king, or were they common blackguards for themselves? The latter was probably the true state of the case, but did it please them to pose as royalists? He took a long chance after a quick prayer because he wanted to live not so much for himself as for the woman.

"I am deserting the Emperor," he said. "I am for the king."

"No king could have brought us to worse straits than we are now in," said the leader, lowering his pistol uncertainly, but still keeping the young man covered.

"Right, my friend," continued Marteau exultantly, realizing that he had made the right choice. "Bonaparte is beaten, Blücher is marching on Paris, Schwarzenberg has the Emperor surrounded. I thought I might as well save myself while I had the chance, so I stole this Russian coat to keep myself from freezing to death, and here I am. I belong to Aumenier."

"You'll join us, then?"

"With pleasure. Who do you serve?"

"Ourselves," laughed the leader grimly. "We're from Fére-Champenoise way. We're all of the village and countryside that the *Cossacks* and the Prussians have left of our families. We're hungry, starving, naked. Do you hear? We were hiding in the woods hard by today. There was a wagon-train. A regiment of *Cossacks* surprised it, killed its defenders, brought it here. We saw it all."

"And where are the *Cossacks* gone?" asked the young man, coolly picking up his pistol from the floor and nonchalantly sitting upon the nearest table in a careless way which certainly belied the beating of his heart. He took careful notice of the men. They were ignorant fellows of the baser sort, half-mad, starving, ferocious peasants, little better than brute beasts, made so by the war.

"An order came for them. They marched away, leaving a company of other soldiers like those yonder." He pointed to the men on the floor.

"And what became of them?"

"There was an attack from the woods at night—a little handful of French soldiers. They beat them off and followed them down the road. They have been gone half an hour. We heard the firing. We came out thinking to plunder the train. We opened wagon after wagon but found nothing but arms. We can't eat steel or powder. We killed two sentries, made prisoners of the officers. We'll set fire to the house and leave them presently. As for this man, we'll kill him, and as for this woman——"

He laughed meaningly, basely, leering at the girl in hideous suggestiveness that made her shudder; and which his wretched companions found highly amusing.

"You have done well," said the young officer quickly, although he was cold with rage at the ruffian's low insinuation. "I hope to have some interest with the king later. If you will give me your names I will see that you are rewarded."

"Never mind our names," growled the leader, still suspicious, evidently.

"Food and drink would reward us better now," shouted a second.

"Aye," yelled one of the others, seconding this happy thought. "We have eaten nothing since yesterday, and as for drink, it is a week since my lips have tasted a swallow of wine."

"And what would you give me if I could procure you some of the fine wine of the country, my friends?" said Marteau quietly, putting great restraint upon himself to continue trafficking with these scoundrels.

"Give? Anything," answered several in chorus, their red eyes gleaming.

"If you've got it we'll take it for nothing," said the brutal leader with ferocious cunning.

"Do I look as if I concealed wine and provisions on my person?" asked the officer boldly, confident now that he had found the way to master these men.

"No," was the answer. "But where is it?"

"And be quick about it," cried a second threateningly. "Those Russians may be back at any moment."

"Is this a jest?" asked a third with a menacing gesture.

"It would be ill-done to joke with men as hungry as you are, I take it," answered Marteau.

"Hurry, then," cried a fourth.

"In good time, my friends. First, a word with you. What are you going to do with those two prisoners?"

"Knock the men in the head, I told you," answered the leader.

"And the woman?"

"We are trying to settle who should have her—first."

"It's a pity there's only one, still——" began another.

"I'll make a bargain with you, then," interrupted Marteau quickly, fingering his weapon while he spoke. "Food and drink in plenty for you, the woman for me."

"And what do you want of the woman?"

"Before I was a soldier I lived in Aumenier, I told you. I served these people. This woman is an aristocrat. I hate her."

It was an old appeal and an old comment but it served. These were wild days like those of the revolution, the license and rapine and ravagings of which some of the older men present could very well recall.

"She treated me like dirt under her feet," went on the officer. "Now I want to have my turn."

"Marteau!" cried the woman for the first time, recognizing him as he turned a grim face toward her, upon which he had very successfully counterfeited a look of hatred. "Is it indeed——"

"Silence," thundered the young soldier, stepping near to her and shaking his clenched fist in her face. "These worthy patriots will give you to me, and then——"

There was a burst of wild laughter throughout the room.

"It's these cursed aristocrats that have brought these hateful Russians upon us," cried one.

"Give her to the lad and let us have food and drink," cried another.

"He'll deal with her," cried a third.

"You hear?" asked the chief.

"I hear," answered Marteau. "Listen. My father kept this house for its owners. He is dead in the village yonder."

"The wine, the wine," roared one, licking his lips.

"Food. I starve," cried another, baring his teeth.

"Wait. Naturally, fleeing from the army, I came to him. My sister is dead too, outraged, murdered. You know?"

"Yes, yes, we know."

"I want to get my revenge on someone and who better than she?"

The young officer did not dare again to look at the young woman. He could feel the horror, the amazement, the contempt in her glance. Was this one of the loyal Marteaux?

"Make her suffer for us!"

"Our children!"

"Our mothers!"

"Our daughters!" cried one after the other, intoxicated with their wrongs, real or fancied, their faces black with rage, their clenched hands raised to heaven as if invoking vengeance.

"Have no fear," said Marteau. "Because of my father's position I know where the wine cellar is, and there is food there."

"Lead on," said the chief. "We've talked too much."

"This way," replied the young captain, lifting the only candlestick from the table. "Leave two men to watch the woman and give the alarm, the rest follow me."

Marteau knew the old castle like a book. He knew where the keys were kept. Chatting carelessly and giving them every evidence of his familiarity, he found the keys, unlocked the doors, led them from room to room, from level to level, until finally they reached the wine cellar. It was separated from the cellar in which they stood by a heavy iron-bound oaken door. In spite of his easy bearing and manner, suspicions had been aroused in the uneasy minds of the rabble, but when Marteau lifted the candle and bade them bring their own lights and see through an iron grating in the door what the chamber beyond contained and they recognized the casks and bottles, to say nothing of hams, smoked meats and other eatables, their suspicions vanished. They burst into uproarious acclamation.

"Hasten," cried the leader.

"This is the last door."

"Have you the key?"

"It is here."

Marteau lifted the key, thrust it in the lock and turned it slowly, as if by a great effort and, the door opening outward, he drew it back.

"Enter," he said. "Help yourselves."

With cries of joy like famished wolves the whole band poured into the wine cellar. All, that is, but Marteau. As the last men entered he flung the door to and with astonishing quickness turned the key in the lock and turned away. The door had shut with a mighty crash, the noise had even stopped the rioting plunderers. The first man who had seized a bottle dropped it crashing to the floor. All eyes and faces turned toward the door. The last man threw himself against it frantically. It held as firmly as if it had been the rock wall. They were trapped. The leader was quicker than the rest. He still had his weapon. Thrusting it through the iron bars of the grating in the door he pulled the trigger. There was a mighty roar, a cloud of smoke, but fortunately in the dim light his aim was bad. Marteau laughed grimly.

"Enjoy yourselves, *messieurs*. The provisions are good and you may eat as much as you like. The wine is excellent. Drink your fill!"

The next instant he leaped up the stairs and retraced his steps. It was a long distance from the wine-cellar to the great room, but through the grating that gave entrance to the courtyard the sound of shots had penetrated. One of the ruffians, committing the woman to the care of the remaining man, started to follow his comrades. He had his pistol in his hand. He went noisily, muttering oaths, feeling that something was wrong but not being able to divine exactly what. Marteau heard him coming. He put the candle down, concealed himself and, as the man came, struck him heavily over the head with the butt of his remaining pistol. He fell like a log. Leaving the candle where it was, the young officer, dispossessing his victim of his pistols, entered the hall and, instead of entering the great room by the door by which he had left it, ran along the hall to the main entrance and thus took the remaining brigand in the rear.

This man was one of those who had seized the Countess Laure. In spite of herself the girl started as the officer appeared in the doorway. The man felt her start, wheeled, his eyes recognized the officer. He had no pistol, but his fingers went to his belt and with the quickness of light itself he hurled a knife straight at Marteau. The woman with equal speed caught the man's arm and disturbed his aim. Her movement was purely instinctive. According to his own words she had even more to fear from Marteau than from this ruffian. The young officer instantly dropped to his knees and as he did so presented his pistol and fired. The knife whistled harmlessly over his head and buried itself in the wood panelling of the door. The bullet sped straight to its mark. The unfortunate blackguard collapsed on the floor at the feet of the girl, who screamed and shrank back shuddering.

"Now, *mademoiselle*," said the young man, advancing into the room, "I have the happiness to inform you that you are free."

CHAPTER 7

A Rescue and a Siege

The woman stared at him in wild amazement. That she was free temporarily at least, could not be gainsaid. Her captors had not seen fit to bind her and she now stood absolutely untouched by anyone. The shooting, the fighting, had confused her. She had only seen Marteau as an accomplice and friend of her assailants, she had no clew to his apparent change of heart. She did not know whether she had merely exchanged masters or what had happened. Smiling ironically at her bewilderment, which he somehow resented in his heart, Marteau proceeded to further explanation.

"You are free, *mademoiselle*," he repeated emphatically, bowing before her.

"But I thought——"

"Did you think that I could be allied with such cowardly thieves and vagabonds as those?"

"But you said——"

"It was simply a ruse. Could you imagine that one of my family, that I, should fail in respect and devotion to one of yours, to you? I determined to free you the instant I saw you."

"And will you not complete your good work?" broke out the man tied to the chair in harsh and foreign but sufficiently comprehensible French, "by straightway releasing me, young sir?"

"But who is this?"

"This is Sir Gervaise Yeovil," answered Mademoiselle Laure, "my attorney, an English officer-of-the-law, of Lord Castlereagh's suite, who came with me from Chatillon to get certain papers and——"

"Why all this bother and explanation?" burst out Sir Gervaise. "Tell him to cut these lashes and release me from this cursed bondage," he added in English.

"That is quite another matter, sir," said Marteau gravely. "I regret that you are an enemy and that I cannot——"

"But we are not enemies, *Monsieur*," cried one of the officers, who had just succeeded in working a gag out of his mouth. "We are Russian officers of the Imperial Guard and since you have deserted the cause of the Corsican you will——"

"Deserted!" thundered Marteau, his pale face flaming. "That was as much a ruse as the other."

"What, then, do you mean by wearing a Russian coat over your uniform and——"

"He is a spy. He shall be hanged," said the other, also freeing himself of his gag.

"Indeed," laughed Marteau. "And do you gentlemen ask me to release you in order that you may hang me?"

"I won't hang you," burst out the Englishman. "On the contrary, I'll give you fifty pounds if you'll cut these cords and——"

Marteau shook his head.

"Countess," bellowed Yeovil angrily, "there's a knife on the table yonder, pray do you——"

The young woman made a swift step in that direction, but the Frenchman was too quick for her.

"Pardon me, *mademoiselle*, I beg that the first use you make of your new life be not to aid my enemies."

"Your enemies, Marteau?"

"The enemies of France, then."

"Not my uncle's France," said the girl.

"But your father's, and I had hoped yours."

"No, no."

"In any event, these gentlemen must remain bound for the time being. No harm shall come to you from me," continued Marteau, addressing the two officers. "But as for these hounds——" He stepped over to the two *Cossacks*, who lay mute. He bent over them with such a look of rage, ruthless determination and evil purpose in his face as startled the woman into action.

"*Monsieur!*" she cried, stepping over to him and striving to interpose between him and the two men. "Marteau, what would you do?"

"My sister—dead in the cottage yonder after—after——" he choked out. He stopped, his fingers twitching. "My old father! If I served them right I would pitch them into yonder fireplace or torture them, the dogs, the cowards!"

"My friend," said the young countess gently, laying her hand on his arm.

Marteau threw up his hands, that touch recalled him to his senses.

"I will let them alone for the present," he said. "Meanwhile——" He seized the dead man and dragged the body out of sight behind the tables.

"Will *monsieur* give a thought to me?" came another voice from the dim recesses of a far corner.

"And who are you?" asked Marteau, lifting the light and staring.

"A Frenchman, sir. They knocked me on the head and left me for dead, but if *monsieur* would assist me I——"

Marteau stepped over to him, bent down and lifted him up. He was a stout, hardy looking peasant boy, pale cheeked, with blood clotted around his forehead from a blow that he had received. Feverish fire sparkled in his eyes.

"If *monsieur* wishes help to put these brutes out of the way command me," he said passionately.

"We will do nothing with them at present," answered Marteau.

"Quick, Laure, the knife," whispered the Englishman.

The Frenchman heard him, however, and wheeled around.

"*Mademoiselle,*" he cried, "on your honour I charge you not to abuse the liberty I have secured for you and that I allow you."

"But, my friends——"

"If you had depended on your friends you would even now be——" he paused—"as my sister," he added with terrific intensity.

"Your pleasure shall be mine," said the young woman.

"If I could have a drink of wine!" said the young peasant, sinking down into a chair.

"There is a flask which they did not get in the pocket of one of the officers yonder," said the young Frenchwoman, looking sympathetically at the poor exhausted lad.

Marteau quickly recovered it, in spite of the protestations of the officer, who looked his indignation at this little betrayal by the woman. He gave some of it to the peasant and then offered it to mademoiselle and, upon her declining it, took a long drink himself. He was weak and trembling with all he had gone through.

"Now, what's to be our further course?" asked the countess.

"I don't know yet. I——"

But the answer was never finished. Shots, cries, the sound of galloping horses came faintly through the open door.

"My men returning!" cried the Russian officer triumphantly. "Our turn will come now, sir."

Two courses were open. To run or to fight. Duty said go; love said stay. Duty was stronger. After a moment's hesitation Marteau dashed for the door. He was too late. The returning Russian cavalry was already entering the courtyard. Fate had decided against him. He could not go now. He thought with the swiftness of a veteran. He sprang back into the hall, threw the great iron-bound door into its place, turned the massive key in its lock, thanking God that key and lock were still intact, dropped the heavy bars at top and bottom that further secured it, just as the first horseman thundered upon the door.

In his rapid passage through the house the young Frenchman had noticed that all the windows were shuttered and barred, that only the front door appeared to have been opened. He was familiar with the *château*. He knew how carefully its openings had been secured and how often his father had inspected them, to keep out brigands, the waifs and strays, the wanderers, the low men of the countryside. For the moment he was safe with his prisoners, one man and a boy guarding a score of men and one woman, and holding a *château* against a hundred and fifty soldiers!

Fortunately, there would be no cannon with that troop of cavalry, there were no cannon in that wagon train, so that they could not batter down the *château* over his head. What his ultimate fate would be he could not tell. Could he hold that castle indefinitely? If not, what? How he was to get away and reach Napoleon with his vital news he could not see. There must be some way, however. Well, whatever was to be would be, and meanwhile he could only wait developments and hold on.

The troopers outside were very much astonished to find the heavy door closed and the two sentries dead on the terrace. They dismounted from their horses at the foot of the terrace and crowded about the door, upon which they beat with their pistols, at the same time shouting the names and titles of the officers within. Inside the great hall Marteau had once more taken command. In all this excitement Laure d'Aumenier had stood like a stone, apparently indifferent to the appeals of the four bound men on the floor and the Englishman in the chair that she cut the ropes with which they were bound, while the French officer was busy at the door.

Perhaps that young peasant might have prevented her, but as a matter of fact, she made no attempt to answer their pleas. She stood waiting and watching. Just as Marteau reëntered the room the chief Russian officer shouted out a command. From where he lay on the floor his voice did not carry well and there was too much tumult outside for anyone to hear. In a second Marteau was over him.

"If you open your mouth again, *monsieur*," he said fiercely, "I shall have to choose between gagging and killing you, and I incline to the latter. And these other gentlemen may take notice. You, what are you named?"

"Pierre Lebois, sir," answered the peasant.

"Can you fire a gun?"

"Give me a chance," answered the young fellow. "I've got people dead, yonder, to avenge."

The brigands had left the swords and pistols of the officers on chairs, tables and the floor. There were eight pistols. Marteau gathered them up. The English baronet yielded one other, a huge, heavy, old-fashioned weapon.

"There are loopholes in the shutters yonder," said the officer. "Do you take that one, I will take the other. They will get away from the door in a moment and as soon as you can see them fire."

"*Mademoiselle*," said the Russian officer desperately, "I shall have to report to the commander of the guard and he to the *Czar* that you gave aid and comfort to our enemies."

"But what can I do?" asked the young woman. "Monsieur Marteau could certainly shoot me if I attempted——"

"Assuredly," said Marteau, smiling at her in a way anything but fierce.

It was that implicit trust in her that restrained her and saved him. As a girl the young countess had been intensely fond of Jean Marteau. He certainly appeared well in his present role before her. In the revulsion of feeling in finding him not a bully, not a traitor, but a devoted friend and servitor, he advanced higher in her estimation than ever before. Besides, the young woman was by no means so thoroughgoing a loyalist as her old uncle, for instance.

"I can see them now, *monsieur*," said the young peasant from the peep-hole in the shutter.

Indeed, the men outside had broken away from the door, groups were running to and fro seeking lights and some other entrance. Taking aim at the nearest Marteau pulled the trigger and Pierre followed his example. The noise of the explosions was succeeded by a scream of anguish, one man was severely wounded and another killed. Something mysterious had happened while they had been off on the wild goose chase apparently, the Russians decided. The *château* had been seized, their officers had been made way with, it was held by the enemy.

"They can't be anything more than wandering peasants," cried an imperious voice in Russian outside. "I thought you had made thorough work with them all, Scoref," continued the speaker. "Your *Cossacks* must have failed to complete the job."

"It will be the first time," answered Scoref, the *hetman* of the raiders. "Look, the village burns!"

"Well, what's to be done now?" said the first voice.

"I don't know, Baron," was the answer. "Besieging castles is more in your line than in mine."

"Shall we fire again, *monsieur*?" asked Pierre within.

"No," was the answer. "Remember we've only got eight shots and we must wait."

"Let us have lights," cried the commander of the squadron. "Here, take one of those wagons and——"

In a few moments a bright fire was blazing in the courtyard.

"The shots came from those windows," continued the Russian. "Keep out of the way and—— Isn't that a window open up there?"

"It is, it is!" came the answer from a dozen throats.

All the talk being in Russian was, of course, not understood by the two Frenchmen.

"One of you climb up there," continued the Russian. "You see the spout, and the coping, that buttress? Ten *roubles* to the man who does it."

A soldier sprang forward. Those within could hear his heavy body rub along the wall. They did not know what he was doing or what was toward. They were in entire ignorance that a shutter had become detached from its hinges in the room above the drawing-room and that they would soon have to face an attack from the rear. The man who climbed fancied himself perfectly secure, and indeed he was from those within. It was a hard climb, but presently he reached the window-ledge. His hands clasped it, he made a brave effort, drew himself up and on the instant from beyond the wagons came a pistol shot. The man shrieked, released his hold and fell crashing to the ground. The besiegers broke into wild outcries. Some of them ran in the direction whence the shot had come. They thought they caught the glimpse of a figure running away in the darkness. Pistols were fired and the vicinity was thoroughly searched, but they found nothing.

The shot, the man's cry overhead, the body crashing down to the ground, enlightened Marteau. He handed Pierre two of the six remaining pistols, told him to run to the floor above and watch the window. The young peasant crossed himself and turned away. He found the room easily enough. It was impossible to barricade the window, but he drew back in the darkness and waited.

Having found no one in the grove beyond the baggage-wagons, the Russians called for another volunteer and a second man offered. Pierre heard him coming, permitted him to gain the ledge and then thrust the pistol in his face and pulled the trigger. At the same time a big *Cossack* coming within easy range and standing outlined between the loophole and the fire, Marteau gave him his second bullet, with fatal effect. There flashed into his mind that the shot which had come so opportunely from outside bespoke the arrival of his friend, the grenadier. He hoped the man would have sense enough to go immediately to Sézanne and report the situation. If he could maintain the defence of the castle for two hours he might be rescued. He stepped to the hall and called up to Pierre. Receiving a cheery reply to the effect that all was well and that he would keep good watch, he came back into the great hall and resumed his ward.

CHAPTER 8

A Trial of Allegiance

Mademoiselle d'Aumenier had seated herself at a table and remained there in spite of the entreaties and black looks of the prisoners. Marteau did not dare to leave his loophole, but the necessity for watching did not prevent him from talking. The men outside seemed to have decided that nothing more could be done for the present. They withdrew from out of range of the deadly fire of the defenders and, back of the wagons, kindled fires, and seemed to be preparing to make a night of it.

The best officers of the detachment were prisoners in the *château*. The subordinate who had been entrusted with the pursuit was young and inexperienced; the *Cossack* commander was a mere raider. They themselves belonged to the cavalry. They decided, after inspecting the whole building carefully as nearly as they dared in view of the constant threat of discharge, that they would have to wait until morning, unless something occurred to them or some chance favoured them. They trusted that at daylight they would have no difficulty in effecting an entrance somewhere. A total of three men dead and one wounded, to say nothing of the sentries and officers, had a discouraging effect on night work. They did not dream that there was an enemy, a French soldier, that is, nearer than Troyes. They supposed that the castle had been seized by some of the enraged country people who had escaped the *Cossacks* and that they could easily deal with them in the morning.

Incidentally, the wine cellars in which the peasants had been shut had openings to the outer air, and through them came shouts and cries which added to the mystification of the besiegers and increased their prudence. The walls of the *château* were massive, the floors thick, the wine cellar far away, and no sound came from them to the inmates of the great hall. Indeed, in the exciting adventure that had taken place, the raiders had been completely forgot by Marteau and the others.

The conversation in the hall was not animated. The Countess Laure, womanlike, at last began to ask questions.

"Monsieur Marteau," she asked persuasively, "will you hear reason?"

"I will hear anything, *mademoiselle*, from you," was the instant reply.

"Think of the unhappy state of France."

"I have had reason enough to think of it tonight, *mademoiselle*. My father and my sister——" his voice faltered.

"I know," said the girl sympathetically, and, indeed, she was deeply grieved for the misfortunes of the faithful and devoted old man and the young girl she had loved. She waited a moment and then continued. "The Emperor is at last facing defeat. His cause is hopeless."

"He yet lives," answered the soldier softly.

"Yes, of course," said the woman. "I do not understand the military situation, but my friends——"

"Will *monsieur* allow me the favour of a word?" interposed the chief Russian officer courteously.

"If it is not to summon assistance you may speak," replied Marteau.

"As a soldier you know the situation as well as I," continued the Russian. "Prince Von Schwarzenberg has Napoleon in his grasp. He will hold him until he is ready to seize him, while Field-Marshal Blücher takes Paris."

"The Emperor yet lives," said Marteau, repeating his former remark with more emphasis and smiling somewhat scornfully. "It is not wise to portion the lion's skin while it covers his beating heart," he added meaningly.

"Not even the genius of your Emperor," persisted the Russian more earnestly, "will avail now, *monsieur*. He is lost, his cause as well. Why, this very convoy tells the story. We intercepted letters that told how pressing was its need. Your army is without arms, without food, without clothes."

"It still has its Emperor."

"Death!" cried the Russian impatiently. "Must we kill him in order to teach you a lesson?"

"You will not kill him while there is a soldier in France to interpose his body."

"Very heroic, doubtless," sneered the Russian, beginning to get angry. "But you know your cause is lost."

"And if it were?"

"Be reasonable. There are many Frenchmen with the allied armies. Your rank is——?"

"I am a Major on the Emperor's staff if you are interested to know."

"Major Marteau, I have no doubt that my interest with my Emperor, the Czar Alexander, with whom I am remotely connected—I may say I am a favourite officer in his guard—would doubtless insure you a Colonel's commission, perhaps even that of a General of Brigade, with my gracious master, or in the army of King Louis after we have replaced him on his throne if——"

"If what?"

"If you release us, restore us to our command. Permit us to send for horses to take the place of those we have killed to take the wagons of the valuable convoy to our own army."

"And you would have me abandon my Emperor?"

"For the good of France," urged the Russian meaningly.

"Will you answer me a question, *monsieur*?" continued the young man after a moment's deep thought.

"Certainly, if it be not treason to my master."

"Oh, you have views on treason, then," said the Frenchman adroitly and not giving the other time to answer he continued. "To what corps are you attached?"

"Count Sacken's."

"And whose division?"

"General Olsuvieff's."

"*Monsieur*," said the young Frenchman calmly, "it is more than probable that before tomorrow your division will be annihilated and the next day the corps of General Sacken may meet the same fate."

The Russian laughed scornfully at what seemed to him the wildest boasting.

"Are you mad?"

"Not so mad as you will be when it happens."

The Russian controlled himself with difficulty in the face of the irritating observations.

"And who will do this?" he asked, at last.

"The Emperor."

"Does he command the lightning-flash that he could hurl the

thunder-bolt from Troyes?"

"Upon my word, I believe he does," laughed the Frenchman.

"This is foolish jesting, boy," broke out the Englishman. "I am a man of consideration in my own country. The lady here will bear me out. I offered you fifty pounds. I will give you five hundred if you will release us and——"

"And I offer you my—friendship," said the countess, making a long pause before the last word.

How much of it she meant or how little no one could say. Any ruse was fair in war like this. Marteau looked at her. The colour flamed to her cheek and died away. It had flamed into his cheek and died away also.

"Gentlemen," he said, "you offer me rank, money——" he paused—"friendship——" he shot a meaning glance at the young girl. He paused again.

"Well?" said the Russian.

"Speak out," said the Englishman. "Your answer, lad?"

"I refuse."

"Don't be a fool," roared Sir Gervaise bluntly.

"I refuse, I repeat," said Marteau. "While the Emperor lives I am his man. Not rank, not money, not friendship, not love itself even could move me. Enough, gentlemen," he continued imperiously as the two Russians and the Englishman all began to speak at once. "No more. Such propositions are insults."

"There is another appeal which ought to be brought to your attention, young sir," said the second Russian officer when he could be heard.

"And what is that?"

"Your life. You know that as soon as day breaks the *château* will be seized. You are a self-confessed spy. You came here wearing a Russian uniform. As soon as we are released we shall hang you as a spy. But if you release us now, on my word of honour you shall go free."

"*Monsieur* is a very brave man," said Marteau smiling.

"Why?"

"To threaten me with death while he is in my power. You are the only witnesses. I could make way with you all."

"You forget the Countess and the English gentleman."

"Although the Countess is the enemy of France——"

"Nay, nay, the friend," interposed the girl.

"Be it so. Although she is the enemy of the Emperor then, I cannot believe that she could condemn to death by her testimony the man who has saved her from worse than death, and as for the English gentleman——"

"*Damme* if I'd say a word to hurt you, if only for what you have done for her, whether you release me or not," cried Yeovil.

"You see?"

"Monsieur Jean," said the countess, "you put me under great obligations to you."

"By saving your life, your honour, *mademoiselle*! I gladly——"

"By giving me your confidence," interrupted the girl, who in her secret heart was delighted at the stand the young officer had taken. She would have despised him if he had succumbed to the temptation of which she herself was part.

"I could do no less, *mademoiselle*," returned Marteau. "I and my forbears have served your house and known it and loved it for eight hundred years."

"I know it," answered the girl. "I value the association. I am proud of it."

"And since you know it and recognize it perhaps you will tell me how you happen to be here."

"Willingly," answered Mademoiselle Laure. "The estates are to be sold. There are deeds and papers of value in the *château* without which transactions could not be completed. I alone knew where they were. With Monsieur Yeovil, my uncle's friend and the father of——" she hesitated and then went on, "so I came to France."

"But with the invading armies——"

"There was no other way. The Czar Alexander gave me a safe conduct. A company of his guards escorted us. Sir Gervaise Yeovil was accredited to Lord Castlereagh, but with his permission he brought me here first. My uncle was too old to come. Arrived here we found the *Cossacks*, the wagon-train. There was a battle, a victory, pursuit. Then those villains seized us. They stole upon us unsuspecting, having murdered the sentries, and then you came."

"I see. And have you the papers?"

"They are—— Not yet, but I may take them?"

"Assuredly, so far as I am concerned," answered Marteau, "although I regret to see the old estate pass out of the hands of the ancient family."

"I regret it also, but I am powerless."

"We played together here as children," said Marteau. "My father has kept it well since. Your father died and now mine is gone——"

"And I am very sorry," answered the young woman softly.

Marteau turned away, peered out of the window and sank into gloomy silence.

CHAPTER 9

The Emperor Eats and Rides

Sézanne was a scene of the wildest confusion that night. It was congested with troops and more and more were arriving every minute. They entered the town in fearful condition. They had been weary and ragged and naked before. Now they were in a state of extreme prostration; wet, cold, covered with mud. The roads were blocked with mired artillery, the guns were sunk into the mud to the hubs, the tired horses could no longer move them. The woods on either side were full of stragglers, many of whom had dropped down on the wet ground and slept the sleep of complete exhaustion. Some, indeed, sick and helpless, died where they lay. Everything eatable and drinkable in Sézanne had vanished as a green field before a swarm of locusts when Marmont's division had come through some hours before.

The town boasted a little square or open space in the midst. A huge fire was burning in the centre of this open space. A cordon of grenadiers kept the ground about the fire clear of stragglers. Suddenly the Emperor rode into the midst. He was followed by a wet, cold, mud-spattered, bedraggled staff, all of them unutterably weary. Intense resolution blazed in the Emperor's eyes. He had had nothing to eat or drink since morning, but that ancient bodily vigour, that wonderful power of endurance, which had stood him in such good stead in days gone by, seemed to have come back to him now. He was all fire and energy and determination. So soon as his presence was known, couriers reported to him. Many of them he stopped with questions.

"The convoy of arms, provisions, powder," he snapped out to an officer of Marmont's division approaching him, "which was to meet us here. Have you seen it?"

"It has not appeared, Sire."

"Has anything been heard of it?"

"Nothing yet, your Majesty."

"Have you scouted for it, sent out parties to find it? Where is the Comte de Grouchy?"

"I come from him, Sire. He is ahead of the Duke of Ragusa's corps."

"Has he come in touch with the enemy?"

"Not yet, Sire."

"The roads?"

"Worse than those we have passed over."

"Marshal Marmont?"

"I was ordered by General Grouchy to report to him and then——"

"Well, sir?"

"He sent me back here."

"For what purpose?"

"To find you, Sire, and to say to you most respectfully from the Marshal that the roads are absolutely impassable. He has put four teams to a gun and can scarcely move them. To advance is impossible. He but awaits your order to retrace his steps."

"Retrace his steps!" shouted Napoleon, raising his voice. "Never! He must go on. Our only hope, our only chance, salvation lies in an instant advance. He knows that as well as I."

"But the guns, Sire?"

"Abandon the guns if necessary. We'll take what cannon we need from the enemy."

And that admission evidenced the force with which the Emperor held his convictions as to the present movement. Great, indeed, was the necessity which would induce Napoleon to order the abandonment of a single gun.

"But, Sire——"

"*Monsieur*," said Napoleon severely, "you are a young officer, although you wear the insignia of a Colonel. Know that I am not accustomed to have my commands questioned by anyone. You will return to Marshal Marmont at once. Exchange your tired horse for one of my own. I still have a fresh one, I believe. And spare him not. Tell the Duc de Ragusa that he must advance at all hazards. Advance with the guns if he can, if not then without them. Stay, as for the guns—— Where is the Mayor of the town?"

"Here, Sire," answered a plain, simple man in civilian's dress standing near.

"Are there any horses left in the countryside, *monsieur*?"

"Many, your Majesty, wherever the Russians have not passed."

"I thought so. Gentlemen," the Emperor turned to his staff, "ride in every direction. Take the mounted escort. Bid them scatter. Go to every village and farm. Ask my good French people to bring their horses in, to lend them to the Emperor. It is for France. I strike the last blow for them, their homes, their wives and children. Fortune smiles upon us. The enemy is delivered into our hands. They shall be liberally rewarded."

"The men are hungry," cried a voice from a dark group of officers in the background.

"They are weary," exclaimed another, under cover of the darkness.

"Who spoke?" asked the Emperor, but he did not wait for an answer, perhaps he did not care for one. "I, too, am hungry, I, your Emperor, and I am weary. I have eaten nothing and have ridden the day long. There is bread, there are guns in the Field-Marshal's army. We shall take from Blücher all that we need. Then we can rest. You hear?"

"We hear, Sire."

"Good. Whose division is yonder?"

"Mine, Sire," answered Marshal Ney, riding up and saluting.

"Ah, Prince," said Napoleon, riding over toward him. "Michael," he added familiarly as he drew nearer, "I am confident that the Prussians have no idea that we are nearer than Troyes to them. We must get forward with what we can at once and fall on them before they learn of our arrival and concentrate. We must move swiftly."

"Tomorrow," suggested Ney.

"Tonight."

"The conscripts of my young guard are in a state of great exhaustion and depression. If they could have the night to rest in——"

Napoleon shook his head.

"Advance with those who can march," he said decisively. "We must fall on Blücher in the morning or we are lost."

"Impossible!" ejaculated Ney.

"I banished that word from my vocabulary when I first went into Italy," said Napoleon. "Where are your troops?"

"Here, your Majesty," answered Ney, turning, pointing back to dark huddled ranks drooping over their muskets at parade rest.

Napoleon wheeled his horse and trotted over to them. The iron hand of Ney had kept some sort of discipline and some sort of organization, but the distress and dismay of the conscripts was but too plainly evident.

"My friends," said the Emperor, raising his voice, "you are hungry——" a dull murmur of acquiescence came from the battalion—"you are weary and cold——" a louder murmur—"you are discouraged——" silence. "Some of you have no arms. You would fain rest. Well I, your Emperor, am weary, I am hungry, I am old enough to be the father of most of you and I am wet and cold. But we must forget those things. You wonder why I have marched you all the day and most of the night through the cold and the wet and the mud. The Prussians are in front of us. They are drawn out in long widely separated columns. They have no idea that we are near them.

"One more effort, one more march, and we shall fall upon them. We shall pierce their lines, cut them to pieces, beat them in detail; we shall seize their camps, their guns, their clothes, their food. We shall take back the plunder they have gathered as they have ravaged France. They have stolen and destroyed and murdered—you have seen it. One more march, one more battle for——" he hesitated a moment—"for me," he said with magnificent egotism and audacity. "I have not forgotten how to lead, nor you to follow. We will show them that at the great game of war we are still master players. Come, if there be one too weary to walk, he shall have his Emperor's horse and I will march afoot as I have often done for France."

He spoke with all his old force and power. The tremendous personal magnetism of the man was never more apparent. The young men of Ney's corps thrilled to the splendid appeal. There was something fascinating, alluring in the picture. They hated the Prussians. They had seen the devastated fields, the dead men and women, the ruined farms. The light from the fire played mystically about the great Emperor on his white horse. He seemed to them like a demi-god. There were a few old soldiers in the battalion. The habit of years was upon them.

"*Vive l'Empereur*," one veteran shouted.

Another caught it up and finally the whole division roared out that frightful and thrilling battle cry in unison.

"That's well," said the Emperor, a little colour coming into his face. "If the lads are of this mettle, what may I expect of the old soldiers of the guard?"

"Forward! Forward!" shouted a beardless boy in one of the front ranks.

"You hear, Marshal Ney?" said Napoleon, turning to his fighting Captain. "With such soldiers as these I can go anywhere and do anything."

"Your Majesty," cried a staff officer, riding up at a gallop, "the peasants are bringing their horses in. There is a section of country to the eastward which has not yet been ridden over by the enemy."

"Good," said the Emperor. "As fast as they come up dispatch them to Marmont. You will find me there by the fire in the square for the next hour. Meanwhile I want the next brigade of horse that reaches Sézanne to be directed to scout in the direction of Aumenier for that missing wagon-train for which we——"

There was a sudden confusion on the edge of the line. The grenadiers forming a circle around the fire had caught a man wearing a Russian greatcoat and were dragging him into the light.

"What's this? *Mon Dieu!*" exclaimed Napoleon, recognizing the green uniform which he had seen on many a battlefield. "A Russian! Here!"

"A soldier of France, Sire," came the astonishing answer in excellent French from the supposed prisoner.

At this amazing remark in their own tongue the bewildered grenadiers on guard released him. He tore off the green cap and dashed it to the ground.

"Give me a *shako*. Let me feel the bearskin of the guard again," he cried impetuously, as his hands ripped open his overcoat, disclosing his uniform. "I am a grenadier of the line, Sire."

Napoleon peered down at him.

"Ah," he said, "I know you. You are called——"

"Bal-Arrêt, your Majesty."

"Exactly. Have you stopped any more this time?"

"There is one in my left arm. Your guards hurt when they grasped it. But it is nothing. I didn't come here to speak of bullets, but of——"

"What?"

"The Russians, the Prussians."

"Where did you get that coat and cap?"

"I rode with Jean Marteau," answered the grenadier, greatly excited.

"What of him? Is he alive?"

"I think so."

"Did you leave him?"

"I did, Sire."

314

"And why?"

"To bring you news."

"Of Marshal Blücher's armies?"

The grenadier nodded his head.

"What of them? Quick man, your tidings? Have you been among them?"

"All day long."

"Where are they?"

"General Yorck with his men is at Étampes."

"And Macdonald?"

"Fighting a rearguard action beyond Château-Thierry."

"On what side of the Marne?"

"The north side, Sire. Right at La Ferte-sous-Jouarre."

"What else?"

"Sacken's Russians are advancing along the main road through Montmirail toward Paris. Olusuvieff's Russian division is at Champaubert."

"And where are Blücher and Wittgenstein and Wrede?"

"Major Marteau will have to tell you that, Sire. He went that way."

"You separated?"

"Yes, Sire."

"You were to meet somewhere?"

"At the Château d'Aumenier."

"Did you go there?"

"I did, Sire."

"And you found?"

"The ground around the *château* filled with wagons."

"A train?"

"Of arms, clothing, ammunition, everything the army lacks."

"What was it doing there?"

"There had been a battle. Horses and men were slain; Frenchmen, *Cossacks*, Russians. I pillaged one wagon," continued the grenadier.

He drew forth from the pocket of the coat a bottle and a handful of hard bread, together with what remained of the roast pig.

"Will you share your meal with a brother soldier?" asked the Emperor, who was ordinarily the most fastidious of mortals, but who could on occasion assume the manner of the rudest private soldier.

"Gladly," said the proud and delighted grenadier, handing the bottle, the bread and the meat to Napoleon, who took them and drank and ate rapidly as he continued to question amid the approving murmurs of the soldiers, who were so delighted to see their Emperor eat like a common man that they quite forgot their own hunger.

"What were the wagons doing there unguarded?"

"I think the men who captured the train were pursuing its guard. Just as I approached the *chateau* they came riding back. I remained quiet, watching them ride up to the door of the house, which they found barred apparently, for I could hear them beat on it with the butts of their sabers and pistols. They built a fire and suddenly I heard shots. By the light I could see Russians falling. It came into my mind that Major Marteau had seized the castle and was holding it."

"Alone?"

"One soldier of yours, Sire, ought to be able to hold his own against a thousand Russians, especially inside a castle wall."

"And what did you then?"

"I made ready my pistol, Sire, and when I saw a man climbing the wall to get in an open window I shot him."

"And then?"

"They ran after me, fired at me but I escaped in the darkness."

"You ran?"

"Because I knew that you must have the news and as Marteau was there it was necessary for me to bring it."

"You have done well," said the Emperor in great satisfaction. "I thank you for your tidings and your meal. I have never tasted a better. Do you wish to go to the rear?"

"For a scratch in the arm?" asked old Bullet-Stopper scornfully. "I, who have carried balls in my breast and have some there now?"

"I like your spirit," said the Emperor, "and I will——"

At this instant a staff officer rode up.

"General Maurice's cavalry is just arriving, Sire," he said.

"Good," said the Emperor. "The brave light-horseman! My sword hand! I will ride with him myself. Tell the Comte de Vivonne to lead his division toward Aumenier, I will join him at once." He turned to those of his staff who remained in the square. "Remain here, gentlemen. Tell the arriving troops that at daybreak we shall beat the Russians at Champaubert. Bid them hasten if they would take part in the victory and the plunder. The rest will be easy."

"And you, Sire?"

"I ride with the cavalry brigade to Aumenier. Tell the men that the wagon-train has arrived. We shall seize it. Food, arms, will be distributed in the morning. Is that you, Maurice?" he continued, as a gallant young general officer attended by a few *aides* rode up.

"At your service, Sire," answered a gay voice.

"Your cavalry?"

"Weary but ready to follow the Emperor anywhere."

"Forward, then. There is food and drink at the end of our ride. It is but a few miles to Aumenier."

"May I have a horse and go with you, Sire?" asked the old grenadier.

"Assuredly. See that he gets one and a Cross of the Legion of Honour, too. Come, gentlemen," continued the Emperor, putting spurs to his tired horse.

CHAPTER 10

How Marteau Won the Cross

For a long time the besiegers had given little evidence of their presence. Through the loop-holes in the shutters fires could be seen burning, figures coming and going. They were busy about something, but just what was not apparent. They had been unmolested by the defenders. Marteau had but three pistols and therefore three shots left. Pierre, upstairs, had but one. To kill one or two more Russians would not have bettered their condition. The pistols should be saved for a final emergency. He had called up to Pierre and had cautioned him. There was nothing to do but to wait.

From time to time the silence was broken by snatches of conversation. As, for instance, the Countess Laure, observing that Marteau wore upon his breast the Grand Cross of the Legion of Honour, thus began,

"You wear a great decoration for a simple——" She stopped awkwardly.

"For a simple peasant you were about to say, *mademoiselle*," answered Marteau, smiling with a little touch of scorn. "In France today even a simple peasant may deserve and receive the favour of the Emperor."

"I am sure that you are worthy of whatever distinction you may have achieved, *monsieur*," said the countess gently, grieved at her lack of consideration and anxious to make amends. "And as one who takes pride in all associated with her ancient house will you tell me how you got that?"

"It was at Leipsic."

"Ah, we beat you there," said one Russian meaningly.

"Yes," said Marteau. "Perhaps after having seen your backs so many times we could afford to turn ours upon you once."

"I was there," said the other Russian triumphantly.

"Were you also at Friedland, at Eylau, at Borodino, at——" began Marteau angrily.

"Gentlemen!" said the countess.

"Forgive, *mademoiselle*," said the Frenchman quickly. "I, at least, will not fight our battles over in the presence of a woman."

"But the cross?"

"It was nothing. I saved an eagle. The Emperor bestowed it on me."

"Tell me about it."

"I was on the bridge at Leipsic when it was blown up by that fatal mistake. The *Port-Aigle* was torn to pieces. The Colonel seized the Eagle as it fell from his hand. I was next to him—afoot. A storm of bullets swept over the river. As the Colonel on his horse was pushed over the parapet by the flying fugitives a shot struck him. He had just strength enough to gasp out, 'Save the Eagle' as he was swept away. I was lucky enough to catch the staff—a bullet had broken it—I seized the upper half with the Eagle and the flag which had almost been shot to pieces during the battle—the Fifth-of-the-Line had done its full duty that day—and I swam with it toward the bank. Really, *mademoiselle*, any soldier would have done as well. I only happened to be there."

"Go on, *monsieur*, I wish to hear everything."

"At your pleasure, then," said Marteau reluctantly, continuing his story.

"The river was filled with men and horses. Marshal Poniatowski was near me. He had been wounded, and guided his swimming horse with his left hand. The current was swift. We were swept down the stream. A cavalryman next to me was shot from his horse. He fell over upon me. I was forced under water a moment. Another horse, swimming frantically, struck my shoulder with his hoof, fortunately it was the left one. My arm was broken. I seized the tatters of the flag in my teeth—you know I am an expert swimmer, *mademoiselle*?"

"I know it," answered the girl, her eyes gleaming at the recital. "Have you forgot the day when, disregarding your warnings, I fell into the river and was swept away and how you plunged in and brought me to the shore and never told my father?"

"I have not forgot," said the young officer simply, "but it was not for me to remind you."

"And I have not forgot, either. But continue the story," said the young countess, her eyes shining, her breath coming quicker, as she listened to the gallant tale so modestly set forth.

"With my right arm I swam as best I could. There was a horse nearby which had lost his rider. I grasped the saddle horn. Somehow I managed to reach the shore with the Eagle. I clambered up the bank, slippery with water and with blood, *mademoiselle*. The Russians were firing at us from the town. A bullet struck me."

"Where?"

"I am ashamed to say, in the back," said the soldier, flushing at the recollection. "But if I had stood up and faced them the Eagle would have been lost."

The Russian laughed scornfully.

"In the back," he cried meaningly, "a fine place for a soldier!"

"Shame," said the countess quickly.

"If I had faced them," returned the French soldier simply, "I should have been shot in the breast and killed, perhaps, but I should have lost the Eagle. It was my business to save the Eagle at all hazards, even though I should be branded with cowardice for having done so," he went on hotly.

"I understand," said the Countess. "I, who have known you from a child, know that you are a brave man, monsieur. Proceed."

"I staggered up the bank. Fortune had brought me to the place where the Emperor stood watching. There were staff officers about him. Oh, very few. The slaughter had been dreadful, the confusion was inconceivable, *mademoiselle*. They made way for me. How well I remember the whole scene," continued the young Frenchman. "The Emperor stood a little apart, his face pale, his head bent. He was frowning and whistling."

"Whistling! *Damme*," burst out Sir Gervaise Yeovil, deeply interested in the unpretentious account of so heroic a deed. "What was he whistling?"

"*Malbrook-s'en-va-t'en-guerre.*"

"By gad," roared the Englishman. "Marlborough beat you. Just wait until we come in touch with you."

"There was no Napoleon there," observed Marteau simply, as if that were adequate answer.

"Napoleon or no Napoleon, wait until Wellington——"

"We shall wait."

"Pardon, Monsieur Yeovil," said the countess, "will you not allow Monsieur Marteau to proceed?"

"There is little more to tell, *mademoiselle*. The Emperor saw me come up. I was wet, my arm hung useless, the bullet had gone through my body. There was blood on my uniform coat. I thought that I was dying, that my end was at hand. My strength was ebbing. I concentrated all my will and power. Holding the Eagle, I lifted it up in salute. 'What have we here?' cried the Emperor, fixing his glance upon me. 'Lieutenant Marteau,' I answered. His voice came to me as in a dream and my own voice sounded far away. 'Of what regiment?' 'The Fifth-of-the-Line, Sire.' 'You have saved the Eagle.' 'Yes, Sire,' I replied. And then consciousness left me. As I fell I heard the Emperor say, 'See that he gets the Legion of Honour if he survives.' People caught me in their arms. When I woke up I was in France. Here, at Aumenier, in my father's house."

Young Marteau did not add to his story that, as he fell, he heard the Emperor, deeply moved, exclaim:

"With such men what resources does not France possess?"

"And did the Emperor give you the cross?" eagerly asked the girl.

"It was forgot until a few days since. When I recovered I rejoined the regiment. To take the duty of an officer suddenly ill I happened to be stationed on service near the Emperor at Nogent. When others were urging him to make terms, I, though a young soldier, ventured to express myself to the contrary."

"And then?"

"His Majesty pardoned the liberty, recognized me, gave me his own cross, made me a Major on his staff."

"And the Eagle?"

"It is still carried at the head of what remains of the Fifth-of-the-Line," said the young man proudly.

"When we have taken your Emperor we will do away with those Eagles, and after we restore her rightful king to France we shall give her back her ancient flag of golden lilies," said the Russian.

"Precisely," said Marteau sharply. "When you have taken the Emperor you may do all that. The men who have made France so great under him will care little what you do, *monsieur*, under such circumstances."

"And why will they be so indifferent, Monsieur Jean?" asked the countess curiously.

"They will be dead, *mademoiselle*, and their Emperor, too, unless God preserve his life for some future use."

"Happy," said the young girl, "is the man who can inspire such devotion, *monsieur*. Although I have been trained differently I think that——"

What the countess thought was never said for at that instant the door at the farther end of the great room was thrown open suddenly with a violent crash, and into the apartment came crowding the score of villains and scoundrels who had been imprisoned below stairs. They had managed to break out in some way and had returned to the great hall to seize again their captives and to wreak their vengeance upon their betrayer. They had got at the wine and were inflamed with drink as well as revenge and savage passion. They had realized, of course, that some enemies were outside but they had not clearly grasped the situation. All they thought of at the time were the people in the great hall. They came crowding through the big doorway, several of them handling pistols and all of them shouting savage and fearsome cries of revenge and triumph.

Instantly the pistols were presented, the triggers pressed and half a dozen bullets swept through the room. Marteau had seen the first movement of the door. He had divined what had happened. Before the pistols had been levelled he was by the side of the countess. The table at which she sat was a huge and heavy one. With one movement he hurled her, chair and all, to the floor, with the other he threw the table on its side in front of her. One of the bullets grazed his cheek, the others swept harmlessly through the room. He seized from another table two of his remaining pistols and discharged them squarely into the face of the crowding mass at the other end of the room at point-blank range. The sounds of the shots still echoed when he cried out:

"The knife, Countess. Cut the bonds of the prisoners. We must fight here for our lives and your honour."

The Countess Laure was quick to understand.

"You are safe now. They have no more shots. Hasten," he urged, reaching down a hand and assisting her to her feet.

He clutched the barrels of his pistols thereafter and hurled them directly into the faces of the infuriated men. Five of them were down and his prompt action had given the people in the room a little respite.

"Gentlemen," cried Marteau, sweeping out his sword and stepping into the open space between the prisoners and the overturned table on one hand and the renegades on the other, "quick, take your swords for the honour of the Countess and for your lives."

The man who led the renegades had some idea of military tactics. He spoke a few sharp words and half a dozen of them backed out of the room, entered the outer hall and ran around to the door on the side of the apartment which gave access to the great hall. The little band of defenders retreated into a corner near the fireplace, which was raised a step or two above the floor of the room.

Meanwhile Laure had cut the lashings of the Russians, the *Cossacks*, and the Englishman. They staggered to their feet numb from their long bondage, but inspired by the frightful imminence of their peril they seized their swords and presented a bold front to the two-sided enemy. There was one pistol left charged. Marteau handed that to the girl.

"The last shot, *mademoiselle*," he said meaningly, "for yourself if——"

"I understand."

"If you could only get to the door," growled the Russian commander, "my men outside would make short work of——"

"It is impossible until we have dealt with these villains," said Marteau. "On guard!" he cried as the marauders suddenly leaped forward.

The big Englishman, burly, tremendously powerful for all his advancing years, dropped his sword for a moment, picked up one of the heavy oak chairs and hurled it full into the face of the larger body at the further end of the room. One stumbled over it, two others fell. The next moment both parties were upon the little group. In their haste, in their drunken excitement, the marauders had not thought to recharge their pistols. With swords, scythes and clubs they fell on the six men. Their numbers worked to their disadvantage. Three of the men surrounding the woman, the Frenchman and the two Russian guardsmen, were accomplished swordsmen. The *Cossacks* were not to be disdained in rough-and-tumble fighting and the Englishman was a valiant ally. Their racial antagonisms were forgot in their common danger and the deadly peril of the woman.

The swords of the soldiers flashed as they thrust and parried. The *cossacks*, less skilful, strove to beat down the attackers by sweeping slashes—not the best method for such close fighting. One *Cossack* was pierced through the breast by a thrust from a renegade and another was cut from his neck almost to his heart by a blow from a scythe. One of the Russian officers was wounded, fell to his knees and was dispatched. The Englishman was hit by a billet of wood and dazed. Marteau and the other Russian were still unharmed. But it was going hard with them. In fact, a fierce blow on his blade from a bludgeon shivered the weapon of the Frenchman. A sword was aimed at his heart. There was a blinding flash, a detonation, and the man who held it staggered back. The countess, the last pistol almost touching the man's body, had pulled the trigger. Marteau seized the sword of the man who had menaced him. The next instant the *château* was shaken by a terrific roar. The Russians outside having constructed a rude bomb had blown up the door.

For a second the combat ceased. The hall was full of smoke. From outside came shots, shrieks, cries, loud curses and groans, cheers, French and Russian voices, the galloping of horses, words of command. The French were there.

"To me," shouted Marteau at the top of his voice. "France!"

The first to heed the call was young Pierre. He descended the hall, watched the conflict a moment and, having possessed himself of a club, battered down the man nearest him, unsuspecting an attack from the rear, then ranged himself by the side of the surviving Russian and the Frenchman. He did not come through scathless, however, for one of the renegades cut him fiercely as he passed. He stood erect by an effort of will but it was evident he could now add little to the defence. The Russian took the pistol from his hand. The next second the great hall was filled with shouting figures of soldiers. Into the smoke and confusion of the room came Napoleon.

CHAPTER 11

An Emperor and a Gentleman

"The Emperor!" cried Marteau.

The Russian officer recognized Napoleon as quickly as the other. The Emperor advanced, the soldiers crowding after threw themselves upon the renegades immediately, while the Emperor strode forward alone. The young Russian noble was a quicker witted man than his countrymen ordinarily were. He saw a chance to end everything then and there, to do his country a great service, although his life would be forfeited instantly in the doing of it.

"My chance," he shouted, raising Pierre's pistol.

The shot was an easy one. It was impossible to miss. Marteau had stepped forward. The thrill in the tones of the man's voice attracted his attention. One glance and he saw all. He threw himself in front of the Emperor just as the Russian pressed the trigger. At the same moment the Countess Laure, who stood nearest him, struck up the Russian's arm. The bullet buried itself in the ceiling above.

"Thank God!" cried Marteau as the sound died away and he saw the Emperor standing unharmed.

Napoleon's keen eye had seen everything.

"It is this lady," said he gracefully, "to whom my safety is due. And I am not unmindful that you interposed your own body between the bullet and your Emperor."

"Your Majesty," cried Marteau, now that his Emperor was safe, fain to discharge his duty, "I have tidings of the utmost importance. I have held this *château* and detained this convoy the Russians had captured. It contains powder, food, guns——"

"I know," said the Emperor. "It comes in the nick of time."

"And I have to report, Sire, that the corps of Wittgenstein, Wrede and of the Field-Marshal Blücher, himself, are strung out at long intervals to the eastward of Champaubert. They have no idea of your proximity."

"Are the divisions in supporting distance of one another?"

"No, Sire. Olsuvieff's division lies isolated at Champaubert. As to the divisions of Sacken and Yorck I think——"

"I have already received information concerning them," said the Emperor, "from your friend, Bullet-Stopper. He should be here."

"I am here, your Majesty," roared the grenadier, stepping forward, "and saving your Imperial Presence I am glad to see the lad. It was I," continued the grenadier, addressing Marteau and presuming on the familiarity with which Napoleon sometimes treated his men, "that fired the shot that brought the man down from the window."

"And that shot saved us," said young Marteau. "This young peasant here——" he bent over Pierre—"he is not dead, Sire, but sorely wounded—he kept them out up there while we held the room here."

"But these?" asked Napoleon, looking at the prisoners.

"Renegades who had taken advantage of the absence of the Russians pursuing the escort to the wagon-train to seize the castle."

"Why did you not impress them for the defence thereof?" asked the Emperor. "They were French undoubtedly——"

"I found them fighting against us."

Rapidly and in few words Marteau told the story of the night, touching lightly upon his own part, but the Emperor was soldier enough to read between the words of the narration and reconstruct the scene instantly. He turned to one of his officers.

"Take those scoundrels out. Put them up against the wall and shoot them out of hand. They disgrace the name of France. Bid the surgeons of the command come here to look to the wounded."

"They are past hope, except the French boy, your Majesty," said Yeovil, who having recovered his own consciousness speedily had been examining them meanwhile. "I have some skill in wounds. One *Cossack* is already dead. It would be a mercy to put that other out of his misery with that horrible scythe slash."

"The Russian officer?"

"Gone, too."

"And who are you?"

"I am a barrister," answered the Englishman in bad but comprehensible French.

"A man of the law. You look it not," said the Emperor, smiling faintly.

"Necessity makes us all resort to the sword," said Sir Gervaise, looking at his bloody blade, for he had fought valiantly with the rest and would have been killed but he had been knocked senseless with that billet of wood which had hit him on the head and felled him to the floor.

"You are, by your language, an Englishman."

"I am, and proud of it."

"The English," said Napoleon slowly, "have been my bitterest enemies."

"Pardon, Sire," said the Russian bluntly, "we children of the white *Czar* will dispute that honour with them."

"And you sought to kill me?" said the Emperor, turning upon the other. "You are a brave man," he added.

"And I would have done so but for——"

"Bah!" interrupted Napoleon contemptuously. "The bullet is not moulded that is destined for me. My career is not to be cut short by the hand of any young boy who wears the uniform of the Russian guard. Silence, *monsieur!* Take him prisoner. See that he be kept under close guard. When we have taken Olsuvieff's division tomorrow and then Sacken's there will be many of his comrades to bear him company to Paris. Did any of the men outside escape?"

"No, Sire," answered General Maurice, entering the room just in time to hear the question. "The wood around the *château* was completely filled with my men. Those we have not killed here we have taken prisoner. Most of them were shot down as they strove to break through."

"That is well," said the Emperor.

"And the convoy?" asked General Maurice.

"Detach a regiment to escort it back to Sézanne. Let it be distributed to the regiments and divisions as they arrive."

"And those who have gone on ahead?"

"Their arms, equipment and provisions are in the hands of the Prussians. We shall march immediately. As for you, *mademoiselle*, what is your name?"

"I am the Comtesse Laure d'Aumenier."

"H'm, the daughter of the Comte Robert d'Aumenier, who made his submission to the Empire and received back his estates, I believe?"

"The same, Sire."

"Where is he?"

"Dead, Sire, these two years."

"And you?"

"I went to my uncle in England."

"To the enemy!" exclaimed Napoleon sharply.

"To the enemy," answered the Countess, looking at him courageously.

"And you came back for what purpose?"

"The estates are to be sold. There were certain papers of which I alone knew the hiding place. There was no way for me to reach them save by the courtesy of the Czar Alexander. He sent me to Field-Marshal Blücher with instructions to provide me with an escort to this *château*. The Field-Marshal did so, and the rest you know."

"And you propose to sell estates that have been in the hands of the family for so long a period? It seems to me that I visited them once when I was a military student at Brienne. Was not your uncle there at the time, an officer in command?"

"I have heard him say so."

"I remember him very well now."

"And he you, your Majesty."

"And he intends now to sell the estates?"

"He did, Sire, but now that there is a possibility of the re—of the——"

"The return of the Bourbons," said Napoleon, divining her thought as the countess paused in confusion, "There is no possibility of that, *mademoiselle*. In three weeks the armies opposing me will have been hurled back beyond the frontier. Your family has forfeited its rights to any consideration at my hands. Your uncle is an *émigré* who has never made his submission. I find you, a Frenchwoman, in the company of my enemies. Your estates are forfeited. Major Marteau, I make you Comte d'Aumenier. The domains are yours."

"I accept them, your Majesty."

"What! Is it possible——" cried the Countess Laure, her face flaming.

"Silence, *mademoiselle*. By the laws of war I could have you shot. It would be a fine example. No Frenchman, however high in rank and station, no Frenchwoman, however young or beautiful, can fight against me and France with impunity. Have you anything to say why I should not mete out to you this well-deserved punishment?"

"Nothing," said the young woman with proud disdain. "The revolution has taken the lives of many of my people. I am not better than they. You are the very spirit of the revolution incarnate, Sire, and——"

"Your Majesty," interposed General Maurice.

"Well, sir?" said Napoleon.

General Maurice, a famous light horseman, otherwise known as the Count de Vivonne, was an old friend and a devoted follower of the Emperor. He had interfered before on occasion between Napoleon and his victims. He knew the Emperor thoroughly and loved him. He realized that it was his time to interpose, or someone's, and he had intuition enough to suspect that his interposition would be most welcome, that indeed Napoleon was playing, as he sometimes loved to do, a little comedy. With a wave of his hand the general checked Marteau, whom he knew slightly, who had sprung forward to protest to the Emperor at the words of the woman he loved.

"Allow me a word, Sire," asked the general with that exquisite mixture of courtesy, deference and resolution which characterized his intercourse with the Emperor.

"I am always glad to hear from you, my good Maurice," said the Emperor familiarly. "What have you to say?"

"This young woman is no traitor to you or to France, Sire, however strange her position."

"How do you make that out?" asked the Emperor, the flickering of a smile playing about his lips.

"It was her hand that struck up the Russian's pistol so that the bullet went there," the General of cavalry pointed upward a moment and then his hand fell until his index finger was trained upon the Emperor's heart, "instead of there," he added meaningly.

"Very good," said the Emperor graciously. "But had she not struck up that hand it was in Marteau's heart that the bullet would have lodged, not in mine, if I remember rightly."

"And if that gives me a claim, Sire, to your consideration——"

"Have I not rewarded you enough," asked the Emperor, "in adding the official stamp of a patent to the nobility of heart which is already yours and by giving you the forfeited lands of Aumenier to boot?"

"And I would give them all for the safety of the lady yonder, whose family mine have served for eight hundred years, with whom I played when a boy, and be content to follow your Majesty as the simple soldier I have always been."

"Brave heart and true," said the Emperor, touched. "*Mademoiselle,* you cannot go back to Blücher. Within two days his army will be no more. I will give you a safe conduct. You can remain here for the night. Couriers will be dispatched to Troyes and to Paris under escort in the morning. They will take you there. You have friends there, I presume?"

"Many."

"You can remain there or, if opportunity arises, I will give orders to have you safely conducted so you can go back to England."

"And me, Sire?" growled out Sir Gervaise Yeovil.

The Emperor laughed.

"I am too good a soldier to fight with men of the law," he said. "You may go with your *protégée* and share her fortunes."

"I thank your Majesty," said the Englishman, touched in his blunt nature by this extraordinary magnanimity. "I will report your consideration to my king and his people and——"

"And say to them that I long for the moment when I can measure swords with the Duke of Wellington."

"And may that moment come speedily," returned Sir Gervaise.

"As for the rest," said the Emperor, turning away in high good humour, "Marteau, you have been continuously on service for two days and two nights and you are wounded——"

"It is nothing."

"Remain here with old Bullet-Stopper, who, true to his name, has had another touch of the enemy's lead. General Maurice, detail a score of the weakest of your command, those slightly wounded, to whom a night's rest would be useful. They shall remain here until the courier stops for the lady and her English friend, and then under Marteau's command rejoin me in the morning."

"Very good, Sire," said General Maurice, turning away.

"I thank your Majesty," said Marteau, "for all you have done for me, and for the Comtesse d'Aumenier."

"And I thank the Emperor also," said the young woman, smiling at him. "Your Majesty's generosity almost wins me to an imperial allegiance."

Napoleon laughed.

"Not even the Emperor," he said proudly, "is as black as he is painted by traitors and the English, *Mademoiselle!*" he bowed abruptly but not ungracefully. "Come, gentlemen," he said, turning on his heel, "we must march."

CHAPTER 12

An Alliance Declined

As the Emperor left the room, followed by the officers and men, a little silence fell over the three people remaining therein.

"Monsieur le Comte d'Aumenier!" exclaimed the Countess Laure, wonder, derision and disdain in her voice. "Your *château*, your domain!"

She looked about the great hall and laughed scornfully. Young Marteau turned crimson. He threw up his head proudly.

"*Mademoiselle*——" he began sternly, his voice full of indignant protest and resentment.

"Don't be too hard on the lad, Countess," interposed the Englishman, his interest aroused. "By gad, he saved your honour, your life, and——"

"And, if I mistake not, I repaid the obligation by saving his life also, sir."

"And I recognize it, and am grateful, *mademoiselle*."

"I am ordered to report to you, sir," said a young man, coming into the room followed by a file of dismounted soldiers, and relieving a situation growing most tense.

"Very good," said Marteau, devoutly thankful for the interruption. "You will dispose your men so as to guard the approaches of the *château* at every hand. You will keep a strict lookout, and you will awaken me at dawn. I think there is nothing to be apprehended from the enemy. The advance of the Emperor will have cleared all this section of even wandering troops of *Cossacks* by this time, but there are masterless men abroad."

"I shall know how to deal with them," said the young officer, saluting.

"You will also send men to remove these dead bodies and clear up this room. Take this poor lad"—pointing to Pierre—"and see that he is cared for. You will find a place for him upstairs. Your regimental surgeon——"

"Is attending to the wounded. I will see that the boy gets every care, sir."

"And Bal-Arrêt?"

"His arm is dressed, and he is the admiration of the camp-fire."

"I suppose so."

"Any other orders, Major?"

"None; you may go."

"*Mademoiselle*," said Marteau, facing the countess as the officer turned away, his men taking the dead bodies and the wounded peasant with them, "you wrong me terribly."

"By saving your life, pray?" she asked contemptuously.

"By—by—your——" he faltered and stopped.

"In what way, Monsieur le Comte?" interrupted the young woman, who knew very well what the young man meant.

In her irritating use of his new-found title, and in the way in which it fell from her lips, she cut him like a whip-lash, and she did it deliberately, too—he, the count, forsooth!

"Call me Marteau," he protested, stepping toward her, at which she fell back a little. "Or, better still, as when I was a boy, your faithful follower, Jean."

"If the Emperor has the power, he has made you a count; if he has not, you are not."

"What the Emperor makes me is of little consequence between us, *mademoiselle*. It is what I am that counts."

"And you remain, then, just Jean Marteau, of the loyal Marteaux?"

"One does not wipe out the devotion of years in a moment. My father served yours, your grandfather, your uncle, your father. I am still"—he threw up his head proudly as he made the confession—"your man."

"But the title——"

"What is a title? Your uncle is in England. He does not purpose to come back to France unless he whom he calls his rightful king again rules the land. Should that come to be, my poor patent of nobility would not be worth the parchment upon which it was engrossed."

"And the lands?"

"In any case I would but hold them in trust for the Marquis——"

"My uncle is old, childless. I am the last of the long line."

"Then I will hold them for you, *mademoiselle*. They are yours. When this war is over, and France is at peace once more, I will take my father's place and keep them for you."

"I could not accept such a sacrifice."

"It would be no sacrifice."

"I repeat, I cannot consent to be under such obligation, even to you."

"There is a way——" began the young Frenchman softly, shooting a meaning glance at the young woman.

"I do not understand," she faltered.

"I am peasant born," admitted Marteau, "but, though no gentle blood flows through my veins, my family, I think, is as old as your own."

"It is so," agreed the countess, trembling as she began to catch the meaning. "Oh, *monsieur*, stop."

"As there has never a d'Aumenier failed to hold the *château* so there has never failed a Marteau to follow him," went on the young man, unheeding her protest.

"I care as little for distinctions of rank as any *demoiselle* of old France, perhaps, but——"

"*Mademoiselle* is right. As for myself, I am a republican at heart, although I follow the Emperor. I, too, care little for the distinctions of rank, for titles, yet I have earned a title in the service of the Emperor. Through him, even humble men rise high and go far. Will you——"

"*Monsieur*, you must not go on!" cried the girl, "thrusting out her hand, as if to check him.

"Pardon," said the young Frenchman resolutely. "Having gone thus far I must go further. Humble as I am, obscure though I be, I have dared to raise my eyes to heaven—to you, *mademoiselle*. In my boyhood days you honoured me with your friendship, your companionship. I have made something of myself. If *mademoiselle* would only deign to—— It is impossible that she should love me—it would be an ineffable condescension—but is there not some merit in the thought that the last survivors of the two lines should unite to——"

"Impossible!" cried the countess, her face flushing. "My uncle would never consent. In my veins is the oldest, the noblest blood of France. Even I could not——"

"Be it so," said Marteau, paling, but standing very erect. "It is, of course, impossible. There is not honour enough or merit enough in the world," he went on bitterly, "to obliterate the difference in station between us. The revolution, after all, changed little. Keep the title, keep the estates, *mademoiselle*, I want them not," continued the young soldier bitterly. "Having aspired to you, do you think these are compensations?"

"You saved my life," said the girl falteringly.

"It was nothing. You did as much for me."

"And my honour," she added.

"I ask no reward."

"By gad!" said Yeovil at this juncture, "I'm damned if I see how you can withstand him. He is a gallant lad. He has fought bravely and he has pleaded nobly. You may not win the Countess—as a matter of fact she is pledged to my son—but you deserve her. I've never been able to understand any kind of women, much less Frenchwomen, saving your presence, *mademoiselle*. Base-born you may be, Major Marteau, but I know a gentleman when I see him, I flatter myself, and, *damme*, young man, here's my hand. I can understand your Emperor better since he can inspire the devotion of men like you."

The two men clasped hands. The countess looked on. She stepped softly nearer to them. She laid her hand on Marteau's shoulder.

"*Monsieur*—Jean," she said, and there was a long pause between the two words, "I would that I could grant your request, but it is—you see—you know I cannot. I am betrothed to Captain Yeovil, with my uncle's consent, of course. I am a very unhappy woman," she ended, although just what she meant by that last sentence she hardly knew.

"And this Captain Yeovil, he is a soldier?" asked Marteau.

"Under Wellington," answered the father.

"Now may God grant that I may meet him!"

"You'll find him a gallant officer," answered the sturdy old Englishman proudly.

"When I think of his father I know that to be true," was the polite rejoinder.

The little countess sank down on the chair, buried her face in her hands and burst into tears.

"Well, of all the——" began the Englishman, but the Frenchman checked him.

"*Mademoiselle*," he said softly, "were every tear a diamond they could not make for me so precious a diadem as they do when I think that you weep for me. I wish you joy with your English captain. I am your humble servant ever."

And Laure d'Aumenier felt very much comforted by those words. It was absurd, inconceivable, impossible, of course, and yet no handsomer, braver, truer, more considerate gentleman had ever crossed her horizon than this descendant of an ancient line of self-respecting, honourable yeomen. She contrasted him with Captain Yeovil, and the contrast was not to Marteau's disadvantage! No, decidedly not!

CHAPTER 13

The Thunderbolt Stroke

On the tenth of February, 1814, for the first time in many days, the sun shone brightly. Nevertheless there was little change in the temperature; the thaw still prevailed. The sun's heat was not great enough to dry the roads, nor was the weather sufficiently cold to freeze them. As the Emperor wrote to his brother, with scarcely any exaggeration, there was still six feet of mud on highways and by-paths.

Napoleon, by rapid marching at the head of Maurice's Squadrons d'Élite, mounted grenadiers, *chasseurs*, hussars and dragoons, had easily attained a position in front of the van of the army commanded by Marmont, which had rested a few hours at St. Prix, where the road crossed the Petit Morin on a bridge. His requisition on the peasantry had been honoured, and great numbers of fresh, vigorous draft horses had been brought in from all sides. There was not much speed to be got out of these farm animals, to be sure, but they were of prodigious strength. The ordinary gun teams were relieved, and numbers of these plough-horses attached to the limbers pulled the precious artillery steadily toward the enemy.

Scouts had discovered the fact that Olsuvieff's division was preparing breakfast on the low plateau upon which was situated the village of Champaubert, which had been observed by Marteau and Bal-Arrêt. Napoleon reconnoitred the place in person from the edge of the wood. Nansouty's cavalry had earlier driven some Russian skirmishers out of Baye, but Olsuvieff apparently had no conception of the fact that the whole French army was hard by, and he had contented himself with sending out a few scouts, who, unfortunately for him, scouted in the wrong direction.

While waiting for the infantry under Marmont to come up, Napoleon sent Nansouty's cavalry around to the left to head off Olsuvieff's advance and interpose between him and the rear guard of Sacken's division. Even the noise of the little battle—for the skirmish was a hot one—a mile down the road, did not apprise the Russian of his danger, and it was not until the long columns of the French came out of the wood and deployed and until the guns were hauled into the clearing and wheeled into action, that he awoke to the fact that an army was upon him and he would have to fight for his life.

With his unerring genius Napoleon had struck at the key position, the very centre of Blücher's long drawn-out line. With but thirty thousand men attacking eighty thousand he had so manoeuvred as to be in overwhelming force at the point of contact! In other words, he had got there first with the most men. Blücher's army was separated into detachments and stretched out over forty miles of roads.

Olsuvieff's division comprised five thousand men with twenty guns. At first Napoleon could bring against him not many more than that number of men and guns, to which must be added Nansouty's small cavalry division. And Olsuvieff, with all the advantages of the position, made a magnificent defence. As a defensive fighter the stubborn Russian took a back seat for no soldier in Europe. But the most determined resistance, the most magnificent courage, could not avail against overwhelming numbers, especially directed and led by Napoleon in person, for with every hour the numbers of the assailants were increased by the arrival of fresh troops, while with every hour the defence grew weaker through casualties.

Olsuvieff might have surrendered with honour at midday, but he was a stubborn soldier, and he realized, moreover, that it was his duty to hold Napoleon as long as possible. Even the most indifferent commander could not fail to see the danger to Blücher's isolated corps. Couriers broke through to the east to Sacken and Yorck, who together had over thirty-five thousand men under their command, and to the west to Blücher, with as many more men, telling all these commanders of the extreme peril of the centre and of the frightfully dangerous situation in which their carelessness and the ability of their great enemy had involved them. The noise of the firing, too, was carried far and wide over the broad open fields and cultivated farms of the rolling prairie of Champagne.

Blücher, however, could not credit the intelligence. He believed it impossible for Napoleon to have escaped from Schwarzenberg. He could not conceive that Napoleon would leave the Austrians unopposed to march to Paris if they would. He could not think that even

Napoleon would venture to attack eighty thousand men with thirty, and, if he did, he reasoned that Sacken and Yorck and Olsuvieff, singly or in combination, were easily a match for him. The messengers must surely be mistaken. This could only be a raid, a desperate stroke of some corps or division. Therefore, he halted and then drew back and concentrated on his rear guard waiting for further news.

Sacken and Yorck were nearer the fighting. They could hear and see for themselves. They at once gave over the pursuit of Macdonald and retraced their steps. Olsuvieff made good his defence until nightfall, when the survivors gave up the battle. Fifteen hundred men of his brave division had been killed on the *plateau*. As many more were wounded and captured, most of whom subsequently died, and there were about two thousand unhurt prisoners. Their ammunition was exhausted. They were worn out. They were overwhelmed by massed charges at last. Blücher's line was pierced, his centre crushed, and one of the finest divisions of his army was eliminated.

In the wagon train recaptured at Aumenier had been found arms and provisions and ammunition. Another Prussian wagon train, blundering along the road, was seized by Maurice's cavalry, which had been sent scouting to the eastward. From the Russian camp the starving French had got food, more arms and clothing. The dead were quickly despoiled, even the living were forced to contribute to the comfort of their conquerors. It was night before the last French division got up from Sézanne, but there was enough food and weapons for all.

A new spirit had come over that army. What had seemed to them a purposeless, ghastly march through the mud was now realized to be one of the most brilliant manoeuvres Napoleon had ever undertaken. The conscripts, the raw boys, the National Guards, many of whom had been in action for the first time that day, were filled with incredible enthusiasm. They were ready for anything.

But the army must have rest. It must be permitted to sleep the night. Accordingly the divisions were disposed in the fields. Those who had fought hardest were given quarters in the village; the next were placed in the captured Russian camp; the others made themselves as comfortable as they could around huge fires. The poor prisoners had little or nothing. The ragged French were at least better clothed than they were in the morning. The defenceless had arms and the whole army had been fed. There was wine, too; the Russian commissariat was a liberal one. There was much laughter and jovialness in the camps that night. Of course, the guard and the other veterans expected nothing else, but to the youngsters the brilliant stroke of Napoleon was a revelation.

As the little Emperor rode from division to division, sometimes dismounting and walking through the camps on foot, he was received with such acclaim as reminded him of the old days in Italy. And, indeed, the brief campaign which he had so brilliantly inaugurated can be favourably compared to that famous Italian adventure, or to any other short series of consecutive military exploits in the whole history of war.

They said that the Emperor had hesitated and lost his great opportunity at Borodino. They said that he had frightfully miscalculated at Moscow, that his judgment had been grievously at fault in the whole Russian campaign. They said that he had sat idle during a long day when the fortunes of his empire might have been settled at Bautzen. They said that, overcome by physical weariness, he had failed to grasp his great opportunity after the victory at Dresden. They said that Leipsic and the battles that preceded it showed that he had lost the ability to see things with a soldier's eye. They declared that he made pictures and presented them to himself as facts; that he thought as an Emperor, not as a captain.

They said that in this very campaign in France, the same imperial obsession had taken such hold upon him that in striving to retain everything from Holland to the end of the Italian peninsula he stood to lose everything. They said that, if he had concentrated all his armies, withdrawn them from outlying dependencies, he could have overwhelmed Blücher and Schwarzenberg, the Czar Alexander, the Emperor Francis and King William, and that, having hurled them beyond the Rhine, these provinces in dispute would have fallen to his hand again. They said that his practical omnipotence had blinded his judgment.

Those things may be true. But, whether they be true or not, no man ever showed a finer strategic grasp of a situation, no man ever displayed more tactical ability on a given field, no man ever conducted a series of more brilliant enterprises, no man ever utilized a small, compact, well-handled force opposed to at least two and a half times its number, no man ever conducted a campaign which stood higher from a professional point of view than this one which began with the march from Nogent and the destruction at Champaubert.

There was no rest for Napoleon that night. Undoubtedly he was not now the man he had been. Paralyzing physical disabilities before and after interfered with his movements. The enormous strains to which he had subjected his body and brain sometimes resulted in periods of mental blindness and physical prostration. It was whispered that a strange malady—was it some form of epilepsy?—sometimes overcame the Emperor so that his faculties and abilities were in abeyance for hours. No man had ever abused such wonderful mental and physical gifts as he originally had possessed by subjecting them to such absolutely impossible strains as he, and Nature was having her revenge. But for that week in February and for a time thereafter there was a strange and marvellous return of the Emperor's physical powers.

He had sustained more fatigue than any man in the army, because to all of the personal sufferings of the march in the long day and the sleepless night and the conduct of the battle had been added responsibility, but he was as fresh as a boy. His pale cheek showed rare colour; his eyes sparkled; his voice was clear and sharp. The nervous twitching of his mouth ceased. The gray look vanished. He was once more the boyish captain of the Army of Italy, at whom the huge grenadiers laughed and the gray-headed veterans marvelled.

The Emperor's scouts had been hard at work during the day. They were constantly coming and going at his headquarters at Champaubert with detailed accounts of the situation of the Russians and the Prussians. The Emperor had a momentous decision to make. From the position he had gained it was equally as easy for him to strike east as to strike west. He decided at last to strike west, realizing that no captain, much less fiery old Blücher, without an absolute forfeiture of his reputation as a soldier could afford to leave his van unsupported, but that the Prussian Field Marshal must advance to its support. If the Emperor's plans worked out, he could destroy that van, and then turn back and mete out the same fate to the main body coming to its rescue.

Just about ten miles away to the westward, on the main road to Paris by way of La Ferte-sous-Jouarre, lay the village of Montmirail. As many miles beyond Montmirail, on the same Paris road, Sacken, with twenty thousand men, had been advancing. From Montmirail a road led northward to Château Thierry and the crossing of the Marne, behind which Macdonald had been driven by Yorck, with perhaps fifteen thousand more. The Emperor decided to seize Montmirail, throw out a corps to hold back Yorck on the northern road, while he crushed Sacken on the other with the remainder of the army, except one corps, which he would leave at Champaubert to delay Blücher's advance. These army corps were in reality nothing more than weak divisions, less than seven thousand strong.

Early in the afternoon Marteau, with old Bullet-Stopper and the little squadron of Maurice's cavalry, had rejoined the Emperor. He had been greatly refreshed by his night's sleep. He had taken advantage of the early hours of the morning to bury his father and sister, saying such prayers as he could remember, in default of the parish priest, who had been murdered. The Emperor having sent a courier with an escort back to Nogent, the Countess Laure and her English friend had elected to go with them. They feared to be left alone in the *château* all day, in the disturbed state of the country, and it was easier, perhaps, to reach Paris from Nogent by way of the Seine than by going direct from Sézanne. Marteau had approved of their decision.

The parting between the young people had been as formal as possible. The Englishman, on the contrary, with true British hospitality, had said that if peace ever came he would indeed be glad to welcome him at his home in England. Marteau had sworn to hold the *château* and its land in trust for the Countess, although she protested she would not hear of anything of the kind. And then he had bade her farewell. He had arrived in time to take part in the hard fighting at the close of the day, and had been busy during the early part of the night in carrying messages and resuming his duties at headquarters.

At two o'clock in the morning Napoleon threw himself down on a peasant's bed in a hut and slept until four. At that hour he awakened and summoned the officer on duty. Marteau presented himself. The Emperor, as refreshed by his two hours of sleep as if he had spent the night in a comfortable bed, addressed the young man familiarly. None could unbend better than he.

"My good Marteau," he began. "But stop—Monsieur le Comte d'Aumenier"—he smiled—"I have not forgot. Berthier has orders to send to Paris to have your patent of nobility made out and to see that the confiscated Aumenier lands are transferred to you."

"I thank your Majesty," said the young *aide*, deeming it wiser to say nothing of his ultimate intentions regarding the patent of nobility and the estates.

"It would be a fine thing," said the Emperor, "if you and that girl should come together. She is the last of her line, I understand, save her old uncle in England, who is unmarried and childless. Is it not so?"

"That is true, Sire."

"Well, you couldn't do better. She is a woman of spirit and resolution. Her prompt action in the *château* last night showed it. I commend her to your consideration. Were I your age and in your station I should like nothing better."

"Your Majesty anticipated my desire, my own proposition, in fact."

"What? You struck while you had the opportunity? That was well."

"But, unlike you, Sire, I struck unavailingly."

"The lady refused?"

"Positively. She is of the oldest family in France, while I——"

"Marteau," said the Emperor sharply, "no more of that. If you cannot be a descendant, be an ancestor. Look at me. My family began at Montemotte, and today the mother of my son is a Hapsburg!"

"But she is engaged to the son of that Englishman, Sire."

"Bah, what of that? Engagements can be broken, marriages even dissolved. The Holy Father at Rome will refuse me nothing. When I have beaten the allies I will take your affair in hand. There are few powers in Europe that will turn a deaf ear to the suggestions of the Emperor of the French, believe me. The lady shall be yours."

"Your Majesty's power," said the young officer dubiously, "does not extend to women's hearts."

"Does it not?" laughed the Emperor grimly. "You shall see. My word shall be law again everywhere. With my favour you will go far. There are no patents of nobility that stand higher than mine, for mine are based on my recognition of merit alone, not on accident of birth. You served me well, and you shall see that I am not ungrateful. Meanwhile, to you a new duty is assigned."

"I welcome it gladly."

Napoleon took an order prepared the night before from a table.

"This to General Nansouty. I want him to march at once. Read it. You will see," he continued, "that Nansouty's cavalry is to hold Sacken in check until I have seized Montmirail. He has guns with him. Let him deploy, attack vigorously. Keep the enemy occupied and gradually fall back upon Montmirail. Ride with him yourself, and rejoin me at Montmirail about ten in the morning. We should be up then. You understand?" said the Emperor, ready to explain his orders more fully, believing that an order could be more intelligently delivered if the purport were explained verbally to the bearer, especially in the case of a skilled and trusted young soldier like Marteau.

"I understand, Sire."

"Away, then. Continue to merit my favour, for upon that favour rests"—he laughed, he was in high good spirits and humour that morning—"the lady."

Marteau saluted. In spite of himself a certain hope began to spring up in his heart. That Emperor was almost a *demi*-god to his men. Whatever he had essayed he had generally achieved in times past, and who could tell? Certainly they were on the eve of great events.

CHAPTER 14

The Hammer of the War God

Nansouty's brilliant cavalrymen were already awake and their general having divined to some extent the part he was to play in the glorious day, the eleventh of February, the trumpets were already calling his horsemen to arms when Marteau delivered the order and took his place by the general as the Emperor's representative, a high position and great responsibility for so young a soldier. They made a hasty breakfast and broke camp. Indeed, there was little to break. The words are only used figuratively, since they had no tents. In half an hour after Marteau had left the Emperor's headquarters, the squadrons were formed. Nansouty, attended by his staff and the young officer, galloped to the head of the column, gave the word of command and the gallant horsemen trotted down the road.

They had been posted near Fromentières, about two miles from Champaubert, for the night. The roads were bad, but they took to the fields, and by six o'clock they had passed through the town of Montmirail, easily driving out a few straggling battalions which occupied it. By eight o'clock they were in touch with the columns of Sacken at Vieux Maisons. A bit of woodland covered their approach. It was not until they were almost upon them that Sacken's advance came in touch with them. The French horse followed the Russian outposts and advance guards at a gallop back to the main column, upon which they fell impetuously. Batteries were also deployed in the woods and opened on the Russians.

Sacken's men had started after breakfast in a rather leisurely way, and they had not progressed very far when Nansouty surprised them. The French rode down the advance regiments, threw the heads of the columns into confusion, and then galloped back to the shelter of the wood. Believing that he was about to be attacked in force, Sacken deployed, wasting much valuable time before he discovered this was only a cavalry feint, whereupon he moved forward. It was ten o'clock before he reached a large farm called Haute-Épine. By that time Napoleon was ready for him. He had left Marmont back at Champaubert to hold back Blücher. He threw Mortier forward on the Château-Thierry road to check Yorck.

He put Friant, the veteran and splendid fighter, in *échelon* along the La Ferte road; withdrew Nansouty's cavalry to cover his own right, and put Ney and Ricard in his main battle line between Friant on the road and the river on the left. The guard, with Maurice's cavalry *d'élite*, he posted on the edge of the woodland, north of Montmirail, ready to throw to the northwestward to Marmont, or to the west to the support of Ney and Friant, as events might determine. These dispositions were barely completed before the battle was joined by the Russian advance.

Sacken, who really outnumbered the forces opposed to him by at least two thousand men, since Mortier's corps, guarding the northwest road, was perforce inactive, and since six thousand men had been left at Champaubert under Marmont to retain Blücher, attacked with the utmost stubbornness and gallantry. He could make no impression on Friant, *écheloned* on the main road, and before the resolute resistance his advancing divisions slowly obliqued to the right toward another walled farmhouse, called Épine-aux-Bois, in a stretch of lowland watered by a brook.

Napoleon, seeing the whole course of the battle clearly, laid a trap for him. He withdrew Nansouty from the battle, and ordered Ricard, in command of his extreme left, to retreat slowly, fighting as if defeated. Sacken, as he saw the wavering on his right, threw his heaviest battalions and regiments upon that point, and attacked with headlong impetuosity. At the same time he had enough men left to keep Friant busy and in check. Napoleon, seeing the success of his ruse, suddenly brought up the Guard. He threw it around the right flank of Friant, and Sacken's left immediately began to give way. Ricard stopped his retreat suddenly and stood like a stone wall. His withdrawing Eagles moved forward.

The advance of the Russian right stopped also, the Muscovite officers and soldiers were greatly amazed by the sudden resistance of an enemy retreating a moment since. One division of the Guard moved out to the support of Friant, who also advanced. The other division joined Mortier, who was in a hot fight with Yorck's cavalry and light infantry. Napoleon now turned to General Maurice, who had ridden up in advance of his horsemen.

"There"—he pointed down the hill toward the dark masses of the Russian right—"there's your chance, General."

The Comte de Vivonne needed but the word. Turning in his saddle he raised his sword. His cavalry had been waiting with unconcealed impatience during the morning. Eagerly they responded to the command. Dashing down the hill they fell on the puzzled Russian infantry around Épine-aux-Bois. Ricard's men opened to give them way. What had been a triumphant advance was turned into a retreat. The retreat bade fair to be a disaster, but the Russians, as has been noted, were splendid defensive soldiers. They formed squares. Although regiment after regiment had been ridden over and beaten to pieces, those who remained fought stubbornly.

Sacken perceived now that his only hope was to effect a junction with Yorck. He withdrew his men under cover of his artillery to Vieux-Maisons, and began to lead them by the left flank, at the same time sending frantic messages to Yorck, imploring him to hasten. But Yorck's guns were mired. He had only the teams attached to them. He could get no other horses. He was unaccountably delayed. He had faced about at the sound of the firing, but the movements of his main body were slow, deliberate. Nansouty, who had opened the battle, was now sent in by Napoleon to deliver the *coup-de-grâce*. With characteristic gallantry he fell upon the Russian columns.

Sacken was driven from the field. In killed, wounded, and prisoners he had lost half his force and all of his guns. His troops streamed westward through roads and woods in wild confusion. He would have been annihilated then and there but for the arrival of Yorck. The Prussian at last fell on Mortier's weak corps and the Guard on the northern road. Mortier's men were outnumbered four to one. They made a desperate resistance, but it was not until Napoleon ordered up the other division of the Guard, which had only been lightly engaged, and Maurice's cavalry, that Yorck's advance was checked.

The short day had drawn to a close. Preparations were made to pass the night on the field and in the town. All of Sacken's baggage train and provisions had fallen into Napoleon's hands. Montmirail had been a more decisive victory than Champaubert. Twenty thousand men had been eliminated from calculations for the time being. Sending couriers to Macdonald to move down the banks of the Marne with all possible speed, to get in the rear of Yorck, with whom he purposed to deal on the morrow, Napoleon, in high spirits, made preparations for the next day's battle.

The next morning, the thirteenth, leaving a heavy force to check any possible attack by Sacken, who had, with incredible energy and labour, partially at least reorganized his shattered troops, but who was too weak to do anything more than lead them away from any possible touch with Napoleon's troops, the Emperor advanced toward the little village of Château-Thierry. Yorck, by this time, had learned the full details of the disaster to Sacken. Indeed, several of Sacken's brigades had joined him, considerably augmenting his force. But he was now no match for Napoleon. To stay meant annihilation. He hastily made his disposition for a rear guard defence and a withdrawal. He made a stubborn rear guard battle of it during the day, and, although he lost heavily in men, guns and supplies, he finally succeeded in crossing the Marne and breaking the bridges behind him.

Macdonald had moved tardily. If he had shown half the enterprise of the Emperor he would have been at the crossing of the Marne in good time and Yorck would have been caught in a trap whence he could not have extricated himself. As it was, Napoleon added largely to the number of prisoners taken and the number of enemies killed. Altogether he had put twenty-five thousand men out of action, in killed, wounded and prisoners. He had taken one hundred and twenty guns—so many that he had to tumble them into the creeks and rivers, because he could not transport them all. He had rearmed and reclothed and provided for his gallant little army at the expense of the enemy. It was an exploit of which even he could be proud. On the other hand, in these operations the French had lost some four thousand men killed and wounded, and, as their army was so small, they could ill afford such a diminution of their forces.

Meantime, Blücher, apprised of these disasters, and at last awakened to his peril, bravely marched westward. He had come in touch with Marmont, and had driven him out of Champaubert after a desperate resistance. The day after the elimination of Yorck, the fourteenth, Napoleon headed his tired but triumphant troops back over the road to Champaubert, sending word to Marmont to hold the Prussians in check as long as possible, to dispute every rod of the way, but not to throw away his precious men or bring on a general engagement until the Emperor arrived.

The morning after that Napoleon fell on Blücher, who clearly outnumbered the French. But the allies were dismayed and disheartened.

The name of the Emperor whom they had defeated and driven across Europe was again full of terror to them. The French were accordingly elated. They would not be denied. Marmont's men, intoxicated with the news of the success of the other divisions of the army, just as soon as they were given the word, which was just as soon as Napoleon could bring up their comrades, fell on Blücher like a storm.

They came in battle contact in the village of Vauchamps. The fighting was of the most desperate character. The battle was harder than all of the others put together. Bavarians, Prussians, and Russians, fighting under the eye of brave old Blücher himself, who recklessly exposed his person on the field, were tenacious and courageous to the highest degree, but the tactics and dispositions of Napoleon, the spirit of his men, his own equally reckless exposure of his person under fire, and a cavalry dash at the allied rear at Janvilliers, finally turned the wavering tide of battle. The allies began to retreat, the French followed.

The French pursued relentlessly, but with splendid skill and determination Blücher himself in command of the rearguard fought them off. Napoleon had foreseen this. He had massed all the cavalry under Grouchy and had sent them on a long round-about march across country to get in Blücher's rear. Just beyond Champaubert, in a dense wood in front of the village of Étoges, the retreating allies found the road barred by the cavalry. Grouchy had been provided with sufficient artillery to enable him to hold the retreat in check; but the mud still prevailed, many horses had been shot and killed, the peasants' horses drawing the guns had been unable to keep pace with the necessarily rapid movements of the cavalry, and the batteries had not come up. Nor was there any supporting infantry. Indeed, the retreat of the Prussians had been so sudden and so rapid that Grouchy's horse had been hard put to it to intercept them.

The regiments leading the allied retreat were formed in squares, and with musketry and cannon animated with the courage of despair, they forced a passage through the charging, barring masses of the French cavalry, not, however, without losing several of the squares in the process. It was their only possible way to safety. As it was, Blücher himself narrowly escaped capture.

Napoleon's soldiers had fought five pitched battles in four days. As a preparation, they had marched thirty miles, night and day, over incredible roads. They were now utterly exhausted. They could do no more. They must have a good rest. Blücher's forces had been scattered, eliminated, defeated in detail. There was now nothing for the Field

Marshal to do but to retreat and rally his men. The success of the Emperor had been brilliant in the extreme.

The fighting was not over, however, for thirty miles to the southward lay the vast army of Schwarzenberg. Napoleon might have pursued Blücher to the bitter end. Military critics say he should have done so. To him, however, on the spot, it seemed proper to leave Blücher for the time being and endeavour to repeat on Schwarzenberg the marvellous tactics of the five days' fight.

The next morning, the fifteenth, he started back to Nogent whence he had come. Victor and Oudinot had been fighting hard with Schwarzenberg, but the news of Napoleon's victories had finally caused the cautious Austrian to stop. He began the recall and concentration of his own scattered divisions. He, at least, would not be caught napping. As usual the enemy learned something, even in defeat.

Speed was still essential to Napoleon. His men had had twenty-four hours of rest. His horses were comparatively fresh. The weather had changed, the roads were frozen, horribly rough, but still much more passable than before. Once again the Emperor resorted to the peasantry. They, too, had been intoxicated with the news of his victories, many of which they had witnessed and, in the plunder resulting, had shared. They brought their horses which they had hidden in ravines and forests when the country was overrun by the enemy. This time, instead of attaching them to the guns which their own teams— recruited from the captures—could draw on the hard roads, Napoleon had them hitched to the big farm wagons. Into the wagons he loaded his infantry. And at the highest speed of the horses the whole force made its way to the southward. To other victories—to defeats—to what?

The Emperor began once again to dream of an empire whose boundaries would be the Vistula instead of the Rhine.

BOOK 2
THE EAGLE'S FLIGHT

CHAPTER 15

The Bridge at Arcis

The long journey was at last over. The last Alp had been surmounted, the last pass traversed. Behind them rose the snowy summit of mighty Mont Blanc itself. Before them lay their wearying journey's end. It was cold even in sunny Southern France on that morning in early spring. Marteau, his uniform worn, frayed, travel-stained, and dusty, his close-wrapped precious parcel held to his breast under his shabby great coat, his face pale and haggard from hardship and heart-break, his body weak and wasted from long illness and long captivity, stood on the top of a ridge of the hill called Mont Rachais, over-looking the walled town of Grenoble, on the right bank of the Isère. The Fifth-of-the-Line had been stationed there before in one of the infrequent periods of peace during the Napoleonic era. He was fa-miliar with the place and he knew exactly where to look for what he expected to see.

More ragged and tattered, more travel-stained indeed, and with only the semblance of a uniform left, was the young lad who stood by the soldier's side. But the boy was in good health and looked strong and sturdy.

"There," said the officer. "You see that square bulk of buildings against the wall beyond the Cathedral church-tower and over the Pal-ais de Justice?"

"I see them, my officer," answered the other, shading his hand and staring over the roofs and walls and spires of the compact little town.

"The barracks will be there unless the regiment has moved. That will be the end of our journey."

"The building with the flag, you mean, *monsieur*?" asked Pierre.

"That one."

Alas! the flag was no longer the tricolour but the white flag of ancient royal France. Marteau heaved a deep sigh as he stared at it with sad eyes and sadder face.

The unexpected, that is, from the young soldier's point of view, had happened. The empire was no more. The allies had triumphed. The Emperor has been beaten. He had abdicated and gone. He was practically a prisoner on the little island of Elba, adjacent to that greater island of Corsica, where he had been born. The great circle of his life had been completed. And all the achievements were to be comprehended between those two little islands in the blue Mediterranean— from Corsica to Elba, the phrase ran. Was that all?

Much water had flowed under the bridges of Europe since that mad ride of the infantry in the farm wagons to face Schwarzenberg after their smashing and successful attacks upon Blücher, although the intervening time had been short. A year had scarcely elapsed, but that twelve months had been crowded with incident, excitement, and vivid interest almost unparalleled by any similar period in modern history. The Emperor had, indeed, fought hard for his throne and against heavy odds. He had fought against indifference, against carelessness, against negligence, last of all against treachery. For in the end it was treachery that had undone him and France. Still, it may be that even had Marmont and Mortier remained loyal the end would have been the same.

The odds were too heavy, in fine. The Emperor did not realize their preponderance until it was too late. If he had assembled every soldier, abandoning everything else but the defence of France, and if he had shown with such an army as he could have gathered under those conditions the same spirit of generalship which he had exhibited in that marvellous campaign against Blücher, he might have saved France, his throne, his wife, his little son, his prestige, everything. As it was, he lost all. But not without fighting. Stubborn, determined, magnificently defiant he had been to the last.

Marteau had often thrilled to the recollection during the long hours he spent in captivity in Austria, and even in the delirium and fever of his long and wasting illness, begot of the foul prison, he had remembered it. In all the hard fighting and hard marching of those mournful if splendid days the young man had faithfully and well borne his important if humble part. There was a great dearth of officers, staff officers as well as the others. He had been very near to the Emperor during those last days.

He remembered the smashing attack upon the van of the allies at Montereau. He could feel once more the thrill of the army, as the circumspect Schwarzenberg stopped his advance, retired, concentrated his columns. He remembered the long, swift march back across the country, after further demonstrations to keep Schwarzenberg in his cautious mood, against the rear of the reorganized and advancing army of Blücher; the desperate, bloody, fruitless Battles of Laon and Craonne, rendered necessary by treachery.

He could recall again the furious rage of Napoleon, the almost despair that filled the Emperor's heart, when the news came of the cowardly surrender of the fort at Soissons by its incapable commandant, which rendered useless Napoleon's cunning plans, and all the hard marching and harder fighting of his heroic soldiery.

He recalled the escape of hard-pressed Blücher again, the return of the French to face the overwhelming main army of the allies, slowly but surely moving toward its goal whenever the withdrawal of the Emperor left it free to advance, the detachment of Marmont and Mortier to defend Paris, the fierce two-day battle at Arcis-sur-Aube, the dash of Maurice's and Sebastiani's gallant cavalry upon the whole Austrian army, the deadly conflict before the bridge, the picture of the retreat that bade fair to become a rout.

He could see again the Emperor, riding down, sword in hand, into the midst of the fugitives crossing the bridge, and, amid a storm of bullets, ordering and beseeching and imploring the men to rally. He had been there on that mad March morning. He would never forget the sight of that figure, the words the Emperor said. It reminded him of the dash of the "little corporal" with the flag on the bridge of Lodi, of which old Bullet-Stopper had often told him and the other young men over the camp-fires.

The Fifth-of-the-Line had immortalized itself that day, adding to the fame it had gained upon a hundred fields, an imperishable crown. Napoleon saw that the battle was lost, that the whole Austrian army had blundered upon that first French division and that, unless their steady advance could be checked, the division itself would be cut to pieces. Men had grown more precious to the Emperor every hour. What would he not have given for those he had spent so recklessly years before? And here was a whole division about to be annihilated, to say nothing of the cavalry, which had performed prodigies of valor.

"What regiment is that?" he had asked Marteau, who was riding at his heels in the midst of the fugitives, and doing his best to second the Emperor's frantic efforts to restore order and bring the men to a stand.

"The Fifth-of-the-Line, Sire."

"Your old regiment?"

"The same, Sire."

"It still stands."

"And it will stand."

"Good! Go to it. Tell them that I, the Emperor, devote them to death, for me and for the army. They must hold the Austrians in check and cover the retreat."

"Farewell, Sire," the young soldier had said, saluting.

"What mean you?"

"I shall not come back with the remainder."

"*Adieu*," said the Emperor, acknowledging the salute and understanding all.

How well Marteau remembered that frightful conflict. The Fifth-of-the-Line had not waited to be attacked. It had gone forward. The Colonel had been shot down. Officer after officer had fallen. The advancing line had wavered, hesitated, halted. The Eagle-bearer fell. Eager hands caught the staff. The Austrian fire was concentrated upon it. The colour guard was shot to pieces. The Eagle itself had the tip of its right wing shot away. Mortal men could do no more. The regiment began to give back.

It was Marteau who sprang to the front, he and young Pierre, who had attached himself to the officer in a sort of unofficial way. It was Marteau who seized the Eagle; it was he who rallied the line. The new men formed up like veterans, the old men settled in their places, cool and ready. They returned the Austrian fire, they checked the Austrian advance, they stood ready while the troops behind them ran for their lives. Napoleon, whose eye nothing escaped, saw it all. He even recognized Marteau carrying the Eagle.

The Fifth-of-the-Line made good that defence until the time came for the retreat. Then it retired slowly, fighting every step of the way down the low hill to the bridge. The men dropped by scores. The Austrians, seeing victory in reach, pressed closer. A charge at the last minute by the cuirassiers of the Emperor Francis' guard almost completed the annihilation of the first battalion of the regiment. The survivors sought to form a square, under a withering gun fire, to meet the uplifted sabres of the heavy cavalry. There were not enough of them left. They were ridden down. Two hundred and fifty of the four hundred who went into that fight lay dead on that field. Of the survivors scarce a handful got across the river. Some of the unhurt men, disdaining quarter and unable to fly, fought until they fell. The wounded, of whom there were many, were all captured out of hand.

Marteau, with the Eagle, had stood nearest the enemy. They had swarmed about him at last. He found himself alone, save for the boy, Pierre. He could see the red-faced, excited, shouting, yelling, passion-animated Austrian soldiers crowding upon him. His sword was broken, his pistols empty and gone. He was defenceless. Retreat was cut off. The Eagle staff had been shot away. The flag torn to pieces. Hands were stretched out to seize it. He could not escape with it, yet it must not fall to the enemy. It was the tradition of the service that the Eagles were to be preserved at all hazards—not the flag, that was a mere perishable adjunct to the Eagle, but the Eagle itself. The river ran but a few feet away. Thrusting aside the nearest Austrian with the stump of his blade, Marteau cleared a path for a second, and into the swift deep waters he hurled the sacred emblem.

He, at least, he thought swiftly, had a right to dispose of it thus, for out of the waters of the Elster he had brought it, so into the waters of the Aube he threw it.

With cries of rage, for the Eagle was the most precious spoil of war, and the regiment or the officer seizing it was distinguished above all others, the Austrians would have cut him down where he stood with arms crossed, facing the enemy, but officers who had ridden up had seen the exploit and had interfered. He had been made a prisoner and Pierre with him. He just had time to whisper to the boy to mark well the spot where the Eagle had disappeared in the waters before they marched away.

While under guard with other prisoners at Salzburg he had heard the story of the end. How Napoleon, trusting the defence of Paris to Marmont and Mortier, had resolved on the bold move of cutting the communications of the allies with his little army, and how the allies had decided to disregard their rear and march on Paris; how Marmont and Mortier had battled for the capital, how the Emperor, hearing of their straits, had begun that mad march toward his beloved city; how he had ordered every soldier that could be reached to march in that direction; how he had stopped at a wayside inn one night for a few hours' rest, after a furious day's ride, only to be told that Marmont and Mortier had gone over to the enemy, that Paris was lost!

The prisoners had learned how the Emperor, not yet despairing, had striven to quicken the spirits of his marshals and soldiers for a last try; how the marshals and great officers had failed him. They had all heard of those lonely hours at Fontainebleau, of the farewell to the Guard, of the kiss on the Eagle, which he surrendered to General Petit, of the abdication, of the exile to Elba, of the restoration of King Louis.

It had made Marteau ill, frightfully so, and but for the tender nursing and loving care of young Pierre he had died. The lad had been devotion itself, but Marteau missed more than anything else the companionship, the sage advice, the bon camaraderie of old Bullet-Stopper. He had never seen him or heard from him after that day at the bridge-head at Arcis. Where was he now?

Oh, yes, those days and their tidings would never be forgot. They all came back to the young officer, as with his humble but devoted companion he stood there on the heights above Grenoble looking at the white flag.

CHAPTER 16

The Gate in the Wall

The two travellers were stopped by the guard at the main gate in the walls that encircled the town. Marteau had drawn his old cloak closely about him, so that it was not evident that he was in uniform. Pierre's nondescript garments were so tattered and torn that neither would they betray the pair. The sentry was clad in the old uniform of the Fifth-of-the-Line, except that he sported a white cockade in his head-gear and every device that referred to the Empire had been carefully eliminated. Still he was the same soldier, and Marteau recognized him at once as one of the veterans of the regiment. The recognition was not mutual. Captivity, illness, privation had wrought many changes in the officer's face. The man looked at him curiously and wonderingly, however, as he challenged him.

"My friend," asked the officer, "of what regiment are you, I pray?"

"The Fifth-of-the——" began the man instinctively, apparently, and then he stopped. "The regiment Dauphiné," he answered, his face clouding.

"And what battalion?"

"The first, sir."

"Are there other troops in garrison?"

"Another regiment of infantry, that was the Seventh. I don't know its new name. And some artillery to man the walls."

"Good. I should like—— Who is in command of the town?"

"There is a new one since yesterday. He has just come down from Paris, the King sent——"

At that instant the gruff voice of the subaltern in command of the detachment at the gate rang out.

"Turn out the guard for the Commanding Officer."

"Back, *monsieur*," cried the soldier, falling into line with his comrades, who came running from the guard-house and ranged themselves in order.

Marteau stepped back into the shadow of the gate, just as a carriage and four, carrying three people and attended by a brilliant cavalry escort, dashed through the narrow street of the town and passed out of the gate, the soldiers of the guard standing at attention in line and presenting arms as the carriage and its following went on into the country by the highroad. The horses had been moving at a fast trot. Marteau had time for but one glance as the vehicle passed. One glance was enough. When the guard had been dismissed and the soldier on post turned again to look at the officer, he was astonished at the change that had come over him. Marteau, pale as death, leaned against the wall, his hand on his heart.

"What's the matter?" cried the soldier, staring at him curiously.

"Has *monsieur* seen a ghost?" asked young Pierre, running toward him in great anxiety.

"Who—who was that?" asked Marteau, who had received a dreadful shock apparently.

"The governor of the town."

"Yes, yes, I know, but his name?"

"I was about to tell you. The Marquis de—— Upon my word, I have forgot it."

"Was it by any chance the Marquis d'Aumenier?"

"That's it," said the soldier.

"And the man with him in the red coat?"

The soldier spat into the dust to show his contempt.

"An English milord."

"And the lady?"

"I don't know. They say, the wife of that Englishman. Things have come to a pretty pass," growled the soldier, turning away, "when our girls marry these English beef-eaters, and—— It was not so in the day of the Em——"

He stopped suddenly, wondering fearfully whether his garrulousness had betrayed him into an imprudence with this stranger.

"No," said Marteau reassuringly. "Will you let me pass, comrade? I am an old soldier of—the Empire." He had no hesitation in avowing himself under the circumstances. "See," he threw open his cloak, disclosing his uniform.

"Why, that is the uniform of this regiment!" exclaimed the amazed soldier.

"Yes."

"And you are——"

"I was Captain Marteau when with the regiment," returned the officer.

"I thought I knew you, sir. Yes, I remember it all now. You were cut down at the bridge at Arcis."

"Yes."

"I, too, was there. I was one of the few who managed to get away alive. But I did not run, *monsieur*. I did not go back until the order."

"I believe it."

"And this boy?"

"He is a young comrade, a faithful companion of my own."

"And you are come back——"

"To rejoin the regiment. I have been months in an Austrian prison, and afterward, ill."

"Pass freely, *monsieur*. You rallied us with the Eagle. We saw it go into the river. The Emperor himself commended us, those who were left. He said we should have another Eagle, but alas, we never got it."

"Have patience," said Marteau. "What is lost may be found."

He touched the small, well-wrapped parcel, which even in his agitation he had not allowed to fall to the ground. The soldier looked at him wonderingly.

"You mean——"

"Never mind. Be silent. Will you call your officer?"

"Corporal of the guard," shouted the sentry, and, when that official appeared, the lieutenant in command of the gate was soon summoned through the usual military channels.

"*Monsieur*," said Marteau, walking up to him, "do you not know me?"

"By heaven!" cried the officer, after a long stare, "is it—it is Captain Marteau!"

"The same."

"We thought you dead. Your name is honoured in the regiment. We knew how you rallied the line; how you took the Eagle; how you threw it into the river rather than permit it to be taken. We thought you were killed."

"My life was spared," was the solemn answer.

"But why did you not rejoin the regiment?"

"I was in prison at Salzburg, and for some reason was overlooked, perhaps because it was thought I was dead, and then for some months

I was helpless, ill of a horrible fever. It was only two months ago that I was set free, with this lad here, who stood beside me before the bridge at Arcis. We learned through unofficial sources that the regiment was here. Having nowhere else to go, I came back, and——"

"They will be glad to see you," said the officer. "The regiment lost heavily. It was almost cut to pieces at Arcis."

"I know."

"But many officers and men of the old regiment have come back, like you, from Russia, from Prussia and from Austria, where they had been held prisoners. They will be glad to welcome you at the barracks yonder. You are permitted to pass. But stop. I must do my duty. What have you in that parcel?"

Marteau looked about him, moved a step away from the sentries and the corporal and sergeant of the guard, and whispered a word into the ear of the officer. He threw up his hands in astonishment.

"*Mon Dieu!*" he exclaimed. "Is it possible?"

"The same," said Marteau, "but say nothing about it until I have seen our comrades."

"Of course not."

"And that carriage and four that just passed?"

"The governor of the town, the Marquis d'Aumenier, the new commander of the regiment."

"I see; and our old Colonel?"

"Dead. The Major commanding the first battalion has been in command until they sent this old noble down here yesterday."

"And the lady?"

"His niece."

"You have met her?"

"Not I. They care nothing for such as we. He treats us as if we were of the scum of the earth, dogs. Oh, if only——"

"Hush," said Marteau. "It is dangerous."

"I know. And he brought with him an Englishman, one of the Duke of Wellington's officers."

"Is he married to the young lady?"

"Not yet, I believe, but betrothed."

"And his name?"

"He has a barbarous name. I can't pronounce it. He had us out inspecting us yesterday—he and that Englishman. Bah! To think of the Fifth-of-the-Line being inspected by such a young red-coated cockerel."

The veteran spat in the dust as the soldier had done and swore roundly. He hated the red-coated English. He had fought them before, and he would like nothing better than to fight them again.

"Patience," said Marteau.

"Do you wish to go to headquarters and report yourself? You were a Major on the Emperor's staff?"

"A Lieutenant-Colonel, by personal appointment that day at Arcis."

"Well, you will be lucky enough if they make you a subaltern. Look at me. I am older than you. I am a veteran of Italy and I am only a sub-lieutenant, I, who was Captain when I was captured."

"Patience, my friend," said Marteau again.

"Here," said the officer, hailing a cabriolet, which suddenly turned the corner.

"I have no money," said Marteau quickly.

"The King pays ill enough," answered the officer, "but what I have is ever at the service of a good comrade."

He assisted Marteau into the cabriolet, allowed Pierre to climb up beside him, paid the driver his fare, and bade him take the two to the headquarters in the barracks.

CHAPTER 17

A Veteran of the Army of Italy

It was noon when Marteau presented himself before the house in which the major of the first battalion, an old veteran named Lestoype, was quartered.

"Who shall I say wants to see him?" asked the orderly before the door.

"A soldier of the Empire," was the bold answer, and it proved an *open sesame* to the astonished orderly.

Lestoype was writing at a table, but he looked up when Marteau came in. He stared at him a moment and then rose to his feet.

"I report myself ready for duty, Major," said the young officer, saluting.

"Good God, is it Marteau!" exclaimed the Major.

"The same."

"We thought you dead."

Rapidly the young officer explained the situation.

"You see," he said in closing, "I survived the Eagle."

"Ah, if we could only have got it back!" exclaimed the Major.

"It is back."

"What do you mean?"

"It is here."

"I don't understand."

"Look," cried the officer, nervously tearing away the wrappings and holding up his precious burden.

The major came to attention, his heels clicked together, his hand went up. He stared at the Eagle.

"*Vive l'Empereur*," he said.

"*Vive l'Empereur*," answered the other, but both of them spoke in whispers, for there was no Emperor, and a mention of the name was treason to the King.

"It is the same?" asked the major, taking the precious emblem in his hand and pressing it to his heart.

"The very same."

"But how?"

"The boy here and I marked the spot where it fell. We took bearings, as a sailor would say; we took them independently, and when we had a chance to compare them we found that we agreed exactly. When I was released from prison and discharged from the hospital as a convalescent, we went back to Arcis, to the bridge, to the river side. The boy here is an expert swimmer. The river was low. He dove into the icy waters again and again until he found it. We were most circumspect in our movements. No one observed us. I wrapped it up, concealed it carefully, learned that the regiment was here, and I surrender it into your hands."

"It is a shame," began Lestoype gloomily at last, laying the Eagle gently down on his desk.

"What is a shame?"

"The order."

"What order?"

"The Eagles of all the regiments and ships are to be sent to Paris to be destroyed."

"Impossible!"

"Nevertheless, it is true. They have taken them wherever they could lay hands on them. It has almost caused a revolt."

"And are you going to send this Eagle to Paris?" asked Marteau threateningly. "This Eagle for which I fought, this Eagle which I rescued from the Elster and the Aube, for which hundreds of brave men have died, this Eagle which has been in the forefront of every battle in which the regiment took part since the Emperor gave it into our keeping before Ulm?"

"What can I do?"

"I will throw it into the Isère first. I will destroy it myself before that happens," cried Marteau, snatching it up and pressing it to his heart. "I have taken no oaths. I am still the Emperor's man."

"Not so loud," said Lestoype warningly. "The men of the regiment may not all be true. You may be overheard."

"You and all the others have taken the oath of allegiance to the King?"

"What else was there to do? Soldiering is my trade. They offered

362

us commissions; the Empire was dead; the Emperor banished. It was a living, at any rate."

"But I am free, I am not bound."

"You must, you will take the oath," urged Lestoype.

"How if he should come back?"

"He will not come back."

"Will he not? It is whispered everywhere," said Marteau. "I have not passed an old soldier who did not voice the hope. It's in the air. 'When the violets bloom,' they say. Even the peasants whisper it. The imperial purple flower—— He will return."

"God grant it may be so."

"And we shall be ready for him, we who have not taken the oath, and who——"

"I am afraid I shall be a forsworn man, in that case," said the veteran, smiling grimly. "Should the Emperor again set foot in France his presence would absolve us from all vows. I only serve under the King's colours because no others fly in France."

"Be it so."

"And you will be with us again in the regiment?"

"How can I?"

"Be advised," said the old soldier, laying his hand upon the arm of the younger, "we must keep together. We must keep our regimental organizations intact. The army must be ready for him. Take the oath as well nigh every soldier high and low in France has done, and——"

"Well, I shall see. Meanwhile, the Eagle there. You won't give it up?"

"Give it up!" laughed Lestoype. "I feel just as you do about it, but we must conceal it. The Seventh, Labédoyère's regiment, in garrison here, concealed their Eagle. At least it has not been found. There was a terrible to do about it."

"Do you vouch for the officer at the main gate? I had to tell him in order to be passed. I know him but slightly."

"The Sub-Lieutenant Drehon."

"He is safe?"

"Beyond doubt. Meanwhile, you require——"

"Everything," said Marteau simply.

"The King's paymasters are a long time in coming. We are left to make shift as best we can. But I am not yet penniless," returned the old Major. He threw a purse on the table. "You will be my guest. With these you can get proper clothes and uniform."

"And the boy?"

"I will turn him over to the men. They will be glad to welcome him. He should have the Legion of Honour for rescuing the Eagle. But stop."

"What is it?"

"He won't talk?"

"I have tested that lad. He will be as close-mouthed as the grave. You understand, Pierre, you are not to say a word about the Eagle until I give you leave," said Marteau to his young comrade. "About our other adventures you can tell."

"I understand. Monsieur knows that I can be silent."

"I know. Goodbye. I shall see you tomorrow. Now," began Marteau, as the orderly who had been summoned had taken Pierre away with instructions to see that he was clothed and fed, "let me ask some questions. Who was in command of the regiment?"

"I was until yesterday."

"And yesterday?"

"The King sent down an old officer to take the command, a Lieutenant-Colonel."

"And the Colonel?"

"Monsieur d'Artois."

"So that——"

"The Lieutenant-Colonel commands the regiment, which is now known as the Regiment Dauphiné, the Comte d'Artois' own," said the major, with fine scorn. "What a name to take the place of the Fifth-of-the-Line," he added.

"And Monsieur d'Aumenier?"

"Oh, he seems harmless enough. He is a trained soldier, too, of royalist days before the Empire. He even told me he had been at the school at Brienne when the Emperor was a student there."

"And who is with him?"

"His niece, the Countess Laure d'Aumenier, engaged to that young English officer."

"And what of him?"

"Well enough for an Englishman, I suppose," was the careless answer. "We were paraded yesterday and the young Englishman inspected us, the lady looking on. Actually my gorge rose, as he handled our muskets, criticized our drill. I heard some of the old moustaches of the regiment say they would like to put a bayonet through him, and, to be frank, I should like it myself. I fought against these English in Spain.

364

There's no love lost between us."

"Did he disparage the regiment?"

"Oh, no, quite the contrary. He was more than complimentary, but I hate them. His father is here, too."

"I see. When is the marriage to take place?"

"How do I know? I was surprised when the old Marquis volunteered any information to the likes of me."

"I must see the Marquis at once; with your permission, of course."

"You have it," returned the other, smiling. "You are not yet reinstated in the regiment, and, so far as I am concerned, you are free to go and come as you will."

"He is not here now, I believe?"

"No. He turned over the command to me temporarily. He is driving out into the country, going out to the gap to reconnoitre for himself, I take it, but he will be back before nightfall, and meanwhile you have much to do. We want to get you well fed, to get some good French wine into you, to put the blood into your veins and color into your cheeks, to give you a bath, to get you clothing—everything," said the generous old veteran.

CHAPTER 18

Almost a Gentleman

"Will you tell the Lieutenant-Colonel, the Marquis d'Aumenier, that an officer returned from the wars desires to see him?" said Marteau to the footman who answered the door at the Governor's palace.

"So many wandering officers want to see His Excellency," said the servant superciliously, "that I have instructions to require further enlightenment before I admit any to his presence."

"Say to your master," replied the other, his face flushing at the insolence of the servant, "that one from the village of Aumenier craves an audience on matters of great importance."

"And even that will scarcely be sufficient," began the lackey.

"Enough!" thundered Marteau. "Carry my message to him instantly," he said fiercely, "or I shall throw you aside and carry it myself."

The servant looked at him a moment, and not relishing what he saw, turned on his heel and disappeared.

"His Excellency will see you, sir," he said, in a manner considerably more respectful when he returned a few moments later. "This way, sir. His Excellency is in the drawing-room, having finished his dinner. What name shall I announce?" he asked, his hand on the door.

"Announce no one," was the curt reply. "Open the door. I will make myself known."

The lackey threw open the door. Marteau entered the room and closed the door behind him. The drawing-room of the Governor's palace was brilliantly illuminated. The Governor was receiving the officers of the garrison and the principal inhabitants of the city that night, but it was yet early in the evening, and none of them had arrived. The young officer had purposely planned his visit at that hour, in order that he might have a few moments' conversation with the

366

Marquis before the invited guests arrived.

There were five people gathered about the fireplace, all engrossed in pleasant conversation apparently. It was the second of March, and the weather made the fire blazing on the hearth very welcome. Four of the five people in the room were men; the fifth person was a woman. It was she whose attention was first aroused by the sound of the closing of the door. She faced about, her glance fell upon the newcomer, a cup which she held in her hand fell to the floor, the precious china splintering into a thousand fragments, her face turned as white as the lace of her low evening gown.

"Marteau!" she exclaimed in almost an agonized whisper.

"*Mademoiselle*," answered the soldier, bowing profoundly.

He was beautifully dressed in the nearest approach to the latest fashion that the best tailor in Grenoble could offer—thanks to the Major's purse—and, although his most becoming attire was not a uniform, his every movement betrayed the soldier, as his every look bespoke the man.

"And who have we here?" asked the oldest man of the group, the Marquis d'Aumenier himself, the attention of all being attracted to the newcomer by the crash of the broken china and the low exclamation of the young woman which none had made out clearly.

"By gad!" bellowed out with tremendous voice a stout old man, whose red face and heavy body contrasted surprisingly with the pale face, the lean, thin figure of the old Marquis, "I am damned if it isn't the young Frenchman that held the *château* with us. Lad," he cried, stepping forward and stretching out his hand, "I am glad to see you alive. I asked after you, as soon as I came back to France, but they told me you were dead."

"On the contrary, as you see, sir, I am very much alive, and at Sir Gervaise Yeovil's service as always," said Marteau, meeting the Englishman's hand with his own, touched by the other's hearty greeting, whose genuineness no one could doubt. "And this gentleman?" he went on, turning to a young replica of the older man, who had stepped to his father's side.

"Is my son, Captain Frank Yeovil, of King George's Fifty-second Light Infantry. By gad, I am glad to have him make your acquaintance. He is going to marry the Marquis' niece here—your old friend— when they can settle on a day. You had thoughts in that direction yourself, I remember," he went on, in his bluff way, "but I suppose you have got bravely over them by now," he laughed.

"I have resigned myself to the inevitable, *monsieur*," answered Marteau with a calmness that he did not feel.

He did not dare to look at the Countess Laure as he spoke. He could not have commanded himself if he had done so. His lips were compressed and his face was paler than before. The girl saw it. She had watched him, fascinated. The Englishman, young, frank, sunny-haired, gallant, stepped up to him, shook him by his unwilling hand.

"I am glad to know you," he said. "I have heard how you saved my betrothed's life and honour, and held the *château*. I have longed to meet you, to thank you."

"And I you," said Marteau. "You English are frank. I shall be likewise," he added. "It was not thus I wanted to meet you, *monsieur*, not in a drawing-room, in this peaceful dress, but—on the field."

"I understand," said the Englishman, sobered a little by the other's seriousness. "And if the war had continued perhaps we might have settled the—er"—his eyes sought those of his fiancée, but she was not looking at him—"our differences," he added, "in the old knightly way, but now——"

"Now it is impossible," assented Marteau, "since my Emperor and I are both defeated."

"*Monsieur*," broke in the high, rather sharp voice of the old Marquis, "that is a title which is no longer current in France. As loyal subjects of, the King the word is banished—like the man."

"I am but new to France, *Monsieur le Marquis*, and have not yet learned to avoid the ancient habit."

"And yet you are a Frenchman," commented the Marquis dryly. "You said you came from Aumenier. I did not catch your name, sir?"

"Marteau, at your service."

"One of the loyal Marteaux?"

"The last one, sir."

"And pray why are you new to France?"

"I have but two months since been released from an Austrian prison and an Austrian hospital."

"I made inquiry," said the countess suddenly, the tones of her voice bespeaking her deep agitation, "I caused the records to be searched. They said you were dead, that you had been killed at the bridge of Arcis with the rest of your regiment."

"I was unfortunate enough to survive my comrades as you see, *mademoiselle*," said Marteau.

"And I thank God for that," said the Countess Laure. "I have never forgot what you did for me, and———"

"Nor has the memory of your interposition which twice saved my life escaped from my mind for a single instant, *mademoiselle*."

"Yes, it was very fine, no doubt, on the part of both of you," said Captain Yeovil, a little impatiently, because he did not quite see the cause of all this perturbation on the part of his betrothed; "but you are quits now, and for my part———"

"What I did for *mademoiselle* is nothing, *monsieur*. I shall always be in her debt," replied the Frenchman.

"Monsieur St. Laurent," said the Marquis, turning to the other oc- cupant of the room, "my new adjutant, Monsieur Marteau," he added in explanation, "was there not a Marteau borne on the rolls of the regiment? I think I saw the name when I looked yesterday, and it at- tracted me because I knew it."

"Yes, your Excellency," said St. Laurent, "he was a Captain when he was detached."

"You were on service elsewhere, *Monsieur mon Capitaine?*" asked the Marquis.

"I was a Lieutenant-Colonel, your Excellency."

"And where and when?"

"On the day at Arcis. Made so by"—he threw up his head—"by him who cannot be named."

"Ah! Quite so," said the Marquis, helping himself to a pinch of snuff from a jewelled box, quite after the fashion of the old *régime*. He shut the box and tapped it gently. "There is, I believe, a vacancy in the regiment, a Captaincy. My gracious King, whom God and the saints preserve, leaves the appointment to me. It is at your service. I regret that I can offer you no higher rank. I shall be glad to have you in my command," he went on. "It is meet and right that you should be there. I and my house have been well served for generations by your house."

"I regret that I cannot accept your offer."

"Why not?" asked the Marquis haughtily. "It is not to every wan- dering officer that I would have made it."

"I should have to swear allegiance to your King, *monsieur*, and that I———"

"Enough," said the Marquis imperiously. "The offer is withdrawn. You may go, sir."

"I have a duty to discharge before I avail myself of your courteous permission," said the young man firmly.

"My uncle," said the girl, "you cannot dismiss Monsieur Jean Marteau in that cavalier fashion. It is due to him that I am here."

"No, curse me, Marquis," burst out Sir Gervaise, wagging his big head at the tall, French noble, "you don't know how much you owe to that young man. Why, even I would not have been here but for him."

"I am deeply sensible to the obligations under which he has laid me, both through the Comtesse Laure, and through you, old friend. I have just endeavoured to discharge them. If there be any other way——*Monsieur* is recently from prison—perhaps the state of his finances—if he would permit me——" continued the Marquis, who was not without generous impulses, it seemed.

"Sir," interrupted Marteau, "I thank you, but I came here to confer, not to receive, benefits."

"To confer, *monsieur?*"

"We Marteaux have been accustomed to render service, as the Marquis will recollect," he said proudly.

He drew forth a soiled, worn packet of papers. Because they had represented nothing of value to his captors they had not been taken. They had never left his person except during his long period of illness, when they had been preserved by a faithful official of the hospital and returned to him afterward.

"Allow me to return these to the Marquis," he said, tendering them.

"And what are these?" asked the old man.

"The title deeds to the Aumenier estates, *monsieur.*"

"The grant is waste paper," said the Marquis contemptuously.

"Not so," was the quick answer. "I have learned that the acts of the late—of—those which were duly and properly registered before the—present king ascended the throne are valid. The estates are legally mine. You reject them. I——" he hesitated, he stepped over to the young woman—"I return them to you, *mademoiselle.* Her dowry, *monsieur,*" he added, facing the Englishman, as he laid the packet down on the table by the side of the Countess Laure.

"Well, that's handsome of you," said the latter heartily.

"I cannot take them," ejaculated the young woman, just a touch of contempt for her obtuse English lover in her voice. "I—— They are legally his. We shall have no need——"

"Nonsense," burst out the young English officer. "They are rightfully yours. They were taken from you by an usurper who——"

"*Monsieur!*" cried Marteau sharply.

"Well, sir?"

"He who cannot be named by order of the king is not to be slandered by order of——"

"Whose order?"

"Mine," said Marteau.

"Indeed," answered the Englishman, his face flushing as he laid his hand on his sword—he was wearing his uniform.

"Steady, steady," cried the old Baronet, interposing between the two. "The lad's right. If we can't name Bonaparte, it is only fair that we shouldn't abuse him. And the girl's right, too. You have no need of any such dowry. Thank God I have got acres and pounds of my own for the two of you and all that may come after."

"It strikes me, gentlemen," said the Marquis coolly, "that the disposal of the affair is mine. Marteau is right and I was wrong. Perhaps he has some claim to the estate. But, however that may be, he does well to surrender it to its ancient overlord. I accept it as my due. I shall see that he does not suffer for his generosity."

"And does *monsieur* think that he could compensate me if he should give me the whole of France for the loss of——"

"Good God!" said the keen witted, keen eyed old Marquis, seeing Marteau's glance toward the young woman. "Are you still presuming to——"

"As man looks toward the sun that gives him life," said the young Frenchman, "so I look toward *mademoiselle*. But have no fear, *monsieur*," he went on to the English dragoon, "you have won her heart. I envy you but——"

"Marteau!" protested the Countess, the anguish in her soul speaking in her voice again.

How different the appearance of this slender, pale, delicate young Frenchman from the coarser-grained English soldier to whom she had plighted her troth, but to whom she had not given her heart. There was no doubt in her mind as to where her affections pointed. Some of the pride of race, of high birth and ancient lineage, had been blown away in the dust of the revolution. She had played too long with the plain people on the ancient estate. She had been left too much to herself. She had seen Marteau in splendid and heroic roles. She saw him so now. She had been his companion and associate in her youth. But of all this none knew, and she was fain not to admit it even to herself.

"Have you anything more to communicate, Marteau, or to surrender?" asked the Marquis coldly.

To do him justice, any service Marteau might render him was quite in accord with the old noble's idea of what was proper and with the ancient feudal custom by which the one family had served the other for so long.

"I have yet something else to give up."

"Another estate?"

"A title."

"Ah, and what title, pray, and what interest have I in it?" asked the Marquis sarcastically.

"I have here," said the young Frenchman, drawing forth another legal document, "a patent of nobility duly signed and attested. It was delivered to me by special courier the day after the battle of Montereau."

"And you were created what, sir?"

"Count d'Aumenier, at your service, *monsieur.*"

"Is this an insult?" exclaimed the Marquis, his pale face reddening.

"Sir," said the young man proudly, "it was given me by a man who has made more men noble, and established them, than all the kings of France before him. No power on earth could better make me Count or Prince or King, even."

"Sir! Sir!" protested the Marquis furiously.

"I value this gift but I do not need it now. I surrender it into your hands. You may destroy it. I shall formally and before a notary renounce it. It shall be as if it had not been."

The Marquis took the paper, unfolded it deliberately amid a breathless silence and glanced rapidly over it.

"Even so," he admitted.

He looked up at the gallant, magnanimous young Frenchman with more interest and more care than before; he noticed how pale and haggard and weak he appeared. He appreciated it for the first time. A little change came over the hard, stern face of the old noble. He, too, had suffered; he, too, had been hungry and weak and weary; he, too, had eaten his heart out longing for what seemed impossible. After all, they had been friends and more than friends, these ancient houses, the high born and the peasant born, for many generations.

"St. Laurent," he said sharply, "we have been remiss. *Monsieur* is ill, a chair for him. Laure, a glass of wine."

Indeed, the constraint that Marteau had put upon himself had drawn heavily upon his scanty reserve of nervous force. St. Laurent did not like the task, but there was that in the Marquis's voice which warned him not to hesitate. He offered a chair, into which the young man sank. From a decanter on the table the girl, her hand trembling, poured out a glass of wine. Swiftly she approached him, she bent over him, moved by a sudden impulse, she sank on her knees by his side and tendered him the glass.

"On your knees, Laure!" protested the young Englishman. "It is not meet that——"

"In gratitude to a man who has served me well and who has set us all a noble example of renunciation by his surrender of land and title here in this very room."

"Rise, *mademoiselle*," said Marteau, taking the glass from her still trembling hand. "The honour is too great for me. I cannot remain seated unless——"

"Very pretty," said the Marquis coolly as young Captain Yeovil helped his reluctant young betrothed to her feet. "Your health, monsieur," he continued, taking up his own glass. "By all the saints, sir," he added as he drained his glass, "you have acted quite like a gentleman."

"'Quite,' my uncle?" quoted the young woman with deep emphasis on the word.

"Well, what more could I say to a Marteau?"

"What more indeed," said the young officer, smiling in proud disdain.

"*Damme* if I wouldn't have left the 'quite' out," muttered the elder Yeovil.

"I have your leave to withdraw now, *monsieur*?" asked the young officer. "You dismissed me a moment since."

"Now I ask you to stay. By the cross of St. Louis," said the old Marquis, fingering his order, "I am proud of you, young man. Take the commission. I should like them to see what sort of men we breed in Champagne and——"

"I feel I shall be unequal to it. I must withdraw."

"Where are you staying?" asked the young woman eagerly.

"With Major Lestoype, an old comrade."

"And I shall see you once more?"

"I cannot hope to see *mademoiselle* again. Our ways lie apart."

"Enough," said the countess imperiously. "It rests with me and I will see you again. Meanwhile, *au revoir*."

She offered her hand to the young Frenchman. He seized it eagerly.

"*Monsieur* allows the privilege to an old and faithful servitor?" he said to the young Englishman, who stood jealously looking on, and then, not waiting for an answer, he bent low and pressed his lips upon it.

Did that hand tremble in his own? Was there an upward movement as if to press it against his lips? He could not tell. He did not dare to speculate. The countess closed her eyes and when she opened them again he was gone.

CHAPTER 19

The Great Honour Roll

At midnight, had there been anyone abroad in the garrison to observe them, a number of men, heavily cloaked, might have been seen drifting through the torrential rain that was falling, toward the quarters occupied by Major Lestoype. They were expected, evidently, for they were admitted without hesitation by the carefully selected old soldiers who kept the door. The usual servants had been dismissed to their quarters, and their places were taken by certain tried and trusted veterans of the regiment.

In the quarters of Major Lestoype was a spacious and lofty hall. Thither the new arrivals were conducted. There was an air of great secrecy about their movements. The occasion was evidently felt to be a solemn one by all. Major Lestoype was not yet present. As they threw off their cloaks it was seen that they were soldiers of the Fifth regiment of the line, to continue to give it the familiar title. Each one was arrayed in his best parade uniform. They were of every rank below that of major, and included among them were several non-commissioned officers and a few private soldiers of reputation and standing. The men were of all ages too, although the non-commissioned officers and privates were, in every instance, veterans. These last stood in a little group by themselves, although there was no attempt on the part of the officers to emphasize any difference in rank on such an occasion.

There were, perhaps, a hundred men in the company when all had been assembled. They had been chosen with the utmost care. The list included all the officers, except certain new officers who had been assigned to the regiment from other regiments of whom Major Lestoype and the veteran captains were not sure. Certain other young officers, sons or connections of influential royalists now in high favour with King Louis XVIII, who had also been assigned to the regiment were of course excluded.

Those who were there were known men, all tried and true. Major Lestoype himself had been a private when the Fifth-of-the-Line had followed the Emperor, then but General Bonaparte, into Italy on that first and most marvellous of the campaigns of the great Captain. He had seen service in Egypt and had been present with the First Consul at the decisive battle at Marengo. Into his hand as a non-commissioned officer thereafter the newly made Emperor had delivered the Eagle. Naturally, he experienced toward it almost the feeling of a father for his child.

Every other man there was associated in some way with that imperial emblem, their regimental standard. As has been said, it was not the flag for which they cared; flags were of perishable silk or cloth; they could be and often were destroyed in battle. They could be replaced. Some regiments stripped the colours from the poles before they went into action. It was the Eagle that was precious and to be defended. It was the Eagle that was in their hearts almost eternal.

It was to receive their Eagle again that these officers and men had been summoned. They did not know that definitely yet, but some whisper of it had been in the air. They were on the *qui vive* for the developments of the evening and full of restless excitement. When the great door was at last thrown open and the Senior Captain caught sight of the tall, lean figure of his commander, he instantly came to attention and said sharply:

"Gentlemen, attention. The Major Commanding."

To be sure, Lestoype no longer occupied that position. His place had been taken by the Marquis d'Aumenier, but in the mind of the Senior Captain and of the others the old major still was supreme and he said the words quite naturally.

The talking ceased at once, the well-drilled officers and men stood at attention, their hands raised in salute. Major Lestoype in full uniform, his breast bright with all his medals and orders—and it was observable that everybody else had adorned himself with every decoration he possessed, even those that had become illegal and valueless, forbidden even, after the fall of the Empire—entered the room, acknowledged the salutes and bowed ceremoniously to the officers assembled. He was followed by a tall slender young man on this occasion dressed again in the uniform of the regiment.

And yet there was a difference between this stranger and the other officers. While from the uniforms of the other officers had been carefully removed everything which in the least degree suggested the Empire, no such deletion had taken place with the equipment of the young man. On the contrary, the buttons, the brasses, the braids, the tricolored cockade; in short, everything was just as it was before the restoration.

The eyes of the soldiers gleamed as they immediately recognized the difference. They looked upon him with a certain envy, because he so boldly sported that of which they were deprived. At first they did not recognize the man who had the hardihood thus to display the insignia of Napoleon in the kingdom of Louis. It was not until he had advanced further in the room and stood in the full light of the chandelier and Major Lestoype turned toward him that one of the veterans recognized him.

"By the living God," cried a deep voice, "Marteau!"

Instantly the name was caught up.

"Marteau! Marteau! Marteau!" came from all parts of the room.

"Gentlemen, comrades," said Lestoype, raising his hand, "I beseech you, silence. Walls have ears. Every man here is tried and true. We are trusting our lives and honour to one another, but what may be outside I know not. We must do nothing to attract any attention. Therefore, restrain yourselves, I beg. Captain Marteau, for it is indeed he, gentlemen, has brought back to the regiment——"

He paused a moment, with an instinctive feeling for the dramatic. Perhaps the little scene had been prearranged. Marteau had carried his hand behind his back. As Lestoype stopped he brought his hand to the front of his body. There in the light of the candles, from the great chandelier above, the officers and soldiers saw the thing which they venerated next to God. For a moment they stared, almost aghast at the gilded emblem in Marteau's hand. Eyes sparkled in some faces, brimmed with tears in others, cheeks paled on one hand and flushed upon the other; breaths came quicker, a low murmur ran through the room—almost terrible in its meaning.

"The Eagle of the regiment, *messieurs*," said old Lestoype solemnly, breaking the silence.

"*Vive l'Empereur!*" suddenly exclaimed a veteran *port-aigle*, or standard bearer, in a low but tense voice, and the mighty battle-cry swept softly through the room from man to man, in low notes, in broken whispers like a great wavering sigh from a multitude of throbbing hearts.

"Is it the same?" asked one as the sound died away.

"The very same," answered Lestoype. "It was given into my hands years ago. I had someone write down the Emperor's words then. I committed them to memory. I can hear him speak now."

"And what were those words we ask you, we, who are young in the regiment," broke out a youth who was yet a veteran of the German campaign of 1813.

"The Emperor, turning to Marshal Berthier, took the Eagle from him, he held it up thus in his own hands."

Lestoype turned to Marteau and suited the gesture to the word. He seized the Eagle and advanced a step and those who watched him so keenly noticed how he trembled. It was to him as if the Emperor were there again. Some mystic aura of his mighty presence seemed to overhang the uplifted Eagle.

"Gentlemen, we were paraded on the Champ de Mars with thousands of others. The Eagles had been marched along the line with the ruffles of drums and blare of bugles. It was raining like tonight, there was no sun, but never saw I a brighter day. The Emperor said:

"'*Soldiers of the Fifth regiment of Infantry of the Line, I entrust to you the Eagle of France. It is to serve to you ever as your rallying point. You swear to me never to abandon it but with life? You swear never to suffer an affront to it for the honour of France? You swear ever to prefer death to dishonour for it? You swear?*'"

As the words of the old officer died away, moved by a common impulse, the hands of the men before him went to their swords. With sweeping gestures they dragged them out of their sheaths, up into the air they heaved the shining blades.

"We swear," they said solemnly, instinctively repeating the ceremony of the past in which some of them had participated and of which all had heard.

As their words died away the gruff voices of the non-commissioned officers and privates standing at salute repeated the acclaim, in accordance with the custom.

"It was so when the Eagle was given," said old Lestoype, deeply gratified by the spontaneous tribute. "Gentlemen and comrades, be seated, if you please. I have called you here for the honour of the regiment to consult as to what is to be done."

"*Mon Commandant,*" said an old veteran, stepping forward as those present sought seats where they could, "I was *port-aigle* of the regiment before Dresden. May I not take in my hand again the '*cou-cou*'?"

That was the cant name which the soldiers gave to the standard, a term of affection, of familiarity, of comradeship which in no way indicated any lack of respect or any diminution of determination to die for it if necessary.

"To you I gladly commit it until we have determined what is to be done with it," said Lestoype, handing it to the old man.

It seemed a perfectly natural and spontaneous act to the officers present when the *port-aigle* pressed his lips reverently upon the number plate below the feet of the Eagle and then, disdaining to sit down, stood at attention, holding it before him.

"Will you not tell us, *Mon Commandant,*" said another of the younger officers, "something more about the Eagle before we discuss its disposition?"

"I was a Sub-Lieutenant at Austerlitz," said Lestoype, only too anxious to comply. "We were under the command of Marshal Soult, club-footed Soult we called him, upon the heights of Pratzen. In the advance we were overwhelmed. The *port-aigle* was killed. I was close at hand. I seized the staff but a bullet got me in the shoulder, here. My arm has been stiff ever since. I fell—a Russian—we were that closely intermingled and fighting hand to hand—seized the staff. I lapsed into unconsciousness. Captain Grenier—you were Sergeant-Major then—finish the story."

"Willingly, Major Lestoype. I cut down that Russian, although wounded myself, and tore the staff from him as he fell. But I couldn't hold it. I fell with it at your feet. Our men had been driven back. There was nobody beside us but the regimental dog."

"Moustache," said one of the other officers, and all eyes turned toward the stuffed skin of a mongrel poodle dog mounted in a glass case hung against the wall. Hands went up in salute. Some of the soldiers laughed grimly.

"The brave Moustache," continued Grenier. "He leaped over my prostrate body. I was conscious still. I saw it all. I would have given worlds for strength, but I was helpless. Still Moustache was enough. He loved the *port-aigle*. He seemed to know the Eagle was in danger. He snapped at the hands of the Russian. The man drew back and cut at him with his sword. Perhaps I should have received that blow. You see where the forepaw of the dog was sliced off? But he had the spirit of a French soldier, that brave dog, and he kept them off until the regiment rallied and came back and drove away the Russians. Marshal Lannes had a collar made for Moustache. You can see it there around his neck, young gentlemen," continued the old Captain. "On one side the inscription reads: '*He lost a leg in the battle of Austerlitz but he saved the Eagle of his regiment.*' On the other side: '*Moustache, a dog of France, who will be everywhere respected and honoured as a brave soldier.*'"

"What became of the dog?" asked another.

"He was carried on the roll of the regiment until he was killed by an English cannon ball at Badajos. We took the skin and it is there, but we buried the brave heart and the rest of him on the rampart where he fell. The soldiers put up a stone above him. 'Here lies the brave Moustache,' it read. I think the English left it standing."

"That Eagle has been in every capital of Europe, *messieurs*," remarked another veteran. "Rome, Berlin, Vienna, Madrid, Moscow."

"It charged with the Guard at Eylau," said Drehon. "You remember, comrades, some of you at least, how we went forward in support of the battalions of the Guard under General Dorsenne?"

"I remember, I remember," came from one and another.

"*Hein*," said a veteran, "he was a bold soldier."

"And a handsome one. They called him '*Le Beau Dorsenne*,'" continued Drehon. "The Guard advanced at arms-aport and so did we. Our drums and theirs were rolling *La Grenadière*. One of his staff said to him as we drew near the ranks of the Russians, 'Hadn't we better begin firing, my General?' 'No,' said the proud Dorsenne haughtily. 'Grenadiers keep your arms aport,' he continued as he saw some wavering. 'The old guard only fights at the point of the bayonet.'"

"And what happened?"

"The Russians seemed to be paralyzed. They stood and watched us. When they finally did fire, in their excitement, they overshot us. The next instant we burst upon them. Our bayonets came down to a charge. They couldn't stand before us, comrades. *Corbleu!* the white snow was red with blood that day! A squadron of cavalry, the Emperor's escort, struck them in the rear at the same time and between us we cut them to pieces. They were heavy, those big Russians, to toss on the bayonet, but we did it."

"Was that when the Emperor called us 'The Terrible Fifth'?" queried a voice.

"That was the time."

"Tell us more," came from the excited assemblage.

"They gave us the gold wreath, there in Paris, after Jena and Eylau and Friedland. They loved the Eagle then, those Parisians," said Adjutant Suraif, taking up the tale. "The women fell on our necks and kissed us when we came marching back. They threw us flowers. They opened their arms to us. They gave us wine. Ah, that was fine."

"At Ratisbon," said the old major, "I commanded the regiment at the bridge-head. We fought the Austrians off all day, giving the Emperor time to make his dispositions. We captured four hundred prisoners, an Austrian battle flag, and three other flags. The firing was terrible, our *cou-cou* lost some leaves of his wreath there. We were alone there and at nightfall our ammunition was all gone. The Austrians were there in thousands. They charged and overwhelmed us."

"But the Eagle?"

"Ah, we had taken precaution," laughed the old Major. "We wrapped the '*cou-cou*' up in the Austrian standard and in the battle flags and buried it in a cellar, so when they captured us they got nothing but the men and, of course, we didn't matter."

"And how did you get it back?" came an excited question.

"The Emperor took the town the day after. They had kept us prisoners there and so we were free. I shall never forget the Emperor on that day. He rode down to us where we had formed in ranks. He looked over us. His glance pierced every man's heart. 'Soldiers of the Fifth,' he said, 'when I heard of the attack on the bridge at Ratisbon I said to my staff, "I am tranquil, the Terrible Fifth is there," and now I see you alive, many of you unharmed, and without your Eagle. What have you done with it?' he thundered out his face black as midnight. 'Sire,' said I, stepping forward and upon my word, comrades, it took more courage to face the Emperor in that mood than to charge an Austrian battery, 'we have not lost our Eagle. We have buried it and having been but this instant released from captivity by your Majesty, we await your permission to dig it up.' 'Go and resurrect it,' he said sharply. 'I will wait.'"

"And did he?"

"Most assuredly. We found it safe and brought it back with the Austrian standard. The Emperor saluted it and commended us. 'I knew I could trust you,' he said, smiling."

"He loved his Eagles," said another voice.

"That did he," answered a veteran. "I have even seen him get out of his travelling-carriage and stand at attention as an Eagle at the head of a regiment marched by."

"I carried the Eagle in Marshal Macdonald's column at Wagram, messieurs," said the old Eagle-bearer, stepping forward. "It was there the bullet struck the wing tip, here." He laid his hand tenderly upon it. "*Mon Dieu*, that was a march! Twenty thousand men in solid columns going across the plain at steady step, with drums beating, the Austrians pouring shot and shell into us. You could hear the bullets crash through the breasts of the division like glass. My arm was numb from the bullet which struck the Eagle, but I changed hands and carried it forward. I can see the big Marshal still. The Emperor was looking on. It was terrible. It didn't seem that mortal man could make it, but we kept on, still, silent, until we came in touch with the Austrians and then we cut them in two. It was magnificent."

"I was with Marshal Mortier when we were caught in the pass of Durrenstein," broke out one of the privates, an old Eagle-guard. "We fought all day and all night in that trap against awful odds, waiting, hoping, until toward morning we heard the thunder of Dupont's guns. We were so close together that we seized the throats of the Russians, and they ours. We begged the Marshal to use a boat we had found to cross over the Danube and escape. 'No,' he said, 'certainly not! I will not desert my brave comrades! I will save them or die with them.' Ah, he was a brave man that day."

"And that such a man could betray the Emperor!" exclaimed another.

"I never could understand it," said one of the soldiers.

"That was the day," said a third, "when our drums were shot to pieces and we had to beat the long roll on the iron cooking cans."

"You remember it well, comrade."

"I was a drummer there. I remember there were but two thousand of the six thousand in the division that answered roll call that day."

"I carried that Eagle into Moscow," said a scarred, one-armed veteran. "I would have carried it back, but I was wounded at Malojaroslavets and would have died but for you, my friend."

"And I carried it across the Niemen after that retreat was over," returned the other, acknowledging the generous tribute of his old fellow soldier.

"*Sacre-bleu!* How cold it was. Not many of you can remember that march because so few survived it. The battalions in Spain can thank God they escaped it," said another.

"It was hot enough there, and those English gave us plenty of fighting," added one of the veterans who had fought against Wellington.

"Aye, that they did, I'll warrant," continued the veteran of Russia. "The Emperor who marched on foot with the rest of us. Before crossing the Beresina—I shudder to think of the thousands drowned then. I dream about it sometimes at night—we were ordered to break up the Eagles and throw them into the river."

"And did you?"

"Not I. That is the only order I disobeyed. I carried it with me, wrapped in my own clothes. One night my fingers froze to it. See!" He lifted his maimed hands. "But I held on. I crossed the Nieman before Marshal Ney. He threw away his musket, but I kept the Eagle. He was the last man, I was just before him," said the man proudly.

"It was Marteau who saved it at Leipsic," said Lestoype, "and again after he had hurled it into the Aube at Arcis he found it and brought it back. And it is here."

Tears glistened in the eyes of the veterans and the youth alike. Hearts beat more rapidly, breaths came quicker, as these brave and fragmentary reminiscences of the part the Eagle had played in past glories were recited.

"What shall we do with it now?" asked Lestoype at last.

CHAPTER 20

When the Violets Bloom Again

Now there was not a man in the room who had not heard of the order to return the Eagles to Paris, where they were to be broken up and melted down, not a man in the army for that matter. Nor was there a man who had not heard some account of the resistance of other regiments to the order, which had been nevertheless enforced wherever possible, although in cases not a few Eagles had been hidden or disappeared mysteriously and had not been given up. There was scarcely a man in the regiment—unless some royalist officer or new recruit—who had not been glad that their own Eagle had been lost honourably in battle and buried, as they believed, in the river. It was more fitting that it should meet that end than be turned back to Paris to be broken up, melted down and cast into metal for ignoble use—and any other use would be ignoble in the estimation of the regiment.

"I would rather throw it into the Isère," growled old Grenier, "than send it back."

"And I, and I, and I," came from different voices.

"Perhaps," said Lestoype, speaking slowly and with deep meaning, for he realized that his words were in the highest degree treasonable, "if we can preserve it by some means we may see it once again at the head of the regiment when——" he stopped. The silence was positively ghastly. He looked about him. The men thrilled to his glance. "——'when the violets bloom again,'" he said, using the mystic poetic phrase which had become so widely current.

"God speed the day!" burst out some deep voiced veteran.

"Amen, amen!"

"*Vive l'Empereur!*"

"Let us save the Eagle!"

The whole room was in tumult of nervous cries.

"*Vive le brave Marteau!*" finally said Drehon when he could get a hearing. "He has given us back our honour, our life."

The emotions of the moment were too much. Reckless of what might happen, the room instantly rang with loud acclaim in response to this appeal. The soldiers sprang to their feet, moved by irresistible emotion. Swords were drawn again.

The officers and men clustered around Lestoype and Marteau. The Eagle was lifted high, blades were upheaved threateningly again. Dangers were forgotten. Intoxicated with enthusiasm they gave free course to their emotions.

"*Vive l'Empereur!*" resounded through the hall, not whispered but shouted, not shouted but roared!

In their mad frenzy of excitement they did not, any of them, notice that the door into the hall had been thrown open and that a young officer of the regiment stood there, his face pale with amazement, his mouth open, staring. He could not take in the whole purport of the scene but he saw the Eagle, he heard the cries, the word "*Vive*" came to him out of the tumult, coupled with the name of Marteau and the Emperor.

"Gentlemen!" he finally shouted, raising his voice to its highest pitch and as the sound penetrated to the tumultuous mass the noise died away almost as suddenly as it had arisen.

Men faced about and stared toward the entrance. There stood young St. Laurent, one of the royalist officers, newly appointed to the regiment, who had been made *aide* to the Governor and commander.

"Major Lestoype," said the youth with great firmness, having recovered his presence of mind and realizing instantly the full purport and menace of the situation, "an order from the Governor requests your presence at once. I was sent to deliver it. The soldiers at the door strove vainly to stop me but I forced my way past them. I am an unwelcome guest, I perceive, being a loyal servant of the King, but I am here. What is the meaning of this gathering, the worship of this discarded emblem, these treasonable cries?"

"Am I, a veteran of the army of Italy, to be catechised and questioned by a boy?" growled Lestoype in mingled rage and astonishment.

"You forget yourself, *monsieur*. I regret to fail in any military duty or in respect to my seniors, but in this I represent the Marquis d'Aumenier, the Governor, aye, even the King, my master. Whence came this Eagle?"

There was a dead silence.

"I brought it, *monsieur*, to my old comrades, to my old regiment," coolly said Marteau, stepping forward.

"Traitor!" exclaimed St. Laurent, confronting him boldly.

"Not so, for I have taken no oath to King Louis."

"Ah, you still wear the insignia of the Corsican, I see," continued the young *aide*, looking more closely. "But how about these gentlemen?"

Again the question was met by silence.

"*Messieurs*," said St. Laurent, "you are old soldiers of the former Emperor. I see. I understand. You love him as I and mine the King. It is as much as my life is worth, as much as my honour, to condone it. Yet I would not be a tale-bearer, but this cannot pass unless——"

"Shall I cut him down where he stands, *Mon Commandant?*" growled the old *port-aigle*, presenting his weapon.

"And add murder to treason!" exclaimed St. Laurent, his face flushing a little but not giving back an inch before the threatening approach of the veteran.

There was good stuff in him, evidently, and even those who foresaw terrible consequences to themselves in his unexpected presence could not but admire him. They were even proud that he was a Frenchman, even though he served the King they hated.

"By no means," said Lestoype, motioning the colour-bearer back. "You shall go as freely as you came."

"And if you do as I suggest I shall go and forget all I have seen, *messieurs*."

"Impossible!"

"Upon my honour I shall do it but on one condition."

"Ah! and that is?"

"That you give me the Eagle."

"Give you the Eagle!" exclaimed old Captain Grenier.

"The Eagle for which our brave comrades died," said Drehon.

"The Eagle which has been carried in triumph in every capital in Europe!" added Suraif.

The whole room was filled with cries again.

"Never! Never!"

The whole mass surged forward, including Marteau.

"Was it to give it up to any servant of King Louis that I brought it

386

back?" the latter shouted threateningly.

"Gentlemen," said the young *aide* so soon as he could make himself heard in the tumult, "the choice is yours, not mine. I am a soldier of the King, *aide-de-camp* to the Governor of this place, an officer under the Marquis d'Aumenier. You have your ideas of duty, I have mine. I have already stretched my conscience to the limit in offering to be silent about this under any conditions. I am doing wrong in concealing it but I do not wish to doom so many brave men to disgrace, to death. You, *monsieur*"—he pointed toward Marteau—"refused a commission in this regiment. You wear the insignia of Bonaparte. You have no place here. Withdraw. Your arrival has disturbed the orderly course of events. These gentlemen were doing their duty contentedly——"

"No, by God, never," roared out a veteran. "Contentedly! We will never be content until——"

"Until what, *monsieur*?"

"Until the violets bloom again," came the answer, accompanied by a burst of sardonic laughter.

"Your interest in the flowers of spring does not concern me, gentlemen," returned the young *aide*, affecting not to understand, and perhaps he did not. "If you will give me the Eagle——"

"And what will you do with it if we should do so?"

"I will be silent as to this."

"And how will you explain your possession of it?"

"I will say that I got it from Monsieur Marteau, who has gone."

"And what will you do with it?"

"That shall be as the Marquis d'Aumenier directs."

"And he?"

"I think he will undoubtedly obey the orders of the Minister of War and send it to Paris to be broken up."

"Gentlemen," said Major Lestoype, endeavouring to quiet and repress the growls of antagonism that arose on every hand, "you hear the proposition of Monsieur St. Laurent. Seeing his duty as he does, I am forced to admit," continued the veteran with great magnanimity, "that it does credit to his heart. What shall we do?"

"Purchase our freedom, purchase our rank, purchase our lives by giving up our Eagle!" said old Captain Grenier. "Never!"

"I vote NO to that proposition," said Drehon.

"And I, and I, and I," acclaimed the soldiers.

"You hear, Monsieur St. Laurent?" said the major. "These gentlemen have signified their will unmistakably."

"I hear," said the young *aide*. "Major Lestoype, forgive me if I have failed in respect or soldierly deference to my superior officer, but I, too, have my duty to perform. I warn you all that when I pass from this room I shall go directly to the Marquis d'Aumenier and report what I have seen."

"When he passes," cried some of the soldiers of lower rank ominously, emphasizing the adverb and rudely thrusting themselves between St. Laurent and the door.

"Pardon me, gentlemen," said the young *aide* quite coolly. "It seems that I spoke unadvisedly in one particular."

"You retract?" said a voice.

"Never. I should have said 'if I pass.'"

Swords were still out, hands were clenched, arms were raised.

"Say the word and he dies where he stands," cried one.

"Gentlemen," said Lestoype sternly, "back, all of you. Free passage for Monsieur St. Laurent. Back, I say. Let him go unharmed, as he came."

"My orders were to request your presence before the Governor of the town immediately," said the *aide*.

"I attend him at once, young gentleman," returned the old soldier, seizing his cloak and covering his head with his *chapeau*. "Gentlemen," he added, turning to the rest, "I leave the Eagle in your hands. Before he departs let me say that Monsieur St. Laurent has borne himself like a brave man, a gallant officer, and a true gentleman. *Monsieur*, you will not take amiss this heartfelt tribute from so old a soldier as I."

"I thank you, sir, and you, gentlemen," said the young *aide*, surveying the men, their sudden temper abated, now looking at him with admiration, some of them with hands raised in salute. "The duty you have imposed upon me by your choice is the most painful I shall ever be called upon to perform."

"This way, Monsieur St. Laurent," said old Lestoype, stepping through the door with his head high, beckoning the young *aide* to follow him.

The door had scarcely closed behind the two when the wild confusion broke out again.

"What shall be done now?" cried Captain Grenier, the senior officer present, as soon as he could be heard.

"*Messieurs*," said Marteau, striving to gain the attention of all, "let me speak a moment. I have a plan. Be silent, I beg of you."

"We will hear Marteau."

"What have you to suggest?"

"Speak!"

"Be quick."

"This. I will take the Eagle, I, who brought it."

"You will throw it into the Isère?"

"No. I know this town like a book. The regiment was once stationed here for a few months. I had time on my hands. I explored many of the ancient buildings. I will—— But ask me nothing. Trust the Eagle to me. I have periled my life for it as have you all. Trust it to me. It shall come to no dishonour in my hands. Say to the Governor that I came here, that I brought the Eagle, that I was asked to surrender it, that I refused, that I took it away, that you know not where I concealed it, nor whither I am gone. Let Monsieur St. Laurent make his report. You can simply tell the truth. Nothing will be done."

"It is well thought on," said Captain Grenier.

"The danger is to you," said another.

"What of that? I have looked danger in the face often since I have been in the army, like all the rest of you."

"I like not to shift the responsibility upon this young man," said the old *port-aigle* dubiously. "He is saving our lives at the risk of his own if they should find him—which is likely."

"*Messieurs*," said Marteau quickly, "I am not preserving your lives for yourselves."

"Why, then?" asked an officer.

"That you may be ready," said the young man, throwing his cloak about his shoulders, seizing the Eagle with his hands, "when the violets bloom again."

As they stared at him he saluted, turned on his heel, opened the door and went out.

CHAPTER 21

Like a Thief in the Night

The reception was over. The last guest had departed. The house had been closed. Sir Gervaise Yeovil and his son and the Countess Laure had bidden the old Marquis good night and retired to their several apartments. There were wakeful hours ahead for the Governor, who repaired to his cabinet and got to work. The tidings which had been brought him by the young Baron St. Laurent were sufficiently grave and perturbing to render sleep impossible, even if he had nothing to do. In great astonishment the Marquis had questioned Major Lestoype closely and from him had received a frank and accurate version of the whole affair. The major would have died rather than betray a comrade, but in this instance the betrayal had already been effected and there was nothing whatever to be gained, from Marteau's point of view or from anybody's point of view, by an attempt at concealment.

The old Marquis had acted with dazzling promptitude. His personal escort had consisted of a troop of loyalist cavalry from the King's household guard and it had not yet returned to Paris. He could depend absolutely upon these men. They had none of them been soldiers of the grand armies of the Emperor. They had been recruited in loyal and long-suffering Vendée. He placed them under the command of St. Laurent, of whose conduct he highly approved, being in ignorance of the offer of secrecy made by that young soldier, Lestoype being too fine a man to attempt to better his case by bringing the Lieutenant into disgrace. This detachment had searched the major's quarters thoroughly. They had found them, of course, deserted.

Captain Grenier, being forthwith summoned to headquarters, had stated truthfully that Marteau had taken the Eagle and gone and thereafter the assembly had dispersed. He declared upon his word of honour that he had no knowledge where he had gone or what he had done with the Eagle. The Marquis had a complete description of Marteau drawn up and sent to every gate in the walled town. The guard was ordered to permit nobody and nothing to pass without the severest scrutiny and the closest search or inspection. The Governor made preparations for public proclamation on the morrow, offering a large reward for the fugitive's apprehension dead or alive, and also an additional reward for information that would lead to the discovery of the missing Eagle.

Promising himself to deal with the matter even more thoroughly in the morning, he had at last dismissed his subordinates and retired. If Marteau was within the city walls—and it was impossible to see how he could have got out of the town without a pass after twelve o'clock at night—he would find him if he had to search every house in the town. The spirit of the old man was high and aflame. To be so braved, to have his command the scene of such an outbreak of disloyalty and treason to the King was more than he could bear with equanimity.

There was another regiment in the town that had formerly been known as the Seventh-of-the-Line, commanded by Colonel Labédoyère, and there were detachments of artillery. The Eagle of the Seventh had never been sent to the War Office in Paris. It, too, had disappeared. But that had been months before the Marquis' time, and he had no responsibility for that. Colonel Labédoyère was more than suspected of lukewarmness, but as he was a young man of great influence, high social standing and much personal popularity no steps had as yet been taken against him. The Marquis determined to have it out with him also at the first convenient season, and unless he could be assured of his absolute devotion to King Louis, he would report to the Minister of War the necessity of the colonel's removal.

The old man was fully alive to the Napoleonic sentiment among the soldiers, a sentiment which arose from a variety of motives. In the first place, war was the trade of most of the soldiers. They lived on it, thrived by it, delighted in it. The permanence of the monarchy meant peace. There would be little chance for advancement and none at all for plunder. Self-interest predisposed every old soldier to continue an imperialist.

In the second place, the finances of France were naturally in a most disordered condition. The pay of officers and men was greatly in arrears; promises made had not been kept, and there was much heart-felt dissatisfaction on that account. The pay of a soldier is in no sense an adequate compensation for the risks he runs, the perils to which he voluntarily and willingly subjects himself, but it is a universal experience that although his pay is in no degree commensurate, yet the soldier whose pay is withheld instantly becomes insubordinate and mutinous, however high or patriotic the motives back of his enlistment.

Again the officers had, most of them, been degraded in rank. Many of them had been retired on pittances which were not paid. Those who were lucky enough to be retained in active service were superseded by superannuated, often incompetent old officers of the old royal army before the revolution, or by young scions of nobility with no knowledge or fitness to command veterans, to whom the gross-bodied, uninspiring, gouty old King did not appeal. Again, the regimental names and associations had been changed and the old territorial or royal and princely designations had been re-established; the Napoleonic victories had been erased from the battle-flags; the Eagles had been taken away.

The plain people of France were more or less apathetic toward Emperor or King. France had been drained of its best for so long that it craved rest and peace and time to recuperate above everything else. It had been sated with glory and was alike indifferent to victory or defeat. But the army was a seething mass of discontent. It had nothing to gain by the continuance of present conditions and everything to lose. It was a body of soldiers-of-fortune held in control temporarily by circumstances but ready to break the leash and respond instantly to the call of the greatest soldier-of-fortune of all.

And while all this is true it must also be admitted that there were many officers and men like Marteau who were profoundly humiliated and distressed over conditions in France and who, passionately wrapped up in and devoted to the Emperor, had spurned commissions and dignities and *preferments*. If they were obscure men they remained in France unnoticed; if they were great men they had expatriated themselves and sought seclusion and safety in other countries, oftentimes at great personal sacrifice of property, ease and comfort.

The King, who was by no means lacking in shrewdness and wit, and his chief advisers in Paris, did not fail to realize something of this, but keen-sighted men like the Marquis d'Aumenier, away from the person of the monarch, realized it much more fully, although even he had not the least idea of the wide extent and depth of this feeling. But the old man knew instinctively that he must control things in Grenoble at least with an iron hand and that no temporizing was possible. The return of Marteau, who was a man of parts and power, he admitted—he recalled how well he had borne himself before the little group in the drawing-room!—followed by the midnight gathering, the joy of the veterans, their worship almost of the Eagle, enlightened him. He would put down sedition with an iron hand, he swore to himself. The King had committed this important place to him. It was, in a certain sense, a frontier city if the impossible happened. Well, the King should find that he had not reposed trust in the Marquis for nothing.

So the old man thought as he lay sleepless during the night. He was not the only one who lay sleepless during the night. Laure d'Aumenier sought rest and oblivion in vain. She had been more moved by Marteau's conduct and bearing and presence in the old Château d'Aumenier, a year ago, than she had been willing to admit until she thought him dead. The Marteaux had always been a good-looking, self-respecting people. Madame Marteau, his mother, had been an unusual woman who had, it was said, married beneath her when she became the wife of old Jean Marteau, although she never in her long married life thought of it in that way. The present Jean Marteau was as handsome and distinguished looking a man as there was in France. The delicacy and refinement of his bearing and appearance did not connote weakness either, as she could testify.

The young woman owed her life and honour to the young soldier. But long before that chance meeting they had been companions in childhood, intimate companions, too. The boy had been her servitor, but he had been more. He had been her protector and friend. In her memory she could recall incident after incident when he had helped her, shielded her. Never once had he failed to show anything but devotion absolute and unbounded toward her.

The proposition of marriage he had made in the old hall, which she had laughed to scorn, had by no means escaped her memory. She had dwelt upon it, she had even speculated upon the possibility of an acceptance of his proposal. Why not? She knew no man more gentle at heart, more gallant in soul, more noble in spirit than he. That, too, she had turned over and over in her mind.

She admired Frank Yeovil. He was a likable man, frank by nature as well as name and brave, sunny in disposition and ardently devoted to her. When the betrothal had been made at her uncle's urgent insistence that she accept Captain Yeovil's suit, it had been a great match for her, for the d'Aumeniers were impoverished exiles, while the Yeovils were a rich family and of a line almost as long as her own. It had been easy enough to plight her troth to the young Englishman at first, but since she had seen Marteau, she realized that it would not be easy to keep that engagement. Fortunately, Captain Yeovil had been on service in Spain and the South of France with the Duke of Wellington's army, and only a few weeks before had he joined her uncle and herself in Paris on leave of absence. He had pressed her to name the day but she had temporized and avoided the issue; not for any definite reason but because as the time drew near she became less and less willing to be the Englishman's wife.

Marteau had been reported killed at Arcis. Perhaps that report had done more to enlighten her to the true state of her affections than anything else. Her pride of birth, her rank and station would never have permitted her, it may be, to dwell upon a living Marteau as a possible husband, but since he was dead there could be no harm in dreams of that kind; and in her grief she had indulged herself in them to the full. It had been a shock to her, of course, but not so great a shock as it would have been if an engagement had subsisted between the two, or she had permitted herself to think that she could ever look favourably on the proposition he had made to her. Nevertheless, it had been a great sorrow. There were some alleviations to the situation, however. Since it had become impossible, since she believed Marteau dead, she could indulge her grief and her mind could dwell upon those attractions which had influenced her so powerfully.

The period was one of intense anxiety and excitement. The old Marquis had lived much alone. He was not versed in woman's ways. Her agitation and grief passed unnoticed. By degrees she got control of herself. Since it was not to be Marteau it might as well be young Yeovil. The whole episode with which the French officer was concerned she viewed from a point of detachment as a romantic dream. His arrival had rudely shattered that dream and awakened her to the reality of the situation. She loved him.

For Laure d'Aumenier to marry Marteau was impossible. The Marquis would never consent. He was her legal guardian, the head of her race. Marriage without his consent was unthinkable. Loving Marteau she would fain not marry Yeovil; yet her troth being plighted in the most public manner and with her consent, the Marquis would force her to keep her word. She knew exactly the pressure that would be brought to bear upon her. Although she had lost some of the pride of her ancestors, she could see the situation from their point of view. There was a deadlock before her and there appeared to be no way of breaking it.

It was a wild night outside. The rain beat upon the casement windows of the old castle. The tempest without seemed fit accompaniment to the tempest within, thought the woman.

A long time she lay thinking, planning, hoping, praying; alike unavailingly. Toward morning, utterly exhausted by the violence of her emotions, the scene she had gone through—and it had been a torture to stand and receive the townspeople after the departure of Marteau— she fell at last into a troubled sleep.

She was awakened by a slight sound, as of a light footstep. She enjoyed the faculty of awakening with full command of her senses at once. She parted the curtains of the bed. With her eyes wide open, holding her breath, she listened. She heard soft movements. There was someone in the room!

Laure d'Aumenier, as has been said, had been trained to self-reliance. She could wield a sword expertly and was an accurate shot with a firearm. She could ride with any woman in England. She had, in full, the intrepidity and courage of her ancestors. Her prowess, so strange and so unusual in that day in a woman, had been a subject of disapproval on the part of her uncle, but Sir Gervaise Yeovil and his son had viewed it with delight. Frank Yeovil had brought her from Spain a beautiful Toledo blade and a pair of Spanish duelling pistols, light, easily handled and of deadly accuracy. The blade hung from a peg in the wall by the head of her bed. The pistols lay in a case on the table upon which her lighted bedroom candle stood. They were charged and ready for use.

Throwing back the cover without a sound, presently she stepped through the hangings and out on the floor. A loose wrapper lay at the foot of the bed, which was a tall old four-poster, heavily curtained. Whoever was in the room was on the other side of the bed, near the wall. The curtains hung between.

She was as light as a bird in her movements. She drew the bedgown nearer, thrust her feet into heelless slippers, placed convenient for her morning rising by her maid, opened the box of pistols, lifted one of them, examining it on the instant to see that it was ready for use, slipped on the wrapper, stepped toward the foot of the bed and waited.

The beat of the rain, the shriek of the wind, the roar of the thunder filled the room with sound, but the woman had good ears and they were well trained. She could hear someone softly moving. Sometimes, in lulls in the storm, she thought she could detect heavy breathing.

The natural impulse of the ordinary woman would have been to scream or if not that, having gained the floor, to rush to the door, or if not that to pull the bell cord and summon help. But Laure d'Aumenier was not an ordinary woman. She knew that any sound would bring aid and rescue at once. There would be plenty of time to scream, to pull the bell or to do whatever was necessary later. And something, she could not tell what, something she could not recognize, impelled her to take the course she did; to wait, armed.

But the wait began to tell on her sensibilities. The sound of somebody or something moving mysteriously to-and-fro behind the curtains over against the wall at the other end of the room began to work on her nerves. It takes an iron steadiness, a passive capacity for endurance which is quite different from woman's more or less emotional courage, to wait under circumstances like that.

Just when she had reached the limit of her endurance and was persuaded that she could stand no more, her attention was attracted by a slight click as of a lock or catch, a movement as of something heavy, as of a drawer or door, and then the footsteps turned and came toward the window. The moment of action had arrived and with it came the return of her wavering courage.

To reach the window the intruder must pass by the foot of the bed where she stood. Now the light was on the table at the head of the bed and the table was far enough from the bed to shine past her into the room. The moving figure suddenly came into view. It was a man, shrouded in a heavy cloak. He did not glance toward the bed. His eyes were fixed on the window. His astonishment, therefore, was overwhelming when he suddenly found himself looking into the barrel of a pistol and confronted by a woman.

CHAPTER 22

In the Countess Laure's Bedchamber

That astonishment was so great when the man recognized the woman that he threw up his hands and stepped backward. As he did so his sodden cloak, which he had gathered closely around him, opened and fell. The next instant his hand tore his hat from his head and he stood revealed in the full light of the candle.

"Marteau!" exclaimed the woman in a surprise and dismay equal to that of the man she confronted.

Her arm that held the pistol dropped weakly to her side. With the other hand she drew the *peignoir* about her, a vivid crimson wave rushed over her whole body. To surprise a man, a thief, in her room at night, was one thing; to confront the man she loved in such a guise was another. Her heart rose in her throat. For a moment she thought she would have fainted.

"You! You!" she choked out brokenly. "*Mon Dieu!*"

"*Mademoiselle*," began the man desperately, his confusion and dismay growing with every flying moment, "I——"

"What do you here," she went on impetuously, finding voice, "in my bedroom at night? I thought you——"

"For God's sake hear me. I came to——" and then he stopped lamely and in agonized embarrassment.

"For what did you come?" she insisted.

"*Mademoiselle*," he said, throwing his head up, "I cannot tell you. But when I was stationed here before this was the bedroom of the Commanding-Officer. I supposed it was so still. I had not the faintest idea that you—that it was——"

"And what would you do in the bedroom of the Commanding-Officer?" asked the woman, forgetting for the moment the strangeness of the situation in her anxiety to solve the problem.

397

"And that, I repeat, I cannot tell."

"Not even to me, who——" she stopped in turn.

"Yes, yes, go on," urged the young man, stepping nearer to her. "Not even to you who——"

"Who espoused your cause in the hall this very night, who befriended you," she went on rather lamely and inadequately having checked herself in time.

"Oh," said the young officer in great disappointment, "that?"

"Yes."

"You see, the Governor——"

"Did you wish to kill him?"

"*Mademoiselle!*" he protested. "I swear to you that I would not harm him for the world but I——"

"Are you in need? He offered you money. I have a few resources."

"For God's sake, *mademoiselle*," interposed the officer desperately, but she went resolutely on.

"Whatever I have is yours. See——" she stripped rings from her fingers and proffered them—"take them."

"*Mademoiselle*," said the young man sadly, "you wrong me."

"Well, if it was not for murder or for gain, for what cause did you take so frightful a risk?"

"Is there no other motive, *mademoiselle*, that makes men risk their lives than revenge or greed?"

"What do you mean?"

"Love."

"But you said you did not know this was my room!"

The words came from her impetuously and before she thought she realized when it was too late.

"Ah, *mademoiselle*, love of woman is a great passion. I know it only too well, too sadly. But it is not the only love."

"Have you another in your heart?" asked the countess with a sinking in her own.

"Love of honour."

"I don't understand."

"And yet I know that you are the very soul of honour yourself."

"I thank you, but——"

"*Mademoiselle*," said the young man, coming to a sudden resolution, "appearances are frightfully against me. That I should be here, in your room, at this hour of the night, under the circumstances, condemns me utterly in your opinion, especially as I have offered no adequate explanation. I am about to throw myself on your mercy, to trust to your honour."

"You shall not trust in vain, *monsieur.*"

"I know that. I trusted to your honour in the Château d'Aumenier and you did not fail me then."

"Nor will I now."

"Will you give me your word not to reveal what I tell you, and not to make use of the knowledge I communicate, until I give you leave?"

"Does it concern the honour or the welfare of those I love?"

"You mean that Englishman?"

"I do not love—I mean the Marquis, my uncle."

"It does not," said the young man, noting with throbbing heart the broken sentence.

"Then I give my promise. Speak."

"I came here to conceal something, *mademoiselle.*"

"What?"

"An emblem."

"Yours?"

"The Emperor's."

"You mean——"

"The Eagle of the Fifth-regiment-of-the-Line."

"Why here?"

"It is a long story. I brought it back, having fished it out of the river Aube, where it had lain since that day——"

"When I thought you killed," said the young woman, her hand pressed to her heart.

"And were you sorry?"

"Sorry? I——But go on."

"I showed it to the officers of the regiment tonight at Major Lestoype's quarters. We were discovered. The matter was reported to your uncle. Rather than give up the Eagle I said that I would hide it."

"And why here?"

"Because being as I thought the quarters of the Commanding-Officer it would be the last place in Grenoble where it would be sought."

"And where did you hide it?"

"Back of one of the drawers in the cupboard yonder."

"And how did you know of the place?"

"I was stationed here when I first joined the regiment. The *château* was untenanted. I rambled all over it. I explored its nooks and corners. I discovered that secret hiding place by chance and now the Eagle is there."

"And there it shall remain until it is discovered or until you give me leave to produce it," said the girl firmly.

"I have your promise?"

"You know well that I shall keep it."

"I thank you, *mademoiselle*. Twice you have saved my life and now, what is more to me than life, the emblem of my faith as a soldier, the honour of my regiment."

"But why keep it, this Eagle, at all," asked the girl, "and run this risk?"

"It may be needed again."

"But by whom?"

"The Emperor."

"The name is forbid."

"But the man is not."

"Ah, you think he will return?"

"I do."

"And when?"

"*Mademoiselle* has all my secrets. I am in her power absolutely. Why keep anything from her?"

"Why, indeed?" assented the woman, thrilling to the acknowledgment of her power over the man she loved as any woman would.

"When the violets bloom again," said the young man, bowing. "Now, *mademoiselle*, I am at your service," he resumed as she stared at him.

"At my service? What do you mean?"

"You have caught me here in your room. You have only to call out to summon assistance. I shall be removed from your pathway forever."

"But the Eagle?"

"I shall find means before I die to tell someone where to look for it if it should be needed."

"And I am to condemn you to death?"

"Why not?" said the young man. "I only lived to bring it back. I never dreamed that I was to have the happiness of seeing you again."

"Happiness? This anguish?" murmured the young woman in daring self-revelation.

She had forgot the hour, her dress, the strangeness of the situation, the awful impropriety of it all, the possibility of discovery. She only saw the man she loved. She saw how he loved her. She hung upon his words, and would fain hear more—more!

"My God!" he responded with a sort of fierce pride that was almost arrogant. "Although I was born a peasant, *mademoiselle*, not the finest gentleman in France or England could love you as I do. Yet it is impossible for you to love me now that the Emperor is no longer here. Your uncle would never consent. You, yourself, love that English gentleman. Why give thought to Marteau? Summon assistance, deliver me up and remember me as one who loved you with all the fervour of his heart, or forget me, if you can."

"I would not have you die," said the woman, shuddering. "God forbid."

"It is best so. Life holds nothing for me now."

"But if the violets bloom again?" asked the other.

"Ah!" exclaimed the man, throwing up his hands and drawing a long breath. "Then!"

"How came you here, *monsieur*?"

"By that window there. There is a ladder without. It reaches most of the way. I am a good climber. The ivy——"

"Go as you came. None shall be the wiser."

"To you always the disposition of my life, *mademoiselle*," said Marteau simply. "I obey your command. Farewell. It is but a postponement, anyway," he added as he turned away. "I can never escape from Grenoble. They will seize me sooner or later and——"

"Stay!" she cried.

Moved by an unaccountable impulse the girl took a step nearer to him. She loosened her clutch upon her garment and held out her hands to him.

"If it is to be farewell," she said tenderly, "know that I do not love that English Captain, no, and that. I——"

He seized her hand and covered it with kisses.

"I can die with better grace now," he said at last.

Not daring to trust himself further he turned to the window again. As he put his hand on the lock of the casement he heard shouts and cries outside, he saw torches. Escape that way was barred. The whole castle seemed suddenly to awake. He realized it all in a moment. He had been traced there. In another minute he would be discovered in the countess's room at that hour of the morning. He turned swiftly to the dismayed girl.

"They are there," he said. "Escape is cut off."

Steps and voices resounded in the corridor.

"Quick," she said, "the closet yonder—you can hide."

She understood the peril as well as he.

"And bring disgrace upon you when they caught me? Never!"

"Marteau, for God's sake, I love you," said the woman agonizingly. "I cannot——"

She stretched out her hands to him again. Very lovely she looked, the *peignoir* falling from her white shoulders, the soft candle-light illuminating and yet concealing in its vague shadows the beauty of face and figure. Marteau did not dare to dwell upon that. He must act and instantly. He rushed toward the woman. He caught her by the hand. He even shook her a little.

"Shriek," he whispered in her ear.

He picked up the pistol from the bed upon which she had thrown it and pointing it upward pulled the trigger. Startled by his utterly unexpected action, the meaning of which she could not fathom, she did scream loudly. The next instant the door was thrown open and into the room half clad, sword in hand, burst the Marquis. With him were Sir Gervaise Yeovil and the young captain, and attending them were servants and guards bearing lights.

The Marquis stared from his niece back to the young officer.

"My God!" he exclaimed. "Is it you?"

Marteau could only bow. He had a few seconds to make up his mind, a few seconds to decide upon the role he must play. Well, his life was certainly forfeit, his reputation he would also give for hers. Any explanation that he could make would be disbelieved unless, of course, he produced the Eagle, which was not to be thought of. Failing the Eagle the more he endeavoured to account for his presence the more deeply would he involve the woman he loved.

"I find you here, you that I treated almost like a gentleman, who, I thought, nearly measured up to the title, in my niece's room at this hour of the morning," continued the enraged old man. "Laure, has he—has he harmed you?"

"You came too quickly, *monsieur*," answered Marteau, himself, giving the young woman time to recover herself. "You heard the pistol shot." He threw the weapon from him. "We were struggling. It went off and——"

"You damned low-born coward," gritted out the English officer, stepping toward him furious with anger.

"Steady, Frank. There is something strange about this," said Sir Gervaise gloomily, catching his son by the arm. "He is no coward. That I'll warrant."

"But to seek entry into a woman's bedchamber!" continued Frank furiously. "If you were a gentleman I'd——"

"That 'almost,'" said Marteau, "saves me in this instance."

"I feel this action almost as if it had been my own son, had God blessed me with one," said the old Marquis, slowly recovering his self-command. "A loyal Marteau, a thief, a despoiler of women! Why, she knelt to you in the hall. She raised her voice in your defence, and now you—you——" His fingers twitched. "'The Count d'Aumenier,'" he added in bitter mockery. "You could not bear the title if it had been left in your hand. I shall have you branded as a thief in the morning and——"

"My uncle," said the woman, "he——"

"*Mademoiselle*," interposed Marteau sharply, resolved to protect her at all hazards, "is not my case black enough without further testimony from you? I beseech you to be silent."

"Speak, Laure," said the old Marquis. "If you have anything to say which will make his punishment surer and harder, I charge you to say it."

"Nothing, nothing," answered the poor young woman. "Oh, if ever a woman's soul was tortured——"

"You tortured her, did you?" cried the Englishman, struggling in his father's arms. "I once thought of meeting you in the field—you—you! I would like to strangle you with my bare hands."

"It is just. I honour *monsieur* for his rage. It is true, I love the woman, and——"

"Is this the way a gentleman shows his affection?" roared out the English captain.

"*Monsieur* forgets that I am almost, not quite, a gentleman."

"And there is another score we have to settle with you," cried the Marquis. "That cursed Eagle—where is it?"

"Before I sought *mademoiselle*," said Marteau, "I placed it in safety and in such keeping as will watch over it. You will never find it. It will only be produced when"—he stopped—"when the violets bloom again."

"What is this damned nonsense about flowers I hear everywhere?" burst out Sir Gervaise.

"Well, *monsieur*," said the Marquis, "it will be produced before that time, or when the violets do bloom they will find some red soil out of which to spring."

"You mean——"

"As I live I will have you court-martialed in the morning and shot for high treason. I stand for the King, for the ancient laws of France. I will have no paltering with traitors, and I am more inclined to deal swiftly and summarily with you since to treason you add theft and this attempt upon a woman. Produce that Eagle, or you die."

"I must die, then," said the young man.

"By heaven," said Sir Gervaise; looking keenly at the officer, "there is more in this than I can understand. Give me leave, my lord," he turned to Marteau. "I have liked you always. I would befriend you now. I do not believe in appearances always. Can you not explain?"

"Sir," said Marteau, "I am grateful to find one here who still believes——" He stopped. "The circumstances speak for themselves. I love *mademoiselle*. I was mad. I came here, I——"

"Gentlemen," said the Marquis, "let us withdraw. It is scandalous that we should be here under such circumstances. You, sir," he turned to Marteau, "this way."

The poor countess had stood in agony and despair. Marteau did not look at her. He bent his head low as he passed her. Two soldiers of the guard grasped him by the arms, the rest closed about him.

"Go, gentlemen. I will see you presently," said the Marquis. "One of you servants yonder send the Countess's women here."

"I thank God," said young Yeovil, "that we got here in time. If he had harmed you, dearest Laure, I would have killed him here where he stood."

Her lover attempted to take her hand, but she shrank away from him. As Sir Gervaise passed her she bent forward and seized the old Baronet's hand and kissed it. He, at least, had seen that there was something beneath the surface.

"Now, my child," said the old Marquis kindly, but with fearful sternness, as the door closed behind the others, "what have you to add to what has been told?"

"What do you mean?"

"I know men. I know that that young man did not come here to assault you, or for robbery. You cannot tell me that the blood of the Marteaux runs in his veins for nothing. And I know you did not invite him here, either. You are a d'Aumenier. What is the explanation of it

404

all?"

But the poor little countess made no answer. She slowly collapsed on the floor at the feet of the iron old man, who, to save her honour and reputation, had played his part, even as Marteau, in her bedroom on that mad March morning.

CHAPTER 23

The Marquis Grants an Interview

The old Marquis was face to face with a terribly difficult problem. That the Eagle had been brought back did not admit of doubt. St. Laurent had seen it, and the officers who had been present at the midnight meeting in the Major's rooms made no attempt whatever to deny it. Marteau admitted it. But it had disappeared. He had not the faintest idea where it was. The most rigorous search had so far failed to discover it. Marteau had been questioned, appealed to, threatened, with no results whatsoever. His lips were sealed and no pressure that could be brought to bear sufficed to open them. He did not deny that he knew where the Eagle was. He simply remained silent, immutably silent, when he was asked where.

From the few loyalist officers in the regiments and in the town a court had been convened and Marteau had been put on trial. He had been found guilty—indeed, there was no other verdict possible, since he calmly admitted everything—of treason, disobedience of orders, a whole catalogue of crimes. The Marquis acted on the old feudal idea that he possessed all the rights of the ancient nobility, the high and low, the middle justice. And, indeed, he represented the King with full powers. The court, completely under his influence, had condemned the young soldier to death. Marteau might have appealed, he might have protested, but he did neither. He accepted the inevitable. What was the difference? No appeal would have been entertained, no protest would have availed. It all came to this, he would either have to give up the Eagle or his life.

Well, life was not worth very much to him, as he had said. Even though he realized from her desperate avowal of the night before that the interest of the countess in him was more than she would have admitted, had not the words been surprised and wrung from her by his deadly peril, he knew that there was absolutely nothing to be hoped for in that direction. Even though his comrades, alarmed by the imminence of his danger, and aroused by the energetic determination of the old Marquis, besought him to give up the Eagle, he refused. He would have considered himself a forsworn man had he done so.

The Marquis had visited the prisoner and had condescended to make a personal appeal to him, imploring him by that old duty and friendship which had subsisted between the families, but his appeals had been as fruitless as his commands and his threats. The old noble was iron hard. He had no sympathy with the Empire or its Emperor, but the determination of the young officer did arouse a certain degree of admiration. He would fain have spared him if he could, but, as he had sacrificed everything he possessed for the King, and counted the sacrifice as nothing, his sympathies did not abate his determination to punish treason and contumacy one whit.

The Marquis was accustomed to having things his own way, and the long period of exile had not changed his natural bent of mind in that particular. He was angry, too, at the stubbornness which he nevertheless admired. In other directions the Marquis was balked. He had seen through the little drama that had been played by Marteau and the Countess Laure in her bedchamber. That was one reason why he would fain have saved him, because he had so gallantly allowed himself to occupy the hideous role which he had assumed, to save the girl's honour. The Marquis had not the faintest suspicion that there was anything wrong in the situation, or even that his niece had actually given her heart to this man. Such a thought could not be entertained at all.

It was inconceivable, but he knew that, however innocent might have been that meeting, if it had been prearranged the world would consider the countess disgraced, unless the explanation which Marteau had suggested was allowed to become current. He had summoned his niece before him, and had sought in every way to force her to tell him the whole truth, but she had partaken, in some degree, of Marteau's stubbornness. All she would say was, that Marteau was innocent of any crime or any wrong. But, when the bewildered Marquis asked her if she had invited him there, and if he was there by her permission, she had indignantly repudiated the suggestion as an insult, which left him more puzzled than before.

The idea that Marteau had come there to hide the Eagle had never entered the Marquis' mind for all his acuteness. He had asked the girl whether Marteau had brought anything into the room or taken any-thing from it, and she had answered truthfully that when she saw him he had been exactly as when they saw him. The testimony of the Marquis and the two Englishmen rendered it unnecessary for the Countess to be present at the court-martial. There was nothing material she could add, and, indeed, it was not for attempted theft, or assault, that Marteau had been condemned—the Marquis had suppressed that as much as possible—but for his conduct with the Eagle.

It was the fifth of March, a warm and sunny day in the south of France, even amid the mountains and hills of ancient Dauphiné. Great things were toward, although the Marquis did not yet know it. The execution of the condemned was set for the next day. At ten o'clock in the morning the regiment was to be paraded and Marteau was to be shot. He had asked that he might be granted a soldier's death, and the Marquis had seen fit to grant the request.

There were very few troops in Grenoble which could be counted as loyal to the King, but there were some. From them the Marquis intended to draw his firing party, and with them he intended to over-awe the regiment if there should be any outbreak. He was too keen a judge of humanity, and too well able to read the characters of men not to realize the whole regiment was in a mutinous temper over the Eagle episode, that they looked upon Marteau as a martyr, and that there might be outbreaks and grave difficulties before he was shot. Well, difficulties did not daunt the stout-hearted, inflexible old noble. He rather enjoyed them. He rather welcomed this occasion, too, be-cause he intended to be master now, and, having once mastered the regiment, he felt he would have no difficulty in controlling it in any future emergency.

To him, as he sat in his cabinet maturing his plans for the morrow, came a message from his niece, asking admittance. The privilege was, of course, instantly granted, and Laure d'Aumenier presently entered the room.

"Have you come, my child," began the old man, regarding her tenderly, for in the few years she had been with him he had learned to estimate the worth of her character and love her as she deserved, "to explain this mystery, to tell me why you declare that the presence of a man in the room of a woman of my house at three o'clock in the morning is innocent? I repeat," he went on reassuringly, "that I can-not conceive of or admit any wrong on your part, and that makes the situation more impossible of explanation."

"My uncle," answered the countess, "I can only say that Monsieur Jean Marteau is not guilty, as he seems."

"And I can quite believe that," said the old Marquis. "Indeed, our English friend, who for all his bluntness is not without discrimination and good sense, has said as much to me. He declared with great emphasis that there was something in it all which he could not understand."

"And you—what did you say?"

"I asked him if that was meant for any reflection on the honour of my family, for if it were I should accord him the pleasure of crossing swords with me and in the end run him through."

"And he said——"

"He disclaimed absolutely the idea. He is as convinced of your sweetness, your innocence and purity, as I am."

"And Captain Yeovil?"

"He lacks his father's insight and *finesse*. He is young. He takes matters as he sees them, and fancies Marteau the common, vulgar thief he appeared."

"Impossible!" cried the Countess. "He is——"

"No doubt he is not especially prepossessed in favour of Monsieur Marteau, who has presumed to love you, and perhaps that accounts for his willingness to believe anything derogatory of him."

"He is blind, and I——"

"But you are not declining his hand on that account!"

"No, the marriage stands. I could wish that it did not," said the woman passionately. "I could be happier if he suspected me of anything, however base, and in his suspicion set me free."

"Hark ye, Laure," said the Marquis earnestly. "I am an old man, and the life I have led has not served to maintain my youth. What I am engaged in now does not conduce to that ease of body and peace of mind which promotes long life. To you I say what I have said to no one else. We are standing, as it were, on a volcano. The army is in no sense loyal to the King. I advised that it be disbanded absolutely, but I was overruled. It is seething with sedition. The envoys of the powers at Vienna are playing, idling, debating endlessly, and while they play and idle and talk in their fools' paradise, the Emperor, he who is so called by misguided France, will return. I should not be surprised at any moment to receive tidings that he has landed."

"And that is what they mean when they speak about the violets blooming again?"

"Yes, that is it. And, do you know as I walked in the garden this morning I found this."

He tossed the first tiny purple violet of the spring on the table before her.

"But he will be dead before the Emperor comes," murmured the woman, her hand upon her heart.

"Put that thought out of your mind, my child," said the old man. "Think rather of Captain Yeovil."

"I hate him," said the Countess, which was most unjust, for he had done nothing at all to deserve such an expression on her part.

"Hate is the passion of old age," said the Marquis slowly, "love that of youth. I told you that my race would soon be run. I am an old man. I have suffered much. I shall be content to die if I can serve my King here a little after all these years of weary waiting. The title-deeds that young man gave back do not cover much. The estate has been divided and granted to strangers. It is practically all gone but the old *château*. I have little or nothing to leave you beyond those small amounts which your father used to send me, which I never would touch because they came from a disloyal France. The Yeovils are true and worthy people. The boy is a gallant lad, a brave soldier, even if not overly acute. Sir Gervaise is a man of consideration and of great wealth. You are portionless. He is most generous. I am very happy in the thought that you will be taken care of. I know what it is to be alone and poor."

"I cannot bear——"

"We have to bear a great many things that we do not wish to in this life. You owe me some consideration. I still retain my faith and confidence in you. I have not pressed you to the wall with hard questions about last night."

"I know, I know, but——"

"And, as the head of the house, I must have even from the children the obedience which is my due."

"I do not wish to fail in my duty toward you, monsieur, but——"

"And your word, the word of a d'Aumenier, has been plighted. You entered into this engagement of your own free will. There was no constraint."

"But there was pressure."

"Yes, certainly, I know what is best for you, but you were not forced in any way, and your troth, having been plighted, your word given"—the old man stopped, looked at her solemnly, his long fingers tapping lightly on the table—"it must be kept," he said, with that air of absolute finality which none could assume better than he.

"It shall be, although it kills me."

"If I live I shall see that it is; and if I die I have your promise?"

"You have."

"That is well. You will live to thank me and bless me. I have fancied, of late, that your heart had been allowed to decline a little to this Marteau. Oh, he is a brave man and true, I know. I take no stock in his confession of theft or assault upon you. Why, I would have cut him down where he stood, or have him kill me if I believed that! But he is of another race, another blood. The Eagle does not stoop to the barnyard fowl. The heart of a woman is a strange thing. It leads her in strange ways if she follows its impulses. Thank God there are men who can and will direct and control those impulses. Put him out of your mind. It is best. Tomorrow he will be a dead man. At any rate, I am rather glad of that," said the Marquis, half reflectively, knowing what trouble he might have made if he were to be allowed to live on. It was cold-blooded, but he could sacrifice Marteau for his niece's happiness, and find abundant justification in the annals of his house, where he could read of many Marteaux who had been sacrificed or had sacrificed themselves for the d'Aumeniers.

"I—I will promise," faltered the girl, "but on one condition."

"I like it not when youth makes conditions with age. Nevertheless, what is in your mind?"

"I want to see Marteau again."

"Impossible!"

"Wait," said the woman quickly. "Is it not true, have I not heard that he is condemned outwardly because he brought an Eagle here and it is gone?"

"Yes, that is true."

"And has it not been said that if he produced the Eagle his life could be spared and he could go?"

"That is also true."

"And would it not allay the dissatisfaction of the regiment and contribute to the establishment of your authority if he gave it up?"

"My authority is established by the King."

"The maintenance of it, then. Would it not enable you to control and hold in check these people, if you could show that you had not been balked?"

"That may be," said the Marquis. "Go on."

"And, if he should produce the Eagle——"

"I would save his life, but he would be a discredited man among his comrades, if I know anything about it."

"Oh, not that, surely."

"Surely; and I may tell you that if I were in his place I would do exactly as he has done."

The woman stepped nearer and put her hand to her head.

"Nevertheless, I must see him. Have mercy!" she entreated piteously.

"Why? Do you think you can persuade him to produce the Eagle—to his discredit, be it remembered?" asked the old man, surveying her keenly, realizing at last the extraordinary interest she took in Marteau.

"But it is his life if he does not."

"Do you care so much for—his life?"

"Yes," answered the woman, looking the Marquis straight in the eyes.

He recognized a will as inflexible as his own. It aroused his admiration. He arose to his feet. He bowed before her.

"*Mademoiselle*," he said firmly, "you have the strength of our house. Perhaps it might be well if he could be induced to produce the Eagle and be thus discredited in the eyes of his comrades. It would tend to make my authority more secure. It would be to the advantage of the King."

"Yes, yes."

"But what argument can you bring?"

"I—I do not know."

"Alas, my child, you know more than you will tell. Oh, I recognize that it is useless to appeal, and impossible to constrain. Well, you give me your word of honour that whatever happens you will carry through the engagement with Captain Yeovil, and that we will together arrange a proper time and that you——"

"I give it."

"Your hand," said the Marquis. "Without there!" He raised his voice. An orderly appeared. "Send Monsieur St. Laurent to me."

"*Monsieur*," continued the old man, as the officer presented himself, "you will conduct the Countess Laure d'Aumenier to the small drawing-room; you will leave her there; you will then go to the guard-house and bring thence the prisoner, Marteau; you will conduct him to *mademoiselle*, my niece, and you will leave them together for half an hour; you will see that the prisoner is carefully guarded, that sentries are posted outside of the windows, and you, yourself, will remain with other escort, in front of the door."

"But out of hearing," said the young woman quickly.

"That, of course. And on your honour, on your duty, on your allegiance, you will say absolutely nothing about this to anyone. Do you understand?"

"I understand, *monsieur*. I shall obey," said St. Laurent, a youth of rare quality, as has been seen.

"Good. You have one half-hour, my child. God grant that you may serve France and induce this wretched prisoner to give up the Eagle. Your impulse of mercy does you credit," he said adroitly, making the best of the situation for St. Laurent's benefit. "Now you may go."

"This way, *mademoiselle*," said St. Laurent, bowing low before her at the open door.

As the countess passed down the long corridor she almost ran into young Pierre, the boy. He had been questioned with the rest, but had absolutely nothing to tell. Of course, he knew about the recovery of the Eagle, but that was all. He had known nothing about the midnight meeting. The Countess Laure had taken him into her service, her uncle being willing. And he had spent a miserable day when not with her, wondering and hoping and praying for Marteau. With others in the regiments he had received important news in the last hour, and had made every effort to get it to Marteau, as had been suggested to him, but he had hitherto failed. No sentry would pass him, and there was no way he could get speech with the prisoner.

He was in despair when he saw the countess approaching, St. Laurent marching ceremoniously ahead, as if to clear the way.

"*Mademoiselle*," he whispered, plucking her gown.

"What is it?" asked the girl, naturally sinking her voice to the other's pitch.

"You will see—him?"

"Yes."

"A message."

"What is it?"

"Give him this."

The boy thrust into her hand two or three flowers like those her uncle had picked, the first purple blossoms of the virgin spring.

"And the message?"

"The violets have bloomed," said the boy, and he was gone.

CHAPTER 24

On the Whole Death May be Better than Life

Marteau realized fully his position, and it would be idle to say that despite his depression he contemplated his fate without regret. Normally he would have wanted to live as much as any man, even though in his more passionate moments he had said that life without Laure d'Aumenier held nothing for him. To be sure, life without her did not look very inviting, and there was nothing in it for which he particularly cared, especially since the Emperor was gone, and Marteau had become a stranger, as it were, in France. If the Emperor had come back, or was coming back, it would be different.

In spite of rumours, originating nowhere apparently and spread by what means no one could say, that the Emperor was coming back, Marteau, in the depressed condition of his mind, gave these statements but little credence. Besides, even if they were true, even if Laure d'Aumenier loved him, even if he had everything on earth for which a man could ask or expect to live, he could not therewith purchase life; he could not even purchase love, at the expense of his honour.

He could not give up the Eagle for the kingdom. It was only a bit of gilded copper, battered and shattered, but it awakened in his nature the most powerful emotions which he was capable of entertaining. His love for Laure d'Aumenier was the great passion of his life. Yet even his love for the woman, or hers for him, if she had returned his devotion with equal intensity and ardour, would not avail to persuade him to give up that battered standard.

Even if she had loved him! Ah, what had she said in that moment of madness in her room that night? It was a moment of madness, of course, nothing else. Marteau put it out of his mind, or strove to. It could not be. Indeed, now that he was about to die, he would even admit that it should not be. But, if it were true, if that impulsive declaration indicated the true state of her regard—the possibility was thrilling, yet reflection convinced him it was better that he should die just the same, because there could be no mating between the two.

He had crossed swords with the Marquis. He had felt the hardness, the inflexibility and temper of the old man's steel. There would be no breaking him, no altering his will. He had made assurance doubly sure in some way, Marteau was convinced. This marriage with this young Englishman, whom the Frenchman regarded with a tolerant, half-amused contemptuousness for his simplicity and bluntness, would have to be carried through. When Marteau was dead the countess would presumably return to a saner frame of mind, and forget the mad attachment, if indeed she had entertained it.

He took a certain melancholy satisfaction in the hope that he would at least become one of her sacred and cherished memories. But no memory can successfully dispute the claim of the living, as a rule. She would eventually marry this Englishman; he would make her a good husband, and by and by she would be happy, and Marteau would not be there to see. And for that he would be glad.

If the Emperor had been there, if the war god had come and summoned his men to arms again, Marteau might have eased the fever in his brain and soul by deeds of prowess on fields of battle, but in peace he should only eat his heart out thinking of her in the other man's arms. There were things worse than death, and this was one. On the whole, he concluded it was just as well, or even better, that he should die.

He was sufficiently versed in military and even civil law to see that his condemnation was irregular in the extreme, but he let it go. He was an obscure officer of a lost cause. There would not be any too rigorous an inquiry into what disposition the Marquis made of him. Nobody would care after it was all over. There remained nothing for him, therefore, but to die like a soldier, and—he smiled bitterly at the thought—almost a gentleman!

He had been informed that any reasonable request he made would be granted. He would fain see a priest of his church, but later, and endeavour to make his peace with man after the time-honoured custom of his religion, and thus insure his peace with God. Meanwhile, a request for a brief interview with the woman he loved had trembled on his lips, but it had found no utterance. He was quite aware how he stood in that quarter. He had come to the conclusion that the Marquis, at least, had seen through the little comedy—or, was it not a tragedy, after all?—which he had played in her bed-chamber, and he had convinced himself that the swiftness, the almost unseemly haste of his trial and condemnation and the nearness of his execution were largely due to a determination on the part of the old noble to get him out of the way before any scandal should arise. Perhaps scandal was certain to come, and gossip to prevail, but it would be less harmful if the man were dead.

To ask to see a woman whom he was supposed to have insulted so deeply and wronged so grievously would have served only to call attention to those things, to have given the whole game away, as it were. Besides, what would be the good of it? She would leave him weaker in his resolution than before. If she had loved him—ah, God, how his heart throbbed—if that impulsive admission had been the truth of her heart! Well, he told himself, he would have gone through the trial, accepted the verdict, received the bullets of the firing-squad in his heart, although it would have been harder. And yet—how he longed to see her.

He had not expected to see her ever again during his long tramp from Salzburg to Grenoble. He had not entertained the least idea that she would be there. He had schooled himself to do without her, contemplate life absolutely sundered from her. But when he did see her his whole being had flamed with the passion he had so long repressed in vain.

And the Countess Laure knew more of his heart than he fancied. During the morning she had had young Pierre before her. She had questioned him, suggesting and even prompting his artless revelations. The boy needed no suggestions. He was quick-witted and keen-eyed. Admiring Marteau extravagantly and devotedly as he did, he could not conceive how anyone could fail to share his feelings. He told the hungry-hearted woman the story of their lives since they had been captured together at Arcis.

Reticent at first, Marteau had finally made a confidant of the lad, who had shown himself sympathetic, discreet, adoring. He had to tell somebody, he had to ease his heart of his burden. And when he had once begun naturally he poured it all out before the boy. He could not have told a man, a woman, perhaps, had one been by sufficiently sympathetic and tender, but, failing that, it was the boy who received the confidences and who never once presumed on these revelations.

Indeed, he had a vein of romance in his peasant heart. He was a poet in his soul. Perhaps that was one reason why the man could confide in him. And then, when Marteau lay in the delirium of fever, the boy had shared their watches with the good Sisters of Charity. He alone had understood the burden of his ravings, for they were all about the woman. And, when she questioned him and gave him the opportunity, he poured forth in turn all the stored treasure of his memory.

And the poor, distraught, unhappy young woman hung on his words with heaving breast and panting heart and tear-dimmed eyes and cheeks that flushed and paled. Glad she was that he had so loved her; sad that it could make no difference. Indeed, young Pierre served his master well in that hour, and earned whatsoever reward, however great it might be, he should receive from him in the future.

How strangely selfish even in its loves is humanity! Although Marteau was intensely fond of the lad, and deeply devoted to him, absorbed in his overwhelming affection for the woman he had forgot the boy until too late to send for him that day. Well, he would remedy that omission on the morrow, he thought, as he abandoned himself once more to dreams of other days, to fruitless anticipations, to vain hopes of what might have been.

To him suddenly came St. Laurent. The young *aide* knew but vaguely of the scene in the countess's bedchamber and, therefore, there was no prejudice in his mind against the officer. Although he was a loyalist to the core, he could sympathize as a soldier with the other's point of view. His address toward him, therefore, was respectful, and even indicated some of that sympathy.

"*Monsieur,*" he began most courteously, "I am sent by the Governor to conduct you elsewhere."

"Shall I need my hat and cloak, *monsieur?*" asked the other, quite appreciative of the young man's treatment of him.

"You will," was the answer.

"Am I leaving this room permanently?"

"You will return to it in half an hour."

"And whither——"

"You will pardon me," was the firm reply, "I have orders to conduct you, not to answer questions."

"Your reproof," admitted Marteau, smiling faintly, "is well deserved. I attend you at once, sir."

Escorted by St. Laurent and two soldiers, he left the building, walked across the barrack yard, attracting instant attention from the soldiers off duty congregated there, and a few officers of the garrison who chanced to be passing. All of them saluted him with the utmost deference and the most profound respect. He punctiliously acknowledged their salutes with a melancholy grace and dignity. There was an air of great excitement everywhere, and he wondered vaguely what could be the cause of it.

To his further wonderment also he found his steps directed to the Governor's palace. Entering, he was ushered through the halls and marched to the door of a room which he remembered was one of the smaller waiting-rooms of the palace. St. Laurent stopped before the door, his hand upon the knob.

"*Monsieur*," he said, "to this room there is but this one door. I remain without with these soldiers. You can see by a glance through the windows that they also are closely guarded. Escape is impossible. In half an hour I will knock upon the door, open it, and escort you back to your place of confinement. Do you understand?"

"Perfectly."

"Enter."

Somewhat bewildered by the mysteriousness of the whole proceeding, and yet with a heart which in spite of himself did beat a little faster, Marteau entered the room, St. Laurent closing the heavy door behind him.

CHAPTER 25

Not Even Love Can Find a Way

Standing in the middle of the room, her closed hand resting upon a table upon which she leaned as if for support, was Laure d'Aumenier. The old Marquis had not noticed it, nor did the young man; that is, the eye of neither took in the details, but both had been conscious of the general effect, for the young countess had dressed herself in her most becoming gown, one that had been newly made for her in Paris before the journey to the south of France and that she had never worn before.

She had spent a miserable night and day. When she had talked with her uncle a short time before, the effects of her sleeplessness and anguish had been plainly apparent. But there, within that room, her colour coming to her face, her eyes shining with excitement and emotion, she looked as fresh and as beautiful as the springtime without.

It was her right hand that rested on the table, and as Marteau approached her left instinctively sought her heart. In his emotion he looked at her with steady, concentrated glance, so keen, so piercing, as if he sought to penetrate to the very depths of her heart, that she could scarcely sustain his gaze. He, too, had forgot cares and anxieties, anticipation, hopes, dreams; in his excitement and surprise everything had gone from him but her presence. Here was the woman he loved, looking at him in such a way, with such an air and such a bearing, her hand upon her heart—was that heart beating for him? Was she trying to still it, to control it, because——

His approach was slow, almost terribly deliberate, like the movement of the old Guard under Dorsenne—*Le Beau Dorsenne!*—against the heights of Pratzen on the glorious yet dreadful day of Austerlitz. His advance was irresistible, but unhurried, as if there must be a tremendous clash of arms in a moment to which haste could lend noth-

419

ing, from the dignity and splendour of which hurry would detract. At another time the woman might have shrunk back faltering, she might have voiced a protest, or temporized, but now, in the presence of death itself, as it were, she stood steady waiting for him. Enjoying the luxury of looking upon him unrestrained, her heart going out to him as he drew nearer, nearer, nearer, she found herself tremblingly longing for his actual touch.

Now his arms went out to her, she felt them slowly fold around her, and then, like a whirlwind released, he crushed her against his breast, and, as she hung there, her throbbing heart making answer to the beating of his own, he kissed her again, again, again. Her heart almost stopped its beating. Beneath the fire of his lips her face burned. Her head drooped at last, her tense body gave way, she leaned upon him heavily, glad for the support of his strong arms.

"Laure," he whispered, "my little Laure, you love me. Oh, my God, you love me. It was true, then. I did not dream it. My ears did not mock me."

"Yes, yes," said the woman at last. "Whoever you are, whatever you are, wherever you go, I love you."

"And was it to tell me this that you came?"

"Yes. But not for this alone."

"What else?"

"I would have you live."

"For you?"

"For me."

"As your husband?"

"And if that were possible would you——"

"Yes, yes, would I what?"

"Give up the Eagle?"

"My God!" said the man, loosening his clasp of her a little and holding her a little away that he might look at her. "Does your love tempt me to dishonour?"

"I do not know," said the woman piteously. "I am confused. I cannot think aright. Oh, Marteau, Jean, with whom I played as a child, think of me. I cannot bear to see you dead outside there. I cannot look upon a soldier without thinking of it. The rattling of the carts in the streets sounds in my ear like shots. Don't, don't die. You must not."

"And, if I lived, would you love me?"

"So long as the good God gives me the breath of life."

"With the love of youth and the love of age?"

"Aye, for eternity."

"And would you be my wife?"

"Your wife?" said the woman, her face changing. "It would be joy beyond all, but I could not."

"Why not?"

"I—you know I am promised to another," she went on desperately, "and but that I might see you I repeated the promise. Otherwise my uncle would never have permitted me this blessed privilege. I told him that I would marry anybody if he would only let me see you—alone—for a moment, even. What difference, so long as I could not be yours? I came to tell you that I loved you, and because of that to beg you to live, to give up that Eagle. What is it, a mere casting of metal, valueless. Don't look at me with that hard, set face. Let me kiss the line of your lips into softness again. I cannot be your wife, but at least you will live. I will know that somewhere you think of me."

"And would death make a difference? High in the highest heaven, should I be so fortunate as to achieve it, I would think of you; and, if I were to be sent to the lowest hell, I could forget it all in thinking of you."

"Yes, yes, I know how you love, because——"

"Because why?"

"I won't hesitate now. It may be unmaidenly, but I know, because I, too——"

"Laure!" cried the man, sweeping her to him again.

"I think I loved you when we were boy and girl together," said the woman, throwing everything to the winds in making her great confession. "I know I loved you that night in the *château*, although I would not admit it, and I treated you so cruelly. And when they told me you were dead, then, then, my heart broke. And when you came here and I saw you two men together—oh, I had made the contrast in my imagination—but last night I saw and now I see. Oh, you will live, live. What is honour compared to a woman's heart? See, I am at your feet. You will not break me. You will live. Something may happen. I am not married yet. The Emperor may come back."

"The boy, Pierre, said last night that it was rumoured——"

"Yes, he gave me a message. I almost forgot it." She held out the violet crushed in her fevered palm. "He said to tell you that the violet has bloomed."

"Does he mean——?"

"I know not what he means."

"It is but an assurance begot of hope," said Marteau.

"And if it were so?"

"He comes too late. Rise, my lady. It is not meet for you to kneel. Let me lift you up, up to my heart. I cannot give up the Eagle. That I have won your love is the most wonderful thing in all the world. It passes my understanding, the understanding of man, but I should forfeit it if I should permit myself this shame."

"Then I will do it, I will betray you," said the little countess desperately. "I alone know where that Eagle is. I will get it. I will bargain with my uncle for your life. Marteau, listen. Do you wish to condemn me to death? I will not, I cannot, survive you. I will not be thrust into that other's arms. I did not know, I did not realize what it was—before. But since I have been here, since you have held me to your heart, since you have kissed me—no, I cannot. It would be desecration—horror. Let me go. I will tell."

"Dearest Laure," said the man, holding her tighter, "think, be calm, listen. It needs not that I assure you of my love. I have proved it. I lie here with the stigma of shame, the basest of accusations in the hearts of those who know of our meeting at night, to save you from suspicion even."

"Not my uncle, not the Marquis. He says there is something back of it all. He knows you are not a thief."

"It takes a d'Aumenier to understand a Marteau," said the young man proudly.

"And I am a d'Aumenier, too," said the woman.

"Then strive to comprehend my point of view."

"I can, I will, but——"

"What binds you to that Englishman?"

"My word, my uncle's word."

"Exactly. And what else binds you to keep my secret?"

The woman stared at him.

"Oh, do not urge that against me," she pleaded. "I must tell all."

"I have your word. That Eagle must remain hidden there until the Emperor comes back. Then you must give it to him and say that I died that you might place it in his hand."

"There must be a way, and there shall be a way," said the agonized woman. "I love you. I cannot have you die. I cannot, I cannot."

Her voice rose almost to a scream in mad and passionate protest.

"Why," said the man soothingly, "I am the more ready to die now that I know that you love me. Few men have ever got so much out

422

of life as that assurance gives me. That I, peasant-born, beneath you, should have won your heart, that I should have been permitted to hold you to my breast, to feel that heart beat against my own, to drink of the treasures of your lips, to kiss your eyes that shine upon me—— Oh, my God, what have I done to deserve it all? And it is better, far better, having had thus much and being stopped from anything further, that I should go to my grave in this sweet recollection. Could I live to think of you as his wife?"

"If you will only live I will die myself."

"And could I purchase life at that price? No. We have duties to perform—hard, harsh words in a woman's ear, common accustomed phrase to a soldier. I have to die for my honour and you have to marry for yours."

"*Monsieur*," broke in the sharp, somewhat high, thin voice of the old Marquis standing by the door, "the court-martial brands you as a traitor. Captain Yeovil and those who were with me last night think you are a thief and worse. But, by St. Louis," continued the old noble, fingering his cross, as was his wont in moments in which he was deeply moved, "I know that you are a soldier and a gentleman."

"A soldier, yes; but a gentleman?—only 'almost,' my lord."

"Not almost but altogether. There is not another man in France who could withstand such a plea from such a woman."

"You heard!" exclaimed Marteau.

"Only the last words. I heard her beg you to live because she loved you."

"And you did not hear——"

"I heard nothing else," said the Marquis firmly. "Would I listen? I spoke almost as soon as I came in. Laure, these Marteaux have lived long enough by the side of the d'Aumeniers to have become ennobled by the contact," he went on naïvely. "I now know the young man as I know myself. It is useless for you to plead longer. I come to take you away."

"Oh, not yet, not yet."

"Go," said the young officer. "Indeed, I cannot endure this longer, and I must summon my fortitude for tomorrow."

"As for that," said the Marquis, "there must be a postponement of the execution."

"I ask it not, *monsieur*. It is no favour to me for you to——"

"Thank God! Thank God!" cried the woman. "Every hour means——"

"And I am not postponing it because of you," continued the Marquis coolly. "But he who must not be named——"

"The Emperor."

"So you call him—has landed."

"Yes, yes; for God's sake, tell me more."

"I have no objection to telling you all. He is on the march toward Grenoble. He will be here tomorrow night. Troops have been sent for and will assemble here. He will be met in the gap on the road a few miles below the town. He will be taken. If he resists he will be shot."

"Yes, the violets have bloomed again."

"And they shall draw red nourishment from the soil of France," was the prophetic answer.

"The Emperor!" cried the young man in an exultant dream, "in France again! The Emperor!"

"And so your execution will be deferred until we come back. The Emperor may take warning from it when he witnesses it," continued the imperturbable old royalist.

"I shall see him once more."

"As a prisoner."

Marteau started to speak, checked himself.

"For the last time," said the girl, "I beg——"

"It is useless."

"Let me speak again. My uncle has a kind heart under that hard exterior. He——"

"A kind heart, indeed," said the old man, smiling grimly, as Marteau shook his head at the girl he loved so well. "And, to prove it, here."

He extended a sealed paper. Marteau made no effort to take it. He recognized it at once. For a moment there flashed into the woman's mind that it was a pardon. But the old man undeceived her.

"Do you give it to him, Laure," he said. "It is that patent of nobility that he gave up. Acting for my King, who will, I am sure, approve of what I have done, I return it to him. As he dies with the spirit and soul of a gentleman, so also shall he die with the title. *Monsieur le Comte d'Aumenier*, I, the head of the house, welcome you into it. I salute you. Farewell. And now," the old man drew out his snuff box, tendered it to the young man with all the grace of the ancient *régime*. "No?" he said, as Marteau stared in bewilderment. "The young generation has forgot how, it seems. Very well." He took a pinch himself gracefully, closed the box, tapped it gently with his long fingers, as was his wont. "*Monsieur* will forgive my back," he said, turning abruptly and calling

424

over his shoulder, "and in a moment we must go."

Ah, he could be, he was a gentleman of the ancient school, indeed. It seemed but a second to youth, although it was a long time to age, before he tore them apart and led the half-fainting girl away.

CHAPTER 26

They Meet a Lion in the Way

Morning in the springtime, the sixth of March, 1815, bright and sunny, the air fresh. The parade-ground was filled with troops. There were the veterans of the old Seventh-of-the-Line, under the young Colonel Labédoyère. Here were the close-ranked lines of the Fifth regiment, Major Lestoype astride his big horse at the head of the first battalion. Grenier, Drehon, Suraif and the other officers with their companies, the men in heavy marching order, their white cockades shining in the bright sunlight in their *shakos*. The artillery was drawn up on the walls, the little squadron of household cavalry was in attendance upon the Marquis. His lean, spare figure looked well upon a horse. He rode with all the grace and ease of a boy.

Yes, there were the colours, too, the white flag of France with the golden lily in the place of the Eagle on the staff, at the head of the column. With ruffling of drums and presenting of arms the flag had been escorted to its place, and from the little group of cavalry had come the words not heard till recently for so many years in France:

"*Vive le Roi!*"

The troops had assembled silently, somewhat sullenly. They stood undemonstrative now. What they would do no one could tell. The couriers who had dashed into the town yesterday night had told the story to the Marquis. Napoleon had landed five days before. He was within a day's march of Grenoble. His following consisted of eleven hundred French infantry, eighty Polish horsemen, and a few guns; troops of the line, and the grenadiers of the Elba guard. The peasants had been apathetic. He had carefully avoided garrisoned towns, choosing the unfrequented and difficult route over the maritime Alps of Southern France. He was marching straight into the heart of the country, to conquer or to die with this little band. The messenger's news had been for the Governor's ears alone, but it had got out. Indeed, the tidings spread everywhere. Every wind that swept over the mountains seemed to be laden with the story. The whole city knew that the foot of the idol was once more upon the soil of France. They saw no feet of clay to that idol, then.

The news had reached Paris *via* Marseilles almost before it was known in Grenoble. The terror-stricken government yet acted promptly. Troops were put in motion, fast-riding expresses and couriers warned garrisons and transmitted orders to capture or kill without mercy. By a singular freak of fate most of these orders were perforce given to the old companions in arms of the Emperor. Most of these were openly disaffected toward the King, and eager to welcome Napoleon. A few were indifferent or inimical to the prospective appeal of their former Captain. Still fewer swore to capture him, and one "to bring him back in an iron cage!" Only here and there a royalist pure and simple held high command, as the Marquis at Grenoble.

The old noble acted with great promptitude and decision. As the Governor of Dauphiné he had an extensive command. Grenoble was the most important town in the southeast. Within its walls was a great arsenal. It was strongly fortified, and adequately garrisoned. No better place to resist the Emperor, if his initial force had grown sufficiently to make it formidable, could be found. Rumour magnified that force immensely. The Marquis gave the order for the concentration of all the troops in the province, to the number of six thousand. He sent out scouting detachments, and companies of engineers to break down bridges and block up roads—none of whom, by the way, obeyed his orders. In short, he did everything that experience, skill and devotion could suggest to stop the Emperor and terminate the great adventure then and there.

The ruffling of the drums in the square ceased. The old Marquis detached himself from his staff and the cavalry and rode out between the regiments. He lifted his hand. There was an intensity of silence on every hand. Even the people of the town had left their places of business and were crowded close to the lines to hear and see what was to be done.

"Bonaparte," said the Marquis, that high, thin, somewhat cracked old voice carrying with astonishing clearness in every direction, "landed from Elba in the Gulf of Juan a few days ago. This usurper, this bloody-minded tyrant, has broken every oath, disregarded every treaty. He is coming to Grenoble. He will be here today. As loyal sub-

427

jects of our gracious and most catholic Majesty, King Louis XVIII, whom God preserve," continued the old man, taking off his hat, "it becomes our duty to seize, and if he resists, to kill this treacherous monster, who had plunged Europe into a sea of blood and well-nigh ruined France."

The old man did not mince words, it appeared! "You, gentlemen and comrades, have all sworn oaths before God and man to be faithful to the King whose bread you eat and whose uniform you wear. It has been said to me that there is disaffection among you. I cannot believe that a soldier of France can be false to his oaths and to his flag. The Fifth Regiment of the Line will march with me to meet the Corsican. The cavalry and my personal escort will keep the gates. If by any chance we should be beaten, which I cannot think possible with such brave men and gallant officers, the town must be held. Colonel Labédoyère, to you I commit the charge. Have your men line the walls. Dispose the troops which will soon be arriving advantageously. See that the guns are double-shotted. If by any chance I do not return, hold the place to the last. Troops are marching to your aid from all over France. Major Lestoype, move your regiment. *Vive le Roi!*" ended the old man.

Again the cry was echoed, but not by many; the household cavalry, one or two of the newer companies of the brigade, some of the citizens. The Marquis noticed it; everybody noticed it. Well, what difference did it make to the old man? They might cry or they might not cry. Fight they must, and fight they should. He had something of the old Roman spirit in him, the Marquis d'Aumenier. Upon him had devolved the conduct of the critical issue. If he could stop Napoleon then and there his venture would be a mere escapade and a sorry one. If he could not, then God help France and the world.

From the window of his prison, which overlooked the parade, Marteau had seen and heard all. The Emperor was coming and he would not be there to extend him a welcome. He forgot that if Napoleon had been a day later it would have made no difference to Marteau if he never came. He would have given years of his life, if it had been possible, to have marched with the column.

Orders had been published that morning postponing his execution until the return of the regiment. Just what was in the Marquis' mind no one could absolutely say, but he was shrewd enough to recognize the possibility of an outbreak or an attempted mutiny among the troops, when the sentence of execution was being carried out. He did not want any difficulties of that kind then. Not because he feared them or felt unequal to them! Oh, no. But because such an outbreak would make the regiment more difficult to control in the greater emergency, and he knew he needed all the influence and moral power and force he could exercise to keep it in line for the graver duty and more tremendous responsibility it must now face. And because he did not wish to leave it with Marteau in Grenoble, he took the regiment with him. If he could force it to do its duty and arrest Napoleon, he could deal with Marteau at his leisure. The Emperor was the greater issue, and Marteau benefited by that fact.

So, with drums beating and flags flying, the Fifth-of-the-Line marched down the road. With the Colonel and his staff rode Sir Gervaise Yeovil and his son. They had asked permission and it had been accorded them. Indeed, the staff was scanty. Young St. Laurent and an orderly, besides the two Englishmen, alone accompanied the old man. Realizing how critical the situation was, and how important it was that the town should be held, he had left every officer and man upon whom he could count with the cavalry, and with instructions to watch Labédoyère particularly, and check any disloyalty, if possible. If the Marquis alone could not effect his purpose with the regiment, no staff officer could aid him. He was a lonely old man and a hard that morning. The odds against him were tremendous, and his weapons were flawed and breaking in his hand. That only made him the more firmly resolute. He knew how sometimes one man could enforce his will on unwilling thousands. Was he that man that day? He would see.

Some miles south of the town the winding road ran along the side of a high and rocky hill. On the side opposite to the hill was a deep morass. This place was known as the Gap. The Marquis, who had apparently thought of everything, had reconnoitred the country, and had decided upon the defensibleness of a place like this in the case of such an emergency as he was about to face, for along that hillside ran the main highway to the coast of France.

The troops reached it about noon-time. The road was high up on the hillside. The Marquis, riding in advance of his regiment, saw far down the long road and across a little river a moving column of men. Above them floated the tricolor flag, the blue and the red vividly distinct in the bright sun, which seemed to be reflected, as it were, from a crown of glory at the top of the staff. There were perhaps twelve hundred soldiers on foot and a few score on horseback. They were coming steadily along the road. The distance was almost too great to distinguish men, but one rode a white horse at the head. The soldiers could see with their minds and hearts better than their eyes, and they recognized that gray-coated figure on that familiar white horse. They could hear the beating of drums faintly. The bridges had not been broken. The fords were not guarded. The advance parties had failed. Presage of disaster!

The Marquis congratulated himself that he was in time to repair the disobedience of orders, which he promised himself to punish at the first opportunity. Instantly he directed Major Lestoype to deploy the men from column into line, so that they filled the road, which was here very broad and spacious. On a sloping hillside he placed flanking companies. The command was given to load, and the ramrods soon rang in the gun-barrels. Major Lestoype's voice shook as he gave the commands, which were repeated hoarsely, brokenly, nervously, by the company and the platoon officers. The dispositions of the men were soon concluded. The place of the Marquis was behind the line, but he rode to the right of it in a little depression cut out by the rains of winter in the side of the hill, underneath a great tree which was just beginning to show its leaves in the soft spring air and sunshine. From there he could command every part of the line with his glance, or move to the front or rear as the occasion might warrant. There he could see and be seen.

He was always pale, his old face seamed and drawn, but to his friends, the Englishmen, he seemed paler and older than ever, as he sat quietly calming his nervous horse. And Sir Gervaise Yeovil was pale, too. Not that he had any bodily fear, but the incident was so fraught with consequences which a man as experienced as he could so easily foresee, appreciate and dread, that its possibilities oppressed his heart. Young Frank Yeovil was all excitement, however. Napoleon had been buried in Elba, but none mentioned his name in any country in Europe without a thrill. Few do it now without a thrill, for that matter. The young man, modestly in the background, as was proper, leaned forward in his saddle and stared at the approaching men and the figure to the fore. So this was the great Bonaparte? He longed earnestly for a nearer view.

"Think you, my lord," whispered the Baronet to the old Marquis, his great anxiety showing in his voice, "that your men are to be depended upon? That they will——"

The Marquis shook his head, stared down the ranks at the men standing grim and tensely silent at parade-rest.

"They look steady," he replied, shrugging his shoulders. "They have taken an oath to the King, and—God only knows."

"What shall you do?"

"The best I can with the means at hand," was the indomitable answer.

"And if——"

"There are no 'ifs,' *monsieur*," was the imperious way in which the Marquis silenced the other.

Recognizing that he had said enough, and indeed pitying the old man so alone, the Baronet drew back a little.

"By heaven," whispered young Frank Yeovil to his father, "I wouldn't be elsewhere for a thousand pounds."

"It may cost you that before you get away, and more," said the old man grimly. "It will cost England millions, unless——"

"*Monsieur le Commandant*," said old Major Lestoype, riding up to the group and saluting respectfully.

"Major Lestoype."

"The command is formed and ready, sir."

"Very good. Take your place and be prepared."

"Will *Monsieur le Marquis* permit me?" asked the old soldier, who had acquired a genuine respect for the old noble.

"Permit you what?"

"To return his advice," was the not unexpected reply.

"The thought of me, which is evidently back of your words, sir, inclines me to overlook their meaning and its impropriety. Know, sir, that I am always ready," was the grim comment of the ancient soldier.

"Indeed, sir—" began the other, but the Marquis cut him short with an imperious gesture and a word.

"Retire."

The Major saluted, resumed his place in the line. No one spoke. The approaching soldiers were nearer now. They were coming. The Fifth-of-the-Line sensed rather than heard a command down the road. They saw the guns of that little army come from their shoulders to a slanting position across the breast—arms aport! It was the habit of the Guard to go into action at arms aport. What had Dorsenne, *Le Beau Dorsenne*, said on that famous day? "The Guard fights at the point of the bayonet!" Would the guns come down to a charge? Would they have to meet bayonet thrusts from these terrible soldiers?

431

There was something ominous in the slow movements of the men, picked men they were, the grenadiers of the Elba Guard especially being of great size, their huge bearskins towering above them. They were marching in columns of fours, but the road was wide; another sharp command and the men with slow yet beautiful precision deployed into a close column of companies at half distance—the very formation for a charge in mass! The brass drums were rolling a famous march, "*La Grenadière*," the grenadier's march. The hearts of the Fifth-of-the-Line were keeping time to the beating of those drums.

Ah, they were splendid soldiers, that regiment of infantry. Even the youths got something from the veterans. They stood still, quiet, at parade-rest, staring. The distance was growing shorter, shorter and shorter. Some of the officers looked toward the Marquis. Even his nervous horse seemed to have caught the spirit of the moment, for he was at last still. The old man sat there immobile, his lips pressed, his eyes fixed on the approaching troops and shining like sword-blades in the sunlight—horse and man carved, as it were, out of the rock of the mountains. Presently that high, thin, sharp voice rang out. Men heard it above the rolling of the drums.

"Attention!" he cried. The men straightened up, swung the heavy muskets to their sides. "Carry arms." As one man the battalion lifted its weapons. "Make ready!" With a little crash the guns were dropped into the outstretched hands.

The approaching men were nearer now. Still they came on with arms aport. Still the drums ruffled and rolled at their head. They were not going to make any response apparently to the fire of the Fifth-of-the-Line. Were they, indeed, to come to death's grapple at the bayonet's point with that irresistible Guard? But no, there was a sudden movement, a change in the approaching ranks.

"Secure arms," cried old Cambronne, and with their guns reversed and comfortably tucked under their arms, the old soldiers came on.

The meaning was plain, the battle was to be a moral one, evidently!

"Aim!" cried the sharp voice of the Marquis, and the guns came up to the shoulders of the long line, as they bent their heads and mechanically squinted along the barrels.

The moment had come! Out in the front had ridden the familiar figure on the white horse. They could see the details of his person now. His pale face was flushed under the familiar black, three-cornered cocked hat with its tricolour cockade, his gray redingote was buttoned across his breast. He suddenly raised his hand. The drums stopped beating, the moving grenadiers halted. Ah, at last!

The Emperor sprang from his horse, not heavily, as of late, but with some of the alertness of a boy. He nodded to the ranks. Old General Cambronne, in command of the Guard, stepped forward. He took from the colour-bearer the Eagle. Four grenadiers of the Colour Guard closed about him—one of them was called Bullet-Stopper, by the way. In rear and a little to the right of the Emperor he moved, holding up the flag and the Eagle. A deep breath, almost a sob, ran down the line of the regiment. Protended guns wavered. Napoleon stepped forward. He threw back his gray overcoat, disclosing the familiar green uniform of the Chasseurs of the Guard, which he affected. The cross of the Legion of Honour glittered on his breast, a shining mark at which to aim.

The flush on his ivory face died as quickly as it had come. He was apparently as composed and as steady as if he had been cut out of granite. But tiny beads of sweat bedewed his brow, shaded by that familiar cocked hat. What would the next moment disclose? Would he be a prisoner, the laughing stock, the jest of Europe? Or would he lie dead in the road, a French bullet in his heart? He had faced the guns of every people in Europe, but he had never faced French guns before. Would any finger in that line press a trigger? Only God knew, but the Emperor would soon find out. Better death than exile without wife, child, friend, or France. On the hazard of the moment he staked all. Yet he who could have looked into that broad breast could have seen that heart beating as never before. Firmly he stepped on.

CHAPTER 27

Comrade! General! Emperor!

"Behold the traitor," shouted the Marquis, his emotion lending depth to that thin voice. "Fire, soldiers!"

No finger pressed a trigger. The silence was ghastly.

Ah! a thrill of hope in the breast of the greater Captain, of despair in the heart of the lesser.

"By God!" muttered Yeovil, "he has lost them!"

The Marquis spurred his horse forward.

"Your oath! For France! The King! Fire!" he shouted.

And now a greater voice broke the silence.

"Comrades! Do you not know me?" said the Emperor. Was there a tremble in his clear, magnificent voice? He paused, his speech stopped. "Behold your General," he resumed. He waited a few seconds again and then finally, desperately, "Let anyone among you who wishes to kill his Emperor fire—now."

He raised his voice tremendously with that last word. It almost came with the force and clearness of a battle-cry. The Marquis sat stupefied, his face ghastly pale.

"There is yet time," he cried hoarsely at last. "Is there none here faithful to his King? Fire!"

But the gun-barrels were coming down. "*Comrade! General! Emperor!*" who could be indifferent to that appeal? Disregarding the old Marquis absolutely, as if he were not on the earth, the Emperor came nearer smiling. He was irresistible to these soldiers when he smiled.

"Well," he said, his hands outstretched and open, "soldiers of the Fifth, who were with me in Italy, how are you all? I am come back to see you again, *mes enfants*," he went on genially. "Is there any one of you who wishes to kill me?"

"No, no, Sire. Certainly not," came the cry.

"Escape," whispered the Marquis to the Englishman, "while there is yet time to take my niece away. To you I commit her. . . . St. Laurent, to the town with the tidings!"

"By God, no," growled Yeovil, as St. Laurent saluted and galloped rapidly down the road. "I am going to see the end of this. The damned cravens!" he muttered, looking at the soldiers.

"And yet," continued Napoleon to the troops, "you presented your guns at me."

"Sire," cried one of the veterans, dropping his musket and running his ramrod down the barrel, "it is not loaded. We only went through the motions."

The Emperor laughed. He was nearer.

"Lestoype," he said, "is it thou, old comrade, and Grenier and Drehon!"

It was astonishing that he should remember them, but so he did. He went down the line, speaking to the men, inspecting them just as of old. The officers could not keep them in line. They crowded about their old leader. Shouts of "*Vive l'Empereur!*" rent the air. Men took off their caps, tore out the hated white cockades, trampled them under foot, and from pockets where they had concealed them for this very moment, they replaced them with the tricolour.

In his movements the Emperor at last confronted the Marquis.

"And who is this?" asked Napoleon, staring up at him curiously.

The Marquis' heart was broken. It was not in the human power of any servant of the King to dominate that scene. A greater personality than his was there. The Emperor had shown himself as of yore, and exhibited his mastery. But no greater ideal possessed any man than that in the heart of the old noble. He hated, he loathed, he abominated the man who looked up at him. He saw in the action of the soldiery a picture of the action of France, the downfall of the King. Well, it flashed into his mind that he at least, and perhaps he alone, might put a stop to it.

From his holster he whipped out a pistol and levelled it at the Emperor. Lestoype, riding near, struck up his hand, the bullet sped harmlessly, the Emperor stood unharmed. A roar of rage burst from the soldiers who came running. Dropping the weapon and reining his startled horse violently back, so as to give himself a certain present and temporary freedom of action, the Marquis drew his other pistol. Lestoype spurred his horse in front of the Emperor, but Napoleon was not menaced.

"Have no fear," said the Marquis almost gently. "I have failed my King. The bullet goes into a truer heart—my own," he added proudly.

Before anyone could stop him there was a flash, a muffled report, the spare figure reeled and fell forward on the saddle. He, at least, after the manner of his house, would not survive a failure which, although he could not prevent it, must inevitably be charged against him.

"A brave man," said the Emperor coolly, staring at him with his hard, bright, gray eyes. "See that his body is cared for in accordance with his rank and his courage. But who are these?" he asked, remounting his horse and facing the two Englishmen, who had dismounted and received the body of the Marquis, stone dead instantly. "As I live, it is the man of law," he said, his marvellous memory serving him well again, "who was at the Château d'Aumenier. It only needs Marteau——"

"He is alive, your Majesty," interposed Lestoype eagerly. "He brought back our Eagle and is——"

"Where is it, and why is he not with you?"

"The Eagle is in hiding somewhere in Grenoble, Marteau in prison. He hid it, and because he would not tell where, the Marquis yonder condemned him to death."

"He has not yet been shot?"

"Not yet, Sire. He waits the return of the regiment."

"Good," said the Emperor. "We will surprise him. Face the men about. We shall go on to Grenoble and see what welcome awaits us there."

He was in high spirits. In this first clash with the troops of King Louis he found that he exercised the old influence over them and from the army, at least, he now realized that he had nothing to fear.

One of the men who had stood nearest the Emperor back of Cambronne was an old grenadier. He had recognized the Marquis d'Aumenier, he had heard the Emperor's conversation and the name of Marteau, and a thrill went through the heart of old Bal-Arrêt when he learned that his beloved officer and friend was yet alive.

The body of the old Marquis—covered with his cloak, and over his heart the now discarded royal standard, for which nobody cared since he was dead—was placed on a farm wagon and escorted back to Grenoble by some of the officers of the regiment and two companies, with reversed arms. He was watched over by the two Englishmen, whom Napoleon freely permitted to follow their own pleasure in their movements, being desirous of not adding fuel to any possible fire of animosity and of showing every respect to every Frenchman, whatever his predilection.

With the Fifth-of-the-Line in the lead, the army moved forward after a halt for noonday meal. The greatly relieved, happy and confident Emperor, riding now with the old regiment of Italy in the van, and now with the grenadiers in the rear, approached Grenoble late in the afternoon. The short March day was drawing to a close when they came in sight of the heavily garrisoned walls of the town.

Labédoyère had obeyed orders in some particulars. The ramparts had been manned, the cannon were loaded, torches were blazing on the walls, and the town was awake and seething with excitement. He had declared for the Emperor, and after a sharp little conflict had disarmed the royalist cavalry and himself held the gates. Every regiment that had come in had cast its lot in with Napoleon. As the soldiers in the town heard, in the twilight, the beating of the drums—"*La Grenadière*" the old march again!—the Colonel of the Seventh, having seized the few royalists, opened the gates, marched out at the head of the troops to receive the Emperor with arms, yes, but with open arms. Amid the shouts of the citizens and the delirious joy of the soldiery, the Emperor entered the city; in his train, first fruits of the war, was the body of the old servant of the unfortunate King.

It was Pierre who burst into the apartment of the little Countess with the news.

"The Emperor is here, *mademoiselle*," he cried enthusiastically. "The soldiers are bringing him to the palace."

"And Marteau?"

"He will be free."

"Thank God!" cried the girl, and then she remembered her uncle. "And the Marquis?" she asked.

"My dearest Laure," said the kindly, sympathetic voice of Captain Frank Yeovil, stepping out of the twilight of the hall into the bright light of the little drawing-room where last night she had bade farewell to Marteau, "prepare yourself for some dreadful——"

"Yes, yes, I know," she interrupted. "The Emperor is here."

"The troops went over to him."

"And my uncle?"

"He——"

"Speak, *monsieur*. What has happened? Did the Emperor——"

"No one harmed him. He could not survive the disgrace, *mademoi-*

selle. Prepare yourself."

"Oh, for God's sake, delay not your tidings."

"He died like a soldier of France on the field, by his own hand rather than survive what he wrongfully thought his shame."

It was the policy of the Emperor to be merciful; it was his wish to be clement. If possible, he wanted peace. If mercy and gentleness could get it he could have it. He gave free permission to Sir Gervaise Yeovil and his son to return to England. He made no objection to their taking with them the Countess Laure, now the last of the line. He, himself, was present at the funeral of the Marquis, who was buried with all the military honours of his rank and station. There were generous hearts among those Frenchmen. As the representative of the King they had hated him, but when he had died so gallantly rather than survive what his nice sensibility believed to be his dishonour, his failure at any rate, they honoured him. If he had been a Marshal of France they could have done no more.

Marteau, restored to his rank and position as *aide* to the Emperor, had but a few moments with the grief-stricken woman.

"No," she said sadly, "it makes no difference. You know my heart. No words that I can utter could add anything more to the testimony I have given you. But I had promised my uncle, and now that he is dead, the promise is doubly sacred. I must go. Thank your Emperor for me for all he has done for me, his enemy, and for my friends, and for what he has done for you. Tell him the story of the Eagle, and the little part in it that I played and—you will not forget me as I will not forget you."

"God grant," said the young soldier, "that I may die for France on some battlefield, my last thought of you."

"Ah, if that should befall you, I should envy you your rest. Would to God I might look forward to such a quick and happy ending," said the grief-stricken woman, turning away.

The next morning, with great ceremony and much rejoicing, the Eagle was brought out, and the Emperor once more presented it to the regiment. He did more than that. He signalized the action of the Fifth-of-the-Line, the news of which had been sent broadcast by couriers and which struck a keynote for the army to follow, by incorporating it as a supplementary Fifth regiment of Grenadiers of the Guard. He promised them a new flag and new bearskins. He promoted Lestoype to be a lieutenant-colonel, Labédoyère to be a general, and promised every veteran officer his old rank or higher in the new army to be formed. The men were promised bounties and rewards, and, with high hopes and glorious anticipations, the march for Paris was begun.

So by the wayside and in the fields around this little army in that springtime, the violets bloomed again.

BOOK 3

THE LAST TRY

CHAPTER 28

At the Stamp of the Emperor's Foot

The wonderful genius of Napoleon, which had been so clearly manifested in so many ways during his varied career, was never exhibited to better advantage than in the three months after his return from Elba. During that period he reorganized the government, recreated and re-equipped an army. The veterans flocked to his standards, and within the time mentioned he had actually two hundred and fifty thousand men under arms.

With the better moiety of this force, the best armed, the best equipped, the best officered contingent, he took the field early in the month of June. The Emperor did not want war any more than France did. He began his new reign with the most pacific of proclamations, which probably reflected absolutely the whole desire of his heart. But the patience of Europe had been exhausted and the belief of rulers and peoples in the honesty of his professions, declarations or intentions, had been hopelessly shattered.

His arrival effected an immediate resurrection of the almost moribund Congress of Vienna. The squabbling, arguing, trifling plenipotentiaries of the powers had burst into gigantic laughter—literally, actual merriment, albeit of a somewhat grim character!—when they received the news of Napoleon's return. They were not laughing at Napoleon but at themselves. They had been dividing the lion's skin in high-flown phrases, which meant nothing, endeavouring to incorporate the Decalogue and the Sermon on the Mount in their protocols and treaties, when they suddenly discovered that the Emperor was still to be reckoned with.

Differences were instantly laid aside and forgotten. Russia, Prussia and Austria immediately agreed to put in the field two hundred and fifty thousand men each. The smaller powers, Sweden, Spain, the

Low Countries, promised contingents. England once more assumed the familiar role of paymaster by immediately placing a vast subsidy at the disposal of the allies. She gave them also what was of more value than a subsidy, a soldier of the first rank to command the armies in the field.

The Duke of Wellington had never crossed swords with the greatest captain of his day and perhaps of all time. But he had measured himself with the ablest and most famous of Napoleon's Marshals. With greatly inferior forces, through four years of desperate fighting, he had defeated the Marshals and armies of France. The dashing and gallant Junot had been routed at Vimiero, Victor had been overwhelmed at Talavera. Wily old Massena with all his ability could look back to the disaster of the blood-stained hill of Busaco, Marmont, the dainty tactician, had been smashed at Salamanca, stubborn Jourdan had been at last decisively defeated at Victoria.

Finally, the brilliant Soult had been hurled out of the Pyrenees and had met his master at Toulouse. Still, great as were these soldiers and highly trained as they had been in the best of schools, not one of them was a Napoleon; all of them together were not, for that matter. Would the lustre of Wellington's fame, which extended from the Ganges to the Ebro, be tarnished when he met the Emperor? It was a foregone conclusion, of course, that Schwarzenberg would command the Austrians; Blücher, the "Hussar General," the hard-fighting, downright old "Marshal Vorwärts," the Prussians; and the Emperor Alexander, with his veteran captains, the vast horde of Russians.

To assemble, arm, equip and move two hundred and fifty thousand men was a great task in those days even for a rich and populous country flushed with victory and in the enjoyment of an abundance of time and unlimited means. The organizing, it almost might be said the creative, ability of Napoleon was not shared by his opponents. Try as they would, June found their preparations still woefully incomplete. The Austrians had scarcely moved at all.

The slower Russians, who were farther away and were to constitute the reserve army, could be discounted from any present calculation of the enemies of the Empire. The English and their smaller allies from the Low Countries, and the Prussians, whose hatred of France and the Emperor was greater than that of any other nation, were quicker to move. Two hundred and fifteen thousand men, half of them Prussians, a third of the other moiety English, the remaining two-thirds Belgians, Hollanders, and other miscellaneous nationalities, had joined the colours on the north-western frontier of France. One-half of this joint assembly was commanded by Blücher and the other half by Wellington.

Leaving the weaker half of his own great army to complete its equipment, and placing strong detachments in fortress and at strategic points to oppose the Austrians should they advance, the Emperor, as has been said, with about one hundred and twenty-five thousand men took the field. Naturally, inevitably, Belgium, the immemorial battleground of the nations, and the great English-Prussian army were his objectives. He saw clearly the dangers that encompassed him, the demands he must meet and the conditions over which he must triumph.

It was by no means certain, even if he decisively defeated his enemies in Belgium and occupied Brussels, that his trouble would be over. There would still be left a possible five hundred thousand trained and disciplined men with whom he would have to deal, under rulers and generals the inveteracy of whose hatreds he could well understand. But at least his position would be greatly improved by a successful preliminary campaign, any success in short, to say nothing of so great a one. If he could show himself once more the inimitable Captain, the thunderbolt of war, the organizer of victory, the Napoleon of other days, the effect upon France, at least, would be electrical. And the world would again take notice.

The Emperor had to admit that, save in the army, there had not been much response from tired-out, exhausted France, to the appeals of its once irresistible and beloved leader. But the spirit of the army was that of devotion itself. There was a kind of a blind madness in it of which men spoke afterward as a phenomenon that could only be recognized, that could never be explained or understood. They could not account for it. Yet it was a powerful factor, the most powerful, indeed, that enabled the Emperor to accomplish so much, and fall short of complete triumph by so narrow a margin.

The spirit of this new army was not that burning love of liberty which had animated the armies of the early republic and turned its tatterdemalion legions into *paladins*. It was not the heroic consecration of the veterans of later years to their native land. It was a strange, mysterious obsession, a personal attachment to Napoleon, the individual—an unlimited, unbounded tribute to his fascination, to his own unique personality. It has not died out, and seems destined to live. Even in death Napoleon, after a century, exercises the same fascination over all sorts and conditions of men! Wise and foolish alike acknowledge his spell. Men hate, men loathe much of that for which the Corsican adventurer and soldier of fortune stood; they see clearly and admit freely the thorough and entire selfishness of the colossal man, but they cannot resist his appeal, even after one hundred years!

Yet in the long run no personal attachment, however deep, however ardent, however complete, can take the place as the inspiration for heroic deeds of that deeper passion of love of country. Nor can any personal devotion to a mere man produce such a steadfastness of character as is brought about by adherence to a great cause or a great land. A great passion like the love of a people for a great country and that for which it stands is eternal. Usually the feet of clay upon which the idol stands have only to be recognized to dissipate the ardour and fervour of the worshipers.

But Napoleon was then an exception to all rules. Though he slew men, wasted them, threw them away, they trusted him. We look at him through the *vista* of years and in some way understand his soldiers. Reason to the contrary, we can experience in some degree, at least, even in the cold-blooded humanitarian materialism of the present, the old thrill and the old admiration. Did his contemporaries love him because they believed he thought in terms of France, we wonder?

So that this body of soldiery was probably the most formidable army in the quality of its units that had ever been mustered on the globe. There was not a man in it who was not a veteran. Some of them were veterans of fifteen years of campaigning with Napoleon. This that came was to be the sixtieth pitched battle in which some of them had participated. Even the younger men had gone through more than one campaign and taken part in much hard fighting. Back from the prisons where they had been confined and the great fortresses they had held until the Emperor's abdication had come the veterans. The Old Guard had been reconstituted.

As a reward for its action at Grenoble, the Fifth-of-the-Line had been incorporated in it as a supplementary regiment, a second Fifth regiment of Grenadiers. The ranks of the Guard had been most carefully culled, the unserviceable had been weeded out, their places taken by men well fitted by their record, their physical prowess and their personal appearance to belong to that famous corps. Not the Immortals of Xerxes, the Spartan Band of Leonidas, the Companion Cavalry of Alexander, the Carthaginians of Hannibal, the Tenth Legion of Caesar, the Spanish Infantry of Parma, or the Ironsides of Cromwell, had surpassed the record of these Pretorians of Imperial France.

The same weeding-out process had been carried out in the rest of the army. The flower of French cavalry, the matchless French artillery and the famous infantry which had trampled down the world were ranged under the Eagles. Other corps had been drained for equipment. But in some particulars the army differed from the Imperial armies of the past. With two exceptions, the great Marshals were not there. Murat, king of horsemen and swordsmen, was a prisoner in his ignoble Neapolitan realm awaiting trial and execution. Marmont and Mortier dared not present themselves before the Emperor they had betrayed. Wily Massena, the wisest and ablest of them all, was old and in convenient retirement. Macdonald, the incorruptible, was with the fat-bodied, fat-witted Bourbon King in Ghent. Berthier, with his marvellous mastery of detail and his almost uncanny ability to translate the Emperor's thoughts even into orders, had not rejoined the Eagles—a terrible loss, indeed.

There were but two of the Marshals of old with Napoleon. Soult, in some respects the acutest strategist and finest tactician, was Chief of Staff. He tried his best to fill Berthier's position and did it acceptably, if not with the success of that master. The other Marshal was pre-eminently the battle-leader, red-headed Michael Ney, the fighter of fighters, a man whose personality was worth an army-corps, whose reputation and influence with the soldiers was of the very highest.

The rest of the officers, while veterans, were younger and less-known men. Drouet d'Erlon commanded one of the corps; Reille another; Grouchy another; Druot was the leader of the Guard; Kellerman, Milhaud, Gerard and Maurice the cavalry. It was an army of veterans, officered by young men, commanded by the greatest of soldiers.

But the army had not yet "found itself." It had no natural coherence and there had been no time to acquire any. It had not yet been welded together. Officers, men, regiments, brigades, divisions were, more or less, new and strange to one another. There was a vast deal of suspicion in the ranks. The discipline was rather because of past habit than present practice. That army needed a few victories, and badly needed them. A welding process was required. Given time and success to shake it together, and it might laugh at the world.

Would it get time and win victory? That was the question. And if it got neither, what then? How would it stand up under the strain? Would the tie that bound hold in defeat? Could the rest of the army live up to the Guard, for instance? Yes, that was the grave, the all-important question.

There was an enormous disparity in numbers between the French army—or it would better be called Napoleon's army—and that of the allies he purposed to attack. The allies were to the French in the ratio of about two to one. Whatever else was lacking, Napoleon had not lost his audacity, nor when his intentions are disclosed by a study of his plans, can it be argued that his strategic intention was lacking in brilliancy or daring.

He determined with his smaller but compact and manageable army to thrust himself between the two wings of the somewhat loosely coherent enemy under its divided command; to hold off one while he smashed the other and then to concentrate upon the surviving half and mete out to it the same hard fortune. In other words, trusting to his ability, he deliberately placed his own army between two others, each of which practically equalled his own. He thrust himself within the jaws of a trap, to use a homely simile, intending to hold one arm of the trap open while he broke up the other. He intended to burst through the allied line and smash up each half in succession.

Of course there was always the danger that he could not burst through that line; or that he could not hold back one half while he fought the other, or that holding back one half he could not beat the other, or having beaten one half he would be too weak to fall on the other. There was always the danger that the trap would be sprung, that he would be caught in its jaws or, to change the metaphor, that he would be like the wheat between the upper and the nether millstone. Still he did not think so, and he did not go into the undertaking blindly. As he had said, in his own case, "War was not a conjectural art," and he had most carefully counted the cost, estimated the probabilities. In short, he looked well before he leaped—yet a man may look well and leap wrong after all.

On these considerations he based his grand strategy. The army of the Prussians had approached the French frontier from the east; the army of the English and allies from the northwest. Napoleon had a complete knowledge of one of the captains opposing him. He knew and accurately estimated Blücher. He did not know and he did not accurately estimate Wellington. He viewed the latter with contempt; the former with a certain amount of disdainful approbation, for while Blücher was no strategist and less of a tactician, he was a fighter and a fighter is always dangerous and to be dreaded. Gneisenau, a much

445

more accomplished soldier, was Blücher's second in command, but he was a negligible factor in the Emperor's mind. The fact that Wellington had beaten all of Napoleon's Marshals with whom he had come in contact had intensified the Emperor's hatred. Instead of begetting caution in dealing with him, Napoleon's antagonism had blinded him as to Wellington's ability.

He also rated the Prussians higher than the English as fighters, and when his officers, who had felt the power of the thin red line which had so often wrecked the French column, explained to him that there were no better defensive fighters on earth than the English, not even the Russians, he had laughed them to scorn, attributing their warnings to the fact that they had been beaten in Spain and had grown timid. The Emperor did not purpose to be beaten in France or Belgium by the stolid English.

In more detail his first plan was to confuse Wellington, who held the right of the allied line, then fall upon him before he had time to concentrate, and beat him or contain him with a detachment under Ney, while the Emperor in person thereafter put Blücher to rout— and all of these things he came very near accomplishing completely. Certainly, he carried out his plans successfully and to the letter until the final day of battle.

He reasoned that if he could beat Blücher and threaten his communications, what was left of the Prussian army, which Napoleon hoped would not be much, would immediately retreat eastward; and that when Blücher had been thrown out of the game for the present, he could turn on Wellington and his English and allies and make short work of him. It did not occur to him that even if he beat Blücher and beat Wellington, provided the defeats did not end in utter routs, and they both retreated, they might withdraw on parallel lines and effect a junction later when even after the double defeat they would still so greatly outnumber him that his chances of success would be faint indeed.

The possibility of their pursuing any other course than that he had forecast for them never entered his mind. His own conception of their action was, in fact, an obsession with him. Yet that which he thought they would do they did not; and that which he was confident they would not do they did!

CHAPTER 29

Waterloo—The Final Review

In a romance like this, in which campaigns and marches, manoeu-vres and battles, however decisive they may be in history, are only in-cidental to the careers of the characters herein presented to the reader, it is not necessary for the chronicler to turn himself into a military historian, much as he would like it. Therefore, in great restraint, he presses on, promising hereafter only so much history as may serve to show forth the sombre background.

In this setting of the scene of the great drama to be played, young Marteau has been necessarily somewhat lost sight of. He was very much in evidence during that hundred days of feverish and frantic activity. Napoleon had distinguished him highly. He had given him the rank of a Colonel of the Guard, but he had still retained him on his staff. Good and experienced staff-officers were rare, and the Em-peror needed all he could get; he could have used many more than were available. And as Marteau was one of those who were attached to the Emperor by the double motive of love of the man and love of his country, believing as he did that the destiny of the two could not be disievered, he had served the Emperor most efficiently, with that blind, passionate devotion to duty by which men give to a cause the best that is in them and which sometimes leads them to almost incon-ceivable heights of achievements.

Suffice it to say that the great strategic conception of Napoleon was carried out with rather striking success in the first three days of the campaign. The Emperor, crossing the Sambre, interposed himself between Wellington and Blücher, completely deceived the English-man, who thought his extreme right was threatened, detached Ney to seize the village of Quatre Bras, where Wellington had at last decided to concentrate, and with eighty thousand men fell on the Prussians at Ligny.

Ney did not seize Quatre Bras; Wellington got there ahead of him and stubbornly held the position. Although Ney had twice the number of troops at the beginning of the battle that the English Field-Marshal could muster, they were not well handled and no adequate use was made of the French preponderance. Napoleon, on the far right of Ney, at Ligny, on the contrary, fought the Prussians with his old-time skill and brilliance. The contending forces there were about equal, the Prussians having the advantage in numbers, but victory finally declared for the Emperor. It was the last victory, not the least brilliant and not the least desperately fought of his long career.

The importance and quality of the battle has been lost sight of in the greater struggle of Waterloo, which took place two days after, but it was a great battle, nevertheless. One of the crude ways in which to estimate a battle is by what is called the "butcher's bill" and eighteen thousand dead and wounded Prussians and twelve thousand Frenchmen tells its tale. But it was not the decisive battle that Napoleon had planned to make it.

The Prussians retreated. They had to. But they retreated in good order. Blücher having been unhorsed and temporarily incapacitated in a charge, the command and direction of the retreat devolved upon Gneisenau. His chief claim to military distinction lies in the fact that he did not do what Napoleon expected, and what Blücher would have done. He retreated to the north instead of the east! A pursuit was launched, but it did not pursue the Prussians. It went off, as it were, into thin air. It pursued Napoleon's idea, his forecast, which owing to the accident to Blücher was wrong!

One reason why the victory of Ligny and the drawn battle at Quatre Bras were not decisive was because of a strange lack of generalship and a strange confusion of orders for which Napoleon and Ney are both responsible. Ney was constructively a victor at Quatre Bras, finally. That is, the English retreated at nightfall and abandoned the field to him; but they retreated not because they were beaten but because Wellington, finding his position could be bettered by retirement and concentration, decided upon withdrawal. But Ney could have been the victor in every sense, in spite of his indifferent tactics, if it had not been for the same blunder that the Emperor committed.

D'Erlon, at the head of perhaps the finest corps in the army, numbering twenty thousand men, through the long hours of that hot June day marched from the vicinity of Quatre Bras to Ligny, whence he could actually see the battle raging, only to be summoned back from Ligny to Quatre Bras by orders from Ney. Retracing his course, therefore, he marched back over the route he had just traversed, arriving at Quatre Bras too late to be of any service to Ney! Like the famous King of France who with twenty thousand men marched up the hill and then marched down again, this splendid corps which, thrown into either battle, would have turned the Prussian retreat into a rout on the one hand, or have utterly cut to pieces Wellington on the other, did nothing. The principal fault was Napoleon's. He saw d'Erlon's corps approaching, but he sent no order and took no steps to put it into the battle.

Well, in spite of the fact that the energies of d'Erlon had been spent in marching instead of fighting, the Emperor was a happy man that night. He had got himself safely placed between the two armies and he had certainly severely if not decisively beaten one of them. Strategically, his operations had been characterized by unusual brilliancy. If things went as he hoped, surmised and confidently expected, all would be well. He was absolutely sure that Blücher was retiring to the east, toward Namur. He dispatched Grouchy with thirty-five thousand of his best men to pursue him in the direction which he supposed he had taken.

Napoleon's orders were positive, and he was accustomed to exact implicit obedience from his subordinates. He had a habit of discouraging independent action in the sternest of ways, and for the elimination of this great force from the subsequent battle the Emperor himself must accept the larger responsibility. But all this does not excuse Grouchy. He carried out his orders faithfully, to be sure, but a more enterprising and more independent commander would have sooner discovered that he was pursuing stragglers and would earlier have taken the right course to regain his touch with his chief and to harry the Prussian Field-Marshal.

He did turn to the north at last, but when the great battle was joined he was miles away and of no more use than if he had been in Egypt. His attack on the Prussian rear-guard at Wavre, while it brought about a smart little battle with much hard and gallant fighting, really amounted to nothing and had absolutely no bearing on the settlement of the main issue elsewhere. He did not disobey orders, but many a man has gained immortality and fame by doing that very thing. Grouchy had his chance and failed to improve it. He was a veteran and a successful soldier, too.

Comes the day of Waterloo. Blücher had retreated north to Wavre and was within supporting distance of Wellington. His army had been beaten but not crushed, its spirit was not abated. The old Prussian Marshal, badly bruised and shaken from being unhorsed and overridden in a cavalry charge in which he had joined like a common trooper, but himself again, promised in a famous interview between the two to come to the support of the younger English Marshal, should he be attacked, with his whole army. Wellington had retreated as far as he intended to. He established his headquarters on a hill called Mont St. Jean, back of a ridge near a village called Waterloo, where his army commanded the junction point of the highroads to the south and west. He drew up his lines, his red-coated countrymen and his blue-coated allies on the long ridge in front of Mont St. Jean, facing south, overlooking a gently sloping valley which was bounded by other parallel ridges about a mile away.

On the right centre of Wellington's lines, a short distance below the crest of the ridge, embowered in trees, lay a series of stone buildings, in extent and importance between a *château* and a farmhouse, called Hougomont. These were surrounded by a stone wall and the place was impregnable against everything but artillery if it were properly manned and resolutely held. Both those conditions were met that day. Opposite the left centre of the Duke's line was another strong place, a farmhouse consisting of a series of stone buildings on three sides of a square, the fourth closed by a wall, called La Haye Sainte. These outposts were of the utmost value, rightly used.

The Duke had sixty-seven thousand men and one hundred and eighty guns. His right had been strengthened at the expense of his left, because he expected Napoleon to attack the right and he counted on Blücher's arrival to support his left. To meet him Napoleon had seventy-five thousand men and two hundred and sixty guns. Off to the northeast lay Blücher at Wavre with nearly eighty thousand more men and two hundred guns, and wandering around in the outer darkness was Grouchy with thirty-five thousand.

The valley was highly cultivated. The ripening grain still stood in the fallow fields separated by low hedges. Broad roads ran through the valley in different directions. The weather was horrible. It rained torrents during the night and the earlier part of the morning. The fields were turned into quagmires, the roads into morasses. It was hot and close. The humidity was great. Little air was stirring. Throughout the day the mist hung heavy over the valley and the ridges which bordered it. But the rain ceased in the morning and Napoleon made no attack until afternoon, waiting for the ground to dry out somewhat. It was more important to him that his soldiers should have good footing than to the English, for the offensive, the attack, the charge fell to him. Wellington determined to fight strictly on the defensive. Nevertheless, precious hours were wasted. Every passing moment brought some accession to the allied army, and every passing hour brought Blücher nearer. With all the impetuosity of his soul, the old man was urging his soldiers forward over the horrible roads.

"Boys," he said in his rough, homely way to some bitterly complaining artillerists stalled in the mud, "I promised. You would not have me break my word, would you?"

Grouchy meanwhile had at last determined that the Prussians had gone the other way. He had learned that they were at Wavre and he had swung about and was coming north. Of course, he should have marched toward the sound of the cannon—generally the safest guide for a soldier!—but, at any rate, he was trying to get into touch with the enemy. No one can question his personal courage or his loyalty to his cause.

Napoleon, when he should have been on the alert, was very drowsy and dull that day at Waterloo. He had shown himself a miracle of physical strength and endurance in that wonderful four days of campaigning and fighting, but the soldiers passing by the farmhouse of La Belle Alliance—singular name which referred so prophetically to the enemy—sometimes saw him sitting on a chair by a table outside the house, his feet resting on a bundle of straw to keep them from the wet ground, nodding, asleep! And no wonder. It is doubtful if he had enjoyed as much as eight hours of sleep since he crossed the Sambre, and those not consecutive! Still, if ever he should have kept awake, that eighteenth of June was the day of days!

So far as one can discern his intention, his battle plan had been to feint at Hougomont on the right centre, cause the Duke of Wellington to weaken his line to support the *château*, and then to break through the left centre and crush him by one of those massed attacks under artillery fire for which he had become famous. The line once broken, the end, of course, would be more or less certain.

The difference in the temperaments of the two great captains was well illustrated before the battle was joined. The Duke mainly concealed his men behind the ridge. All that the French saw when they came on the field were guns, officers and a few men. The English-Belgian army was making no parade. What the British and Flemish saw was very different. The Emperor displayed his full hand. The French, who appeared not to have been disorganized at all by the hard fighting at Ligny and Quatre Bras, came into view in most splendid style; bands playing, drums rolling, swords waving, bayonets shining even in the dull air of the wretched morning. They came on the field in solid columns, deployed and took their positions, out of cannon-shot range, of course, in the most deliberate manner. The uniforms of the army were brand-new, and it was the fashion to fight in one's best in those days. They presented a magnificent spectacle.

Presently the Duke, his staff, the gunners and the others who were on the top of the ridge and watching, saw a body of horsemen gallop rapidly along the French lines. One gray-coated figure riding a white horse was in advance of the rest. The cheers, the almost delirious shouts and cries, told the watchers that it was the Emperor. It was his last grand review, his last moment of triumph.

It was after one o'clock before the actual battle began. More books have been written about that battle than any other that was ever fought. One is tempted to say, almost than all others that were ever fought. And the closest reasoners arrive at different conclusions and disagree as to many vital and important details. The Duke of Wellington himself left two accounts, one in his dispatches and one in notes written long afterward, which were irreconcilable, but some things are certain, upon some things all historians are agreed.

The battle began with an attack on the Hougomont Château and the conflict actually raged around that *château* for over six hours, or until the French were in retreat. Macdonell, Home and Saltoun, Scotsmen all, with their regiments of the Household Guard, held that *château*, although it was assailed over and over again, finally, by the whole of Reille's corps.

They held that *château*, although it burned over their heads, although the French actually broke into it on occasion. They held it, although every other man in it was shot down and scarcely a survivor was without a wound. It was assaulted with a fury and a resolution which was only matched by the fury and resolution of its defence. Why it was not battered to pieces with artillery no one knows. At any rate, it occupied practically the whole of Reille's corps during the whole long afternoon of fighting.

The space between Hougomont and La Haye Sainte was about a thousand yards. La Haye Sainte was assaulted also but, to anticipate

events, it held out until about five o'clock in the evening, when, after another wonderful defence, it was carried. The French established
themselves in it eighty yards from Wellington's line.

Waterloo—The Charge of d'Erlon

Meanwhile the French had not confined their efforts to the isolated forts, if they may be so called, on Wellington's centre and left centre. After a tremendous artillery duel d'Erlon's men had been formed up for that massed attack for which the Emperor was famous, and with which it was expected the English line would be pierced and the issue decided. The Emperor, as has been noted, had intended the attack on Hougomont as a mere feint, hoping to induce the Duke of Wellington to reinforce his threatened right and thereby to weaken his left centre. It was no part of the Emperor's plan that an attempt to capture Hougomont should become the main battle on his own left that it had, nor could he be sure that even the tremendous attack upon it had produced the effect at which he aimed. Nevertheless, the movement of d'Erlon had to be tried.

It must be remembered that Napoleon had never passed through the intermediate army grades. He had been jumped from a regimental officer to a general. He had never handled a regiment, a brigade, a division, a corps—only an army, or armies. Perhaps that was one reason why he was accustomed to leaving details and the execution of his plans to subordinates. He was the greatest of strategists and the ablest of tacticians, but minor tactics did not interest him, and the arrangement of this great assault he left to the corps and its commander.

Giving orders to Ney and d'Erlon, therefore, the Emperor at last launched his grand attack. One hundred and twenty guns were concentrated on that part of the English left beyond the westernmost of the two outlying positions, through which it was determined to force a way. Under cover of the smoke, which all day hung thick and heavy in the valley and clung to the ridges, d'Erlon's splendid corps, which had been so wasted between Quatre Bras and Ligny, and which was burning to achieve something, was formed in four huge parallel close-ranked columns, slightly *écheloned* under Donzelot, Marcognet, Durutte and Allix. With greatly mistaken judgment, these four columns were crowded close together.

The disposition was a very bad one. In the first place, their freedom of movement was so impaired by lack of proper distance as to render deployment almost impossible. Unless the columns could preserve their solid formation until the very point of contact, the charge would be a fruitless one. In the second place, they made an enormous target impossible to miss. The attack was supported by light batteries of artillery and the cavalry in the flanks.

Other things being equal, the quality of soldiers being the same, the column is at an obvious disadvantage when attacking the line. It was so in this instance. Although it was magnificently led by Ney and d'Erlon in person, and although it comprised troops of the highest order, the division commanders being men of superb courage and resolution, no valor, no determination could make up for these disadvantages. The tremendous artillery-fire of the French, which did great execution among the English, kept them down until the dark columns of infantry mounting the ridge got in the way of the French guns which, of course, ceased to fire.

The drums were rolling madly, the Frenchmen were cheering loudly when the ridge was suddenly covered with long red lines. There were not many blue-coated allies left. Many of them had already laid down their lives; of the survivors more were exhausted by the fierce battling of the preceding days when the Belgians had nobly sustained the fighting traditions of a race to which nearly two thousand years before Caesar himself had borne testimony. As a matter of fact, most of the allies were moved to the rear. They did not leave the field. They were formed up again back of the battle line to constitute the reserve. The English did not intend to flee either. They were not accustomed to it and they saw no reason for doing it now.

Wellington moved the heavy cavalry over to support the threatened point of the line and bade his soldiers restrain their fire. There was something ominous in the silent, steady, rock-like red wall. It was much more threatening to the mercuric Gallic spirit than the shouting of the French was to the unemotional English disposition. Still, they came intrepidly on.

Meanwhile, renewed attacks were hurled against the *château* and the farmhouse. Ney and d'Erlon had determined to break the English line with the bayonet. Suddenly, when the French came within point-blank range, the English awoke to action. The English guns hurled shot into the close-ranked masses, each discharge doing frightful execution. Ney's horse was shot from under him at the first fire. But the unwounded Marshal scrambled to his feet and, mounting another horse, pressed on.

The slow-moving ranks were nearer. At point-blank range the English infantrymen now opened fire. Shattering discharges were poured upon the French. The fronts of the divisions were obliterated. The men in advance who survived would have given back, but the pressure of the masses in their rear forced them to go on. The divisions actually broke into a run. Again and again the British battalions spoke, the black muskets in the hands of the red coats were tipped with redder flame. It was not in human flesh and blood to sustain very long such a fire.

It was a magnificent charge, gloriously delivered, and such was its momentum that it almost came in touch with the English line. It did not quite. That momentum was spent at last. The French deployed as well as they could in the crowded space and at half-pistol-shot distance began to return the English fire. The French guns joined in the infernal tumult. The advance had been stopped, but it had not been driven back. The French cavalry were now coming up. Before they arrived that issue had to be decided. The critical moment was at hand, and Wellington's superb judgment determined the action. He let loose on them the heavy cavalry, led by the Scots Grays on their big horses. As the ranks of the infantry opened to give them room, the men of the Ninety-second Highlanders, mad with the enthusiasm of the moment, caught the stirrup-straps of the Horse and, half running, half dragged, joined in the charge.

The splendid body of heavy cavalry fell on the flank of the halted columns. There was no time for the French to form a square. Nay more, there was no room for them to form a square. In an instant, however, they faced about and delivered a volley which did great execution, but nothing could stop the maddened rush of the gigantic horsemen. Back on the heights of Rossomme Napoleon, aroused from his lethargy at last, stared at the great attack.

"*Mon Dieu!*" he exclaimed as he saw the tremendous onfall of the cavalrymen upon his helpless infantry, "how terrible are those gray horsemen!"

Yes, they were more terrible to the men at the point of contact than they were to those back of La Belle Alliance. No infantry that ever lived in the position in which the French found themselves could have stood up against such a charge as that. Trampling, hacking, slashing, thrusting, the horses biting and fighting like the men, the heavy cavalry broke up two of the columns. The second and third began to retreat under an awful fire.

But the dash of the British troopers was spent. They had become separated, disorganized. They had lost coherence. The French cavalry now arrived on the scene. Admirably handled, they were thrown on the scattered English. There was nothing for the latter to do but retire. Retire they did, having accomplished all that anyone could expect of cavalry, fighting every step of the way. Just as soon as they opened the fronts of the regiments in line, the infantry and artillery began again, and then the French cavalry got its punishment in its turn.

It takes but moments to tell of this charge and, indeed, in the battlefield it seemed but a few moments. But the French did not give way until after long hard fighting. From the beginning of the preliminary artillery-duel to the repulse of the charge an hour and a half elapsed. Indeed, they did not give way altogether either, for Donzelot and Allix, who commanded the left divisions, were the men who finally succeeded in capturing La Haye Sainte. And both sides suffered furiously before the French gave back.

There was plenty of fight left in the French yet. Ney, whatever his strategy and tactics, showed himself as of yore the bravest of the brave. It is quite safe to say that the hero of the retreat from Russia, the last of the Grand Army, the star of many a hotly contested battle, surpassed even his own glorious record for personal courage on that day. Maddened by the repulse, he gathered up all the cavalry, twelve thousand in number, and with Kellerman, greatest of cavalrymen, to second him and with division leaders like Milhaud and Maurice, he hurled himself upon the English line between Hougomont and La Haye Sainte. But the English made no tactical mistakes like that of Ney and d'Erlon. The artillerists stood to their guns until the torrent of French horsemen was about to break upon them, then they ran back to the safety of the nearest English square.

The English had been put in such formation that the squares lay chequerwise. Each side was four men deep. The front rank knelt, the second rank bent over at a charge bayonets, the third and the fourth ranks stood erect and fired. The French horsemen might have endured the tempest of bullets but they could not ride down the *chevaux de frise*, the fringe of steel. They tried it. No one could find fault with that army. It was doing its best; it was fighting and dying for its Emperor. Over and over they sought to break those stubborn British squares. One or two of them were actually penetrated, but unavailingly.

Men mad with battle-lust threw themselves and their horses upon the bayonets. The guns were captured and recaptured. The horsemen overran the ridge, they got behind the squares, they counter-charged over their own tracks, they rode until the breasts of the horses touched the guns. They fired pistols in the face of the English. One such charge is enough to immortalize its makers, and during that afternoon they made twelve!

Ney, raging over the field, had five horses killed under him. The British suffered horribly. If the horsemen did draw off to take breath, and reform for another effort, the French batteries, the English squares presenting easy targets, sent ball after ball through them. And nobody stopped fighting to watch the cavalry. Far and wide the battle raged. Toward the close of the day some of the English squares had become so torn to pieces that regiments, brigades and divisions had to be combined to keep from being overwhelmed.

Still the fight raged around Hougomont. Now, from a source of strength, La Haye Sainte had become a menace. There the English attacked and the French held. Off to the northeast the country was black with advancing masses of men. No, it was not Grouchy and his thirty-five thousand who, if they had been there at the beginning, might have decided the day. It was the Prussians.

They, at least, had marched to the sound of the cannon. Grouchy was off at Wavre. He at last got in touch with one of Blücher's rear corps and he was fighting a smart little battle ten miles from the place where the main issue was to be decided. As a diversion, his efforts were negligible, for without that corps the allies outnumbered the French two to one.

Telling the troops that the oncoming soldiers were their comrades of Grouchy's command who would decide the battle, Napoleon detached the gallant Lobau, who had stood like a stone wall at Aspern, with the Young Guard to seize the village of Planchenoit and to hold the Prussians back, for if they broke in the end would be as certain as it was swift. And well did Lobau with the Young Guard perform that task. Bülow, commanding the leading corps, hurled himself again and again upon the French line. His heavy columns fared exactly as the French columns had fared when they assaulted the English. But it was not within the power of ten thousand men to hold off thirty thousand forever, and there were soon that number of Prussians at the point of contact. Frantic messages from Lobau caused the Emperor to send one of the divisions of the Old Guard, the last reserve, to his support.

It was now after six o'clock, the declining sun was already low on the horizon, the long June day was drawing to a close. The main force of the Prussians had not yet come up to the hill and ridge of Mont St. Jean. Wellington, in great anxiety, was clinging desperately to the ridge with his shattered lines wondering how long he could hold them, whether he could sustain another of those awful attacks. His reserves, except two divisions of light cavalry, Vivian's and Vandeleur's, and Maitland's and Adams' brigades headed by Colborne's famous Fifty-second Foot, among his troops the *de luxe* veterans of the Peninsula, had all been expended.

Lobau was still holding back the Prussians by the most prodigious and astounding efforts. If Napoleon succeeded in his last titanic effort to break that English line, Blücher would be too late. Unless night or Blücher came quickly, if Napoleon made that attack and it was not driven back, victory in this struggle of the war gods would finally go to the French.

Hougomont still held out. The stubborn defence of it was Wellington's salvation. While it stood his right was more or less protected. But La Haye Sainte offered a convenient point of attack upon him. If Napoleon brought up his remaining troops behind it they would only have a short distance to go before they were at death's grapple hand to hand with the shattered, exhausted, but indomitable defenders of the ridge.

CHAPTER 31

Waterloo—The Last of the Guard

Long and earnestly, one from the heights of Mont St. Jean, the other from those of Rossomme, the two great Captains scanned the opposing line. Napoleon seemed to have recovered from his indisposition. Indeed, he had undergone frightful fatigues which would have been incredible if sustained by a younger man, and which would have been impossible to any other man than he. To add to his fatigue, he was ill. He could not sleep and the nature of his illness was such that it was agony for him to mount a horse. This condition had been aggravated by the awful exertion, physical and mental, he had made and the strain of that long afternoon of desperate fighting. Nor had he eaten anything the livelong day. Yet at about half after six that night he did get into the saddle again. Conquering his anguish, he rode down to the fifteen battalions of the Guard still held in reserve at La Belle Alliance, all that was left intact of that proud and gallant army.

"My children," he said hoarsely in last appeal, "I must sleep in Brussels to-night. There is the enemy. Go and break the English line for me."

Cambronne, to whom nature and education alike had denied every attribute of grace or greatness except unbounded devotion and stubborn courage, mustered the Guard. Ney, *le terrible Rougeaud*, the soldiers' idol, his torn uniform covered with dust, one of his epaulets slashed from his shoulder, his coat open, his shirt likewise, his bared breast black with powder, his face red-streaked with blood, for many bullets had grazed him, his hair matted with sweat—the weather had grown frightfully hot, the air was terribly humid—his eyes blazing, flecks of foam about his mouth, placed himself in the lead. Every staff officer left joined the great Marshal.

With the brass drums beating "*La Grenadière*," that famous grenadier quick-step, the great Guard moved out. Here, again, in the excitement of the conflict, an opportunity was overlooked. They could have gone up in rear of La Haye Sainte with practically no danger, but they went straight out into the open, between farm and château. Up the road, over the fields of bloody grain, through the torn hedges, trampling over the bodies of their comrades, the last hope advanced to meet the enemy.

All over the field the tide of battle ebbed and flowed. The armies came together for the last try. Off to the right Lobau still held his appointed station, but now the Prussians in great masses were swarming on the field about Planchenoit. Division after division, avoiding Lobau meanwhile, mounted the ridge to join the English line. It had almost been broken by d'Erlon at La Haye Sainte. Mouffling, Wellington's Prussian aide, had galloped over to Ziethen in command of the advance with the news that unless the English were reinforced heavily at once their line would be pierced and they would be routed. On to the field opposite La Haye Sainte came the Prussians. Still raged the battle around Hougomont and the English right, but the eyes of every spectator not engaged in fighting for his life were concentrated on the advance of the Guard.

Napoleon had ridden down from Rossomme to La Belle Alliance. He sat his horse within easy cannon-shot of the English as the devoted Guard passed by in its last review. His physical pain was forgot in the great anxiety with which he watched them. The battle was practically lost. This was the last desperate throw of the gambler, the last stake he could place upon the board. He knew it, every officer knew it, perhaps even the more experienced grenadiers like old Bullet-Stopper of the Guard knew it. That did not matter to them. They were his men and at his word, for him, they were going forward to conquer or die.

Tramp, tramp, tramp, keeping time to the long continuous rolling of the drums whose notes were heard even above the roar of the cannon and the tumult of the battle, the Guard, from whose lips came one continuous cry of "*Vive l'Empereur!*" marched forward. Covered as usual by the fire of one of those great batteries of concentrated guns so conspicuous in Napoleonic tactics, through the smoke and the mist and the shadows of the evening, they passed on. Napoleon himself with three battalions in reserve followed a little distance behind them.

Now they were mounting the hill, now they were abreast of La Haye Sainte; now the ridge in front of them was topped with Eng-

461

lish. Away off could be heard the thunder of the oncoming Prussian horsemen, the roar of the Prussian guns. Back of the ridge the brigades of light cavalry stood ready. The infantry reserve with brave Colborne and the Fifty-second, thirteen hundred strong, in the lead, were quivering with excitement. Even the stolid British phlegm had vanished. This was the last supreme moment. Throbbed wildly the usually steady hearts of the cool islanders. If they could stop this grand advance the battle would be gained. The hill would be held. Could they do it? And if not——!

Out of the smoke and mist opposite the English soldiers of the Royal Guard came their Imperial enemies. The waiting British saw the black bearskins of the tall Guard, the imperial insignia on cross-belts and uniforms. They were so near that they could see the grim faces of the old soldiers, their moustaches working, their lips drawn back over their teeth, snarling, sputtering like savage beasts. Here and there mouths were tight shut in a firm line. Here and there men came silently, but mostly they were yelling. And they came up, arms aport, after the precept and example of Dorsenne, *le beau Dorsenne*, alas, no longer with them, to try conclusions for the last time with the soldiers' white weapon, the bayonet, cold steel! Would the English wait for that? They would not.

"Fire!" cried an English voice just when the suspense had become unbearable.

The heavens were shattered by the discharge. Ney pitched from his horse, the sixth that day to be shot under him. He was up in a moment, his sword out. He advanced on foot at the head of the Guard. It was his last charge. He was to face muskets again, but in Paris, in the hands of a firing-squad, with his back to the wall. He was not given the coveted privilege of dying on that stricken field, though he sought for it wildly everywhere, but when he did die it was as he had lived, undaunted. Now, his great voice uplifted, he led forward the devoted and immortal band. His sword was shot out of his hand. Seizing a gun and a bayonet from a falling grenadier, he fought in the ranks as in Russia.

Again, the tactics were faulty, as d'Erlon's men the Guard came in solid columns. Right in front of the rapid-firing English, the muskets and cannon in one continuous roar now, they sought to deploy and return that terrible withering fire. The Prussian infantry, panting like dogs, now gained the crest of the ridge and, animated by more than human hatred, fell into disorderly but determined lines and opened fire. Harsh German oaths and exclamations mingled with hearty English curses and cheers. The Guard was firing rapidly now, straight into the faces of the English. And still the columns came on. Like a great wave which rushes forward at first swiftly and then goes slower and slower and slower as it rolls up the beach it advanced. By and by it stopped. The end was at hand. With bent heads the men stood and took the hail of lead and iron.

"Come!" said Ney, frantic with battle fever. "Come! See how a Marshal of France can die."

Now was the crucial moment. The Iron Duke saw it. The two armies were face to face firing into each other. To which side would the victory incline? He spoke to Maitland, to Adams, to Colborne. That gallant soldier threw his men on the exposed flank of the column which had obliqued, bent to the right. Before they could face about out of the smoke came the yelling English! They found the men on the flank of the column the next morning just where it had stood lying in ordered ranks dead.

Still they did not give back. Vivian and Vandeleur, daring light horsemen, were now hurled on the devoted division. At it they ran. On it they fell. Still it stood. It was incredible. It was almost surrounded now. The attack had failed. To advance was impossible, to retreat was dishonour. They would stand! Their case was hopeless. Appeals were made for the survivors to lay down their arms and surrender. Into the faces of the assailants vulgar but heroic Cambronne hurled a disgusting but graphic word. No, nobody said so, but the Guard would not surrender. It would die.

Back of his Guard, the Emperor, having stopped not far from the *château*, watched them die. He was paler than ever, sweat poured from his face, his eyes and lips twitched nervously and spasms of physical pain added their torture to the mental agony of the moment. He muttered again and again:

"*Mon Dieu! Mais ils sont mêlés ensemble.*"

Now the Prussian horsemen, the Death-head Hussars, added their weight to Vandeleur's and Vivian's swordsmen and lancers. Other regiments supplemented the withering fire of the advancing Fifty-second and the reserve brigades. Now, at last, the Guard began to give back. Slowly, reluctantly, clinging to their positions, fighting, firing, savage, mad—they began to give way.

"*Tout est perdu,*" whispered Napoleon.

"The Guard retreats!" cried someone near the Emperor.

463

"*La Garde recule!*" rose here and there from the battlefield. "*La Garde recule!*" Men caught up the cry in wonder and despair. Could it be true? Yes. Back they came out of the smoke. Now was the supreme opportunity for the allies. The Duke, recklessly exposing himself on the crest of the hill, bullets flying about him, as they flew about Napoleon, yet leading apparently a charmed life, closed his field-glass and turned to the red line that had made good its defence.

"Up!" he cried, waving his hand and not finishing his sentence.

They needed no other signal. Their time to attack had come. Down the hill they rushed, yelling, followed by Belgians, Netherlanders, and all the rest, pressing hard upon their heels. La Haye Sainte was recaptured in the twinkling of an eye. The shattered broken remains of the Guard were driven in headlong rout. The assailers of Hougomont were themselves assaulted. At last numbers had overwhelmed Lobau. The survivors of an army of a hundred and thirty thousand flushed with victory fell on the survivors of an army of seventy thousand already defeated.

At half-past seven the battle was lost. At eight the withdrawal became a retreat, the retreat a rout. At set of sun lost was the Emperor, lost was the Empire. Ended was the age-long struggle which had begun with the fall of the Bastile more than a score of years before. Once again from France, with the downfall of Napoleon, had been snatched the hegemony of the world.

There was no reserve. There was nothing to cover a retreat. Someone raised the wild cry not often heard on battlefields overlooked by Napoleon, and it was echoed everywhere:

"*Sauve qui peut.*"

The army as an army was gone. Thousands of men in mad terror fled in every direction. Still, there were left a few battalions of the Guard which had not been in action. They formed three squares to receive the English and Prussians. Into the nearest square Napoleon, bewildered, overwhelmed, stricken by the catastrophe, was led on his horse. His sword was out. He would fain have died on that field. Doubtless, many a bullet marked him, but none struck him. For a little while these squares of the Guard, Napoleon in the centre one, another square on either side of the centre one, stayed the British and Prussian advance, but it was not to be. "The stars in their courses fought against Sisera!" The Emperor gave no order. Bertrand and Soult turned his horse about and the squares retreated.

It was night. They were the sole organized body left. Well, they upheld their ancient fame and glorious reputation and untarnished honour. Through the calm and moonlit night pursuers and pursued could hear the rolling of the brass drums far and wide over the countryside as the Guard marched away from that field back to stricken France, to that famous grenadier march, "*La Grenadière*."

Again and again they stopped to beat off the furious attack of the cavalry. Again and again the Prussian pursuers hurled themselves unavailingly on quadrangles of steel, worked up to a terrible pitch of excitement by the possibility that they might seize the Emperor at whose behest and for whose purpose fifty thousand men lay dead or wounded on that fatal hill, in that dreadful valley. Happy the fate of those who were dead—horrible the condition of those who were wounded. English, Prussians, Germans, Bavarians, Hollanders, French, trampled together in indistinguishable masses. Horses, guns, weapons, equipment—everything in hopeless confusion. Every horror, every anguish, every agony was there—incense burned about the altar of one devouring ambition.

CHAPTER 32

At Last the Eagle and the Woman

Nearest the crest of the hill immortalized by the great conflict, in advance of but in touch with the regular dead lines of the Guard, a little group, friend and foe, lay intermingled. There was a young officer of the Fifty-second infantry, one of Colborne's. He was conscious but suffering frightfully from mortal wounds. One side of his face where he had been thrown into the mud was covered with a red compound of earth and blood; his bright head was dabbled with the same hideous mixture. Blood frothed out of his mouth as he breathed. He murmured from time to time a woman's name. "Water," was sometimes the sputtering syllable that came from him.

His left hand clutched uneasily at his breast, where his torn uniform showed a gaping wound. But his right hand was still. The arm was broken, paralyzed, but the fingers of his right hand were tightly closed around a broken blue staff and next to his cheek, the bloodstained one, and cold against it, was a French Eagle. He had seized that staff in the heat of battle and in the article of death he held it.

At the feet of the English officer lay a French officer wearing the insignia of a colonel of the Guard. He was covered with wounds, bayonet thrusts, a sabre-slash, and was delirious. Although helpless, he was really in much better case than the young Englishman. He, too, in his delirium muttered a woman's name.

They spoke different tongues, these two. They were born in different lands. They were children of the same God, although one might have doubted it, but no one could mistake the woman's name. For there Frank Yeovil and Jean Marteau, incapable of doing each other any further harm, each thought of the same woman.

Did Laure d'Aumenier back in England waiting anxiously for news of battle, fearing for one of those men, hear those piteous, bro-

466

ken murmurs of a woman's name—her own?

Around these two were piled the dead. Marteau had seized the Eagle. Yes, he and a few brave men had stayed on the field when the great Ney, raging like a madman, and seeking in vain the happy fortune of a bullet or sword-thrust, had been swept away, and on him had fallen Yeovil with another group of resolute English, and together they had fought their little battle for the Eagle. And Marteau had proved the Englishman's master. He had beaten him down. He had shortened his sword to strike when he recognized him. Well, the battle was over, the Eagle was lost, the Emperor was a fugitive, hope died with the retreating Guard, the Empire was ended. Marteau might have killed him, but to what end?

"For your wife's sake," he cried, lowering his sword, and the next minute he paid for his mercy, for the other English threw themselves upon him.

But Frank Yeovil did not get off scot free. There was one lad who had followed Marteau, who had marched with the Guard, who had no compunctions of conscience whatever, and with his last pistol Pierre gave the reeling Englishman the fatal shot. Yes, Pierre paid too. They would certainly have spared him, since he was only a boy, but maddened by the death of their officer, half a dozen bayonets were plunged into his breast.

Thither the next day came Sir Gervaise Yeovil, who had been with the Duke at the Duchess of Richmond's famous ball in Brussels. Young Frank had left that ball at four o'clock in the morning, according to order, only to find that later orders had directed the army to march at two and that his baggage had gone. He had fought that day in pumps and silk stockings which he had worn at the ball; dabbled, gory, muddy, they were now.

Sir Gervaise Yeovil was an old friend of the Duke of Wellington. The Iron Duke, as they called him, was nevertheless very tender-hearted that morning. He told the Baronet that his son was somewhere on the field. Colonel Colborne of the Fifty-second had marked him in the charge, but that was all. Neither Vivian nor Vandeleur could throw any light on the situation. There were twenty thousand of the allied armies on that field and thirty thousand French.

"My God," said Sir Gervaise, staring along the line of the French retreat, "what is so terrible as a defeat?"

"Nothing," said the Duke gravely. Then looking at the nearer hillside he added those tremendous words which epitomized war in a way in which no one save a great modern captain has ever epitomized it. "Nothing," he said slowly, "unless it be a victory."

They found the Guard. That was easy. There they lay in lines where they had fallen; the tall bearskins on their heads, the muskets still clasped in their hands. There, too, they found young Yeovil at last. They revived him. Someone sought to take the Eagle from him, but with a sudden accession of strength he protested against it.

"Father," he whispered to the old man bending over him, his red face pale and working, "mine."

"True," said the Duke. "He captured it. Let him keep it."

"O God!" broke out the Baronet. "Frank! Can nothing be done?"

"Nothing. Stop." His lips moved, his father bent nearer. "Laure——"he whispered.

"Yes, yes, what of her?"

"That Frenchman she loved——"

"Marteau?"

The young Englishman closed his eyes in assent.

"He could have killed me but spared—for her—he—is there," he faltered presently.

"There is life in this Frenchman yet," said one of the surgeons, looking up at the moment.

"My Lord!" said old Sir Gervaise Yeovil, starting up, choking down a sob and endeavouring to keep his voice steady. "My boy yonder——"

"Yes," said the Duke, "a brave lad."

"He's—— It is all up with him. You will let me take him back to England, and—the Frenchman and the Eagle?"

"Certainly. I wish to God it had never happened, Yeovil," went on the soldier. "But it had to be. Bonaparte had to be put down, the world freed. And somebody had to pay."

"I thank God," said the old man, "that my boy dies for his King and his country and for human liberty."

"Nor shall he die in vain," said the soldier.

Frank Yeovil died on the vessel Sir Gervaise chartered to carry him and Marteau and some other wounded officers of his acquaintance back to England. They did not bury him at sea. At his earnest request they took him back to his own land to be laid with his ancestors, none of whom had spent themselves more gloriously or for a greater cause than he.

Marteau, frightfully weak, heart-broken and helpless, by Sir Gervaise Yeovil's command was taken to the Baronet's own house.

"I did my best," he said brokenly from the bed on which he lay as Laure d'Aumenier bent over him, Sir Gervaise standing grim and silent with folded arms in the background.

"For France and the Emperor," whispered the woman.

"Yes, that, but for your husband as well. He fell upon me. I was trying to rally the Guard—the Eagle—he was beaten down—but I recognized him. I would not have harmed him."

"He told me," said the Baronet, "what you said. 'For your wife's sake,'" he quoted in his deep voice, looking curiously at the girl.

"Sir Gervaise," said the countess, looking up at him entreatingly, "I am alone in this world but for you. I was to have been your daughter. May I speak?"

"I wish it."

"Marteau—Jean," she said softly, "I was not his wife. Perhaps now that he is dead it would have been better if I had been, but——"

"And you are free?"

Again the countess looked at the Englishman. Simple and homely though he was, he showed the qualities of his birth and rank.

"*Mademoiselle,*" he began gravely, almost tenderly. He looked a long time at her. "Little Laure," he continued at last, taking her slender hand in his own great one, "I had hoped that you might someday call me father but that hope is gone—since Waterloo. If I were your real father now I should say——"

"*Monsieur!*" whispered the woman, her eyes brightening, her hand tightening in the clasp of the other.

"And I think the old Marquis would say that it is the will of God, now——" He bit his lip. It was all so different from what he imagined.

"Go on, if you please," whispered Marteau. "I am ill. I cannot bear——"

"If she be guided by me she will be your wife, young sir," said Sir Gervaise decisively.

He dropped the woman's hand. He turned and walked heavily out of the room without a backward glance. He could do no more.

"And will you stoop to me?" pleaded Marteau.

For answer the woman knelt by his bed and slipped her arm tenderly under his head. She bent and kissed him.

"When you are stronger," she replied, "you shall raise me up to your own high level of courage and devotion and self-sacrifice, but meanwhile it is upon my bosom that your head must lie."

"Alas," said Marteau, after a little, "the Emperor is taken, the Empire is lost, my poor France!"

"I will go back with you and we will help to build it up again," said the woman.

That was the best medicine that could be given to the young man. His recovery was slow but it was sure and it was the more rapid because of the gracious care of the woman he loved, who lavished upon him all the pent-up passion of her fond adoring heart.

Sir Gervaise Yeovil, whose interest at court was great, exerted himself to secure a reconfirmation of Marteau's patent of nobility and to see that no difficulties were placed in the way of the young couple in obtaining repossession of their estates. So that once more there should be a d'Aumenier and perhaps a renewal of the ancient house in the old *château* in Champagne. This was easier since Marteau had never taken oath to King Louis and therefore had broken no faith.

At the quiet wedding that took place as soon as Marteau recovered his strength a little, Sir Gervaise continued to act the father's part to the poor woman. After the ceremony he delighted the heart of the soldier by giving to him what he loved after the woman, the Eagle which had been Frank Yeovil's prize.

"You will think of the lad, sometimes," said the old Baronet to the girl. "He was not lucky enough to win you, but he loved you and he died with your name on his lips."

"I shall remember him always," said the new-made wife.

"His name shall be held in highest honour in my house as a brave soldier, a true lover and a most gallant gentleman," added the new-made husband.

Marteau would never forget the picture of the Emperor sitting on his horse at La Belle Alliance that June evening, stern, terrific, almost sublime, watching the Guard go by to death. He was glad he had not seen him in the retreat of which he afterward heard from old Bal-Arrêt. But that was not the last picture of the Emperor that he had. Although he was scarcely strong enough to be moved, he insisted on being taken to Portsmouth with his young wife. Sir Gervaise went with him. He had no other object in life it seemed but to provide happiness for these young people. He could scarcely bear them out of his sight.

One day, a bright and sunny morning late in July, they put the convalescing soldier into a boat with his wife and the old baronet and the three were rowed out into the harbour as near as the cordon of guard-boats allowed them to approach to a great English ship-of-the-line, across the stern of which in gold letters they read the name, "*Bellerophon.*"

"Bonaparte gener'ly comes out 'n the quarter-gal'ry of the ship, 'bout this hour in the mornin'," said one of the boatmen. "An' if he does we can see him quite plain from yere."

There were other boats there whose occupants were moved by curiosity and various emotions, but when the figure of the little man with the three-cornered cocked hat on his head, still wearing the green uniform of the *chasseurs* of the Guard stepped out on the quarter-gallery, his eyes, as it were instinctively, sought that particular boat.

"Help me up," said Marteau brokenly.

The boat was a large one and moving carefully they got the young officer to his feet. He was wearing his own battle-stained uniform. He lifted his trembling hand to his head in salute. The little Emperor bent over the rail and stared hard at the trio. Did he recognize Marteau? Ah, yes! He straightened up presently, his own hand returned the salute and then he took off that same cocked hat and bared his brow and bent his head low and, with a gesture of farewell, he turned and re-entered his cabin—Prometheus on the way to his chains at St. Helena!

LEONAUR

ALSO FROM LEONAUR
AVAILABLE IN SOFTCOVER OR HARDCOVER WITH DUST JACKET

IRON TIMES WITH THE GUARDS *by An O. E. (G. P. A. Fildes)*—The Experiences of an Officer of the Coldstream Guards on the Western Front During the First World War.

THE GREAT WAR IN THE MIDDLE EAST: 1 *by W. T. Massey*—The Desert Campaigns & How Jerusalem Was Won---two classic accounts in one volume.

THE GREAT WAR IN THE MIDDLE EAST: 2 *by W. T. Massey*—Allenby's Final Triumph.

SMITH-DORRIEN *by Horace Smith-Dorrien*—Isandlwhana to the Great War.

1914 *by Sir John French*—The Early Campaigns of the Great War by the British Commander.

GRENADIER *by E. R. M. Fryer*—The Recollections of an Officer of the Grenadier Guards throughout the Great War on the Western Front.

BATTLE, CAPTURE & ESCAPE *by George Pearson*—The Experiences of a Canadian Light Infantryman During the Great War.

DIGGERS AT WAR *by R. Hugh Knyvett & G. P. Cuttriss*—"Over There"With the Australians by R. Hugh Knyvett and Over the Top With the Third Australian Division by G. P. Cuttriss. Accounts of Australians During the Great War in the Middle East, at Gallipoli and on the Western Front.

HEAVY FIGHTING BEFORE US *by George Brenton Laurie*—The Letters of an Officer of the Royal Irish Rifles on the Western Front During the Great War.

THE CAMELIERS *by Oliver Hogue*—A Classic Account of the Australians of the Imperial Camel Corps During the First World War in the Middle East.

RED DUST *by Donald Black*—A Classic Account of Australian Light Horsemen in Palestine During the First World War.

THE LEAN, BROWN MEN *by Angus Buchanan*—Experiences in East Africa During the Great War with the 25th Royal Fusiliers—the Legion of Frontiersmen.

THE NIGERIAN REGIMENT IN EAST AFRICA *by W. D. Downes*—On Campaign During the Great War 1916-1918.

THE 'DIE-HARDS' IN SIBERIA *by John Ward*—With the Middlesex Regiment Against the Bolsheviks 1918-19.

LEONAUR

ALSO FROM LEONAUR
AVAILABLE IN SOFTCOVER OR HARDCOVER WITH DUST JACKET

FARAWAY CAMPAIGN *by F. James*—Experiences of an Indian Army Cavalry Officer in Persia & Russia During the Great War.

REVOLT IN THE DESERT *by T. E. Lawrence*—An account of the experiences of one remarkable British officer's war from his own perspective.

MACHINE-GUN SQUADRON *by A. M. G.*—The 20th Machine Gunners from British Yeomanry Regiments in the Middle East Campaign of the First World War.

A GUNNER'S CRUSADE *by Antony Bluett*—The Campaign in the Desert, Palestine & Syria as Experienced by the Honourable Artillery Company During the Great War .

DESPATCH RIDER *by W. H. L. Watson*—The Experiences of a British Army Motorcycle Despatch Rider During the Opening Battles of the Great War in Europe.

TIGERS ALONG THE TIGRIS *by E. J. Thompson*—The Leicestershire Regiment in Mesopotamia During the First World War.

HEARTS & DRAGONS *by Charles R. M. F. Crutwell*—The 4th Royal Berkshire Regiment in France and Italy During the Great War, 1914-1918.

INFANTRY BRIGADE: 1914 *by John Ward*—The Diary of a Commander of the 15th Infantry Brigade, 5th Division, British Army, During the Retreat from Mons.

DOING OUR 'BIT' *by Ian Hay*—Two Classic Accounts of the Men of Kitchener's 'New Army' During the Great War including *The First 100,000 & All In It*.

AN EYE IN THE STORM *by Arthur Ruhl*—An American War Correspondent's Experiences of the First World War from the Western Front to Gallipoli-and Beyond.

STAND & FALL *by Joe Cassells*—With the Middlesex Regiment Against the Bolsheviks 1918-19.

RIFLEMAN MACGILL'S WAR *by Patrick MacGill*—A Soldier of the London Irish During the Great War in Europe including *The Amateur Army, The Red Horizon & The Great Push*.

WITH THE GUNS *by C. A. Rose & Hugh Dalton*—Two First Hand Accounts of British Gunners at War in Europe During World War 1- Three Years in France with the Guns and With the British Guns in Italy.

THE BUSH WAR DOCTOR *by Robert V. Dolbey*—The Experiences of a British Army Doctor During the East African Campaign of the First World War.

LEONAUR

ALSO FROM LEONAUR

AVAILABLE IN SOFTCOVER OR HARDCOVER WITH DUST JACKET

THE 9TH—THE KING'S (LIVERPOOL REGIMENT) IN THE GREAT WAR 1914 - 1918 *by Enos H. G. Roberts*—Mersey to mud—war and Liverpool men.

THE GAMBARDIER *by Mark Severn*—The experiences of a battery of Heavy artillery on the Western Front during the First World War.

FROM MESSINES TO THIRD YPRES *by Thomas Floyd*—A personal account of the First World War on the Western front by a 2/5th Lancashire Fusilier.

THE IRISH GUARDS IN THE GREAT WAR - VOLUME 1 *by Rudyard Kipling*—Edited and Compiled from Their Diaries and Papers—The First Battalion.

THE IRISH GUARDS IN THE GREAT WAR - VOLUME 1 *by Rudyard Kipling*—Edited and Compiled from Their Diaries and Papers—The Second Battalion.

ARMOURED CARS IN EDEN *by K. Roosevelt*—An American President's son serving in Rolls Royce armoured cars with the British in Mesopatamia & with the American Artillery in France during the First World War.

CHASSEUR OF 1914 *by Marcel Dupont*—Experiences of the twilight of the French Light Cavalry by a young officer during the early battles of the great war in Europe.

TROOP HORSE & TRENCH *by R.A. Lloyd*—The experiences of a British Life-guardsman of the household cavalry fighting on the western front during the First World War 1914-18.

THE EAST AFRICAN MOUNTED RIFLES *by C.J. Wilson*—Experiences of the campaign in the East African bush during the First World War.

THE LONG PATROL *by George Berrie*—A Novel of Light Horsemen from Gallipoli to the Palestine campaign of the First World War.

THE FIGHTING CAMELIERS *by Frank Reid*—The exploits of the Imperial Camel Corps in the desert and Palestine campaigns of the First World War.

STEEL CHARIOTS IN THE DESERT *by S. C. Rolls*—The first world war experiences of a Rolls Royce armoured car driver with the Duke of Westminster in Libya and in Arabia with T.E. Lawrence.

WITH THE IMPERIAL CAMEL CORPS IN THE GREAT WAR *by Geoffrey Inchbald*—The story of a serving officer with the British 2nd battalion against the Senussi and during the Palestine campaign.

www.ingramcontent.com/pod-product-compliance
Lightning Source LLC
Chambersburg PA
CBHW030748030726
47497CB00001B/183